TENDER TOUCH

Praise for Lynn Emery's work:

NIGHT MAGIC

"NIGHT MAGIC is one of those powerful novels that block-buster movies are made of—complete with a fiery, passionate heroine, a strong determined hero and a plot that rivals a . . . roller coaster with all its twists, turns and unexpected tunnels. . . . A read of a lifetime." 4½ stars (Exceptional)

—*Romantic Times*

AFTER ALL

"Sweet, glorious, triumphant . . ."

—*Romantic Times*

TENDER TOUCH

Lynn Emery

Pinnacle Books
Kensington Publishing Corp.

http://www.pinnaclebooks.com

PINNACLE BOOKS are published by

Kensington Publishing Corp.
850 Third Avenue
New York, NY 10022

First Printing: December, 1997
10 9 8 7 6 5 4 3 2 1

Printed in the United States of America

This book is dedicated to Jean Paul, my loving husband, who is unfailing in his support of my dreams; to my mother, Mildred Emery, who is a role model of strength; and to my brother, Wayne Emery, who wins the prize as my most determined promoter! Last but not least, to Brian Emery, my talented and handsome nephew.

A big thanks to my wonderful friends, Pat and Stephanie— you guys are the greatest.
Hugs to my good pal, Becky, a real sweetheart.

Chapter 1

Nervous energy caused Jade to pace for several seconds before she realized what she was doing. "Relax, it doesn't have to be a bad sign that the new boss wants to see you," she mumbled in an effort to calm herself.

It did not work. She knew only too well a change in administrations always meant out with the old, in with the new. Of course as a state employee with permanent civil service status, she could not be fired. Still she could be assigned new duties—duties that were dull. The title would be the same—administrative coordinator—but she would, in actual fact, be a well-paid secretary for several staff and maybe supervise one or two clerical workers. Jade had waited for the ax to fall for several days now. But why meet with her? Most big guns left such staff decisions for their assistants to handle.

She glanced around the corner office. The view from the sixth floor was spectacular. Mid February in Louisiana was a mixture of cold, rainy days and warm, sunny ones. Through a sparkling clean picture window, the governor's mansion was visible. The lake behind it shimmered in the late winter sun. Jade turned back to the room.

So this is the seat of power. She peered at a row of framed documents, one of which was a Master of Public Administration degree from Xavier University in New Orleans.

"Checking out my credentials before the interview, eh?" Bill Lang stood in the open door of the office wearing an impeccable charcoal gray suit and a half smile. Just over six feet tall, his dark brown face had a chiseled look. Heavy eyebrows framed eyes the color of black coffee. His black hair had a touch of premature gray at the temples. At thirty-four, his career achievements were the envy of many.

"Oh, I . . . I was just *admiring* all your credentials." Jade felt foolish that she was caught in effect snooping on one of the most powerful appointed state officials. "You've accomplished quite a lot even before becoming deputy secretary of the Department of Health & Hospitals." She tried to recover her composure.

Lang gave a slight nod in acceptance of the praise then closed the door. "A lot of paper—that means I had to work twice as hard to get where I am, earning half what I could in the private sector." He chuckled.

"That rural health program you set up is a model still being studied by experts all over the country. And the Healthy Babies—Happy Mothers project in the Bottoms has resulted in a decrease in infant mortality in one of the poorest parts of East Baton Rouge Parish. It's obvious your rewards don't just come from money." Jade spoke with intensity, forgetting her embarrassment.

"Thank you, Ms. Pellerin. You're well informed—just one of the many good things Madeline Craig had to say about you."

"She gave me opportunities to grow professionally." Jade thought of the previous occupant of this office. The new governor had lost little time replacing her with a new appointee.

"Ms. Craig did the best she could under difficult circumstances." Bill Lang sat down in the high-back chair behind his large mahogany desk—a desk that had become legendary in the few short weeks he'd moved it into this office.

Here it comes. Jade steeled herself for the inevitable. Madeline Craig had been a much embattled secretary for the last year. Cuts in federal funding and scandals of uncovered Medicaid fraud had made all their lives miserable. The Baton Rouge *Morning Advocate* had run major stories about politically connected companies who benefited from money targeted for the poor. Favors were given, connections between state staff who regulated programs and owners of various health agencies were exposed. The new governor was swept into office by angry voters who responded to his message of reform and running the state like a business. Jade knew all Department of Health and Hospitals high-level staff were considered damaged goods. Might as well get it over with. Jade cleared her throat.

"I've organized all the pending memoranda that deals with requests by providers to increase their hospital beds. They're divided into acute care, psychiatric and extended care." Jade referred to the small notepad she'd brought in with her.

"I see. Very good." Bill Lang nodded.

"Then there are messages from the top aides of two legislators who wish to schedule appointments to meet with you. I have this and some minor items that need attention within the next few days printed up in priority order so there won't be any confusion." Jade started to rise when Lang raised a hand.

"Just a minute, Ms. Pellerin. I realize that change is tough on everyone even in the best of circumstances. And this department can in no way be said to be in the best of circumstances."

"No problem, Mr. Lang. As a state employee for the past twelve years, I know very well about change in state government. If you or your new assistant need any help, just give me a call." Jade stood up. She was sincere in her offer.

"You're very thorough. But you've made a serious mistake."

"Well, I'm sorry. Just let me know what it is and I'll be sure to correct it before I leave." Jade frowned and opened her pad again.

"Good. Tell my new assistant not to jump to conclusions." Lang held out his hand. The corner of his mouth lifted in amusement at her nonplussed expression.

"Me?" Jade was so stunned, she shook his hand without realizing it.

"Every one of your former bosses has high praise for your abilities. Of course Mike Testor will be my confidential assistant."

"I . . . uh," Jade stammered. She must have misunderstood him.

"But you will be my administrative assistant, a new civil service title with more responsibility and work. But more money, too," Lang went on as though he had not heard her. "That is, if you want to work for me."

"Oh, it isn't that—not at all. It's just that I worked closely with Ms. Craig, and I thought you'd want to pick your own staff."

"And I have. Look, I'll be frank. More than one person confided that Ms. Craig and you had heated words before she left. You disagreed with some of the practices of providers."

"Ms. Craig was a fine person, who as you said had a difficult situation to deal with." Jade spoke quickly. Despite the tension between them in the last nine months, she still had respect for her former boss.

"Which proves even more what kind of person you are, Ms. Pellerin. That one statement shows you not only have integrity, but discretion and good professional judgment as well. Well, what do you say?"

"Yes, I accept." Jade smiled back at him.

"Good, now let's get to work. I've got a meeting at one o'clock this afternoon about a new program. I want you to attend with me."

"Yes, sir." Jade began taking notes as Lang rattled off a string of instructions.

For the next twenty minutes, Jade wrote at a furious pace. Then for another two hours, she walked him through standard operating procedures. Lang asked detailed questions then made a few changes that he found more acceptable. On the whole, Jade was impressed with her new boss. Things were looking up after all.

"Whew! Another killer staff meeting. I thought I'd never get to eat lunch." Shaena pulled a chair up to Jade's desk and set a brown bag down on it.

"Hey, all you lawyers are long-winded *and* argumentative. What's new?" Jade patted her lips with a paper napkin. "Shaena, we were supposed to be eating healthy these days." She shook her head at the grease stains and smell of french fries.

Shaena Greene had been Jade's best friend at work since they met seven years earlier. Working in the legal department kept her so busy, they rarely had time for anything but quick lunches. Mostly they went out after work or met on the weekends.

"After the morning I've had, I needed one of those juicy burgers from downstairs in the cafeteria. Don't give me that look. Tomorrow, I promise." Shaena shrugged a halfhearted apology.

"Yeah, sure you will."

"But forget about that, how was *your* morning?" Shaena gave her an appraising look.

"Fine." Jade nodded slowly at her friend's raised eyebrows. "I'm his new administrative assistant."

"Get outta here!" Shaena almost dropped the french fry halfway to her mouth. "And I made a point to come down here and console you."

"My pay is going up quite nicely, too."

"Touchdown! A title don't mean a thing if it ain't got cha-ching! Congratulations, girlfriend." Shaena grinned at her.

"Thanks. And he's working my butt off all ready. But Mr. Lang is one sharp dude, just like I've always heard." Jade took another bite of her shrimp salad.

"Yeah, but what's he *really* like? Come on, nobody's around." She peeked out the door to Jade's office to make sure they were alone.

"Like I said, he's smart. It took him no time to start making decisions that will help things run a lot more smoothly around here. Minor housekeeping stuff, you know—but still things that make a difference in an office this busy.'' Jade stuffed the empty plastic container with a few lettuce leaves left of her lunch into her garbage can.

"Oh, come on. You know what I mean. Give me the dirt.'' Shaena hitched her chair closer, a gleam in her eyes.

"There is no dirt.''

"They say he's full of himself. And he moved up by becoming a master at guerilla warfare.'' Shaena munched on a corner of her hamburger.

"Shaena, you've been around this place long enough to know that most successful people get called arrogant. Usually it means the person had the guts to work hard and got recognition for it,'' Jade said.

"Yeah, well, just be careful. There's usually some truth to even the wildest rumor. That's something else I've learned working in state government.'' Shaena shook a finger at her for emphasis.

"Damn, it's twenty after. Gotta go—it's another meeting on getting back money from Health Tech.'' Shaena scooped up the food she had left back in the bag. "Tell you about that later. Bye.''

"Oops! Me, too.'' Jade sprang up and grabbed her cosmetics bag at the same time.

It was fortunate for her they were meeting in the conference room right down the hall. Jade combed her shoulder-length hair, put on lipstick and popped a breath mint in record time. She was even able to walk into the room with her notepad and not seem out of breath. The receptionist ushered in a short, stocky man with blond hair at the same time. He held out a chunky hand.

"Hello, I'm Steve Franklin with Second Start.'' He gave her a warm, moist handshake.

"Good afternoon. Have a seat. I'm sure Mr. Lang will be here soon.'' Jade resisted the urge to wipe her hand when he let it go. Once seated, she eased a tissue from her jacket pocket and blotted her palm beneath the conference table.

They were soon joined by two women and another man.

They introduced themselves as administrators of agencies that provided health and social services. One of the women, Connie Mason, seemed very friendly with Franklin. Susan Taylor was Franklin's staff. The other man, Eddie Simon of Gracie Street Center, sat quietly. Lang came into the room with an air of brisk authority. They all helped themselves to coffee from a pot on a nearby table.

"Sorry I'm late. A meeting at the legislature ran late." Lang shook everyone's hand. "Thank you for coming on such short notice."

"No problem, Bill." Connie Mason beamed at him. Her silver hair and expensive business suit were in perfect order.

Lang smiled back. "Let's get started then. There are three large grants that we stand a good chance of getting. The purpose—"

The door to the conference room opened, causing all heads to swivel around. The newcomer paused momentarily. Dark eyes the color of mahogany scanned the room. He seemed satisfied to see Eddie Simon.

"Come in, Damon. Damon Knight, this is Connie Mason of Quality Medical Services; Steve Franklin, you know. Miss Taylor is his program coordinator." Lang pointed to the plump brunette.

"Sorry—I got here as fast as I could." Damon Knight stood at least an inch taller than Lang at six foot three. The dark gray jacket he wore over a striped shirt open at the collar did not seem at all out of place beside Lang's dark silk suit and tie. "I wanted to be here even though Eddie is my administrator. But I hope you didn't wait for me."

"It's okay. We were just starting. This is Jade Pellerin from my office," Lang said. "Mr. Knight is not only the vice president of the Gracie Street Center Board of Directors, he founded it."

"I had help from a lot of good people—including Eddie," Damon said with modesty. His gaze moved around the table until it rested on Jade's face.

Jade caught her breath when those eyes focused on her. Even

at five foot seven, she was craning her neck at a towering figure when he crossed the room to grasp her hand. Unlike Franklin's sweaty greeting, the touch of his hand was velvet smooth. Full lips and a strong nose that flared gave his face a sensuous look that shook her. She searched for just the right description for the color of his skin. Pecan? No, not quite right. Almond? That did not seem to be it, either. Then it hit her. Dark honey, the gourmet kind she'd seen in a small shop in the mall . . . clear and sweet. Jade felt dazed by the still warm tingle from his touch that tickled the palm of her hand.

Damon let go of her hand and sat down abruptly. "Nice to meet you, Miss Pellerin." He dipped his head in acknowledgment and looked away.

Jade felt a rush of embarrassment. She hoped no one sensed her reaction to this striking man. Then she became incensed. He seemed to take his magnetic effect for granted. A real cool customer, he was ready to get down to business while she was mooning like a teenager in heat. Well, forget him. Another conceited lover-boy was the last thing she needed after what Nick had put her through. Jade looked down at the materials she'd prepared for the group. She assumed her best professional demeanor.

"I was just saying, Damon, it looks like the department will be getting the three-million-dollar grant. That's over a five-year period of course and statewide."

"But it's to work with teen parents. Right, Bill?" Connie Mason asked.

"Yes, but the description really means the scope can be broader to include some prevention of teen pregnancy and even health services," Lang said.

Franklin assumed a sincere expression. "A terrible problem in this state. But we at Second Start have done some work in this area. We are committed to helping these youngsters get a better start in life."

Damon sat forward. "How do you propose the money be committed? Three million statewide isn't much." He frowned at Lang.

"That's why I wanted input from you folks. You've got some of the most successful programs in Louisiana, in the southern region even. I think with proper planning, we can have a positive impact."

"There are ways to get matching federal dollars from other sources and maximize the dollars we get." Franklin spoke with eagerness. He blinked at Damon Knight's sharp glance. "To spend on the kids of course."

Damon turned to Lang. "You don't even know if the grant will be awarded to DHH yet, and we're already talking about using it to get more money?"

Jade gazed at Damon first then her boss. The muscle along Lang's jaw jumped a few times as he looked down at the table. It was not her imagination. There was some tension between these two men. An expectant silence hung heavy in the room.

"We're here to examine all options. Including ways to help as many people as possible. I'm sure you would agree, with a problem as big as this, we'd want to hit the ground running. It makes sense to do some preliminary planning." Lang spoke in a measured tone, one that said he was only trying to be prudent.

"Oh, certainly. It's just us and Arkansas in the running for the funding now. The proposal we submitted is far superior. I think it's a very smart move to begin work now, Bill," Connie Mason said. She tapped a manicured finger on the tabletop.

"We're only here to talk about a strategy, Knight. To build on what you folks are doing and how *you* can help improve services. Frankly I expect a call at any minute giving us the award," Lang said.

"Really?" Franklin perked up again.

Lang nodded. "Arkansas was asked for additional information about support services that they don't have in place. We do, that is, through agencies such as yours." He looked at Damon. "That's why we're here—to talk about the money we can use now. You're right, anything else is premature at this point. I'm sure Steve meant that as just a brainstorm idea for now."

"Absolutely, just added in as food for thought on down the line," Franklin put in quickly. He seemed just as eager to play down his earlier suggestion. "Might not even be necessary."

Jade watched Damon Knight, fascinated with the way he pursed his lips when deep in thought. How would it feel to press her lips against them? When his gaze met hers, she felt a rush. Those smoky eyes sent a thrill through her she'd never experienced before. Not even with Nick. She looked away. *No thank you, Mr. Heartbreak. I will not give in to hormones this time.*

Damon dropped the pen he was holding and sat back in his chair. He turned away from Jade. "Fine. Then I suggest we concentrate on teenage fathers with equal emphasis and work with local school systems to offer programs as either part of their health education curriculum or as an elective."

"Okay, that's a good place to start," Lang said.

For the next hour, the group went back and forth debating the merits of various approaches. They agreed to very general goals but decided to wait until the grant award was made official. Throughout the meeting, Jade avoided making eye contact with Damon—a difficult task since he sat directly across from her. Despite the distance of several feet, he seemed too close for comfort. His presence was a palpable force that she had to make a conscious effort to resist. At last the meeting came to a close, with Lang thanking them again for coming. Jade suppressed a huge sigh of relief. She hoped Lang would not include her in future meetings. Damon and Lang stood talking even though the others had left.

"Ms. Pellerin, could you come back please?" Lang called out to her.

Jade reluctantly went toward the two men. Damon did not look in her direction. His square-jawed face was impassive.

"Yes?" Jade forced her voice to be cool, the picture of a together nineties kind of woman who was not impressed with his superficial charm.

"Mr. Knight has some excellent ideas. In fact, his programs aimed at teen dads is one of only two in the state. I'd like you to work with him once the grant comes in, which I'm sure it will." Lang nodded at Damon.

Jade clamped her jaws shut to keep from blurting out a loud refusal. Why was she afraid? "Yes, Mr. Lang."

"Eddie Simon can give you all the information you need." Damon smiled at her. "But of course if you need anything from me, just ask." He looked down at her legs then cleared his throat. "I'll make myself available."

Jade felt a charge of aggravation. So he thought a lift of his dark eyebrow in her direction would make her melt, did he? "Thanks, but I doubt I'll need to bother you, Mr. Knight. I'm sure Mr. Simon, as the director, has all the information I'll need," Jade said in a clipped tone. She took a step back to stand behind her boss.

Damon picked up his leather portfolio. "Of course." He shook Lang's hand and strode off without another word.

Jade forced herself not to smirk at putting him in his place. His long stride was a study in fluid motion. A tiny prick of regret grew as Jade watched him go. *Stop it, fool. Be glad he's gone.* She made a determined vow not to think of him again. Yet forgetting those eyes would take great concentration. Bill Lang's high energy level helped. She juggled assignments the rest of the day with no time to daydream about full brown lips and strong arms.

By the time she fought rush hour traffic to arrive at her condo at six that evening, Jade was spent. She kicked off her pumps and plopped down on her sectional sofa. Before she could relax with a diet soda and watch the network news, the doorbell rang. Her mother's face was magnified in the glass of the peephole.

Jade rested her forehead against the door. This was not the way to end a long day. She opened the door. "Hello, Mama. Hi, Lanessa."

Clarice Pellerin swept in ahead of her oldest daughter. Her gold lightweight wool cape hung just so on her shoulders. Neatly coiffed hair dyed a dark auburn fell in soft curls swept away from her face. Lanessa looked to be a younger version of her mother. They were frequently mistaken for sisters and turned male heads when they made an entrance either together or separately.

"Hello, baby." Clarice gave Jade a peck on the cheek. "We saw a simply stunning sofa at Rosenfield's that would do wonders for this room. Wouldn't it, Lanessa?"

Jade clenched her teeth. "I'm not looking for new furniture. I bought this set only two years ago."

"Hi, Jade." Lanessa gave her sister a look of apology. "I've always loved this sofa and love seat. That soft fawn color is perfect with those drapes."

"Thanks, Nessa." Jade shot her a look of sister-gratitude.

"Hmm, well . . ." Clarice cast a critical gaze that said she did not agree. "So what are your plans this evening, Jade?"

"To curl up with a good book and enjoy a cup of herbal tea. I'm really beat tonight. Getting to bed real early will feel so good." Jade stretched, hoping her mother would take the hint. Clarice took off her cape and settled in.

"With that jazz concert down in the Atrium at eight, you should be going to that. I swear, you'd think you were my age. Lanessa has a date with Alex what a catch!" Clarice beamed at her oldest daughter with pride.

"To tell you the truth, I'd just as soon stay home myself. Alex St. Romaine isn't exactly Mr. Excitement." Lanessa crossed her long legs.

"Nonsense, he's perfectly wonderful. He's a computer program analyst or something high-tech like that." Clarice waved a hand, dismissing her statement. "He makes a ton of money, too."

"Too bad he can't buy some personality," Lanessa said with a snigger.

Jade started to giggle, but both daughters stifled their mirth at a sharp look of disapproval from Clarice.

"Lanessa, Alex cares a great deal for you. I hardly think you should be making fun of him behind his back," Clarice scolded her.

"Oh, come on, Mother." Lanessa tossed her hair, dark reddish brown hair. It set off her cocoa brown skin beautifully, and the long curls fell just below her shoulders. "Alex is no Prince Charming by any stretch of the imagination—but he'll do in a pinch."

"Baby, he's perfect for you. The right family and a good profession. You've known him practically all your life, since grade school. You should appreciate what you've got." Clarice tried to reason with her.

"Whatever," Lanessa quipped. "So, Jade, what's up with your superfine new boss? I hear he's got it." A gleam was in her eyes.

"Well . . ."

"Oh, don't embarrass her, Lanessa. You know she won't keep that position with her old boss gone." Clarice gave Lanessa a significant look before turning to her youngest daughter. "Now, Jade, you'll get another little job. Why, maybe your daddy can help."

"I have a job. In fact, I'll be working for Mr. Lang as his administrative assistant," Jade said with an edge to her voice. Clarice always managed to belittle anything she did.

"Why, that's nice, baby. Isn't that nice, Nessa?" Clarice nudged her Lanessa.

"Great, kiddo. Keep climbing. I admire the way you make it in that jungle out there." Lanessa took a deep breath. "I doubt I could do it."

"With that hefty settlement from your second divorce, I don't know why you work at all." Clarice pursed her lips at Lanessa. "I mean really, Lanessa, wasting your time."

"Hey, there are lots of fine, well-to-do businessmen hanging around the state capitol these days. More and more African-American men, Mother." Lanessa smoothed her dress over her curves.

"Re-ally?" Clarice lost her frown as she contemplated this fact. "I hadn't thought about it like that."

Jade looked from her mother to her sister. Clarice had groomed Lanessa from the cradle to be the wife of a wealthy man. Lanessa seemed to have the perfect temperament for it. She hated getting up early or any activity that required too much work on her part. Males of all ages had raced each other trying to make life easy for her since kindergarten. Jade, on the other hand, was the "competent one" as her mother loved to tell anyone who would listen.

To Jade this meant unattractive and that she needed to pursue a career since her marrying prospects were slim. Jade had taken her height and build from her father's side of the family, taller than average with healthy curves. Lanessa, at five feet three, had a lean frame and looked like Clarice had at her age. Not ony that, but Lanessa shared her mother's termperament. An outsider, that was what she was in her own family.

Alton Pellerin doted on his baby girl but was gone much of the time, tending to a successful dry cleaning business. The familiar feeling of sad resentment flooded her as she watched the two of them in easy camaraderie discuss men.

"I guess we should be going if you're going to have time to get ready for your date." Clarice stood and lifted her cape to her shoulders. Jade jumped up and helped her. "Don't work too hard, sugar." She pressed her lips to Jade's cheek then rubbed the smear of lipstick from her skin. "Such lovely skin runs in our family."

"Bye, Jade-girl," Lanessa said. "Really, it's great about your promotion. You deserve it." She held Jade's hand a moment before letting go.

"Thanks, Nessa." Jade felt a rush of affection. A fleeting shadow of . . . something passed over her sister's face. Sadness? Regret? "Are you okay?"

"Hey, fine as wine." The old Lanessa, confident and self-possessed flashed a dazzling smile. "Child, I've got a sweater dress that is going to have old Alex's tongue hanging out all night. With any luck I'll have a diamond necklace this Christmas. Then it's so long, sucker."

Jade laughed in spite of herself. "You ought to be ashamed of yourself, girl." Even with all her vanity and being favored by Clarice, Jade could not help but have a deep sister-love for her.

"Don't you sit around alone every night. With your looks you could have a dozen fine men to choose from." Lanessa shrugged into her leather pant coat.

"Oh, yeah. I had to change my phone number three times to avoid them," Jade said with a snort. "Besides, I've had my fill of men for a while."

"Hey, your divorce was final a year ago. Forget about Nick, he didn't deserve you."

"I'm over Nick. My life has gotten one hundred percent better since he's out of it. And no other look-so-good brother is going to mess with my mind again," Jade blurted out with force—too much force not to make Lanessa take note.

"Who have you met? Some man has got you more turned on than you want to be." Lanessa was never so self-involved that she could not read her little sister like a book. The accuracy never ceased to amaze Jade, or annoy her.

"Don't be ridiculous," Jade said. She looked down at the carpet. "I'm just making a general statement."

"Uh-huh." Lanessa started to say more when Clarice called out.

"Lanessa, you and Jade can talk about me behind my back later. Now come on."

"That woman thinks she's the center of the universe." Lanessa rolled her eyes up to the ceiling. She gave Jade a quick hug.

"And the apple doesn't fall far from the tree," Jade murmured with good nature as she watched the dove gray Lincoln Continental drive off.

Finally able to enjoy a peaceful night, Jade put on her big nightshirt with matching knee socks. A steaming cup of Sleepy Time tea sat on the end table near the sofa. As she flipped through television stations looking for some bland old movie that would not tax her thoughts, Lanessa's words came back to her. Even hours later it seemed the stamp of Damon Knight's powerful and magnetic effect on her was visible. The man was sexy, no use denying it. Just sitting a few feet across from him had set her body thrumming with the desire to feel his hard chest pressed against her. What was this? Until now, abstinence had been an easy choice. Now she had to feel a sensual ache because of one encounter.

"It's just the natural effect of being without a man for so long. Nothing more," she said out loud as though hearing her own voice would make it so. But even as she spoke the words, she felt a small glow at the possibility she might see him again very soon.

Damon sat in the second-floor office of his carpet and floor covering store on Coursey Boulevard. The store manager, Joe Kinchen, and other employees had locked up long ago and most were gone now. He'd reviewed the inventory and sales reports at least three times in the last hour. To his deep dismay, the face of that gorgeous assistant of Lang's kept coming back, sending his mind off on a very unbusinesslike reverie. Just his luck she sat right across from him. One look at those dark lashes and eyebrows framing the most startling cocoa brown eyes made his libido come alive.

Joe stood anxious to leave. "Everything in order, Mr. Knight? I mean, you got any questions . . . ?"

"Hmm? Oh, sorry, Joe. No, everything is fine." Damon rubbed his eyes.

"If you need to get the shipping lists, they're right here." Joe went to a metal file cabinet.

"Damon, I thought you were at the Main Street location today. Hi ya, Joe. How's that new baby?"

Damon's younger brother strode in and gave Joe a handshake. Trent Knight had the same good looks stamped on his nut brown face as his older brother and father, but the similarity stopped there. Oliver Knight was a dour workaholic. Damon did share his trait of being serious and hard working, though he was not as humorless. On the other hand, Trent always had a joke or was ready to laugh at himself. He owned his own business, cleaning up construction sites and commercial buildings. That he did not follow in the family business was a constant source of tension in the family.

Damon felt a rush of guilt. Here it was almost seven o'clock at night, he was keeping Joe from his family. All because he could not keep his priorities straight and stop mooning over some woman he had seen only once.

"Go on home, Joe. I'm sorry for keeping you here so late." Damon jumped up from the chair and crossed to him. "I'll finish up. Tell Beryl hello for me."

"Thanks, Damon. Night." Joe waved a hasty goodbye.

"Give that sweet baby girl a kiss for me, man!" Trent yelled after the fleeing proud papa. A muffled replied came back. "Can you believe how he turned his life around in two years?"

"Sure. Even when I met him in jail, I could see Joe was a man who wanted something more in his life." Damon began to organize the papers in brown file folders.

"And he's got it. A lovely wife and baby."

"Uh-huh. How's business with you?" Damon did not want to talk about happy nuclear families. It brought too much pain at what he did not have.

"Great. That new Lancaster Estates development has been keeping my crews busy." Trent sprawled his lanky frame in the large leather chair opposite his brother.

"You'll be adding more employees soon then?" Damon paused in his task of arranging the documents.

Trent held up a hand. "Yes, and I'll interview a couple of boys from your program." He laughed. "Always putting the touch on me for those little scamps, as Grandma would call them."

"You get as much of a kick giving those kids a break as I do, so don't even try it." Damon gave him a playful punch as he passed to get to the file cabinet.

"That's true. Well, I'm on my way to pick up Carliss. Say, you ought to join us. Her friend—"

"Forget it," Damon cut him off.

"But she's a fabulous lady. A corporate attorney." Trent twisted around in his seat.

"Sure. Just what I need after being taken to the cleaners by Rachelle in that divorce settlement: to spend time with another lawyer. No, thanks."

"Come on, bro. Don't get all bitter on me."

"I'm taking a time-out from the mating game for a while. When I start dating again—and it won't be soon—I'll take it slow."

Damon thought of Jade's lips, touched with lipstick the color of dark red wine. Her hair, parted down the middle, was a soft coal black frame to that lovely face. No, he was not falling into that tender trap again. Not him. He shook his head and went back to the desk.

"I see."

"Real slow. No more getting turned around by a fine woman who . . . uh, anyway I'm doing okay. I don't need it."

Trent watched him for a while before speaking. "Who is she?"

"Who is who?" Damon shuffled the files in front of him.

"I got a strong impression that you had one particular female in mind. That wasn't a theoretical fine woman that put a spark in your eyes just now."

"The point is, it's only been a year since I finally had Rachelle surgically removed from my life. I don't mind telling you it's been a peaceful twelve months." Damon heaved a sigh.

"Yep, you had it rough."

"Ten years of The Marriage from Hell. I'm happy to be lonely these days. So let's talk about something else."

Damon did not want to dwell on the memory of Jade. What had she done to him to leave such an indelible mark of arousal that came back at the mere thought of her? He needed to put a halt to any weakening in that direction. Beautiful women were trouble. And pain. An image of Rachelle, cold and calculating, made his stomach clench. Rachelle was as heartless as she was beautiful. No way. Jade Pellerin had heartache written all over her.

Trent took a melodramatic deep breath. "Okay, I'll let Carliss know she'll have to give up trying to find you a new love."

"Definitely. Now have you seen Dad lately?"

"Have I! Will he ever get over me not running these stores with you?" Trent let out an exaggerated groan.

Damon snorted. "You know the answer to that. At least he's following the treatment plan these days."

"Yeah, he's got more movement in his left arm than ever before. But it's been a long way back for him." Trent lost the irritated expression at the reference to how ill their father had been.

"That stroke could have killed him." Damon spoke in a sober tone, saying what Trent would not. "A year of treatment and he's still weak. But a least he's doing better."

"Sure, nothing wrong with his mind—or his *mouth,*" Trent said.

"Don't let it get to you. Besides, fussing and carrying on is his hobby. I think it helps him stay alert." Damon grinned at the grimace his comment caused Trent.

"Oh, so having him chew on my rear end is medicinal. Well, then he ought to be himself in no time," he said with a twinkle in his eyes. He glanced at the clock on the wall. "Let me get outta here. Sure you don't want to—"

"Goodbye, Trent." Damon pushed him toward the door. "Have a nice time."

Damon spent another fifteen minutes putting things in order for Joe. He glanced at his watch: eight thirty already.

He decided to stop by Mario's for take-out Italian food on his way home. It seemed there were couples everywhere: in the cars alongside his at every stop sign or red light, in the restaurant while he waited for his order. Damon tried to ignore them, yet seeing them made him feel an emptiness that he had not felt before. Jade Pellerin . . . Somehow not only his body but his heart told him she would be a perfect fit to fill that void. There was a seductive grace about the way her hair swung when she turned her head. She had a habit of tilting her head to the right when considering something said to her. It made

Chapter 2

"For the last three days I've been doing damage control. That idiot Steve Franklin is shooting his mouth off all over the state." Mike Testor slapped an accordion file down on Lang's desk. The tall man still had his summer tan. His blue eyes flashed with annoyance. He brushed back perfectly combed black hair.

"No one really listens to Steve, Mike." Lang seemed undisturbed. "You know what's going on in the finance section. Just do what you always do. Tavis is on top of things there, too."

Lang nodded to a thin black man standing at his shoulder. Tavis Collins worked as a program analyst in the finance section of the Medicaid office. He and Lang had worked together before. Tavis perched on the edge of Lang's desk and gazed at Mike.

"Sure, Mike. Besides, there is nothing—no executive bulletin or published rule—that prohibits anything you're doing."

"You mean anything we're doing, don't you?" Mike shot back.

"Whatever." Tavis did not lose his composure as he returned Mike's stare with his own cool gaze.

"Bill, the governor is real sensitive to this type of stuff. Remember, he was in the legislature for five years. He knows the ropes." Mike drummed his fingers with nervous energy.

"He's also got his hands full with the gambling issue. Between the gambling lobby and the anti-gambling lobby, he can't take come up for air long enough to notice much else." Lang stirred his mug of coffee. He was as relaxed as Testor was nervous.

"But Dr. Chauvin isn't consumed with the gambling thing. The governor named him secretary of this department for a good reason. The man is not only considered a brilliant doctor, but he's an expert in health care services with an international reputation."

"Yes, yes." Lang showed mild irritation. Walter Chauvin had the kind of stature and power he wanted badly. "Walter walks on water."

"Not to mention Chester Howard. He's not in charge of the Office of Budget and Finance for nothing. And he's keeping close watch on the Medicaid division."

"I know all that, Mike. They both interviewed me, remember?"

"All I'm saying is, we've got to be careful."

"And you've said it four times already. I got the point. You think I got where I am by being sloppy?" Lang took a long sip of the hot liquid.

"But those rule changes—" Mike was still unconvinced.

"Are so complicated and obscure, no one will figure them out for at least a year," Tavis broke in.

"Yeah, but one of Chester's hotshot new assistants is making waves. He's been complaining to me for the last two months. He's figured it out real fast." Mike chewed on his bottom lip.

"I've got another meeting, Bill." Tavis brushed at the lapels and sleeves of his wool jacket. His manner conveyed he was bored with this conversation. "By the way, I handled that problem you told me about the other day. It's cool. See you at the club later?''

Lang wore a amused expression at the look of annoyance on Mike's face at being dismissed with disdain. ''Yes. Dinner at six.'' He watched Tavis stroll out past Mike.

''Who does he think he is anyway? If he thinks Howard will be put off because some low-level bean counter—'' Testor fumed.

''Mike, nobody listens to Dave. He's been around for years, singing the same old song. That's why he's shuffled away in that cramped cubicle, tracking some obscure statistics.'' Lang chuckled.

Mike's frown relaxed a bit. ''Guess you're right. He has that slumped shoulder profile from bending over stacks of computer sheets. Yeah, nobody listens to old Dave anymore.''

''If they ever did. Now what have you heard from Sherman Ortego?''

''Things are going well. He's very pleased with what we've done thus far.'' Mike nodded.

''He should be,'' Lang grunted. ''Those rule changes mean he can expand beds with new certificates. I'm looking forward to my vacation to Cancun.''

''Ortego has rented a yacht to take us down the coast. It's a great trip.'' Mike rubbed his hands in anticipation.

''Hmm, I wonder if my new assistant would like to go?'' Lang stared at the door to his office as though picturing her.

''Jade is one fine lady. She'd be a real . . . asset.'' Mike actually smacked his lips.

''*Ms. Pellerin* to you,'' Lang snapped. He stood up. ''Good-bye, Mike. I have work to do.''

Mike sprang from his seat. ''Sure, Bill. Didn't mean to offend . . . I mean, the young lady is very attractive is all—''

''Give me a call on that home health issue. The board of nursing has been on my back about it for the last three weeks.'' Lang opened the door.

Testor shrugged and accepted the dismissal. ''Sure thing. Oh, Ja—Ms. Pellerin, how are you?'' With his back to Lang, he let his gaze wander down her body before looking at her face again.

Jade nodded to him. The man was handsome, but there was something about him that made her a bit uneasy—a feeling that she would not like to be alone with him.

"Hello, Mike. Here are the reports you needed." Jade nodded to him. "And if you need me to clarify anything, let me know."

"I'll be sure and do thát." Mike flashed a dazzling smile. "You are so helpful."

"I'm sure that won't be necessary. Besides, Ms. Pellerin will be tied up pretty much. Goodbye again, Mike." Lang gave him a pointed look.

"Bye, Mike," Jade said. She wondered what Mike had done to annoy the boss. Lang's voice cut through her musings.

"Ms. Pellerin, can we get to work on that report for Secretary Chauvin?" Lang motioned her into his office.

"Yes, sir, but I'm still waiting for legal to give me the statute that applies. They promised to have it by this afternoon at the latest."

"That's cutting it close, but I guess it can't be helped. That leaves the meeting with the Office of Public Health. I'd like the report on laboratories."

"Yes, Mr. Lang." Jade got up to leave.

"Listen, let's not be so formal with this 'yes, sir—no, sir' stuff. Besides, I feel like an old man when you call me Mr. Lang."

"Yes, sir, I mean . . ." Jade laughed.

"Come on, now—you can call me by my first name," Lang coaxed her.

"Okay . . . Bill. That will take getting used to." Jade shook her head.

"With as closely as we'll be working for the next four years, you'll get lots of practice. I already think of us as a working team, Jade." Lang put a hand on her elbow.

"I see you've gotten settled into your new office." A petite woman gazed at them with eyebrows raised. She wore an elegant fuschia suit with black lapels. Her black leather pumps and purse were stamped with a small gold design of a leading fashion house. Her skin was the color of smooth café au lait.

"Hello, Kathy. This is my administrative assistant Jade Pellerin. My wife, Kathy." He let go of Jade's elbow and moved away from her by just a fraction.

"A lovely name. Pleased to meet you." Kathy held out her hand in a regal manner.

Jade smiled at her tentatively. "Hello, Mrs. Lang. Nice to meet you."

"So how long have you been working here?" Kathy's voice was cool, but her question seemed to have some other purpose.

"Almost twelve years now. I've worked in a couple of the sections since I started." Jade sensed that Kathy was not pleased to see a female so close to her husband. "Mostly making sure the bosses have what they need to run things."

"And I'm sure you do an excellent job at whatever you do." Kathy eyed Jade in a less than complimentary way.

"Thank you, Jade. You can go now." Lang stepped between the two women. He ushered Kathy ahead of him into his office and shut the door with a firm thud.

Jade blinked at the closed door. Muffled voices engaged in an intense exchange sounded through the heavy wood. "Whoa! Honey, pull those fangs in." She hurried to make herself scarce.

"I see you met the First Lady." Shaena appeared from around a corner, carrying a stack of files.

"Miss Thang is something else. She all but accused me of being hot for her husband." Jade took some of the folders that threatened to fall. "Let me help. Is any of this the statute I so desperately need for Bill's report?"

"Nah, Warren is still working on that one. He'll be through in about twenty minutes, he said to tell you. Back to Kathy the Dragon Slayer." Shaena followed Jade into her office.

"She's a piece of work."

"Well, maybe she's got cause."

"I haven't heard anything like that about him," Jade said in defense of him. "Bill has been nothing but professional with me."

"Saint William?" Shaena squinted. "I don't think so."

"Oh, stop it. Besides, it's none of our business." Jade shook a finger at her.

"Okay, but I have a feeling we'll be hearing more about this as time passes." Shaena switched gears. "By the way, Aline tells me a real honey was up here, and lucky you got to meet with him. Damon Knight."

"You know him?" Jade tried to keep her voice matter-of-fact.

"By reputation."

"Oh, a real woman chaser. It figures." Jade shut the file drawer with a bang. She should have known not to trust her instincts when it came to men.

"No, I mean he was a track star in high school and college. And his father has a string of carpet and tile stores. The Knight family has been prominent for at least one hundred years." Shaena pulled out half a granola bar.

"Really?"

"Yep. Damon's from an old Louisiana family with money." Shaena munched on the remains of the snack.

"Wait a minute. As in Hezekiah Knight?" Jade's eyes went wide.

Shaena nodded. "His great-great-grandfather. Made a fortune selling hardware and with his own carpentry business. He's in the Louisiana history books for being one of the most influential black men during Reconstruction."

"Wow." Jade remembered the way he walked, shoulders back, head high. Damon Knight was from a family mentioned in black history books on Louisiana. This intrigued her about the man even more.

"Say, you've got a dreamy look on your face. Yep, Dynamite Damon strikes again." Shaena snickered.

"Get real. I am not bowled over by Damon Knight." Jade spoke sharply. She brushed a stray tendril of hair from her face and turned away from her friend.

"Hey, stronger women of all ages have fallen under his spell. The man is superfine, you must admit."

"I'm through judging men by what's on the surface. I didn't pay close attention to the man anyway." Jade's voice cracked.

"Liar. You're trying too hard to convince me, and yourself." Shaena gazed at her.

"You and Lanessa have overactive imaginations."

"Well, let's consider the evidence," Shaena said. "When I mentioned his name, your eyes got that gleam in them. Also, Damon Knight is one fabulous brother with beaucoup charm."

Jade waved her hand. "I hope you do better defending some poor sucker in court. That is a pitiful case."

"And most important, you haven't been with a man since Heck was a pup." Shaena folded her arms.

"Like I said, pitiful. You've been out of the courtroom too long. Even I could blow that out of the water." Jade lifted her chin in defiance.

"Oh, really? Go ahead then."

"One, we were in a meeting discussing the driest of topics for all of two hours, during which my attention was on the business at hand."

Shaena looked dubious. "I'll bet."

"Two, Damon Knight is trouble wrapped up in nice packaging—something I got my fill of with Nick." Jade held up two fingers.

"So because Nick was selfish and cruel, all men are trash? Come on."

Jade clenched her teeth in aggravation. "No, but I could spot his kind a mile away. Damon Knight is too sure that every woman he meets would crawl through jagged glass to get into his bed. It's written all over him."

Shaena giggled. "Honey, he'd be right. At least two dozen women in this town would jump at the chance. I've met him a couple of times at social functions. He's got a body that won't quit."

"Yeah, and he knows it. You should have seen the way he strolled around like he was some kind of king." Jade turned the memory of how his fluid movement sent shivers through her into a negative, or at least she was trying hard to so as to counteract the powerful attraction.

"Brother was steppin', eh?"

"Sitting there with that I'm-too-cool look on his face." Jade remembered the strong set of his jaw. The way those dark brows came together when he was deep in thought. His lips looked like velvet milk chocolate. It would be so nice to see if they were as sweet as . . . Jade shook herself to clear the hot vision that had formed.

"Let me get this straight: You were with him a short time, and your mind was only on business." Shaena lifted an eyebrow at her.

"You got that right," Jade cracked.

"But you noticed his walk, his look and what kind of expressions crossed his face." Shaena sat back in her chair. "Sounds to me like you were checking the brother out and—"

"I was not—"

"And you liked what you saw." Shaena looked pleased with herself. "Prosecution rests, your honor."

"You're hallucinating," Jade snapped. She got up to put away a large binder. What she really wanted was to conceal how on-target her friend's assessment had been.

"Hey, you ought to know better than to try and fool me. We lawyers are trained to ferret the truth out of witnesses."

"Don't you have work to do somewhere else?" Jade gave her a baleful look. "You have a habit of picking on my nerves until I could strangle you."

"Now, now—what are friends for?" Shaena's lips twitched with suppressed mirth. "Seriously, go on after the man. You want to anyway, right?"

Jade was dumbfounded at how her bald statement shook her. The phrase "want to" sent a delicious jab of fire down her spine that spread to her hips. She needed to move this conversation to a safer topic, and fast.

"This subject is closed, Shaena."

"Fine. But after spending more time with Damon Knight, we'll see how long you can fool yourself into believing—"

"Closed, I said," Jade said with a warning glare.

"I'm through with it." Shaena held up both hands in a gesture of surrender. "By the way, here's the *State Register*. We just finished it."

The *State Register* announced proposed changes in state regulations. State law required that before any new rule took effect, a public hearing had to be held with notices published in newspapers around the state.

"Thanks." Jade put it aside.

"There's a piece in there about hospital beds. I thought there was a moratorium on issuing certificates." Shaena wore a slight frown. "Of course I'm only guessing at what it means. Whoever wrote it sure emptied out his legal thesaurus."

"Humph, you lawyers can turn an order for a burger with fries into a ten-page brief. Bill said something about a problem with one of the regs that limits the department from responding to the need based on hospital use." Jade flipped through a stack of sheets with tiny black print on them. "Who can keep up with all this paper?"

"You've got that right. Between executive bulletins, written interpretations and stupid memos from bosses, I don't even pay attention to most of it anymore. Well, I better get moving."

"See you later for our usual Thank God It's Friday, after-work dinner?"

"You got it." Shaena picked up the stack of folders and headed off.

With a sigh, Jade buried herself in the mound of paper they had just complained about. Quitting time would not come soon enough.

"Moving up in more ways than one?" Kathy Lang settled into the leather chair across from her husband. She crossed her legs.

"What are you talking about?" Lang gazed at her without expression.

"A great office with a lovely view and another nice view

right outside the office. Ms. Jade Pellerin is a nice ornament to have around.'' Kathy tossed back her thick dark brown hair.

''She's more than ornamental.'' Lang's voice was tight with irritation.

''I don't doubt that for one minute,'' Kathy said. Her lips turned down in a slight sneer.

''Kathy, how many times have we gone through this? If I slept with only a third of the women you've accused me of, I'd be busy twenty-four-seven. Jade is my assistant, nothing more.''

''Bill, I—''

Lang began sorting notes Jade had left for him. ''Now I'm very busy. I'll see you tonight.''

Kathy leaned forward with a contrite look. ''Baby, I'm sorry. It's just . . . you know how much I love you. I just want us to be together.'' The cold, sophisticated veneer was gone, replaced by a vulnerable woman desperate for the attention of the man she adored.

''To the exclusion of everything else.'' Lang's voice had a hard edge that sliced through the space between them. ''Even spending time with my son. I had to fight like crazy to get my ex-wife to let him spend three weeks a year with me.''

''You know how much I enjoy having little Derrick visit.'' Kathy failed to sound sincere.

Lang gave a snort of skepticism. ''Yeah, sure you do. That's why you throw temper tantrums whenever he asks to spend time with me.''

''His mother uses it as an excuse to call my house and throw herself at you!'' Kathy snarled. ''That witch still wants you.''

''Now you're back on this kick about Ileen. What is it with you anyway?'' Lang gazed at her with a sour look.

''Bill, please. I didn't come here to fight.'' Kathy tried to appease him.

''Then why are you here, Kathy?'' Lang went back to scanning the papers in front of him.

''I thought we could . . . Honey, let's take a long lunch

together.'' Kathy got up and crossed to stand beside him. She stroked his hair. "Like we used to."

"I've got too much to do today." Lang ignored her.

"You're the boss, take the rest of the day off. I set us up an appointment at Crown Travel. There is a wonderful trip to Jamaica that would be just heaven."

"No." Lang still did not stop reading.

"I have pictures of the suite we'd have. It has a view of the beach and this fabulous king-sized bed." Kathy leaned down to nibble his ear. "I always could make you forget work with a certain touch in just the right place." She reached down toward his lap.

Lang pushed her hand away. "I can't get away right now. Excuse me." He reached to open the desk drawer next to her hip. "I need to get something."

Kathy jumped back. "Why can't we go? It's not like you don't have able assistants." She perched on the desk edge again when he closed the drawer.

"Because there is a lot going on right now that I personally have to attend to. Why don't you run along so I can get back to work?" Lang gave her a brief glance before picking up another report.

Kathy's face became rigid with anger. "Just like that. Run along, Kathy." Neither paid attention to the knock on the door.

"Bill, Warren is going to bring you that . . . Oh, I'm sorry." Jade stopped just inside the door when she saw Kathy. The look on the woman's face made her back up. "It can wait."

"Come in, Jade. Kathy is on her way out." Lang stood up and took his wife's arm. He walked her out. "Goodbye, dear." He gave her a perfunctory kiss on the cheek.

"We'll continue this discussion later." Kathy scowled at him then directed her ire toward Jade. "Goodbye, *Ms. Pellerin.*" There was no mistaking the belligerence in her voice. She stalked off.

Jade cleared her throat. "I'm really sorry for interrupting. I didn't stop to think Mrs. Lang might still be with you."

"Don't worry about it." Lang seemed to have already dismissed his wife from his mind. "Come in."

Jade followed his lead and got back to business. "As I was saying, Warren is going to come down this afternoon."

"Good. We can get started preparing for the next legislative session. Now what about this note you left on Senator Boudreaux?"

They spent well over an hour sorting through notes from legislators who wanted to discuss health care issues in preparation for committee meetings. The phone rang every ten minutes it seemed. By four thirty Jade was still busy even as she waved goodbye to the secretarial staff on their way out.

"Jade, it's been a long day," Lang said. He leaned against the door frame of her office.

"A long week, Mr.—"

"Ah-ah." Lang held up a forefinger.

"I mean Bill. The weekend didn't come too soon for me." Jade arranged items on her desk in a neat configuration so as to make her day start off right on Monday. "Oh, here are some more reports for you, but they can wait until next week."

"Thanks. Got big plans, I suppose." Lang spoke in a casual voice. He followed Jade toward the elevators.

"Yeah, dressing real comfortably and doing nothing." Jade laughed.

"Hmm . . . some of us are going out for dinner and drinks. Why not come along?" They stopped in front of Lang's office.

"Thanks, but I'm meeting a friend."

"Oh? Well, I see. Have a good weekend then." Lang smiled at her and walked away waving.

"You, too," Jade called out. She turned in time to see the elevator door open with Shaena standing inside.

"Taxi, ma'am?" Shaena beckoned to her with energy. "Come on, let's get out of this place and pretend we don't have to come back."

*   *   *

They were settled in at their favorite seafood restaurant, Uncle Joe's, savoring the aromas. Jade nursed a diet soda while Shaena sipped iced tea. These were their drinks since both were driving.

"Ah-hhh, that hit the spot." Shaena smacked her lips. She waved to several people who passed.

"What would we do without Uncle Joe?" Jade let out a sigh of contentment.

Both women gazed around at the dining room that had been a fixture since the early sixties in the black community. An old jukebox blared blues tunes by Buddy Guy and Tabby Thomas. Friends, some who had known each other since childhood, laughed and talked with great animation. Waitresses called customers by name.

"There would be a riot if Joe Junior ever closed this place. And I'd be the ringleader." Shaena switched her attention to Jade. "Now about your social life."

"Say what? How did we get onto this subject?" Jade folded her arms in a defensive pose.

"I brought it up, that's how. I just hate seeing you acting like the Lone Ranger, girl." Shaena put her elbows on the table. "Listen, being lonely is not the cure for being hurt by one man."

"Thank you, Miss Ebony Advisor," Jade quipped.

"I'm being serious, work and more work is no life. This guy I'm dating has a real fine friend. His name is Norman." Shaena sat forward.

"No, thank you."

"Look, if Damon ain't your speed, give Norman a go. He's very serious, a churchgoer and never been married."

Jade groaned. "What part of 'no' don't you understand?"

"Well, if not Norman, then . . . Hey, over here!" Shaena stood up and gestured to someone.

"Is that Latonya with our order? About time," Jade said. She put a napkin in her lap.

Jade twisted around, expecting to see a tray of food balanced by their waitress. Instead Damon walked up with the fluid movement of an athlete sure of every step. He was wearing dark green corduroy pants with a matching plaid shirt open at the collar. His tan jacket was slung across his shoulder. His dark hair was a frame of tight curls like lamb's wool framing his face. She let out a tiny gasp at the sight of him, so fine and smiling down at her.

"Good evening. You ladies addicted to this place like three-fourths of the black folks in Baton Rouge, eh?"

"You bet. Join us." Shaena maneuvered him onto the seat next to Jade in the booth.

"I was just going to get take-out . . . but I guess I could stay." Damon hesitated only a few beats before sitting next to Jade. "How are you, Ms. Pellerin?"

"Okay," Jade replied. Her mouth felt like cotton. Having him so close sent tiny jolts of delight through her. A wild urge to inch closer until their thighs touched seized her. In response, she moved toward the wall away from him.

Damon noticed her discomfort. "They'll have my order ready soon. I should be going anyway." He turned away to stare across the restaurant. "I have someplace to go."

"Don't be silly. Stay and eat with us. Right, Jade?" Shaena shot her a look of disapproval at her behavior.

Jade felt a tinge of guilt at his reaction and Shaena's admonishment. "Yeah, sure. No need to rush off."

Right, stay here and help me make a pure idiot of myself. Jade wondered if she could resist the strong magnetic field this man radiated. No surprise women flocked to him. A long moment of awkward silence stretched.

"Latonya, he's going to eat in after all, so bring his food with ours." Shaena took control of the situation. "Now that's that. So y'all are going to be working on some project I hear." She looked from one to the other.

Jade cleared her throat. "Not exactly, he—"

"Actually Ms. Pellerin will be working with the director of the Gracie Street Center. I, uh, I'm on the board of directors is all." Damon darted a glance at Jade from the corner of his eye.

Shaena suppressed a smile at the two of them studiously avoiding eye contact. "I hear you helped get the place started. It's given kids a safe, clean place to hang out. Not a small thing in that area of town."

Damon's dark eyes brightened. "Eddie has worked real hard to give that neighborhood a center where people could come together and be a real community again. I haven't done much really."

"Don't be modest. Why, you've given more time and money than a lot of people have in this town. You even sent a couple of those children to junior college." Shaena studied Jade. She smiled when Jade turned to Damon.

"That's what kids living in such poor neighborhoods need, a place to have some hope—which is why I'm so glad about these grants we'll be getting," Jade joined in.

Damon nodded. "Yes, the most dangerous person in the world is someone who feels he has nothing to lose. Those kids are so talented. But so are their parents. They deserve a chance, too."

"Exactly, when parents have a dream they can be better parents. Your adult literacy program is tops in the state. I mean, the program at Gracie Street," Jade said.

"We've had a couple of the adult students go on to more training and better jobs." Damon took obvious pride in the work being done at the center he helped create.

"And with the grant, you could direct more center funds to helping Meals on Wheels to the elderly and the Early Intervention Program. Why, the center could really grow," Jade continued enthusiastically.

"We hadn't considered that—I guess because grant money can dry up." Damon shrugged.

"But you could start with grant money, then switch to a combination of United Way and Community Care funding. Neither of those will seed new programs. But they do fund programs with a track record that could end without their help." Jade felt excited, thinking about all of the great things the center could do.

"Now there's an idea. Well, Ms. Pellerin, I think you and Eddie will make a heck of a team." Damon wore an expression that said he was impressed.

Shaena stared at them for a few seconds. "Whew, too much iced tea. Excuse me." She slid from the seat. She winked at Jade as she walked off. Instead of rushing to the ladies' room, she lingered to chat with a laughing group at a table several feet away.

Jade watched her with a jaundiced eye. She would get that little sneak later. Damon's voice brought her back to her predicament. She was determined to hide how attractive she found him—an even harder task now that they were alone.

"You've got a real solid grasp on program implementation and funding. You a social worker?" Damon looked at her.

"No, my degree is in management. But I've had extensive training in public health policy in the last eight years."

"So how did you get into human services? I thought all you management grads went into business to make big bucks." He smiled at her. Smooth brown lips parted to reveal teeth like pearls.

Jade fought to slow her breathing. Damon Knight could melt icebergs with that smile. She braced herself before speaking.

"I worked in the private sector for a while. But one of my father's friends recruited me to work with him when he was appointed as regional manager for the Department of Social Services. I got hooked on helping to shape public policy and stayed."

"Lucky for the state of Louisiana . . . and me. What I mean is, your expertise on this project will be a real asset," Damon added quickly. He tugged at his collar.

Jade did not look at him. She tried to press down the rise of pleasure his words evoked. How many times had this bashful act worked? "Thank you, but it is my job after all," she replied in a business tone. *Darn, that sounded too prissy even to me.*

Damon sat erect. "Of course."

Another of those awkward silences stretched between them. Jade decided she could at least be more cordial to the man.

Especially since Shaena was determined to take her sweet time getting back to the booth. The waitress refilled their drinks, giving Damon a big smile and lingering as long as possible.

"I mean, I'm glad to have the opportunity to work with you on this project. It will mean a lot to those folks." Jade twisted the drinking straw between her fingers.

Damon relaxed next to her. "It will. Look, I'll be at Gracie Street on Wednesday. Maybe you could schedule to visit then"—he stared into his glass of root beer—"if you're not tied up."

Jade's heart went thump at the simple invitation. Her mind shouted "yes!" but she forced out a composed, "I'll check my calendar Monday and let you know."

"What's happening Wednesday?" Shaena seemed to pop out of nowhere, a gleam of mischief in her light brown eyes.

"Setting up a meeting is all," Jade blurted out.

"About the project," Damon added a little too quickly, he thought. He shifted in his seat.

"Yeah, right." Shaena arched an eyebrow at them both. "Well, here is the food, thank goodness. I'm starved."

For the rest of the meal, Shaena helped jump start a steady stream of conversation between Jade and Damon. They talked about all kinds of topics. Jade could now see why women were so wild about Damon Knight. He was not only charming and handsome but almost courtly in his treatment of women, yet he did not make it seem artificial. Jade found keeping her thoughts of him neutral to be increasingly difficult.

Damon glanced at his watch. "Wow, look it's almost seven thirty. Ladies, I'd better get moving. My parents are probably wondering what happened to me. It's really been nice talking to you," he said, gazing at Jade for several seconds.

"Yes, nice seeing you, too. I'll call you Monday . . . about the site visit." Jade wanted to keep looking into those eyes for just a few moments longer. She let out a sigh as he walked away. Several female heads swiveled to watch him as he passed through the dining room.

As though he finally came back to himself, Damon turned around. "Good to see you again, Ms. Greene." He waved.

"See ya around, Damon," Shaena called after him. She wore a smirk. "Damn! The man was so mesmerized by you, he forgot I was even in the room."

"You're crazy." Jade was exhilarated at the thought despite her protest.

"Maybe, but I ain't stupid. That man wants you bad." Shaena leaned toward her.

"Damon Knight comes on to a lot of women. I want more than a casual thing."

"There is nothing casual in it. I saw the look in his eyes. The man is down with some serious feelings for you." Shaena shook a finger at her.

Jade held herself in check. "Don't be silly, Shaena. You don't know what he's thinking—or are you psychic now?"

"Girl, I don't need gris-gris or tea leaves to tell me Damon is hot for you in more ways than one. The man cares what you think. That's a sign." Shaena sat back with a wise look.

"A sign of what?"

"In my experience any man who takes time to find out what you think on some dry, serious subject wants more than a slam-jam, thank-you-ma'am kinda thing." Shaena nibbled on a corner of french bread. "Don't waste time. Bag it up!"

"You are hallucinating, darlin'. Besides, I'm not going to get involved. So there." Jade stared at her friend with a resolute expression.

"Save that act for somebody who might be fooled by it, okay?" Shaena waved away her declaration with a manicured hand.

"I'm not acting. I'm not going to be the same fool twice. And that's all there is to it."

"Yeah, right," Shaena said, her tone dripped skepticism.

Jade ignored it and went on to talk of something else. Yet for the rest of the evening, she kept getting flashes of the way his lips, so full and inviting, curved when he smiled. Damon Knight had left an impression that was like a hot brand on her consciousness. A growing anxiety mixed with anticipation at seeing him again took root. She could keep him in check, but could she resist the temptation to give in to his allure. The picture of how those other women looked at him brought her up short. Yes, she would have to be strong. Damon Knight would have fun with her and move on to someone in his league—probably a long-legged beauty from another old Louisiana family. Better to face reality now than be hurt again. Time to end this silly, teenage fantasizing. Jade went home with a new determination to protect herself.

"What about that office building job? Did that new carpet come in time for you to meet the contractor's schedule?" Oliver Knight sat across from Damon in a large easy chair. His salt and pepper hair was still thick despite his age and recent illness.

The elder Knight held himself erect, though his right hand curled slightly and he leaned to his left. It was apparent which side of his body had been affected by the stroke he'd suffered two years ago. Still he'd made a good recovery by most standards. He was only a half inch shorter than his oldest son. Dressed stylishly in an expensive long-sleeved sport shirt with olive green chino pants, he was still a striking figure at fifty-nine.

"Come on, Pops. Forget the business. You should just relax now. How was your golf game?"

"Damn game," Oliver muttered. "And Larry Mayew is foul-tempered fool!"

Damon suppressed a smile. "You've been saying that for twenty years now. Why don't you guys just quit playing with him?"

"We did quit. We changed to a later tee-off time. But he shows up every once in a while just to irritate us. Now what about that Lancer job I just asked you about?" Oliver switched back to his favorite subject, Knight and Sons, Inc.

"We were right on time, Pops. Say, that fishing rod Trent

gave you for Father's Day is gathering dust. We ought to take a trip down to Old River some time.''

Oliver blew hard. "Sitting outside in the sun all day to catch one little old sorry fish. Forget that!"

"You need to develop some interests to keep you busy. You used to love collecting stamps and coins. There's a big show coming to the Centroplex Saturday." Damon tried another way to divert his father's attention to some activity that would make retirement easier for him to accept.

"Son, when I expanded to five stores here and in Lafayette, I didn't have time for much else. I put my life's blood into that business. So don't think I'm just going to be put out to pasture." Oliver wagged a finger at his son's nose.

"Pops, the doctor made it clear you can't work anymore. Besides, you've more than earned a rest," Damon said in a calm voice.

"Hey, I'm your father, not some little kid. Don't patronize me, young man."

"Well, you're acting like a little boy who won't take his medicine, the medicine in this case being rest and relaxation." Damon wanted to laugh at the way his father's frown deepened into a perfect pout. But he knew better than to give in to that particular urge.

"Damn doctor. I'll probably be at *his* funeral!" Oliver glowered as though the doctor was in the room with them.

"Pops, the stores are doing fine. I've got good managers." Damon said, knowing that the doctor was not the real issue.

Oliver jabbed a finger in the air between them. "That doesn't mean you can just leave everything to them. You've got to be a hands-on businessman, son. Many a man has lost everything, letting someone else run his business."

Damon groaned inwardly. He did not feel up to one of Oliver's lectures on running a business. "I know, Pops. Say, Trent came by the store last night. He and Carliss seem to be very serious." He patted Oliver's arm. "Before you know it, you'll have grandchildren running around here."

"Hope they have a wedding first," Oliver grunted. "And

that's another thing, Trent has no sense of family responsibility. He's letting you run those stores alone.''

''Come on now.'' Damon wondered if there was any subject he would pick that would not lead to complaints.

''Why in the world he went off on his own is a mystery to me.''

''Pops, the problem is Trent is too much like you. He's independent and marches to his own beat.''

Oliver shook his head. ''Yeah, but I never questioned my duty to take over my father's legacy. A slap in the face is what it is.''

''Now hold on, Trent has nothing but respect for you, and you know it. Why else does he come to you for advice, even with all your barking at him? And you give it to him.'' Damon knew Oliver was just hurt that his younger son wanted to be on his own. Yet Oliver admired Trent's courage, though he'd never admit it.

''As for getting married, humph! How many women has he dated in the last two years? Six or seven.'' Oliver waved a hand. ''I'll grow old waiting for the boy to settle down.''

''I don't know. He's talking commitment this time.''

Oliver brushed away his comment with another grunt of skepticism. He twisted around to stare at Damon with an intense expression. ''What about you? That Monique Benoit has been asking about you, so your mother says.''

''That's right.'' Marlene Knight swept into the room, wearing a floor-length lounge dress. Her hair was black without a hint of gray. At fifty-four she moved with the same self-possessed confidence she had at eighteen.

''Hello, Mother.'' Damon gave her a respectful kiss on the cheek.

''Hello—and your father is right.'' Marlene arranged her dress after sitting down on the love seat across from her husband.

''Mother, I'm a little old for matchmaking.'' Damon swallowed the rising irritation that threatened to force a sharper response.

As usual, Marlene went on without commenting on his protest. Any disagreement with what she wanted was ignored. "Monique is quite devoted to you. Her parents were in school with us."

"Monique is devoted to money more than anything, Mother."

"So she's used to the finer things in life, what's wrong with that? Her family has been prominent in this city and Point Coupee Parish for the last ninety years. She's perfect for you, dear." Marlene ran a hand over her perfectly styled hair.

"Let's not get into this again," Damon mumbled low.

"I heard that." Marlene tilted her head back to stare at him. "Why shouldn't you find her attractive? She's beautiful, smart and from a good family."

"Mother—"

"She comes from the same background as you. Tell him how important that is, Oliver." Marlene prodded her husband with a darting glance.

"Philip Benoit has the most successful insurance bonding company in south Louisiana, not to mention a string of funeral homes. Thriving concerns run by *all three of his sons,*" Oliver said with more than a trace of envy.

"I know, Pops." Damon had heard it all before, several times.

"Just think of what that would mean in terms of advancing African-American presence on the business scene in this state." Oliver rubbed his hands together in anticipation of forging a commercial empire with his schoolmate Philip Benoit. "Something we could leave our grandchildren with pride."

"Choosing the right wife is important," Marlene added.

Damon gazed at his parents. Marlene Cormier Knight came from a prominent family in West Baton Rouge Parish. His parents met at a charity ball when they were still in college, she at Xavier University and Oliver home from Morehouse. They married with the approval of their parents, mainly because both were old-money families. She and Oliver were not a passionate couple by anyone's standards.

Damon wondered how his mother had overcome her distaste for anything as untidy as lovemaking long enough to have two sons. And though not an unfeeling mother, she was not the warm maternal type. Now Damon realized why he'd been so captivated by Rachelle with her penchant for emotional drama. She seemed so gay and warm compared to what he was used to at home. But Rachelle required constant admiration. She resented anything, including his business or commitment to helping others, that took his attention away from her. Her solution had been to find a lover. His mother's voice cut into the painful memories.

"So when are you going to call her?" Marlene spoke in a firm tone that was more a command than a question.

"Remember how you pushed Rachelle and I together for the same reasons, Mother?" Damon said with bitterness.

"Well, you can't compare Rachelle to Monique. I mean the Balleaux side is fine, but on her mother's side . . ." Marlene shrugged. "They made their money from saloons for goodness' sakes."

Damon barked out a harsh laugh. "Her great-grandfather owned a bar a hundred years ago, Mother. And you didn't seem to care about that when you introduced us ten years ago."

"Let's put that behind us, dear. There is no value in dwelling on the past." Marlene was untouched by his implied criticism of her.

"It's getting late," Damon said in a clipped tone. "I've got a long day ahead of me. Good night."

"Call me, son. I want to visit the Thibodaux location since I haven't been there in a while. I know you're due to go there next week," Oliver called after him.

"Sure, Pops." Damon did not bother to argue with his stubborn father.

On the drive to his apartment, Damon mulled over his father's words. Settling down was something he had been sure he could live without for the foreseeable future. Yet a pair of big brown eyes framed by black hair parted in the middle to frame a lovely face had changed all that in a heartbeat. Jade Pellerin inspired a physical reaction so strong Damon could feel it even now. His breath caught just at the tilt of her head in his direction. He wanted to be the one to make her smile. What would it take? Damon imagined the taste of her skin, rich and sweet like expensive chocolate.

Whoa, brother. This is how you got taken out last time, remember? But even as the thought pushed through the heated fantasy, something told him that Jade was so much more than a fine body. Damon shook his head as though trying to clear the confusion filling it. His head told him not to risk the hurt again. His body and heart said *go for it!* With a sigh, he determined to steer clear of Ms. Jade Pellerin. That seemed the best plan all around. He would concentrate on his business, making sure his father followed his physician's orders and expanding his philanthropic interests. Let Eddie meet with her. Damon would make it a point to be too busy.

"Yeah, I'll let Eddie keep me informed. Besides, I really should spend time at the store in Thibodaux. Might as well be Thursday, right?" Damon spoke out loud.

But as the sound of his voice died in the car, doubt tugged at him. Damon let out a loud groan of exasperation at his own uncontrolled emotions. Jade Pellerin had no idea what trouble she was causing.

Chapter 3

Jade watched her sister pace the floor in front of her. They were in Jade's condo on a Saturday night. Lanessa alternated between being outraged at Alex and blaming their mother for pushing them together.

"Calm down, Nessa. You're not making any sense. Now what did Alex do?" Jade was used to her sister's mood swings, but she'd never seen her this agitated. Something about the way she was behaving caused a small tickle of worry.

"Said maybe we shouldn't see each other for a while. Can you believe the nerve of that punk? I'm doing him a favor and he dumps me!" Lanessa pulled out a cigarette and lit it.

"Uh-huh, not in here you won't." Jade snatched it from her hand and went into the powder room. She flushed it down the toilet. "I thought you'd stopped smoking, Nessa."

"I'm under stress here. Come on. Just one." Lanessa fumbled in her purse for the pack again.

"There are no ashtrays in my house for a reason." Jade crossed her arms. But she felt a shiver of concern at the way Lanessa's hands were shaking. "Come over here and sit down."

"I need a drink." Lanessa went to the kitchen and poured

herself two fingers of scotch straight up. She downed it in two quick gulps then poured more.

Jade watched her take a tiny sip. "Lanessa, you've got to drive home, so slow down on that stuff."

Lanessa smiled at her. She seemed more relaxed. "Hey, I'm steady as a rock."

"Lanessa, I'm going to drive you home if you keep this up."

"Now, you chill," Lanessa said with a laugh. "I'm doing okay. And to hell with old Alex." Her voice shook despite the bold words as a dark look shadowed her features.

"Did you two have a fight or something?"

Men had always a been a means to an end with her sister. Lanessa got men she wanted and those she did not care about. While Jade felt unattractive and awkward around handsome men, Lanessa was in her element. Lanessa accepted men chasing after her as a given. Jade felt a knot of anxiety now, seeing her like this, yet she could not put her finger on what was wrong. Maybe it was just that she'd never seen her beautiful older sister rattled by the rejection of a man. In fact, Jade could think of only a few men who had been unaffected by Lanessa's beauty, and Nessa had dismissed them anyway since she had so many devoted admirers.

"No, I mean we disagreed a couple of times." Lanessa shrugged. She did not offer any more information but looked away from Jade's questioning gaze.

"Was the disagreement over something serious?"

Lanessa stared at her glass and took another sip. "I don't really remember. Anyway it doesn't matter now."

"You don't remember? Oh, come on, Nessa. What did you do? I know you have a sharp tongue. Tell me—"

"Look, forget it, okay?" Lanessa cut her off and started pacing again. "It's over so it's pointless to rake up history now. Besides, Keith Darensbourg has been flirting with me for months now. He's got more money than Alex—the nerd."

"Lanessa . . ." Jade did not like the direction she was headed. "Don't you think you're a little old for this wild girl, let's partee act? Not to mention how dangerous jumping from one man to another is these days."

This seemed to touch a nerve. "I'm only thirty-four! I'm not old. Look at this body. There are eighteen-year-olds who work out every day to look like this," Lanessa said, her voice rising with each word.

"I didn't say you were old—"

"There are men younger than me who have thrown platinum credit cards down to get my attention. I am not old." Lanessa stood with her feet apart in front of Jade.

Jade stood to face her. She was annoyed and troubled at the same time by her reaction. "Get a grip, sister. You've still got men breaking out in a sweat just by walking by. I'm talking about maturity up here"—Jade tapped her forehead—"not chronological age."

Lanessa glared at her for a few moments, then slumped down into the chair opposite the sofa. "Don't pay attention to my ranting, Jade-girl. I'm just stressed out with work. Not only is this thing with Alex getting on my nerves, but my boss is on my case now."

"Listen to me, it's just your pride that's hurt. You didn't even care for Alex that much. You said so yourself only a few days ago."

"You're right." Lanessa chewed on a fingernail for a few seconds before realizing she would ruin her expensive silk wrap. "Let me pull it together, acting stupid over Alex of all men." She gave a brittle laugh.

"Tell you what, let's go get something to eat." "I'll drive." Jade got up and gave her a pat on the shoulder.

"I guess, but I'm not that hungry."

"You will be when we get to Bamboo Gardens. They've got this shrimp and snow peas entree that is fantastic." Jade got her purse and car keys.

"Chinese would be good. I don't want anything heavy. Gotta keep this fine frame for Keith." Lanessa stood and pulled at her form-fitting dress.

"Lanessa, what did I just say about that?" Jade put both hands on her hips.

Lanessa laughed. "I know, I know. But I can still let him savor what he might get in the future. You know he's on the board of Louisiana National Bank?"

"Oh, Lanessa!" Jade shook her head with a chuckle.

For the rest of the evening, Lanessa seemed her old self again. Jade began to think she had been imagining things. Her sister was fine. They talked on about a variety of subjects since Lanessa knew all the latest gossip about the prominent families around town.

"And Mrs. Louvillier was bragging on her daughter. You know how she is, 'Queisah did this and Queisah did that.'" Lanessa spoke in an exaggerated imitation of a patrician accent.

Jade rolled her eyes. "She is sickening with that snob act."

"Well, finally Mama looked at her and said, 'I'm so glad to hear Queisah's doing better after that unfortunate library incident. So they let her return this semester?' "

"No—she didn't!" Jade sat forward.

"She did. Mama smiled at her in that way she has, and Mrs. Louvillier kept her mouth shut for the rest of the luncheon." Lanessa sat back with a grin. "Of course then everybody started whispering about how the librarian caught Queisah with some guy, panties down around her ankles, back in the history stacks. She got kicked out of school."

Jade wiped tears from her eyes. "Stop, please." She gasped for air in-between giggles.

"And then there's—"

"You are too much. Now hush before I choke." Jade took a long drink of water to recover. "Is there anything you don't know?"

"Sure. I don't know why it's Saturday night and a fine lady like you is out with her sister." Lanessa looked at her.

"You don't have a date, either. So there."

"I have an excuse. Don't try to change the subject back to me. Why are you making yourself suffer like this?"

Jade let out a sigh. "I'm not suffering. I'm taking time to get myself together is all."

"Almost two years without a man? Please! That's some kind of self-penance."

"A year and a half. And not everyone thinks grabbing the next available man is the way to recover from a failed relationship," Jade retorted.

"I know you, sister. You're scared of choosing the wrong man again. Nick was a self-centered you-know-what who made himself feel big by putting you down. But you can do better."

"Yeah, right." Jade pushed her teaspoon around in a circle. "I don't think I'll get serious about anyone else anytime soon."

"Are you telling me there isn't one man in this town worth having? No way."

"Why do women always end up talking about men whenever they get together?" Jade said.

"Because as much as we complain about them, they are endlessly fascinating. Face it, there are some brothers that leave a mighty big impression." Lanessa picked up her menu. "We even love sitting around fussing about them."

Jade could not block the image of Damon Knight that flashed in her mind. His strong jaw, the way his eyes brightened when he smiled came back to her with a vividness that made her heart speed up. This was not the first time she'd thought of him in the past few days since their first meeting. She would see him in a few short days. Her lips curved up as she remembered something funny he'd said the other evening at Uncle Joe's.

"Hel-loo," Lanessa said as she waved her hand in front of Jade's face. "The waitress is ready for your order."

Jade blinked up at the woman standing with pen poised over her pad. "Uh, I'll take a number sixteen."

Lanessa was quiet until the waitress left. "My oh my, little sister. Whoever he is, go for it if he sends you into a daze like that." She leaned across the table.

"I don't know what you're talking about." Jade sniffed.

"Like hell you don't." Lanessa spoke with confidence.

"Remember what you said a little while ago: there is very little that gets by me."

"Take a sniff of reality, sugar. There is no 'him' to hear about." Jade steered her to another a subject.

Jade made a silent vow to get this adolescent fog she seemed to keep slipping into under rein. Damon Knight was not in her personal future. Period.

"Got that last set of figures for me, Jade?" Lang beckoned to her as he came back from a big meeting with the other top cabinet officials. He used her first name with ease.

"Sure do. Looks like the cost of Medicaid billings has gone down at about six percent in the last three months." Jade handed him a green folder.

"Good. Every little bit helps." He unbuttoned his jacket and slumped into his chair. "Sitting in there with Howard is like being put through a wringer."

"He's determined to make every dollar count. Mr. Howard has been talking about the problems with the state budgets for years, but no one listened." Jade could picture the dark, bushy brows made even more prominent against his pale skin. Chester Howard had a reputation for being honest and not willing to say what politicians wanted to hear. "Too bad or we wouldn't be in this fix."

"Well, we are. And some of the cuts will hurt, no way around it. Speaking of which, set up a meeting with the four assistant secretaries. We need to give them the bad news on how much of a hit their programs will take."

"Yes, sir. By the way, I'll be at the Gracie Street Center tomorrow."

Lang frowned. "Hmm, I'd forgotten about that. Look, if you really don't want to be bothered, send someone from the planning section."

"No, no—I'm looking forward to it," Jade blurted out. A tickle of embarrassment went up her back at his questioning glance. "I mean, it will give me a chance to see firsthand what I'll be writing about in the grant revisions."

"I see." Lang gazed at her for a moment. "Damon and I were in school together. He's a very impressive guy."

"Oh? I don't know much about him. Anyway, Mr. Simon sent over a brochure they just had done describing the center. I left a copy on your desk." Jade avoided making eye contact with him. Instead she busied herself arranging papers on his desk. "These are for your signature, and these are copies of memos sent out by the assistant secretaries."

"Thank you, Jade."

Something about the way he said her name made Jade pause. When she looked up, he smiled at her briefly then began scanning the spreadsheets on home health billing of Medicaid and state funds. She gave a slight shake of her head. Her imagination was running wild these days.

The phone on her desk was ringing when she got to her office. She snatched it up. "Yes, I'll hold." Shaena came in and leaned against her door.

"I'll come back," Shaena whispered.

"No, this won't take long, just someone confirming an appointment." Jade place a palm over the mouthpiece. A male voice sounded, causing her to jump. "Oh, hello, Mr. Simon. Yes, we're on for tomorrow at ten o'clock in the morning. I look forward to seeing Gracie Street Center. I see. All right then, goodbye."

"What's wrong?" Shaena crossed her legs. "You look like the wind got taken out of your sails."

"I don't know what you're talking about." Jade forced a nonchalant tone to her voice.

"Eddie Simon is the director at Gracie Street. You're going over there, right?" Shaena looked the part of an attorney questioning a reluctant witness.

"Yes."

"Damon Knight going to be there?"

Jade waited a few seconds before answering. "No."

"Oh?"

"He has some business to take care of and won't be there. But Eddie Simon has all the information," Jade put in quickly.

"Umm." Shaena kept her face blank.

"Simon is the director. Actually there was no need for Damon Knight to be there at all. I'll get the information we need." Jade fidgeted with items on her desk. What was this? First Lang and now Shaena making her feel like a schoolgirl caught passing notes to a boy.

"You're disappointed. Admit it, girl."

"Shaena, will you give it a rest?"

Jade wanted to protest she felt no such thing. But the truth was she'd felt a marked lack of enthusiasm about her visit when Simon broke the news that Damon would not be at the center. This was getting out of hand.

"Jade, why don't you give the strong independent don't-need-a-man act a rest. I love you like the sister I never had. Let it happen and be happy."

"He has so many good-looking women throwing themselves at him, he hasn't given me a more than a glance." Jade felt the familiar hollow feeling of being not quite good enough gnawing at her.

"Jade . . ." Shaena took a deep breath.

"Not that I care," Jade said with force.

"There are men who'd give up a finger just to get you to look their way. Girlfriend, you've got a lot going on with you. I just wish you could see it."

"A finger isn't exactly what they're thinking of giving me, Shaena." Jade snorted. "Getting that kind of attention from a man is no big accomplishment."

Shaena laughed out loud. "Well, a few maybe. I'll just bet Damon Knight is checking you out. He's playing it cool after that nasty divorce, I'll bet."

"He can be as cool as he wants, all right? I'm about business, not getting a date. So if Mr. Knight thinks I'm going to follow the old pattern of every other woman he meets and throw myself at him, he can just think again."

Shaena gave a groan of exasperation. "Fine. I'm through with it then. You are one tough nut to crack when it comes to this."

"Thank you," Jade answered.

"Say, did you get a chance to see that memo on home health agencies? Strange stuff."

"Not really. Bill is trying to avoid even greater costs when people have to be hospitalized. I mean, care at home reduces the number of folks who end up in the emergency rooms." Jade had long wanted to see more home-based health care.

"I'll buy that. But this new rule seems really vague to me. Sets up the opportunity for abuse of the system. I mean, the guidelines for home psychiatric care are . . . loose." Shaena drummed her fingers on the arm of her chair.

"Well, Bill and Mike worked with the Medicaid folks on it. They said they didn't want to make them too exclusionary. Anyway, the costs are coming down." "Man, look at all this paperwork." Jade slapped a pile of memos and reports on her desk.

"Yep, we kill a lot of trees in this department. Back to the salt mines for me, girl." Shaena heaved herself out the chair. "Have a good tour at Gracie Street."

"Thanks."

"But since Eddie Simon stuck a pin in your balloon, it won't be as good since Mr. Wow-He's-Fine! won't be there. Bye." Shaena winked at her then darted down the hall with a chuckle.

"I'm not—He's—I'll get you!" Jade yelled after her. She fumed for the rest of the afternoon.

"Thanks, man. I don't think I should miss being at court with LeVonne. He's messed up, but I think his probation officer will ask the judge to give him another chance if we agree to work with him." Eddie sat in the small conference room next to his office with Damon.

"I understand. No problem," Damon assured him.

"But I know you had other things with your stores to take care of today. I'm sorry to put this on you, but Christine had to be at the mayor's office this morning." Eddie explained for the third time why the assistant director could not take over for him.

"Eddie, I said it's no problem. It wasn't anything that was life and death." Damon felt guilty at being the source of Eddie's discomfort.

The fact was, the tasks could easily be handled by his district manager. Damon had told himself he should stop dumping dull tasks on his subordinate and spend more time attending to the family business. Yet he'd been pleased when Eddie called.

"Well, it shouldn't take more than an hour and a half. At least you won't spend too much time here."

"Don't worry about it, man. Besides, I'm looking forward to it." Damon traced a line on the table with his forefinger.

"Yeah, Jade Pellerin is quite a woman: brains and beauty in one nice package." Eddie gazed at his old pal with amusement.

"Who? Oh, I guess," Damon said with a false casual tone. "She seems nice."

"Uh-huh. So you didn't notice that great-looking lady?" Eddie prodded him, trying to get a reaction. Damon blinked rapidly at his words.

Damon cleared his throat. "Yeah, but I meant it's been a while since I've had a chance to see the staff during the day what with just dropping in for a few minutes here and there."

"Sure." Eddie's expression did not change.

"And the board meetings are in the evenings when the staff have left." Damon shifted in his chair. He cleared his throat several more times during the long moment of silence.

"I'm sure they'll enjoy seeing you, too." Eddie's mouth twitched with the effort not to laugh.

"So LeVonne is in serious trouble?" Damon shifted back to the subject of the young man Eddie was concerned about. He did not like the way his friend was probing so close to the sensitive area of his erotic bone-shaking response to the enticing Jade Pellerin.

Eddie's face transformed into a grimace of worry. "He hasn't been to school in two weeks. And a police officer picked him up in a neighborhood after a woman reported a suspicious man peering into windows."

"Peeping Tom charge?"

"Nah, it was during the day when most of the residents were at work. He was probably getting ready to burglarize those houses." Eddie shook his head. "That's what he's been arrested for over ten times."

"Man, he's heading straight for some serious time. When he turns sixteen, they can charge him as an adult." Damon had seen the same pattern countless times in his work with troubled teens.

"The thing that gets me is how sharp this kid is. He has so much potential." Eddie looked at the clock on the wall. "Twenty to ten. I better get a move on if I'm going to be in Judge Taylor's court on time." He got up to leave just as the door opened.

"Mr. Simon, Ms. Pellerin is here to see you." Eddie's secretary, Tisha, stood in the door.

"Show her into my office. Thanks," Eddie said.

"Come on in, ma'am," Tisha said a few seconds later.

Damon smoothed his jacket, tugged at his tie and adjusted the cuffs of his shirt all in quick succession. He was thrown off balance by the rapid arrival of the disturbing female presence whose effect on him he'd been unable to neutralize. Damon stopped in the act of patting his hair when he glanced up to see Eddie grinning at him.

"Let's go," Damon snapped softly as he brushed past him. Eddie was still smiling when he extended a hand to Jade. "Morning, Ms. Pellerin."

Jade went breathless for a split second at the sight of Damon right behind Eddie. One thing she had to admit, he wore a suit like few other men could. The charcoal gray wool fabric was set off very well by the colors of dark red, blue and gray in his silk tie and the light blue shirt. Jade felt a warm flood of pleasure at seeing him. His deep voice turned up the heat.

"Good morning." Damon reached out a large hand to her also.

Jade took his hand and felt her body begin to melt at the touch of satin flesh. "Hello," was all she could manage.

Did her voice actually crack and shake? Did they notice? When Eddie turned to offer her a chair, she felt weak with relief. Maybe she had not made an utter fool of herself. Jade squared her shoulders and took control . . . she hoped.

"I'm afraid something urgent has come up. One of the young people we're working with has a court hearing this morning. I feel I have to be there," Eddie said.

"I see. Well, if you'd rather we reschedule . . ." Jade was careful not to look at Damon.

"No, no. I've asked Mr. Knight to give you the grand tour. I'm sorry I won't be able to stay and show you around." Eddie watched her closely.

Jade sensed this was a test of some sort by the searching look he gave her. She affected a cool, professional demeanor. "I certainly understand, Mr. Simon. But really, I can come another time. I know Mr. Knight had other obligations today." *He isn't having silly daydreams about seeing you again. He's here only out of necessity, so snap out of it.*

"Not at all. Today is just fine. I've made more than adequate arrangements with my employees," Damon put in.

"Then you're all set, right?" Eddie looked from Jade to Damon.

"Yes," Jade said with a nod. She finally looked at Damon again. She was already tired at the thought of struggling to hide her strong physical reaction to the man for the next couple of hours. "I appreciate this, Mr. Knight."

Eddie's dark eyes held a glint of mischief. "Listen to us. We're being so formal. I'm Eddie. May we call you Jade?" He included Damon in his request.

Jade blinked at him. "Certainly, Eddie."

Damon had watched her lips move and the swing of her

thick hair with each movement of her head. "Well, Jade, let's get started." He surprised himself with the ease that her name popped out. There was no denying the rush just saying that lovely name gave him. He held open the door for her.

"Goodbye, you two," Eddie called out.

"See ya," Damon shot back. He gave him a sharp scowl that told his friend he knew what he'd been up to. To his chagrin, Eddie gave him a thumbs-up sign then darted off down the hall before Damon could respond.

"Where would you like to go first?" Damon walked beside her down the hall leading from the main offices deeper into the center.

Jade felt good being near him. "You choose," she said with a smile.

Damon forgot about Eddie or his annoyance as he looked into her eyes. "Let's start with the large community room. It's where we have lectures and workshops open to the folks in the neighborhood."

Jade followed him into a room that could seat up to fifty people. Rows of chairs were set up. At the opposite end of the room, across from the double doors leading inside, a podium with a microphone was set up. Several large tables were scattered around with pamphlets spread on them.

"What kind of workshops?" Jade forgot to be uneasy. It seemed quite natural to be here with Damon.

"We have speakers on a wide variety of topics. Mostly we set up events based on our surveys of the folks and comments we get from them. For instance, you can see the last lecture was on crime prevention." Damon pointed to a brochure on home security.

"That's great."

"Yeah, a prominent police chief from North Carolina credited with turning his city's crime problem around came. He talked about making the community better with recreation, neighborhood events for families and things like that as a way to reduce crime. We had a tremendous turnout," Damon said with pride.

Jade strolled around reading the few brochures left scattered along the tables. "Yes, but what I meant was how you based your programs on what the people who live here said they wanted. That's unusual. Most of the time, a group of professional social workers decide what kind of programs they think are needed."

"Well, Eddie and the other social workers here have a very grassroots approach to their work. After all, this is really their center—which is why our policy requires that at least fifty percent of the board members live in the Gracie Street area."

"That must make a difference in how this center is run compared to more traditional programs." Jade could not help but catch his excitement at what was happening here in one of the poorest, most neglected parts of the city.

"A huge difference." Damon launched into a full-fledged description of the governing body as he led her toward another section of the center.

For another thirty minutes, he talked about services offered such as the day-care center and parenting classes. They met staff and some of the neighborhood residents. Jade marveled at how the relatively modest center seemed to compare to full-service agencies in cities twice the size of Baton Rouge in terms of its comprehensive approach.

She felt a growing appreciation for this man, who seemed as dedicated as any social worker she'd ever met. Strange for a businessman to take such a personal interest. He had not grown up facing the hurdles of those who lived in the inner city. Yet he showed genuine compassion for the poor people who faced daily hardships—something quite exceptional in most of those born to a family with money and status.

Jade watched his face brighten when they were surrounded by the toddlers in the Headstart class. He was relaxed with the elderly students in a nutrition class. This caring man intrigued her more than ever. Damon Knight seemed a far cry from the wealthy playboy she'd built him up to be in her mind. Jade began to think Shaena was right.

"I must say, the people in this area are fortunate that you made your vision a reality." Jade turned to him.

Damon blushed. "It was a shared vision. I couldn't have done it alone."

"But you were the guiding force. And you put your money where your mouth was, exact quote from Eddie." Jade matched his slow pace as they walked back toward the administrative offices. She followed him into the conference room.

"They're both special people. In fact, everyone from the janitor up to the president of the board put their heart and soul into this place. It's not just me." Damon pulled out a chair for her to sit down. When she was seated, he poured them both a cup of coffee.

"Come on, Mr. Knight—"

Damon waved a finger at her. "Now, you heard Eddie give specific instructions before he left. Call me Damon."

Jade's professional demeanor slipped just a notch. He looked adorable with that teasing glint in his eyes. "Damon, accept the accolades. You have reason to be proud. You've shown leadership, a valuable commodity in the face of the kind of obstacles this area of town faces."

"Thank you, Jade," Damon said. He looked at her for a long moment with a thoughtful expression.

His voice saying her name was like a hot brand against her skin. She watched his mouth in fascination. Her whole being longed to make him call her name but for a very different reason. She imagined guiding those wonderful, long hands toward her.

"Ms. Pellerin, I have a call for you on line two. Ms. Pellerin?" Tisha looked at her then at Damon.

Jade blinked and came back to her surroundings with reluctance. "What?"

"You can take it in here." Tisha pointed to a phone on the credenza along the wall behind the large table. "That is if y'all aren't too involved to be disturbed."

"No, no." Jade went to the phone on legs that felt like cotton.

Damon coughed and stood up. "I'll give you some privacy. Let me know when you're through." He passed Tisha without returning her gaze.

Jade punched the button. "Yes. Oh, hi, Aline. Yeah, tell him they're in that blue binder on the second bookcase of the library. I see." She found great difficulty paying attention to the clerk's message from Bill. The woman seemed to drone on forever, asking questions so Bill could find a policy he needed urgently.

Something important had happened in the last few minutes, a sort of culmination of what meeting Damon Knight for the first time had set in motion. In one moment, with one simple phrase, a certainty that she could be close to this man took hold deep inside her. Now she was anxious to be with him again. If only this phone call would end!

Damon came back into the room and started to leave when he saw her still talking on the phone.

"Wait, I'm almost through," Jade called out and cut off the clerk on the other end of the line in midsentence. "I'll see you in a little while and take care of it. Bye." She hung up before the long-winded staff person could start talking again.

"Well, it's eleven thirty already. You, uh, probably have plans for lunch." Damon cleared his throat and glanced out the window.

"I need to grab something at a drive-through and get back to the office. A minor crisis is brewing," Jade said. She picked up her purse and leather portfolio.

"Sure. I understand. That's a busy place these days." Damon stood next to the door but did not open it. "Bet you'll be working late, too."

"Not tonight," Jade said with great vigor. *Take it easy, girl.* But her heartbeat was like a small drum going double-time.

"There's a reception tonight for a new faculty exhibit at the Frank Hayden Gallery on campus at Southern University. I have an invitation. Would you care to join me? If you're into art, that is."

"I love going to art galleries. In fact, I've started my own modest private collection."

"Really? Then I'll pick you up at a quarter to six. We can have dinner afterward." Damon wore an animated look.

Jade smiled at him. "Sounds good." She managed to restrain herself from shouting *ya-hoo!* With a steady voice, she gave him her address.

For the rest of the day, she breezed around light of heart. Nothing altered her splendid mood. Things that might have left her frazzled at the end of the day were no match for the magic Damon had worked on her. At quitting time Jade eased by her boss's office careful not to make noise lest he stop her. She breathed a sigh of relief as the elevator doors shut. It was almost five when she got to her condo. Jade made a mad dash to the bedroom and began searching her closet. Red dress? Too bold a statement for the first date. Black jersey dress? Too prim and proper. Time was getting short. After several minutes of muttering and searching, she uttered a cry of delight. Of course—she should have thought of it at once. Her gold cotton cashmere sweater, long slim black skirt with a side split and wide black belt. Perfect. When the door chimes sounded, she jumped. Even though she was dressed, Jade felt far from ready. Butterflies of doubt fluttered in her stomach. What if she was moving too fast? Well, it was too late for second thoughts now.

Damon's confidence faltered at the echo of the chimes within the condo. He wondered if he'd lost his mind. Being close to this woman in a cold government office building had set off his fire alarm like crazy, and here he was at her doorstep. The attraction was not just physical, though Lord knows the way she moved in a skirt made his brain sweat. Well, he'd just have to put the brakes on his emotions. He had been with other good-looking women in the last year.

"Hey, I've dated since my divorce. No biggie." Damon tried to convince himself with a suave shrug of his shoulders. Then the door swung open, and a silent blast blew away his resolve to play it cool. "Have mercy," he murmured at the sight that greeted him.

"Hi. Come on in."

Jade stood there like a work of art herself. Damon was rooted to the spot at sight of her in gold and black. The outfit she wore was a wonderful showcase of the womanly curves that set him on fire.

"You look magnificent," Damon said in a voice filled with awe. He sounded like a lust-struck adolescent, but he could not help it. The woman had it all together.

"Thank you." Jade gave him a shy smile.

Damon kept up a running dialogue in his head to convince himself that he could maintain control in the face of such tremendous temptation. He looked around at the fawn, slate blue and red color scheme of her living room. The soft fabric of the sofa conspired to make him feel right at home sitting next to her. When she lifted her arm to brush back a stray strand of hair, the delicate, spicy fragrance of Red made him quiver. He mentally surrendered.

"I've been looking forward to this evening all day, Jade." Damon felt a weight lift, then a sinking feeling began when a long moment of silence stretched as Jade considered his words. Oh, well, at least he'd get the bad news early this time.

Jade gazed at him. "So have I."

"Damn, I'm glad to hear you say that," Damon said. "I mean, uh . . ."

"I know exactly what you mean." Jade's lips lifted just a bit at the corners.

Damon took a deep breath. "I've been through a really rough divorce. And I'm kinda taking it easy where relationships are concerned."

"Me, too. Divorce can leave you a little ragged around the edges, can't it?" Jade faced him.

"Tell me about it. But you're something I didn't count on." Damon searched for a way to explain the feeling that they were the right fit somehow, that they could be good together. "I'm not saying this very well." He ran his fingers over his hair in frustration.

"Let me try. We enjoy talking to each other and seem to

have common interests. Neither of us is ready to get into a heavy thing right now, but we'd like to spend time together. How's that?'' Jade watched him closely with a twinkle in her eyes.

''That's it exactly.'' Damon leaned toward her just a fraction. ''I definitely want to spend time with you, Jade. But . . .''

''Yes?'' Jade stiffened a bit.

''I understand if you're seeing someone else. That is, I'm not saying we're seeing each other exclusively.'' Damon stared at the carpet. He cringed at the clumsy way he tried to find out if there was another man in her life, but he did not want to know about him, for he felt sure such a fabulous woman was dating.

''Of course. Naturally,'' Jade put in quickly. ''Well, shall we go? The reception starts at six thirty, so we have fifteen minutes to get there.''

''Yeah, right. I hear there are some outstanding new pieces in this new exhibit.'' He helped her into a gold and black cropped jacket.

Damon felt a damper put on the night ahead. So there was someone else—no problem, he assured himself. In fact, it was just as well. That would keep him from jumping into a serious relationship too fast. Yes, all things considered that would work just fine.

Jade rode beside the Damon in his Buick Riviera. The soft leather seats were like a glove fitting her body, and he'd popped in a compact disc of jazz. The exhibit had been wonderful, yet she could not get the thought that Damon wanted to see other women out of her mind. Even as they walked around, admiring the powerful sculptures and paintings, Jade kept hearing him say they should see other people. *You should be relieved, dummy. This way you know where you stand. Besides, you don't need to throw yourself into a big-deal love affair.* She gazed at his profile in the muted glow of the dashboard lights. He was not preoccupied with it; that was obvious as he went on about the art gallery and his knowledge of the artists. After a pleasant dinner, they returned to her condo. Damon stood just inside her living room with an air of indecision.

"Would you like coffee? I have a special blend from Colombia." Jade turned away to take off her jacket. Was he searching for a way to make a graceful exit?

"Sure," Damon said. He sat down on the sofa with a sigh.

Jade felt a rise of irritation. "Are you sure? I'll understand if you need to leave."

Damon got up and crossed to her. "No, Jade. This is where I want to be. The truth is, I'm having a hard time keeping myself in check around you."

Excitement tickled through her. "What do you mean?"

"Look, I know I said we'd spend time together and see other people. And I thought I meant it at the time. Well, I tried to mean it because of my ex, and what happened with her. But . . . ah, hell. I'm not making any sense." Damon raked his fingers over his hair for the second time that evening. No woman had ever made him feel like a babbling idiot—not even Rachelle. He could not string two coherent sentences together, especially when what he wanted to do was stop talking and kiss her.

Jade stepped up to him and touched his arm. "Damon, I know exactly what you mean."

Damon took her hand. "I'm not seeing anyone else, not now. Not after meeting you that first day, Jade. Maybe I'm rushing things, but I'd like us to get to know each other without distractions. I know you didn't have this in mind, but . . ."

"You thought I wanted to see other people?" Jade was light-headed with relief. "When you brought it up, I agreed because I thought you wanted it."

"Let's start over," Damon said with a chuckle low in his throat. He lifted her chin with a forefinger. "I think you are one magnificent woman, Jade Pellerin. And I want to be with you in every way."

"Agreed," was all Jade could manage. Her breath was short from the thrill of seeing the desire in his eyes. She lifted her mouth to his and pulled his head down. The cool, smooth taste of him filled her with a hunger that roared through her body like a wildfire.

The kiss stretched out for a long, delicious time. They stood wrapped in each other's arms, lost in a world of mutual passion. When it ended, they both took a deep breath in satisfaction.

"Woman, you've got a Ph.D. in Kissology. Lord have mercy!" Damon cradled her to him and stroked her arms.

"Thank you, professor, but you must have written the book." Jade giggled. Then she looked up at him with a sober expression. "I don't think we should act too quickly and get serious too fast right now—"

"Let's just go with it for now. This feels so good, I don't want to talk about doubts or dwell on what happened in the past for either of us." He looked at her, his dark brown eyes intense. "I'm willing to take it slow and easy. I'll accept wherever this leads."

Jade rested her head on his chest with a feeling of quiet joy she'd never felt before with any man, including Nick. "So am I, Damon Knight. So am I."

Chapter 4

"Jade, come here!" Lang yelled. "Jade!"

She rushed into his office with a feeling of dread. "What is it? What's wrong?"

"Not a thing. We got more of the grant money than even I expected on my most optimistic day. A grand total of 3.8 million dollars." Lang waved a sheet of paper in the air.

"That's fantastic." Jade read the award letter when he handed it to her.

Lang rubbed his hands together. "But now the real work begins. We've got to set up a task force immediately to select a permanent project director." He came to stand in front of her. "I'm going to recommend you."

Jade's mouth hung open. "Oh, but—"

"Wait a minute before you say no. I watched you in the meeting the other day. Even though it was the first time you'd met those folks, you had a way of pulling all their thoughts together and directing them toward a focus of effort."

"I don't know what to say, Bill. Naturally it's a wonderful compliment." Jade's mind was in a whirl. This was a great opportunity, but the work would be all-consuming.

"You'll get to meet some of the top people in the field of human services. We have a substantial budget for travel and attending national and even international conferences." Lang watched her reaction.

"I'm not sure I have the experience. . . ."

"You'll be working closely with folks who are more than willing to help. Me, for example." Lang looked down at her with an intent expression. "Say yes."

Jade knew she'd be crazy to pass up such a chance. She pushed away self-doubts and lifted her chin. "Of course I'll do it. And thanks for having confidence in me."

Lang stared at her for several seconds. "Jade I . . . You're quite welcome." He stepped back and went around to sit behind his desk again. "Speaking of conferences, there is one next month in Washington, D.C., on community intervention. I'll be going and so will Mike. I want you to come also."

"Fine," Jade said in a calm voice. Inside she was as happy as a kid going off to Disney World. "How long will we be there?"

"About four days." He wore a slight smile. "Yes, you'll have time to visit the Smithsonian and wander through art galleries. I might even come along—if you don't mind."

"Fantastic," Jade answered without really hearing him. Already she was planning to log on to the museum's web site so she could plan which exhibits she would make sure to see. "I'll get back to work."

For the rest of the day, Jade interspersed planning her trip with taking care of details related to the project. The hours passed, and she was preparing to leave when the phone on her desk rang.

"Hello, Mother." Jade propped the phone against her ear with one shoulder while she sorted through files. "How are you?"

"Okay, I guess. I haven't heard from Lanessa since Monday. Have you?" Clarice had a petulant tone reserved for times when she felt neglected.

Jade felt a brush of aggravation. They had not spoken in

four days. "No, I haven't, Mother. Lanessa's a big girl. And I'm doing fine, too. Thanks for asking."

"What? Oh, now, Jade. Even though you're younger than your sister, you've always been the strong one. I don't worry about you as much." Clarice repeated the same explanation Jade had heard all her life, it seemed.

"What a compliment," Jade murmured.

"I couldn't hear you, dear. Stop muttering into the phone and speak clearly."

"I said call her at home, she's probably there by now." Jade looked at her watch. "It's almost four thirty. Lanessa makes it a practice to be home by four."

In fact her official schedule was eight to four thirty like all ordinary civil servants. But Lanessa, as usual, did not have to follow the same rules as everyone else. Her job in documents at the state capitol was a plum position. Somehow Lanessa had charmed the boss, a grim workhorse with a reputation for being unbending when it came to following rules.

"I'm sure she's just fine. Lanessa always manages, Mother." Jade paid more attention to stacking her work for the next day than to her mother's voice. Then something caught her attention. "What was that?"

"Since you're obviously too busy to talk to your mother now, then maybe we'll have more time later tonight when you come over," Clarice snapped.

"Tonight?" Jade blinked. She did not remember making plans to visit her parents. She'd promised to meet Damon for dinner. "Well, I have plans."

"Oh?" Clarice's voice sharpened with interest. "You have a date with a young man. Well, well. When will your father and I get to meet him?"

Jade groped for a way out of this predicament. "Uh, just dinner with a friend, Mother. Listen, my boss is calling me. Gotta go, bye." Clarice barely had time to say goodbye before Jade hung up. "Whew, dodged that bullet."

Shaena stood with her arms folded. "But not for long."

"Eavesdropping is beneath you, Shaena."

"Well, I was just coming to see if you wanted to have a midweek celebration. Wednesday means only two more days of toiling. But since you have plans . . ." Shaena shrugged and eyed her.

"Yes, I do. So how have you been? That legal work on new department policies must be a real challenge." Jade tried to deflect the direction of this conversation.

"More like a real pain. So you and Gail going out to eat? Gee, I haven't seen her for at least two months. How is she?" Shaena sat down across from Jade.

Gail Malveaux was an old college friend. She and Jade made it a point to have dinner or lunch at least every few months. "Gail is fine." Jade avoided the first question. "Girl, I must have returned a dozen phone calls since lunchtime."

"Gee, I wouldn't mind seeing good old Gail. Maybe I'll stop by and have a cup of coffee with y'all later at the Café Rouge."

"I'm not having dinner with Gail." Jade avoided her gaze.

"You're seeing Damon Knight again," Shaena stated with certainty. "Why not just admit it? You've got a date."

"Okay, Sherlock Holmes. You figured it out," Jade retorted. First her mother, now Shaena.

Shaena wore a smug look. "It wasn't hard. You told me how fabulous it was being with him on your first date—"

Jade tapped her long fingernails on the desk. "Me and my big mouth."

Shaena ignored her remark. "I knew it was the first of many. Honey, you'll have all those other women foaming at the mouth with envy when they find out. Go, girl."

"I'm unsure about this, Shaena. I mean, it's good between us—almost too good to be true. You know what I'm saying?" Jade struggled to describe how she felt.

"Now there you go. Don't start being suspicious of the man before you have reason to be."

"I don't want to assume too much"—Jade looked at her friend—" and repeat the same mistake. I thought I knew Nick, too."

"Baby, as you know I've had my share of experiences with low-down men. Please don't get me started," Shaena said with a sigh. "But Nick is a special breed of dirty dog. Don't use him as a guide to judge Damon."

"They are completely different people. I mean, Nick came on with the charm. He'd go to any lengths to impress."

Jade remembered the extravagant evenings Nick would plan that included roses and trips to plays in New Orleans. But for him, the chase and conquest were a thrill. He needed constant doses of such dramatic evenings with a new audience each time. But Nick was also good at deception. He enjoyed having a wife to come home to despite his craving for variety. A spike of that familiar pain went through her at the memory of finally facing the truth.

"That kind of man can get in your blood like a drug, girl. Been there, done that, got the T-shirt," Shaena said as she waved a hand in the air.

"Damon is so . . . real. He's charming but not like Nick."

Shaena grunted. "You mean he's not flashy and superficial. When he says something, you can believe it."

Jade felt as though a light had come on. "That's it. I've been thinking about Nick a lot. And compared to Damon, he seems so phony. Nick thinks only of himself. Damon seems like someone you can count on."

"Sounds like a reason to hang on to him. So why are you hiding the man like a bad habit you don't want folks to know about?"

"It may not lead to anything. So I don't want to share it just yet. Especially not with Mama." Jade shuddered at the thought of Clarice getting into her business.

"Or Lanessa," Shaena said with her customary shoot-from-the-hip style. "She'll wrap herself around a fine man like a python."

"Don't be so hard on her," Jade put in weakly. In a lot of ways, Jade was closer to Shaena than she was to her older sister. Over the years they had shared long conversations about family relationships.

"You know it's true, Jade. Really, I don't think she's vicious. Lanessa just tends not to think of how going after what she wants affects other folks."

"But if I don't trust him, maybe we shouldn't even be together." Jade frowned.

"Quit worrying about all that, girl. You've had only one date so far. Already you're coming up with reasons not to see the man." Shaena handed Jade her purse. "It's almost five o'clock. Get out of here so you can be on time. And stop making problems that don't exist." She pushed her out the door.

"Maybe you're right. Hey, we might not see each other for very long anyway," Jade said.

"Uh-huh." Shaena folded her arms and stared at her hard.

"What?"

"The last time you dated a guy, you didn't have that glow whenever you said his name. You'll be seeing Damon Knight for more than a few dates. He's hot for you and you're hot for him." Shaena chuckled at the blush her words caused. They got into the elevator with three other people.

Jade considered her remark as they rode down to the first floor. "Is it that obvious?" she whispered as they passed the security guard on the way out the door.

"Honey, y'all could set off the sprinkler system with the way you look at each other," Shaena said.

Jade took a deep breath. "Shaena, he is one sexy man—I have to admit."

"Then relax and enjoy the ride." Shaena gave her a wink. "Pun intended."

"You ought to quit." Jade tried to sound shocked but failed when she giggled.

"Now go. Have a great time." Shaena headed for her car. "And ask him if he's got a friend for me."

Jade laughed all the way home. She dashed in for ten minutes to freshen up then headed for the restaurant, Chez Irene. They had agreed to meet there. Damon was waiting for her just inside the door when she arrived.

"Hello there." Damon gave her a quick kiss. "You look lovely as usual."

"Thanks," Jade said. The deep satisfaction a simple compliment from him brought was a source of amazement. Never had anyone made her feel so . . . wanted.

They followed the hostess through the crowded restaurant to a table. Jade nodded to several acquaintances. Chez Irene was a hit with the up-and-coming young professionals in town. Steak and seafood were the main fare.

"Wow, this place is packed tight. Lots of familiar faces." Damon gazed around and waved to several men with their families.

"You know folks in south Louisiana know good food when they find it. And Miss Irene can dish it out." Jade giggled.

"Cute," Damon said with a mock groan. "Umm, wouldn't a prime-cut steak hit the spot?"

"Not to mention the garlic shrimp pasta dish. It is out of this world."

"Yes indeed. And the seafood platter?" Damon stared at the menu with anticipation.

"Say, why don't we just order everything?" Jade wore the expression of a kid looking forward to being naughty.

"Don't tempt me. But I'll settle for prime rib and a baked potato this time."

"I've got to go for the light entrees these days. All those fat grams and calories have a way of multiplying when they get in this body. A dirty trick my metabolism plays on me, or at least that's my alibi." Jade sighed and put the menu down.

Damon took her hand. "Babe, whatever you're doing is working. Keep it goin' on just like that." His dark brown eyes held a soft gleam of affection.

"You're going to spoil me. Two compliments in less than thirty minutes. Can I take it?" Jade was fascinated at the way his fingers curled around her hand and the feel of his warm flesh pressing hers. Her teasing tone was an attempt to maintain some kind of equilibrium in the face of such a powerful assault on her senses.

"Spoiling you is something I very much look forward to over the next few weeks," Damon murmured. He raised her hand and brushed his lips across her fingers.

A tingle of fire shot up her arms and wrapped around her heart. "Oh," Jade said with a gasp.

"Y'all want me to come back?" The waiter raised an eyebrow at them. When Damon nodded, he gave him a thumbs-up sign. "Gotcha, brother. I'll just fade on back to the kitchen for a few."

"Jade, I really like you. A lot." Damon still held her hand.

"Wow, Damon. I'm kind of at a loss right now." Jade used her free hand to bring the glass of ice water to her lips. Maybe that would help her cool down enough to think straight. This man had the ability to take her from a normal temperature to a fever pitch at the speed of light.

"Me, too. Feels nice though."

"Slow down," Jade pleaded. She needed time to recover, or she'd be all over him right here and now.

Damon released her hand. He wiped his brow with his handkerchief. "I'm sorry. You said you needed time, and I'm pushing you. Believe me, I'm as stunned by this as you." Indeed, he did seem a little off balance.

Jade was touched by the sincere look of bewilderment on his handsome face. "It's okay, really."

"Look, for the past two years since my divorce I've been dating but nothing heavy. I was sure a serious relationship was not something I'd want for a long, long time. But now . . ."

"But now?"

"Now I feel like I've finally met a woman who is not only beautiful and intelligent, but . . . real. Someone with a sense of purpose—a woman I could be with in every way."

"With all the women you've met, how can you be sure?" Jade traced an invisible line on the tablecloth between them. She thought of all the gorgeous women who moved in Damon's social circle. How could he find her more attractive than them?

"Contrary to rumor, I haven't dated every woman in town," he said with amusement.

"That's good to know," she quipped.

"You're special to me, Jade. The armor I put up after my divorce was like steel, until you."

"I . . . I don't know what to say," Jade stammered. She felt as though they were alone in a private space.

"Don't respond right now. Listen, I was as hard a case about romance as you. But I'm willing to give it a try if you are." Damon looked at her intently as he waited for her response.

This time it was Jade who reached out to touch his hand. "I'm willing." Still the old caution kicked in. A painful memory of just such a moment with Nick pushed through. "But still let's take time to really know each other before we . . ."

Damon squeezed her hand. "I agree. Over the next few weeks, let's have some quality time."

"Yes. We'll have time before I leave." Jade smiled at him

"What do you mean?"

"Oh, I didn't tell you. We're going to Washington, D.C., to a big conference. It's going to be great."

"You and Lang?" Damon's jaw muscle jumped.

"Yes. Some of the country's leading experts in social services will be there. There will be a special day-long seminar on community intervention in inner-city neighborhoods. You should send Eddie."

"Humph, guess so," Damon said. The waiter returned and took their order. "How long is this conference?"

"Four days. But Bill and I are going down a few days early. He's going to introduce me to some congressmen and top Health and Human Services officials. I'm so excited," Jade said.

His brown eyes flashed with annoyance. "Guess Bill still has the connections to make a big impression."

"Hey, works for me. We got the grant because of his inside knowledge."

"Yeah, Bill always had a way of going around the rules." Damon took a deep drink from his water glass.

"What do you mean . . . ? Oh, no," Jade blurted out. "Please, Lord, let me be hallucinating."

"Alton, look. It's our Jade. Hello, sweetie!" Clarice pulled her husband along in her powerful wake like a battleship. Alton Pellerin wore a look of apology. "Why, isn't this something."

"Hello, Mama." Jade tried not to sound as horrified as she felt. "Hi, Daddy. How've you been?"

"Fine, darlin'." Alton bent down to kiss her.

"Now who is this?" Clarice fixed Damon with an appraising gaze that took him in from head to toe. A small nod signaled her approval based on first impression.

"Mama, Daddy, this is Damon Knight. Damon, my parents."

"Happy to meet you, Mr. and Mrs. Pellerin." Damon stood up and shook hands with Jade's father. "Please join us."

Jade groaned inside. She was trapped in date hell with no hope of escape. "Yes, do," she said with a forced smile.

For several minutes they exchanged small talk. Clarice was the picture of grace as she skillfully extracted information about how long Jade and Damon had known each other and where they'd first met. Damon seemed not to notice he was being pumped for details by a master. As she watched her mother, Jade was sure anything she ate now would sit in her stomach like a hard rock.

The waiter came back. "What'll you folks have?"

"Oh, no, no, no." Clarice held waved a hand with great drama. "We wouldn't dream of intruding on these young people. Besides we're meeting the Monroes for dinner. There they are. Telma, over here."

Telma and Caspar Monroe had been friends of Jade's parents for years. The handsome older couple played tennis with the Pellerins, and they even took short vacations together on occasion.

"This is Jade's . . . friend," Clarice said with a significant look to Telma. "Marlene and Oliver Knight's oldest son."

"My, my. How do you do." Telma looked at him with frank interest.

Damon seemed not to notice the stir he was causing. He even seemed to be enjoying the attention of the women as they made a fuss about his family tree. Caspar Monroe was a retired professor who knew his father quite well. He went on to tell several amusing anecdotes about Oliver's exploits on the golf course years ago. While Clarice and Damon were distracted, Jade's father leaned over to her.

"I tried to talk her out of this," he said in a low voice.

"It's okay, Daddy," Jade mumbled. Her tone suggested just the opposite. "How in the world did she figure out where . . . ?"

"She's better than any psychic. First place she named when Telma asked where we wanted to go." Alton kept an eye on his wife to make sure she did not suspect he was talking about her. "You know how your mother is, baby."

"Oh, boy, do I," Jade said. She watched her mother with a growing sense of dread. When Clarice turned to her, the feeling deepened.

"Why have you kept this darling young man such a secret, Jade? He just has to come over for dinner." Clarice turned back to Damon. "Of course you will." She patted his arm as though to say that it was settled.

"Mama, we . . ." Jade wanted to pull herself from this sinkhole. But how?

"Next Wednesday?" Clarice pretended not to have heard her.

Damon smiled at Clarice. "Sounds fine, Mrs. Pellerin. I'm looking forward to it."

"Excellent." Clarice beamed back at him. "Now we'll leave you two alone. Bye now."

The foursome made their farewells and swept off into another dining room. Jade began thinking of excuses to cancel the dinner within seconds of her parents' departure.

"Your parents seem very nice. And your mother is charming," Damon said.

"Yes, charming."

"I'm looking forward to next Wednesday already."

"Oh, well. If you're busy, I'll understand. I mean . . . don't feel you have to come." Jade took a deep breath.

"You scared I'm going to do something awful and embarrass you? I promise not to lick my fingers," he teased.

"No, that's not it." Jade moved her dinner fork around on the tablecloth. "I just don't want you to think I'm pushing you to something more serious. Meeting parents takes things to a whole new level."

Damon put an arm around the back of her chair and spoke close to her ear. "Sweetheart, I don't think you're rushing me into anything. I want to go."

"Really?" Jade looked up into eyes that reminded her of warm summer nights and soft music.

"Really." He grinned at her. "Things are right on time."

Jade was afraid to put too much into his statement. Such enticing words could turn out to be lies. The pain of another letdown would be unbearable.

"Then let's agree that this dinner has no significance attached to it. It's only dinner." Jade made herself pull back from him.

"Fine. Now do you feel safe?"

"I didn't feel threatened," Jade blurted out in a defensive tone then blushed.

"I understand," he whispered low. "I've felt the same. Getting your heart stepped on will do that to you."

"Oh, Damon." Jade wanted to grab this man and drag him home to her bed. He was everything she wanted: sensitive, sexy and kind. Those three attributes were like a powerful aphrodisiac, working on her body with the force of a nuclear blast.

"Like we said before, let's take our time. I'm looking forward to going slow with you," he said, his voice deep and sensuous.

"Yes—me, too." Jade rested her temple against his. The need to be near him was so strong it pulled her to him like a magnet.

He rested a hand on her thigh and caressed it underneath the long, white tablecloth so no one else could see. "But I've got to be honest, Jade. I've never wanted a woman the way I want you. From the first day, I've thought about all the ways I'm going to please you. You know what I mean?"

A little voice way down inside told Jade she should be offended and slap his hand away. But that voice was soon shouted down by the desire coursing through her. Another voice said, "I felt it, too." Jade was startled to hear the words come out of her mouth. But the dark desire in his eyes made her glad she'd said it.

The rest of the evening was more relaxed. Jade marveled at how they could talk with ease about everything. There were no awkward silences, no desperate search to fill in with mindless chatter. Damon talked about his business with a sense of pride in his father's accomplishments. But his enthusiasm really showed when he spoke of the Gracie Street Center. His commitment to making life better for the residents of that neighborhood was genuine. They talked at great length about the hopes and dreams he wanted to come true for them, especially the children. Jade wanted to do everything she could to help him. She now looked forward to working on the grant like never before.

"I can't wait to learn more in Washington. People like Karl Dennis will be there. He's got a fantastic program that's built on unconditional care and wrap-around services," she said.

"Tell me about it."

"Unconditional care means they don't discharge people from their programs. In other words, some agencies draw the line— say, if kids get arrested or pregnant—and stop serving them. His agency makes a commitment to stick with that child no matter what."

Damon sat back and folded his arms. "That's an awesome concept. What's wraparound services?"

"It means you design the services to meet whatever needs will help that child or the family. If they need better housing, child care, whatever, you get it. You don't just focus on changing the child's behavior or the parents', too, for that matter," Jade said.

"That sounds like something we'd want to get into."

"Then send Eddie. Like I said, this is a tremendous opportunity for him. He could learn about other agencies and network with experts." Jade munched on the remains of her french bread.

"We'll see. Now are we ready for coffee?"

"Bye, Jade. Damon, we'll see you next week," Clarice called to them as she passed by. The others in her party waved as well.

"I'll be there," Damon called back.

"Bye, Mama." Jade's cheerful goodbye was genuine, much to her own surprise.

"Now I've got some of the best Jamaican coffee you ever want to taste. Shall we?"

"I thought you meant . . ."

"No demands, remember? I promise not to bite." Damon stood up and held out his hand. Jade took it and followed him out.

The drive took them through an exclusive neighborhood of luxury town homes and garden homes. Jade watched the tail-lights of his Mercedes Benz. *Woman, you have lost your mind going over to the man's apartment.* Jade waited behind him at a red light. Damon waved to her, smiling in his rearview mirror. Yet she did not think of turning the car down a street and running off into the night. That would be rude, she reasoned. She dodged the thought that she was curious to see where he lived. The tiny warning voice so familiar said he might be a crazed pervert for all she knew.

"Now I'm really tripping," Jade murmured. "Why do I have to add mad drama to everything? This is a normal invitation to end a pleasant evening with a congenial cup of coffee."

Jade considered the change of heart toward her mother's obvious intention to insert herself into Jade's love life. Clarice would no doubt try to interfere. Of course her mother would see it as helping nurture a desirable match. Still Jade did not feel the annoyance or grim resignation her mother's machinations usually inspired. Somehow she felt in control this time. With Damon the pace of their relationship would not be dictated by anyone—not even so formidable a woman as her mother. That she could think of having a date over to her mother's home without getting a sick, dizzy spell was proof positive of the magic Damon Knight had worked on her. When she got out of her car to walk with him, Jade giggled to herself.

"Okay, share the joke." Damon led the way into his living room.

"I was just thinking of my mother. She's probably already planning next Wednesday's dinner. I get shivers at the thought of what she'll come up with." Jade could well imagine Clarice would pull out all the stops to impress Damon.

"Can't cook?"

"Oh, she's a great cook. But she has made matchmaking her mission. And not just for her own daughters, though we're her top priority." Jade shook her head.

"That simply means she loves you and wants the best for you." Damon brought her a cup of coffee.

Jade had seldom seen her mother's efforts to mold her in that light. "I suppose so. Still, it can be very aggravating." When Damon sat close to her on the sofa, she forgot her mother. And everything else.

"Tell me about it. My father can be a real bull when he decides he knows what we should do. Trent, my younger brother, still hasn't been forgiven for not joining the family business."

"I see." Jade did not see anything but the even color of his skin. The delicate scent of his cologne—she played a game of trying to identify it—was like heated spices. *Better think of something else quick or I'll be all over him.* "I love your place." She took regular breaths in an attempt to slow her racing pulse when he turned away to look around.

"Thanks. My own feeble decorating efforts."

Jade admired the earth tones of red, forest greens, beige and brown that blended so well. The sofa was brown fabric with a pattern of leaves in fall colors. The carpet was a dark green that blended well with the green and brown draperies. Several small African sculptures were arranged with great taste on the tables. She admired two prints of popular black artists that were on the walls. He used a few items to great advantage. The apartment was individual and inviting.

"Don't be so modest. I love what you've done." Jade's heart began to thump hard when a swell of a mellow blues tune floated from the compact disc player. Johnnie Taylor's voice flowed like warm honey, making her squirm. When Damon came back to sit beside her again, Jade sat rigid with determination.

"I'm glad you like my place. Maybe that means you'll visit often." Damon sat relaxed with his arm across the back of the sofa. He did not attempt to touch her.

"Yes, it is attractive." Jade was too flustered to respond to his last statement. She made a great show of looking at her watch. "Goodness, I hadn't realized how late it is. I'd better be going."

Damon pulled her arm to him before she could get up. He held her arm and took his time staring at the watch face. Looking into her eyes, he stroked her skin. "Umm, only nine. You have to rush off so soon?"

Jade's throat went dry. Words would not come. For several seconds she sat transfixed by his hypnotic gaze. "Well, I've got lots to do at the office," she said, forcing her voice to work. "Um-hmm, I need to get an early start before Bill gets there."

"I see," he said in a quiet voice. Damon's gaze never wavered.

"Once he's in the office, things get so hectic," Jade said in a small voice. Her heart was beating so hard, she was sure folks in the next apartment must hear it.

"Guess you can't stay a little while longer." Damon leaned toward her.

"I really should be going." Jade's voice was no more than a whisper as Damon touched her bottom lip with his thumb. His warm breath brushed her cheek as his face came within an inch of hers. She shivered. "Damon."

"Yes," he murmured. Slowly he teased her by rubbing his bottom lip against hers.

Jade could not stop the gasp she uttered as a blast of hot energy surged down her back to spread through her hips. The desire to have his hands on her body left her weak, too weak to pull away when his tongue flickered over her mouth. He kissed her with a slow, sweet searching movement of his lips and tongue. But soon an urgency took control as his hands gripped her shoulders tighter. Jade could feel the rest of the world slip away until there was only the touch of his skin and the warm, tangy scent of him. Her mind filled with a kaleidoscope of pastels that swirled. All she wanted was for this to go on forever. She wanted more than to just be with him, she wanted to be inside him. No, she needed to have him inside her. Close was not enough. This man moved her to a place so wondrous, so delicious it was almost supernatural. His large hands moved with a gentleness that drove her wild. Damon was not just holding and kissing her, he possessed her the way a powerful spirit might possess a poor mortal. The certainty that they were meant to be together, emotionally and physically, flashed into her consciousness like a blinding bolt of lightning.

"Jade, baby," Damon moaned. "You taste so good." He kissed her face and neck.

She wrapped both arms around him. "We shouldn't . . ." Yet even as she spoke, she pressed her body to his.

Damon nuzzled her cleavage. "Take it slow, you mean?" he said in a soft voice.

"Oh, my—I mean yes," Jade said. She shook her head in an attempt to clear it. When he kissed the base of her throat, she melted into him again.

"Don't make me wait too long," Damon whispered in her ear before leaning back against the cushions. A sheen of perspiration made his face glisten. He took out a handkerchief.

"Mercy, mercy me." Jade got up from the sofa on legs like soft putty. She had to move away from the force of him. It was more than she could resist for much longer. Walking to the fireplace, she sought to steady herself by holding on to the cool marble of the mantel. Her back was to him.

"Please don't be angry with me. I know I got carried away," Damon said in a voice laden with anxiety after several long minutes of silence.

"Damon, it's so fast." Jade wanted laugh and cry at the same time.

"I'm sorry, I went too far. But please don't turn away from me." Damon stood beside her but was careful not to touch her.

"What?" Jade blinked with confusion. The haze of desire still clouded her mind.

"How can I explain it?" Damon paced in front of the sofa. "I feel like a man stumbling out of the desert to find a cool stream of spring water. A little sip only makes me that much more thirsty for you."

"Damon—"

"I know. Getting heavy is not on your agenda right now."

"Damon . . ." Jade was so full of emotion that all she wanted to say crowded her mouth until she could not say anything. The old fear that she was not worthy of him slammed back with a vengeance. This was too good to be true, which meant it could not, would not, last. She backed away from him. "Maybe I'd better go now."

Misery painted his features with a grim frown of resignation. "Have I lost you?" he asked.

Jade could not bear to be the cause of that look. She came back to stand before him, a hand on his arm. "No, no! It's just that I need some time to sort through all I'm feeling." She gave him a smile of reassurance and touched his cheek. It was hard not to pour out her heart to him.

Damon placed his hand over hers. "I don't want to do anything to make you go away." He smiled at her with a gleam of amusement in his eyes. "Besides, I need a little time to recuperate from you, too. Now I truly understand the expression 'You rock my world.'"

Jade laughed. "I can testify myself, brother-man." She planted a chaste kiss on his chin then moved away fast before the spark ignited between them again. She picked up her purse and coat on her way out. "I'll see you soon."

He was beside her in a few long strides and stood close. Damon brushed her face once more then opened the front door. "Count on it."

Chapter 5

"Thanks for meeting with me on such short notice." Lang shook hands with Damon.

They were in Damon's suite of offices in the Knight-Cormier Building. An office complex built with financing from both of his grandfathers in 1960, not long after his parents were married, it was three stories high. Titus Knight wanted his son to make a big impression on the business community. Aubin Cormier wanted his new son-in-law to continue to provide for his much treasured youngest daughter in the style she was accustomed to and deserved.

Located in the heart of what was known from the early thirties as the heart of the black upper-crust business district, it was made of gray brick with large windows facing the street. A large sculpture by Frank Hayden, a leading black artist, greeted visitors as they entered the lobby. Prints of famous paintings by Henry Ossawa Tanner, Clementine Hunter and others lined the halls leading to offices. Tenants included attorneys, an insurance company and even a black dentist. Damon's offices were on the top floor with a nice view of tree-lined Harding Boulevard.

"No problem, Bill. Have a seat. Now what can I do for you?" Damon sat opposite Lang in a dark red leather chair that matched three others arranged around a cherry wood table set in an alcove of his spacious office. A window let in late winter sunshine that brightened the room.

Lang accepted a cup of coffee from Damon's secretary, Marius. "Thank you, son. I think it's great the way you've given jobs to the young brothers in need."

"Marius has done well for himself. He's got more of a focus than ever before."

"Marius is from Easy Town, right? Gangs have really gotten to be a problem in that area."

Damon gave a solemn nod. "One of his brothers is on death row at Angola State Prison. I think Marius has made up his mind to live a different kind of life."

"Good for him. Good for him." Lang took a sip of coffee. "This place never goes out of style." He gazed around the office building.

Damon wondered about the purpose of this visit. Just what was Lang leading up to now? He'd known him since they were teenagers, and disliked him for just as long. "Bill, you didn't come here to talk about gangs or admire my office building." He sat back and waited.

Lang smiled. "Still the same serious, get-to-the-point Damon Knight. How long have we known each other? Sixteen, seventeen years?"

"Longer. We met when we were juniors in high school. Then again at Morehouse." Damon remembered how the fresh-faced young man could charm his way into any woman's bed or gain the trust of other men.

"Yes, those were some good times."

"Mostly," Damon replied. He also remembered how he learned that Lang was willing to do whatever was necessary to get what he wanted. Lang would not break laws, if he could help it. But bending rules or changing them to suit his needs came easy to William Jefferson Lang.

"You're still not holding a grudge about that incident with

the vice chancellor are you? Man, we're grown-ups now. Besides, I talked you out of trouble." Lang put his cup down.

"I didn't have anything to do with faking those lab results in the first place. And Thomas St. George was expelled, while you were only suspended for two semesters." Damon wore an expression of displeasure. Thomas had gone home in disgrace. He'd later completed his education at a small college in Virginia.

"Wonder how old Thomas is doing?" Lang seemed curious but not the least bit regretful that the impressionable young man had suffered because he'd been led into trouble by him.

"Quite well," Damon said. *No thanks to you.* "He's running his uncle's hardware store chain in West Virginia."

"Splendid."

"Bill, I'm still wondering why you're here." Damon now wanted him out of his office.

"There have been several meetings with Mike and Steve Franklin about the grant that you haven't attended. Why?"

"I didn't think it was appropriate to meet with them just yet. I thought we were going to set up a steering committee to include community members." Damon had explained all this to Mike Testor when he'd called him a month ago.

"We're working on it."

"Apparently key decisions will be made and then handed to them to be rubber-stamped."

"Certainly not. But as a businessman you know that not everything can be done by committee. We'd never get this project rolling if some groundwork was not done to help them get a solid start." Lang was all reason.

"What kind of groundwork?" Damon wore a skeptical expression.

"Starting with a policy and procedures manual for their review—but first putting together an orientation for them. This committee could become a permanent advisory board. These are just a few of the details we need to discuss," Lang said. He sat forward with an earnest look to his suave features. "Let's get down to the real deal, Damon."

"Which is?"

"You don't trust me." Lang held up a hand to forestall a reply. "With good reason, I admit. But like I said, I've grown up a lot since college."

"Look, I'm not accusing you of anything." Damon was still wary. He'd seen Lang in action too many times over the years.

"You don't have to, brother. All I'm asking is that you look over my career for the last twelve years."

Damon could not dispute him. He'd watched Lang rise in state government with a solid reputation for getting things done. "You've done some good things," he said finally.

Lang sat back. "I've been active in the community. I want to change some of things that have gone wrong for all poor people, though of course the plight of black people touches me at a deeper level."

This time Damon sat forward. "Which is why we can't afford to lose any opportunity to reach out. Conservatives have been more successful than most folks realize in cutting back on programs. But so-called liberals have gone along with a lot of their agenda as well."

"We're in total agreement. So you're afraid I'll do something to squander a chance to make an impact?" Lang raised an eyebrow at him.

"Steve Franklin has a reputation for putting profit before quality services. With his interests in nursing homes and psychiatric hospitals, he's made millions." Damon stopped short of mentioning recent revelations about overbilling Medicaid funds. Four psychiatric hospitals run by Franklin's health care company were responsible for much of it.

"Steve can be an aggressive business hound, sure. But his facilities have come through audits and survey reviews with only a few minor citations."

Damon knew this was true since it had been reported in the newspapers. Even with a lot of digging, investigative reporters had not turned up any wrongdoing that involved Franklin. Maybe he was being too paranoid. Lang was right, they were almost twenty years older now.

"I'm sorry, but it's just that those folks are so used to having their hopes crushed," Damon said. "Too many grants end up providing high-paying jobs for a few of the already-haves."

"I'm going to be straight up, Damon. We need you because the people around Gracie Street, Easy Town and Banks trust you. For our efforts to really be effective, we need that credibility factor. If you ever have any questions about something we've done, don't hesitate to ask. You'll be kept fully informed." Lang's tone was decisive and meant to inspire confidence.

Damon still hesitated. "Eddie should be more of a player than I."

"Of course Eddie can represent you. I know how busy you are running one of the most successful black businesses in the state. I don't expect you to make every meeting," Lang put in quickly.

"It's not so much that . . ." Damon thought of Jade. Lang was right about his time being at a premium with the stores and Gracie Street Center activities. But Jade was now an important factor. She worked long hours and so did he, but Damon had no intention of missing out on such a fabulous woman. Meeting with Lang and the others would take precious hours away from his already scarce private life.

"Besides, the best way you can know we're doing the right thing is to be present. Right? And we'll meet at my office, which is just a ten-minute drive from here."

The prospect of seeing more of Jade turned Damon's hesitation into decision. "When is the next time you get together?"

Lang smiled broadly. "Next Thursday at ten thirty. We should be through by lunchtime at least." He stood up and pumped Damon's hand. "I'm glad we had this talk. We're going to make a great team, Damon."

Steve Franklin swiped at his mouth with a linen napkin. "That guy bothers me, Mike. He's always pulling on Bill's chain about something.'' He sat across from Mike Testor in the dining room of the exclusive City Club restaurant.

"Let him. He doesn't know squat.'' Testor chewed on the portion of prime rib.

"But he could get Lang to thinking about those certificates too much.'' Franklin suppressed a burp then dove back into his pasta dish.

"Look, Bill knows the deal. He's more than willing to see this thing through. Now what have you heard from your people?''

Franklin put down his fork and leaned forward. "Medicaid funding guidelines are definitely going to change within the next nine months. Disproportionate share is history.'' He wore a sour look.

"Damn! Couldn't our man in Congress do anything about this?'' Mike Testor drummed his fingers on the table.

"No way. He wasn't going to stick his neck out in an election year. Besides, once those other congressmen realized just how much Medicaid money we were drawing down, that was all she wrote.'' Franklin lifted both hands in the air.

"We were able to increase our Medicaid allocation quite nicely over the past six years. Too bad.'' Mike wore a pained expression like a child who'd lost a favorite toy.

"Yeah. Calloway was a genius.'' Franklin referred to the former secretary of the Department of Health and Hospitals with a tinge of awe in his tone. "Only a few understand those Medicaid regs like him. He figured out how to get more Medicaid money.''

Testor nodded. "The health care industry took off.''

What he did not need to say was that private health care businesses raked in millions of dollars in Medicaid money and made their owners rich in a few short years. Now it seemed the party was over, thanks to a vigilant congressman and his staff, who realized what a huge loophole had done to the national budget. As taxpayers complained about the out-of-control welfare spending, Congress learned that a few states had parlayed nonspecific wording in the regulations into huge increases. They were shocked and not a little embarrassed. The benefactors were evenly divided between liberals and conservatives who owned businesses that profited.

"Well, we can kiss that gravy train goodbye," Franklin said with a grunt.

"Maybe, but we can shift our focus so that we don't lose much in the long run. We've still got home health, nursing homes and the psychiatric beds, you know." Mike's mood lightened. He sawed at the meat and put another small chunk in his mouth.

"I guess so. We're not having much trouble getting approval for admissions. But Chester Howard is a real bloodhound about waste in state government. What if he—"

"You worry too much, Steve."

Franklin glanced over his shoulder. "Howard is eventually going to figure out that gaps in the system allow for less than meticulous decision making when it comes to eligibility."

"So what? Most of those are clinical decisions based on professional judgment. If your doctor says a kid needs sixty psychiatric inpatient days, who's to say he's wrong?" Mike continued to eat with gusto.

"Yeah, but in some places extensions have been given so a kid has been in the hospital nine months. Longer in some instances." Franklin lowered his voice even more.

"Give me a break. Some little criminal who's been stealing or selling crack is locked away. Nobody is going to complain. Trust me." Mike waved his fork for emphasis.

"I know but—"

Testor put down his fork. "Steve, we go back what—fifteen years? I swear, you're getting downright timid in your old age. Relax."

"The climate has never been like this before, Mike. All that reform talk wasn't just for the campaign this time. Governor Foster means it."

Mike chuckled. "The Department of Health and Hospitals is the largest agency in this state. And it's such a complicated bureaucracy, it'll take them the next four years just to find out which end is up."

"You've got a point," Franklin said. His frown smoothed out a bit. "There are so many sections, rules, policies and stuff it's like a jigsaw puzzle ten miles wide with ten million pieces."

"And by the time you get one part put together and try to see the whole picture, another part of the thing changes. All we need to do is step carefully and don't get skittish."

"And Lang? He's more of a wild card than I like." Franklin's frown deepened again.

"He has his uses." Mike wore an unpleasant smirk. "Bill is going to be more of a help to us than even he realizes. Let him think he's in control."

"Lang is no dummy, Mike. He could figure it out."

Mike shook his head with a look of disdain. "We'll throw him a few crumbs. They don't need much in the way of money before they rush off to buy flashy clothes and a fancy car."

Franklin barked out a harsh guffaw. "Yeah, you got a point there. Man, did you see him strutting around in his silk suit the other day?"

"But remember, they do have their uses nowadays, Steve. They still have their uses." Mike raised his glass of iced tea laced with gin to Franklin in a mock toast.

"You've been seen running around with some young woman." Oliver Knight got straight to the point. He stared at Damon hard.

"I'm dating Jade Pellerin," Damon said in a taut voice.

They had hardly sat down in the elder Knight's large den before his father blurted out his gruff comment. Damon was used to being grilled about the business during his visits to check on his father, but this probing into his personal life really grated. His parents never let him forget that they had opposed his divorce from Rachelle. Her father and brothers ran the most successful General Motors dealerships in the region. In addition, they had a thriving equipment rental business. To them, her affair was no more than a regrettable indiscretion of an immature young woman.

"Pellerin . . . I know that name." Oliver rubbed his chin.

"Her father is Alton Pellerin, Dad." Damon felt a prick of irritation at himself. Out of habit, he began to talk of her family. He'd always despised the preoccupation with pedigree of the black upper crust, old money. What did it matter who her parents were?

"Hmm, yes, of course. Had his start in real estate. A few shotgun houses over in Easy Town. His daddy was a yard man." Oliver's heavy black eyebrows formed two arches over his deep-set eyes.

"What is this about the yard man?" Damon's mother came in and sat down in a billow of silk. The soft material of the burnished gold lounge dress could be worn out to dinner with ease.

Oliver gazed at his wife with a pointed look. "We're talking about Alton Pellerin, Marlene. Damon is dating their youngest daughter."

Marlene gave Damon her full attention. "Is that so? Well." She brushed back her soft layered hairstyle. "Well, well. And where did you meet her."

"She's the top aid to Bill Lang in the Department of Health and Hospitals. It looks like Gracie Street Center will benefit from grant funds to serve at-risk populations," Damon said with resignation in his voice. This conversation was inevitable but had come sooner than he'd hoped.

"Oh, she works for the state." Marlene pressed her lips together and let her comment speak for itself.

"In a very high-ranking position, Mother," Damon said in a sharp tone.

"Yes, well . . ." Marlene wore a stiff smile that faded after a split second.

"Okay, let's get this over with right now." Damon looked from her to his father.

"Oliver, do you know what your son is talking about?" Marlene ignored his question and looked at her husband. It was a habit she had when not pleased with the way she'd been addressed that she spoke to a third party.

"Mother, Jade Pellerin is intelligent, attractive and a good person."

"Yes, I'm sure she's nice but . . ." Marlene let her expression finish the thought. Jade's family background was unacceptable.

"I don't need to trace her roots back to some rich ancestor to know that she's someone I want to be with." Damon spoke with force.

Marlene looked down at her manicured fingernails. "I see."

"Watch how you speak to your mother, young man. I can tell this Pellerin girl is already having a bad influence on you," Oliver shot back at him with a scowl.

Damon pushed down the rise of anger in his chest. "I'm no teenager in danger of hanging with the wrong crowd."

"You're right of course, dear," Marlene said, cutting off her husband before he could respond. "I'm just concerned about your happiness. You've moved in a certain circle all your life. Your friends and family come from the same background."

"Which has nothing to do with making new friends." Damon heaved a sigh.

"Don't take it so lightly, Damon. Having experiences in common can become very important after the first flush of romance dies."

"Mother, I don't see my circle, as you call them, very much these days. And it's in Jade's favor that she doesn't fit the mold of those people," Damon retorted.

"Don't be silly. The boys you went to school with are prominent men today." Marlene lifted her chin. "And the young women have certainly made names for themselves socially and professionally." She was quick to defend those she considered as her social clan.

"They're all snobs of the worst kind. And I could tell you stories about some of their escapades that would rival any Eddie hears down on Gracie Street." Damon gave a wicked laugh. "In fact, you could probably tell me things I don't know."

"Now you're being downright uncouth—" Despite her words, Marlene had a gleam in her light brown eyes that said he was right. But she would never admit it and give him ammunition.

"The point is, son, this young woman may not be right for you. Don't let your hormones rule your head." Oliver broke in, impatient to drive home his thought on the matter.

"I'll be the judge of that. And it won't have anything to do with her family tree."

"I don't know how much longer I've got on this earth. I'd like to see at least one grandchild before I die. And I'd like to know he's got a solid foundation to build on in this world." Oliver spoke in a grave voice.

"Remember, Dad, I took you to your last doctor's appointment. You're making remarkable progress. An exact quote."

"Smart-mouth kids," Oliver grumbled.

Yet once again Damon was shaken by his father's reference to his own death. Damon had been leaning toward a career in human services after taking several undergraduate courses in social work and sociology. The field placements he'd worked in a couple of social service agencies led him discover a love of making life better for others. Naturally his parents had been appalled at this development. Only a deep sense of family loyalty, especially after Trent rebelled and refused to join the business, had brought him back to work with his father. And when Oliver became ill, all thoughts of another career were pushed aside. Damon had only mild regret. His work with Eddie and the Gracie Street Center gave him much satisfaction.

"So don't even try it. And no visit to the stores this week, either." Damon turned the tables on his father and became the parent.

"Damn, doctor. He's as much a quack as his old man," Oliver muttered.

Marlene cleared her throat. "Damon, we have overstepped our bounds. You're entitled to conduct your life as you see fit."

Oliver gaped at his wife. "Did I hear you right?"

"Yes, dear. Damon is a grown man and can make his own

decisions without you second-guessing him.'' Marlene seemed to scold Oliver, as though she had not tried to interfere.

"Me?'' Oliver stared at her, speechless.

"I'd love to meet this remarkable young lady. When can we get together? I think at the Century Club for dinner would be just the thing.''

Damon felt a pinprick of suspicion. "Are you serious?'' The Century Club was sacrosanct to the black society of Baton Rouge. Money alone was not enough for membership, family background was more of a factor.

"Yes, talk to her soon. I'll make the reservations.'' Marlene gave him a warm, maternal smile. "If she means so much to you, I'm sure we'll like her. Right, Oliver?''

"Uh-humph,'' was his father's only reply. He shook his head.

"I'll let you know.'' Damon kissed her forehead. "Mama, you can still surprise me.''

He felt a glimmer of hope that his parents would see reason where Jade was concerned. If Marlene came around, Oliver would give in without much of a struggle. When he left for home, Damon felt a soaring lift of joy he had not felt for a long time. A beautiful, desirable woman was now in his life. And a battle with his family over their attempts to pick his mate seemed a thing of the past. The grant would bring a welcome boost to the Gracie Street Center, and Lang seemed to be a sincere brother trying to help. Life had never been better.

"Shaena, will you stop grinning at me like that,'' Jade said. She sat down with a plate of low-fat gingerbread squares.

The two friends had decided to eat in and watch a movie for their Wednesday midweek get-together. Cold, wet and windy weather made being inside with a nice fire going more inviting than fighting traffic to get to a restaurant. They headed over to Shaena's elegant garden home, which was only ten minutes from Jade's condominium. Shaena had cooked a simple chicken stir fry with vegetables. Now they settled in for dessert. Two steaming mugs of coffee sat on an oak serving tray.

"I know you like a book, girl. When I saw you and Damon together, I said to myself 'Self, he's the one!' " Shaena popped a piece of gingerbread in her mouth.

"Do you have to be so obnoxious about being right?" Jade nudged Shaena.

"Yes." Shaena cackled. "Especially since you were so biggity about how he didn't mean anything to you, and you weren't impressed with him."

"All right, okay." Jade smiled. She was too happy to really be irritated with anyone right now. "So maybe I was trying to convince myself that I wasn't attracted to him."

"Honey, there was more electricity crackling between you two than in a power plant. Now tell me everything," Shaena said with a gleam of interest in her eyes. She settled back with her mug. "Start from beginning. What does his place look like? How long did it take for y'all to get in the groove?"

"We did not get in the groove, I'll have you know. We've only just started seeing each other," Jade said in a prim voice.

Shaena looked a little disappointed. "Oh, yeah?"

"Apart from wanting to know a man is the kind of person I can stand to be with outside the bedroom, these days you have to be careful," Jade said.

"Yeah, yeah sure." Shaena brushed aside the threat of a lecture from Jade on men and safe sex. "Don't try to change the subject. You've got scorch marks still on your body, sugar. Some kinda heated activity took place. Now spill it."

"Well . . ." Jade leaned back against the plush overstuffed pillows with a secretive smile.

"Girl, don't do this to me!" Shaena bounced on the sofa with frustration.

Jade giggled. "Much as I love seeing you squirm, I'm dying to tell you more." She closed her eyes and took a deep breath. "Shaena, it was fabulous. Damon is all man."

"Go, girl!"

Jade opened her eyes and stared into the flames. "I don't

just mean sex appeal. He's got a depth that I've never known in a man before. He's so much more than good looks.''

"Whoa, this is heavier than even I thought it would get this fast." Shaena lost her joking demeanor. "You're really into this guy, aren't you? In a serious way, I mean."

"Yes, and it terrifies me."

Jade had been avoiding men for that very reason. Not only did she fear being used again, she did not trust her own ability to choose the right man. Look at how Nick had been so successful in deceiving her. She suspected her need for love and approval made her prey to wearing blinders when it came to romance. How else could she explain not seeing what was so obvious in Nick? And those little devils from the past were not gone simply because she now knew they existed.

"I could lie to you and say from now on you won't get hurt. But hey, love is a gamble—plain and simple." Shaena shrugged.

"Thank you for those words of comfort, Dr. Ruth," Jade retorted.

"However," Shaena said in an exaggerated accent, "ven you give your heart, the joy it vill bring is worth the risk. Only ven vee love are vee truly alive." She held up a forefinger for emphasis.

"Don't quit your day job, babe. Show biz ain't for you." Jade gave a shudder.

"That's gratitude?" Shaena wore a smirk. Then she turned serious. "But straight up, I've got a feeling this is a real special thing between you. I hear it in your voice when you talk about him."

"I'm scared, Shaena," Jade said in a quiet voice.

Shaena grabbed her hand. "I've been there, too. Don't push away a good man. Happiness is too hard to find. I'm still looking."

"We've been through it, huh?" Jade patted her friend's hand.

They had comforted each other through painful breakups with men they thought would be in their lives forever. Shaena had said goodbye to a married man who'd promised to leave his wife for three years. Jade helped her gather the strength to tell him goodbye. Not long after Shaena held a sobbing Jade when she learned of Nick's affair and illegitimate child—a child that had been conceived and born within the first two years of Jade's marriage to Nick.

"And we survived," Shaena said. "Stronger and wiser."

"I hope so, but I'm still not sure." Jade wanted to believe more than she could express. "Am I right about Damon? That's a question that echoes in my head at least once a day."

"What do you think?"

"He's handsome, has lots of money and is from a prominent family. What does he want with me? I'm on the wrong side of thirty, not a size six and no supermodel." Jade rubbed her hands together.

"You're only thirty-two, a baby. And the man's no snob or fool, either. He knows a good woman when he sees one." Shaena put down her empty coffee mug.

"I know, I know. Deep down I do feel good about myself most of the time. It's just . . ."

"Okay, time for the exercise." Shaena tapped her arm. "Let's hear it."

"Aw not now." Jade groaned and let her head fall back on the sofa pillow.

"Let's hear it. Our self-love exercises made a big difference for both of us. Go on, you know the drill," Shaena said in a commanding voice.

"No, no, no," Jade whined.

"I'm going to be a real nuisance until you do it."

"Oh, all right!" Jade heaved a sigh. "My job is . . . stimulating. I've just been promoted."

"You were promoted because . . . ?" Shaena prompted her.

"Bill said he was impressed by the good things my former boss said about me." Jade sat up.

"Which was?"

"That I was smart, creative and took initiative." Jade felt pride in saying those words.

"And you did something to make him say those things." Shaena nodded.

"There was this one big project with the feds, and I was able to work out a big problem that saved the whole thing. I can't believe all those brains in policy and planning missed it." Jade looked at Shaena.

"So you're not stupid."

"And Nick was pretty slick with the way he fooled me. Could that man tell a good lie! When I think of how naive I was then." Jade looked up at the ceiling and shook her head.

"Y'all started dating when you were nineteen. Then you got married right out of college. What did you know?" Shaena lifted a shoulder.

"Since meeting Damon, I don't feel anything when I think of Nick. It's weird."

"What do you mean?" Shaena reached for another piece of gingerbread.

"No anger or resentment, nothing. I can even laugh at how ridiculous he was at times. The man couldn't pass by a window or mirror without checking his look." Jade chuckled. For the first time in years, she could make a joke about him that was not tinged with bitterness. She felt an emotional freedom, like a weight had lifted. "Carrying around that kind of animosity saps a lot out of you, Shaena."

"Tell me about it. I'm still not over mine yet." Shaena stared ahead.

"Hey, now don't you start. Gerald wasn't worth it any more than Nick." Jade gave Shaena a nudge with her elbow.

Shaena blinked and smiled. "You're right. Now let's stop wasting time talking about them. Feel better?"

"As usual you know exactly how to make me snap out of the old self-pity trance. Thanks, sis." Jade gave her a quick hug.

"You've been there for me, too." Shaena squeezed Jade's hand then let go. A twinkle lit her eyes. "So when do you and Damon move this thing to a higher level of intensity?"

"We're taking it one step at time. Damon has been hurt

badly like me. And I know that isn't an act. I've heard the gossip about his ex-wife, Rachelle." Jade fiddled with her mug.

Shaena jumped on her last sentence. "Uh-huh! You've been scoping out the man's past all the time, trying to make me think you were being so cool. Reel him in, honey." She laughed at the look of chagrin on Jade's face.

"Oh, hush. Maybe I did want to know more about him. That's not strange." Jade lifted her nose in the air. Still she had to suppress a giggle.

"Good for you. You've got a bit of Lanessa in you, child." Shaena gave her a playful shove. "She knows how to finesse a man."

At the mention of her sister, Jade grew sober again. "Speaking of Nessa, she's got me worried. She's seems kind of shaky these days."

"In what way?"

"I can't put my finger on it. She's just not herself." Jade tried to sort out the jumble of little incidents that bothered her. "For instance, she's always on edge. You can say the least thing to her, and she freaks."

Shaena waved a hand in dismissal. "Lanessa has always been high strung. She's a diva used to getting her way. She'll get over it. She always does."

"I don't know, Shaena. She's acting different this time. I've never seen Lanessa like that over anything, especially a man. Even after her divorces, she bounced back."

"Lanessa has the will of an ox, baby. I've no doubt she'll be just fine."

"But what bothers me is the way she's just drifting. Let's face it, at thirty-four it's time to settle down. I think even she wants to find a lasting relationship." Jade had only an intuition of this since Lanessa had not confided in her.

"What Lanessa wants is a man who will give her anything she asks for," Shaena said. "The girl will land on her feet wearing two-hundred-dollar Italian leather pumps, and not get one scuff mark on 'em."

"You think so?"

"Sure. Isn't this the woman who convinced Patrice Lawrence that she was better off without her fiancé? And this when the woman had tracked Lanessa down to whip her butt for stealing him!" Shaena howled with laughter.

Jade joined her until they were both in tears. "After Patrice had stolen him from another woman. Patrice didn't realize she'd been played until two weeks later, girl. By that time Lanessa had moved on to somebody else."

"Lanessa has more smooth moves than anybody I know." Shaena wiped her eyes. "She'll be just fine."

"I guess you're right." Jade recovered and took a deep breath. "But I'm going to give her a call all the same. Now what have we got?" She pointed at the movie cassettes.

"Shaft!"

For the rest of the evening, they enjoyed a succession of classic black films and chattered away. Yet in the back of Jade's mind was the memory of sweet, brown lips covering hers and strong hands that sent tremors of desire down the length of her body. For the first time in years, the days ahead held the promise of something wonderful.

"Marlene, I think you're going too far," Oliver said with a slight frown. He stared at his wife, who sat across from him.

"Do you want him to end up with this girl?" Marlene's lip curled in an expression of distaste. "Jade Pellerin."

"I don't see why n—"

"And that mother of hers. So pretentious with her fake cultured accent. She still has farm dirt under those acrylic nails."

"Nothing wrong with farming. Your grandfather was one." Oliver corrected her. "And so was my great-grandfather."

"Oliver, my grandfather was one of the richest black farmers in Rapides Parish, who inherited land from his white grandfather. Hardly the same thing as a sharecropper digging sweet potatoes out of the dirt," Marlene said with a toss of her head.

"Is the girl after Damon for his money and position?" Oliver had more concerns than pedigree. He worried about the Cormier-Knight family fortune. Marlene had substantial money from her family. Oliver not only passed on a thriving business to Damon, but interest in several successful family business run by his brothers in which he'd invested.

"Well, of course she is," Marlene said in an impatient tone. "Anyone can see it—*except* Damon. I'm sure he'd eventually come to his senses, but it could be too late."

"But I don't know about this, Marlene. If Damon finds out . . ."

"He won't for a long time. By then he'll thank me for rescuing him. Now let's see. Ah, here it is." She glanced down at an address book with a floral fabric cover.

"Are you sure you should?" Oliver grew more uneasy as he watched her punch in the number.

"Yes, now stop pestering me." Marlene smiled but not at him. "Hello, dear. How are you? Yes, it's Marlene Knight. Just wanted to see how you've been, Rachelle."

Chapter 6

Lang crossed his arms. "Mike is on a short leash, Tavis. Stop worrying. I've known him for a long time. Is that why you came down here?" His voice held a note of amusement. "I could have saved you a trip."

Tavis tugged at the designer silk tie he wore, even though it hung perfectly. He sat in one of the leather chairs facing Lang's desk. "Mike is a master schemer, Bill. I don't trust the man one bit."

"He can't do anything without us knowing, now can he? I have the authority, so my signature has to go on any changes in our plans. Mike's okay—just likes to hedge his bets for maximum benefit." Lang was the picture of ease, sitting back against the soft dark green leather captain's chair.

"Yeah, maximum benefit for himself."

"I've known Mike a long time, Tavis. He's not what I'd call a bosom buddy, but we've worked together on at least six major projects in the department. We understand each other. Besides, if push comes to shove, he's got as much to lose as I do."

"You think that's enough to keep him from selling you out?" Tavis still looked skeptical.

"You're being too pessimistic. It won't be an issue because there won't be a problem." Lang got up to admire the view from his window. "I have Secretary Chauvin's complete confidence since that meeting three months ago."

Tavis sat forward with interest. "Tell me about it."

"We discussed the situation with hospital beds and the critical need in communities like Easy Town, the Ninth Ward in New Orleans. I can make exceptions to the moratorium on approving more." Lang turned back to smile at him.

"But . . ."

"No one cares about this stuff, Tavis. That's the beauty of it. The process is so boring and dry, no one pays attention when certificates are issued," Lang said. "Not even Chauvin thinks much about it."

"But what about Howard?"

"Got his hands full with straightening out other messes in the department. And don't forget our esteemed lawmakers. Having legislators who own all or part of some of these places helps quite a bit."

Tavis rubbed his chin. "Yeah, I forgot about that. They won't be too anxious to have committee hearings or even be receptive if anybody tries to bring it up."

"Exactly. Those hospital and nursing home beds bring in millions of medicaid dollars. They'll be happy and I'll have a rewarding consulting career in another ten years. So will you." Lang sat down again and tilted the chair back. He crossed his long legs. "Feel better?"

"Somewhat. Just thinking of a way to keep an eye on Mike. It doesn't hurt to be extra careful." The handsome man lifted an eyebrow at his mentor.

"Son, you've got a keen sense of survival. I've taught you well. But in this case, Mike is the least of our worries. By the time we get back from D.C., we should be well on our way to getting set for the next year." Lang picked up the phone and dialed a number. "Jade, bring me the procedures on bed certificate requests and approvals."

"Are you sure enough time has passed?"

"Plenty." Lang glanced past Tavis when Jade knocked then came in. "Jade, you know Tavis Collins."

Jade shook hands with him. "Sure. How are you today, Tavis?" She went to place the papers before Lang.

"Fine," Tavis said. He gazed at her from head to toe. "Mighty fine," he murmured low.

"Excuse me?" Jade looked at him again.

"Nothing." Tavis wore a slight leer.

Jade turned her attention back to the file and did not notice. "I've got the procedures with timelines on top, Bill."

"Good. I'm pretty familiar with this. But I just want to make sure. I'll go over these then have you prepare them. Oh, did you get delegation of authority ready for me?"

Tavis looked at him hard. "Delegation of authority?"

"Since Jade is my assistant, I checked and she can give approvals in my absence so things won't come to a standstill simply because I'm out of town. You know how much I have to travel in this position." Lang smiled up at Jade.

Tavis looked at Lang then Jade. Both thick eyebrows arched high on his light brown face. "Hmm. I see."

"But maybe I shouldn't go to the conference then, Bill. I mean with both of us out of the office for over a week . . ." Jade wore a slight frown. "I hadn't thought about it before now."

"I'll have everything squared away by then, Jade. So don't even think about abandoning me. In fact, take my suggestions and leave early to shop for the trip," Lang said.

"Oh, I've got a million things to do."

"I can't believe this, Tavis. Any other woman would jump at the chance to buy new outfits to impress them in our nation's capital." Lang held out both hands as though perplexed.

"She's obviously not any other woman, boss," Tavis replied. "One hard-working lady."

"Very dedicated." Lang glanced back at Jade.

Jade laughed. "The truth is, I don't want to come back to a desk piled high with work."

"Well, it's your call. I offered."

Jade went to the door. "And I appreciate it, Bill. You're one great boss-man. See you later, Tavis."

"Bye," Tavis said. When she was gone, he looked at Bill. "Be cool, my brother. Kathy is on the alert these days."

Lang gave a grunt of scorn. "I can handle it, man. Besides, some things you just can't pass up." He stared at the closed door.

"Aline, be sure these get put in Mr. Lang's 'in' tray. These can come to me for my signature." Jade went over the instructions with Lang's secretary for the third time.

The petite blonde looked at the ceiling. "Jade, I've been an administrative assistant for three years now."

"You're right. But go through my messages every day. Let's see what else?"

"You'll be gone only a few days for goodness' sakes. And thanks for taking *him* with you." Aline nodded toward Bill's office.

"I know he can be a little short at times, but he doesn't do it to be mean," Jade excused. Bill did have a high-handed way with clerical staff.

"Yeah, sure. All the same, he doesn't have to rush back as far as I'm concerned," Aline grumbled low.

Jade snatched up a long gold envelope. "This is from legal. The regional office staff didn't send in that summary of evidence yet. I'm going to call them right now. I could be here late if this keeps up." She ran her fingers through her hair.

"I'll call them. I always do, Jade." Aline faced Shaena with a look of relief. "Will you talk to her? She's driving everyone nuts," she whispered. With one last look of exasperation, she made a hasty retreat.

"What's up with you?" Shaena put both hands on her hips.

Jade searched the top of her desk then the open file drawer

behind her. "Takin' care of business before I get out of here. Where did I put—Hey, get your foot off that!" Jade dove to the floor and snatched a large pocket envelope.

Shaena leapt aside just in time to avoid being tackled. "Girl, pul-leeze! You *have* lost your mind."

"Oh," Jade said with a sheepish look. "I'm sorry." But still she paid more attention to the prized item than to Shaena. "You okay?"

"Don't overwhelm me with your concern," Shaena retorted.

"This trip has got me all shook up. Only a few weeks on the job, and now I'm leaving for almost two weeks!" Jade shuffled more papers.

"Get a grip. You'll be gone only a week. What is the matter with you, really?" Shaena placed a hand down on the papers firmly. "Well?"

"It's got nothing to do with Damon, if that's what you're getting at." Jade pressed her lips together, knowing she'd just given herself away.

"Now we get to the heart of the matter, pun intended." Shaena pushed her down into her chair and sat on the desk close to her. "Tell me all about it. And don't bother trying to wiggle out of this one."

Jade sucked air then plunged ahead. "With all the fine women he can choose from, I just know he'll play while I'm away. Why shouldn't he?"

"We've had this conversation, Jade. I'm losing patience with you." Shaena gave her a slap on the back of her hand.

"Ouch! Cut that out." Jade rubbed a growing red spot and scowled at her friend. "I didn't mean it like that. But men with looks *and* money don't lack for company just because one woman isn't available—"

"Some men," Shaena cut in.

"They like the hunt-and-conquest game. Most men don't even try to resist women who throw themselves at them," Jade went on as though she had not spoken.

"Jade, check yourself. You've lumped all men into one big pile of canines. My dad and yours are not like that. Never have been.'' Shaena got a mint from the candy jar on Jade's desk. She popped it into her mouth.

"Daddies don't count," Jade said with a stubborn, little-girl expression. Seeing Shaena's sideways glance, she relented. "Okay, so I'm getting a little weird about this."

"A *little* weird?"

"But we're barely at the starting gate, and I've got to back out now with this darn conference."

Shaena sat down in a chair. "You were so enthused about it two weeks ago. What a change."

Jade sighed. "Yeah, and for the last two weeks, it's dawned on me how many women would love to get their hands on Damon even when I'm in town. Women like Lila Castille."

"Lila's got more miles on her than a Greyhound bus. Damon would never go for that type," Shaena said with a catty snort.

"But her family dates back to the time when Louisiana was a Spanish colony. Royalty even." Jade wore a miserable expression.

"Give me a break. Royal thieves who spent most of their time stealing from everybody in sight." Shaena chuckled. "Her ancestor was only one of many mistresses. In fact, I heard she was a hooker."

"Really?" Jade brightened for a second with the juicy gossip over two hundred years old. Then she swung back to the present. "Anyway, she's just one of many. Maybe I should break it off now."

"Sure, dump him before he dumps you. At least it's safe."

"Don't give me that tone," Jade shot back at her.

"Yeah, as a matter of fact who needs the attention of a fine, sensitive man who thinks you're gorgeous, right? No need to wait until he's done something wrong. Drop-kick the dude now." Shaena ignored her smoldering look.

"I'm warning you—"

"Guilty until proven innocent. He's a man, that's evidence enough."

"Shaena, you're on thin ice with a big crack down the middle." Jade glared at her.

"Hey, it's not like good men aren't a dime a dozen after all. Watch it!" Shaena dodged a rubber band shot at her head.

"I get your point." Jade laughed again, this time harder. "What is the matter with me? I'm losing my mind like you said."

"At least you can laugh about it, sugar. Look, a bad experience can make it hard to trust again. I know how it feels."

Jade grew thoughtful again. "I swore I'd never let any man mean that much to me again."

"You put your faith in someone you loved and he lied. That kind of heartbreak takes a long time to heal. I'm just learning how to move on."

For several minutes the two women sat silent, each reviewing a painful past. Jade thought of the ardent, sincere look on Damon's face when he spoke of wanting to have someone in his life he could be close to. He'd been hurt like her. Having been hurt in the way only a lover can, Jade knew the shadow of sorrow in those stunning eyes was not fake. His tender touch was that of a man who wanted to love and be loved in return. A man who wanted true love, not a conquest. And Jade needed the same.

"Maybe I should, too. Damon doesn't talk or act like any other man I've ever been with, Shaena." Jade looked up with a glow of warmth in her expression.

"That's right, honey. I've been doing the tough, don't-need-no-man thing long enough to realize that. But no more." Shaena waved a hand.

"I'm going to stop making myself crazy about this. Damon is coming over tonight, and we're going to have a wonderful time." Jade gave a decisive nod.

"Good for you, girl. A nice cozy evening is just the tonic you need." Shaena grinned at her.

Jade wore a puzzled frown for a few seconds. "Say, hold up. What did you say about not being without a man anymore?"

Shaena's eyes shifted to the left then right. She cleared her throat then got up to leave. "Let me get back up there and finish this brief."

"Freeze!" Jade jumped up and caught her arm. "Don't even think about leaving until you tell me who he is."

"Hey, my boss is going to wonder where I am soon." Shaena tried to shake loose without success.

"So you don't want to tell me? And I thought we were closer than sisters." Jade assumed a hurt expression. "Okay. I understand . . . I guess." She turned away.

"Stop with the guilt trip." Shaena glanced around before shutting the office door. "Promise you won't laugh," she said so low Jade leaned forward.

"Speak up, I don't read lips. Why would I laugh?"

Shaena bit her lip and paused before speaking. "It's Brad Pittman."

"Brad Pittman!" Jade yelled and slapped her head. "Tell me this is a nightmare sequence from *The Twilight Zone*. Tall, reddish-blond on the sixth floor Brad Pittman?"

"Lower your voice, mega-mouth," Shaena said through clenched teeth. She stared at Jade with a stonelike gaze. "I didn't know you had a hangup about interracial dating."

"I have a hangup about dating outside your species. The guy is arrogant and condescending. I've always suspected he was a bigot, too."

"Scratch that last theory, hon." Shaena giggled.

"But Shaena, Brad Pittman?" Jade dropped into one of the two chairs for visitors that faced her desk.

"He doesn't have patience with a lot of idiot bureaucrats. But neither do we. And his reputation is undeserved." Shaena lifted her nose in the air.

"Brad Pittman," Jade said with astonishment still in her voice.

"Have you ever seen him be rude to someone without cause? Think about it."

Jade sat without speaking. "Okay, you have a point. But still . . ."

"We've had only one date so far, so don't make a big deal." Shaena tried to look nonchalant.

"Then why act so undercover when I asked you about it?"

Jade fixed her with a critical gaze. "Nah, I'm not buyin' it, girlfriend. It's my turn to tell you that you're not fooling anybody, except maybe yourself. You got a jones for the man."

"No way." Shaena shook her head with vigor.

"Don't run away from love," Jade said with a smirk. "Be honest about your feelings. I'm sure you recognize your own advice."

Shaena groaned. "I asked for that."

"And more—" Jade broke off to answer her phone. "Oh—hi, Damon. Working hard to get things cleared up before I leave. You are?" Jade broke into a wide grin. "That's marvelous! I'll see you tonight."

"What good news have you gotten?" Shaena asked.

"Damon is going to the conference, too. Oh, happy day!" Jade got up and did a little dance.

"Bet you won't be so grouchy about leaving here now." Shaena laughed at her.

"No, indeed."

Lang knocked on the door before opening it. "Jade, here are the letters I've signed. Hello, Ms. Greene."

"Hello, Mr. Lang." Shaena got up to leave. "I'll talk to you later." She waved goodbye and left.

"Count on it," Jade called after her. She chuckled at the face Shaena made at her. "Uh, Bill I think I *will* leave early today to do some shopping."

"See? I knew you'd want to get something special to wear. Go right ahead." He smiled at her. "I'm sure you'll wow them in D.C." Lang went back toward his office.

"Thanks, Bill."

Jade arranged the papers on her desk. In a few minutes she was ready to leave. She hummed a favorite blues song as she locked the door to her office. She already had in mind what she wanted to get. With one last set of memos to distribute, she went into Lang's office on her way out.

"Here you go. I've gotten the last mail out." Jade nodded to Tavis, who was still in Lang's office.

"Efficient as always. Happy shopping."

When Jade was gone, Lang leaned back in his chair. "She's looking forward to our trip as much as I am."

"Oh?" Tavis gazed at him with an amused look.

"Yes. Jade is on her way to buy new clothes. I'll bet lingerie is on the list." Lang wore a smug grin.

Jade closed her eyes and held on for a lovely ride. The slow blues tune wrapped around them like a warm blanket. It was magic being with him with all of her senses working overtime. She savored the feel of having Damon's arms around her in the dark. Her ears hummed with the slow beat of the bass being strummed with such precision. Damon's cologne was a tangy spice that tickled her nose in a delicious way. The dance floor was packed, but Jade no longer noticed or cared.

Dorothy Moore crooned. Her rich throaty voice poured out the words to a blues love song, AT LAST MY LOVE HAS COME ALONG making the old R&B standard sound new.

The Blues Cabaret was a nightclub in downtown Baton Rouge that catered to the true blues aficionado. Some of the best guitar players and singers came there regularly, mainly because many of them were Baton Rouge or Louisiana natives. They loved coming home to jam with friends. Local audiences were the happy beneficiaries.

"Having a good time?" Damon said in a soft voice close to her ear.

"Hmm," she purred. Jade rubbed against him, wishing there was a way to get even closer. "I'm at one with the universe."

Damon chuckled. "So love can be a mystical experience, eh?"

Jade shivered at the word. She looked up at him. "We're falling in love?" The way his lips curved up at the corners made her weak in the knees. He needed to be kissed—or rather she needed it, badly.

"What do you think?" Damon nibbled her bottom lip with a gentle tugging motion. "Tell me."

"Damon," Jade gasped.

A delicious hot hunger spread up her thighs and hugged her hips. The movement of her gentle rocking motion against him was involuntary. Instinct made her press forward. That he was just as aroused became obvious when she felt his erection through the fabric of his slacks. The music seemed designed to push them into sweet insanity.

"Tell me you want me, too," Damon said. "Say it."

"Yes," Jade whispered. Her voice was hoarse with the effort to hold on to what little conscious control she had left. She trembled as a tiny explosion rocked her body. "Oh, yes."

"Say it," he urged. His hands traveled up and down her back, making her tremble more. "Please."

"I want you so much, Damon." Jade groaned with the sweet sensation of arousal. She gave a tiny cry of dismay when the song came to an end.

"Time to go back to our table." Damon held her still on the dance floor. His eyes were smoky with passion.

"Have mercy on me," Jade said. Her heart was pounding like a drum in her chest.

They walked back to their seats with their arms encircling each other's waist. An alert waiter appeared. He handed Jade a cardboard hand fan with an advertisement for a soul food restaurant nearby.

"Nice cool drink oughta go down just right after that one." He winked at Damon. "How about it, my man? Looks like you could use something with ice in it."

Damon nodded in a numb fashion. "Yes, indeed."

"I'll have another diet cola, please." Jade worked the fan back and forth. The cool breeze helped calm her.

"That was some dance." Damon wore a look of amused affection.

"I had a great partner helping me keep time," Jade said with a saucy tilt of her head to one side.

She was amazed at her boldness. Jade had always considered herself inept at this kind of erotic flirtation. This was her first experience with a man who so enjoyed making love long before consummation. Damon was bringing out a side of her she had no idea existed. Jade liked it a lot.

"I feel like we're communicating perfectly on every level. I can't wait to tell you about even little things that have happened to me. But sometimes just sitting next to you at the end of the day is enough." Damon locked her in a loving gaze. He sat with an arm draped around her.

"I know." Jade felt a soaring of her emotions as she leaned into the crook of his arm.

At that moment the waiter brought their drinks. Damon paid him. "Keep the change." He waved the man away, impatient to have him gone.

"Thanks, brother." The waiter glanced at Jade with masculine appreciation. He backed off. "I understand. Yes, indeed."

"Can we leave now?" he murmured, his lips brushing against her cheek. Damon's question was one with a charged double meaning.

Jade could no longer resist. She kissed him full on the mouth, not caring that they sat in the middle of the crowded nightclub. So intent on the delicious taste of him, she did not hear the scattered applause from those around them.

"People are watching," Damon said, his lips still pressed to hers.

"What people?" Jade replied. She eagerly touched the tip of her tongue to his. With perfect timing, they parted just as the music came to a dramatic end with a long guitar solo that ended abruptly.

"Jade?"

A loud male voice directly above them broke the spell of passion. Recognition tugged at the corner of her consciousness. She looked up to find her ex-husband, a pouting beauty on his arm, standing two feet away. The look of slack-jawed amazement on his face made her want to laugh out loud.

"Come on, Nicky," the woman said. She shot Jade a glance that could curdle milk. "You promised to take me to Chez Irene."

"Hello, Nick." Jade's manner was cool and offhand.

Yet she could not help but feel a teeny thrill. This could not have been better had she arranged it! All the nights of smarting from blows to her self-esteem dealt by Nick came back in an instant. There were also moments of rage at her treatment. Moments when she fantasized about showing him a thing or two. *I wish I had a camcorder!*

"It's been a long time." Nick glanced at Damon then back at her. "A very long time."

"A few months." Jade smiled at him. "This is Nick Guillory, Damon. My ex-husband. Nick, Damon Knight. And this is . . . ?" She nodded to the woman.

"Oh, uh, Tiffany—" Nick broke off, a befuddled crease in his handsome brow.

"Monroe," Tiffany snapped. She dug her long nails into Nick's coat sleeve, causing him to jump.

"Yes, Monroe," Nick said with an embarrassed laugh. "Sorry, it's just I'm surprised to see you here." He stared at Damon.

"Nice to meet you. Great band, eh?" Damon did not look happy at the way Nick kept glancing at Jade so possessively.

"Hmm, yeah, yeah. Really good music." Nick did not seem as though he was thinking of music at all. "You two been coming here awhile?"

Jade almost lost control at the obvious attempt to find out how long they had been dating. Before she could speak, Damon began.

"Awhile," he said. His expression challenged further efforts to probe.

Nick drew himself up and became the imperious man so familiar to Jade. "We usually go to New Orleans but decided to stick around the old town for once."

Damon was not impressed. "Oh, yeah."

"In fact what was that club I used to take you to down near the French Market, Jade? You loved it. We'd stay up until two in the morning then wander over to Café du Monde—"

"Nick, this trip down memory lane is simply fascinating,

but I'm ready to leave. *Now.*'' Tiffany spoke in a tight voice of fury.

"We're on our way out, too." Jade lifted her royal blue cape from one of the extra chairs at their table.

"Listen, if you're hungry, join us for dinner," Nick spoke up. He made a point of not looking at Tiffany. "No reason we can't be friends and get acquainted—or reacquainted as it were, ha-ha."

Damon stood up and helped Jade into her cape. "No, we're going to *my place.*" He wrapped an arm around Jade and pulled her close. "But thanks anyway."

"Oh. Then goodbye." Nick had the wide-eyed expression of a man who had just had cold water thrown in his face.

They were silent for the long drive to Damon's apartment. Jade's mood of amusement slipped to one of worry at the dark scowl on Damon's face since they had left the club. Once they were inside, Damon turned on his compact disc player and began preparing café au lait. Several minutes went by before she worked up the courage to speak.

"As usual the Blues Cabaret had the best jam in town." She craned around from her position on the sofa to see him in the kitchen just off the living room.

"Yep," came his clipped reply.

"I'm glad you suggested we go there. It was one fabulous evening, honey." Jade hoped the tension that hung in the air between them like a thin curtain would lift. But it did not.

"Well, it started out to be anyway." Damon marched in with a teakwood tray bearing two beautiful white cups with an African kente cloth pattern as a border around the rims.

Jade bit her lip. "How do you mean?" She was not prepared for the rush of anger that followed.

"I mean, your ex showed up and stood scoping out every inch of your body. Right in front of me." Damon did not touch his mug.

"Nick isn't interested in me, Damon."

"That's not the way he acted tonight. And you seemed to eat it up." Damon turned to her with a look of accusation.

"Damon I . . ." Jade searched for a way to explain.

"So that means you still care about him." Damon got up and stood with his back to her, hands jammed into his pockets.

Jade was well acquainted with the sting of feeling insecure. Knowing how he'd been hurt by his ex-wife helped her to be understanding. Jade stood behind him and put her arms around his waist.

"Damon, I admit I enjoyed seeing that dumbstruck look on Nick's face. Not very admirable, I know. But it's not because I still have feelings for him." Jade forced him to turn and face her. She lifted her face to his. "You're the one and only man in my heart."

"Are you sure? You were together for a long time. How can I compete with all the memories?" Damon searched her face for an answer.

"Nick was not only unfaithful to me, he constantly belittled everything I did. Most of my memories of being with him are unpleasant, some downright horrible," Jade said in an intense voice.

"I didn't realize he'd hurt you so much." Damon's face softened. He touched a fingertip to her mouth.

"About one year after he finished law school, he announced that he'd outgrown me. Well, not exactly in those words, but that's what it amounted to."

Nick had joined the thriving family insurance business. The heady life of meeting some the South's most wealthy and powerful only made his oversized ego bigger. He went from treating her with mild condescension to outright contempt. Jade stared off. Even that hurt had faded. She felt nothing at the image of that last ugly scene which led to the end of her marriage.

"Are you sure there isn't at least a trace of love left?" Damon spoke just above a whisper. His expression was one of fearful expectation.

"No," Jade said with confidence. After all this time, this was a moment of revelation to her. Nick meant nothing to her now. "He's the past. I can't even get mad at him anymore."

Damon gazed into her eyes for several long moments. "Then let's forget about the past. For us, the present is sweet enough." He traced a line from her lips down her throat.

Jade's pulse jumped to double-time as she watched his finger stop just at the point her cleavage began. "More than sweet."

She guided his hand to her breast and let out a gasp when he teased her nipple beneath the fabric of her blouse. Her mouth opened to his with eagerness. Damon kissed her in short urgent bursts that trailed down her neck to the tops of her breast. Jade unbuttoned her blouse.

"Only if you're ready," Damon said. He paused in the act of unhooking the front clasp of her lace cup bra.

Jade's answer was to discard her blouse completely and pull him down to the sofa. "Now. Now," she murmured.

With soft words of love, Damon undressed her then let her undress him. When flesh met flesh, they both sighed with pleasure at the satisfaction of a long-waited desire fulfilled. To her delight Damon began to nuzzle her nipples with tiny bites using his lips. From there he brushed his lips down the length of her.

"I want you from the top of your head," Damon whispered. He looked up at her with eyes dark with desire. "To the bottom of your feet." He planted a hot kiss on the smooth skin of her ankle. He let out a satisfied chuckle at the vibration that rippled through her.

Jade tingled all over, her mind filled with the wonder of how luscious sex could be with a tender lover who took his time finding all the right places to touch. This was a dream come true. Jade ran her hands over the solid, muscular arms as he worked his way back up and licked her breast with long strokes. Damon was so kind. And his lovemaking was a reflection of his generous nature. His attention to pleasing her brought small cries of joy from Jade. She feared she would lose consciousness as he again rubbed his lips up and down her thighs. Damon pulled away.

"Don't dare move." He sought to quiet the gasp of dismay that came from the loss of contact.

Jade clenched her teeth to keep from shouting for him as

the few seconds he was gone seemed like hours. She ached with the need and feel him. But he appeared over her, holding a small foil square.

"We should—" he began.

Jade nodded then watched him tear open the package. His hands shook as he shoved the remaining oversized pillow from the back of the sofa. He took a small throw pillow and placed it under her bottom. Gazing into her eyes, Damon guided her hands as she gently rolled the condom into place. She pulled him down on top of her and pressed his mouth to hers. As their tongues met, he entered her. Slow rhythmic motions rebuilt the smoldering embers into a roaring flame that seared through them. They talked to each other, at first in soft words of desire. But soon the urgent need to satisfy a roaring hunger took control. Their soft murmurings became cries of ecstasy. With one long, shuddering moan Damon let go. Jade screamed his name as she felt herself release. They lay holding each other a long time, wrapped in a cocoon of contentment.

Damon went to the hall closet and brought back a soft cotton blanket. "Here, now that we've cooled off—"

"Speak for yourself." Jade giggled. Even so, she allowed him to cover them both with it. Damon sat up and pulled her to snuggle against his chest. "Of course you wouldn't be chilly if you put on some clothes. Wicked thing."

"Me?"

"Uh-huh. Had your way with me right here on the sofa. You couldn't even be bothered to seduce me into the bedroom." Jade rubbed her cheek against the hair of his broad chest.

"I'll never be able to sit in here again without a big smile on my face," Damon said with a chuckle as he gave the arm of the sofa a pat. "But I don't regret one minute. Do you?" He became serious.

Jade hugged him tighter. "No, indeed! By the way, thanks for keeping your word." Her eyes sparkled when she looked up at him.

"Which promise was that?"

"To go real slow and take your time. Just what I needed, baby." Jade laughed deep in her throat.

"Thank you, ma'am." Damon grinned at her. "I aim to please. Now would you like to see the bedroom?"

"Hmm, I'm getting sleepy." Jade yawned. "Maybe I'd better go home now, or I'll be here all night." she stretched.

"Exactly," Damon whispered. With a playful pat on her buttocks, he pulled her down the hall.

They kissed with tender affection before dozing off. But only a few hours later, they were once more riding a tidal wave of lust. It was a night that left them both happily exhausted and sure of their love.

Chapter 7

Clarice tapped out a rhythm with the tip of her ink pen as she sat at the small desk in a corner of the den. "Damon Knight," she said for the fourth time.

Alton did not lower the newspaper. "Hmm, hope the Jaguars beat Grambling good this year. Tired of listening to Burrell shooting off his mouth about his alma mater stomping on our team."

"He's one fine young man." Clarice put away the stamps and envelopes she'd been using to pay bills. "Wonder how far it's gone."

"Bayou Classic is going to be better than ever. They've got the Neville Brothers to play at the Alpha Kappa Alpha dance that Friday night. Gonna be a blast." Alton ignored her comment.

"The Knight family has been prominent in the state for over a hundred years at least, Alton. And to think Jade was the one that snared him." Clarice sounded surprised at the fact. She settled on the plush sectional sofa.

Alton lowered the newspaper with a deep sigh. "Stay out

of it, Clarice. It's none of your business. When Jade tried to squirm out of that dinner, you should have taken the hint.''

"She didn't squirm out of anything. We're going to have it in another week and a half. On a Friday night before her trip.''

"Strong-armed her into it anyway, huh?'' Alton's mouth turned down in disapproval. "Shoulda known you'd get your way come hell or high water.''

"We're having a roast," Clarice said. "Jade made the selection.''

"Didn't have much choice once you cornered her.''

"Damon went through a real bad marriage and divorce. Lanessa told me all the gory details. And they're the same age," Clarice went on as though her husband had not spoken.

"Clarice," Alton said in his gravellike voice. "Our daughters are grown women who should be capable of running their own lives.''

"He seems a little . . . ahead of Jade, if you ask me. I mean even with his bad experience with Rachelle Balleaux, he's not exactly been slow to bounce back. From what I hear, he's been seen with some of the most elegant young women in the past year. All old money of course.''

Alton grunted. "Of course.''

"I hear that Marlene Knight—she was one of the St. Landry Parish Cormiers you know—makes sure her sons date and mate the 'right' girls. The woman is very demanding.'' Clarice wrinkled her nose with disapproval. "One of those people who always insist on having her way.''

"Humph, sounds familiar," Alton grumbled in an undertone.

"So Jade is going to have to pass her inspection. Poor dear, Jade is going to fold or get smart with her. You know how she is," Clarice said.

"That's my baby girl. Jade has a dozen low-key ways of telling folks to go jump.'' Alton chuckled.

Clarice shot a reproachful glance at him. "I don't think we should encourage that behavior, Alton.'' She sat in thought for several minutes. "The more I think about it, the more it seems that those two won't be together long.''

"What are you saying?"

Clarice pursed her lips and was silent for several seconds "Damon and Jade are completely incompatible. But now Lanessa and Damon would make a perfect pair."

"Wait just one minute—" Alton slapped down the section of newspaper he was holding.

"He's got the kind of sophistication that Lanessa can handle with ease. She's a high-stepper for sure as my grandmother used to say." Clarice spoke of her older daughter with pride.

"Clarice!" Alton snapped in a commanding tone. Clarice stared at him in wide-eyed surprise. "This is too much even for you!"

"Why Alton, I . . ." Her voice trailed off at the stern look of ire on his face.

"Jade seems happier than she's been in almost three years. You'd try to sabotage that?" Alton let her see just how loathsome he found the notion.

"Alton Earle Pellerin, how dare you even think I'd do such a thing?" Clarice drew herself up in outrage. "I said nothing about trying to cause them to break up."

"I know you too well, woman. You've decided he's right for Lanessa and thinking of other men for Jade right now. Some sort of consolation prize for the child. I won't have it." Alton did not back down from her. Once in a great while he took a stand against his wife's more blatant meddling.

"I only meant that it's clear Jade and Damon won't be together long. You know I have a feel for these things," Clarice tried to explain.

"And your feelings have been wrong before. Jade and Nick are a prime example."

"But what about Lanessa's husband? Everyone else thought he was so wonderful. I tried to tell her, but would she listen? And look how that turned out." Clarice shook a finger at him.

"Yeah, I still say Brandon wasn't such a bad guy. Lanessa did her part in messing up that marriage," Alton said.

"Nonsense. But I'm not going to argue with you about that again."

"Good." Alton got up to retrieve the remote and turned on the television.

"You're wrong as usual. Anyway, there is no reason Lanessa can't date Damon when they break up—only after a decent interval of course."

"*If* they break up, Clarice. From the way they looked at each other the night we saw them together, I think you're way off base on this one." Alton was losing interest now. He punched the buttons until he found the sports cable channel. "Just leave it alone."

"Well, we'll see. I give it three months tops—and that's stretching it." Clarice folded her arms wearily.

"Our children are grown. Let them handle their lives."

"I want both my girls to be happy, Alton. They've been hurt, and I want to see that they find a man who will give them a good life. What's wrong with that?" Clarice had repeated this question numerous times when her husband or daughters were critical of her attempts to help them.

"Sure, baby. I know deep down you do, but they're not little girls anymore. They have to make their own way."

"Yes, yes." Clarice had heard all this before.

He gazed ahead. "Jade doesn't have enough self-confidence, and Lanessa seems to be drifting somehow." Alton shook his head as though the effort to fathom his daughters was too great a task. "Anyway, sticking your nose in their love lives won't help matters for either of them."

"Yes, dear," Clarice said in an indulgent manner. "Of course you're right. Oh, look, the game is about to start." She pointed to the big-screen television. A smile of satisfaction curved her lips when he turned to watch it.

"Dallas against Oakland." Alton propped his feet up on the leather ottoman that matched his favorite recliner. He had forgotten the discussion already. "This is gonna be good."

"Jade needs a stable man in her life." Clarice held a novel in her lap without looking at it.

"Uh-hmm." Alton was engrossed in the announcer's pre-game comments on the line-up.

''Someone like ... Dorothy VickNair's son'' Clarice said with a snap of her fingers.

Alton glanced back at her for a second. ''What was that?''

''Nothing, honey.'' Clarice watched him turn his attention back to the muscular men who bounded out onto the field. ''Nothing at all.'' She smiled to herself.

''Sure you don't mind going without me? I know what an ordeal tearing yourself away from the business will be.'' Eddie Simon gazed at Damon with an amused gleam in his eyes. He had stopped by Damon's office on his way back from a meeting.

''Don't worry about it. At first I hesitated to leave Joe with all the work, gearing up for year-end inventory, but we'll handle it.'' Damon cleared his throat. He worked hard not to let the anticipation show on his face or in his voice.

The truth was, he had been unable to concentrate on business, or anything else for that matter, for the past three days. The quarterly sales reports, operating budgets and marketing reports were no match for the memory of Jade. Damon could still taste the tangy-sweet trace of her lips just by closing his eyes. He could not wait to show her all his favorite places in Washington. Already he was thinking of at least two days when they would skip the latest workshops to visit a few galleries. Most of their days would be busy. But the nights? A finger of heat tickled through him at the thought of holding her close while they danced.

''Ahem.'' Eddie cleared his throat in a loud dramatic fashion. ''Come back to earth, my brother. You'll be with her and across state lines soon enough.''

Damon's eyes went wide with embarrassment. He gave up the vain attempt to disguise the reason for his distraction. ''Eddie, she got to me, man.''

''Yeah, and I can see how upset you are about being caught.'' Eddie gave him an amused look. ''Fighting like crazy to get away from her.''

''Real funny,'' Damon shot back. He took a deep breath.

"But you're right. I thought suffering through Rachelle was a strong vaccine against any kind of lovebug."

"Come on. Relax and be happy. Jade seems to be a wonderful woman."

"Jade who?" Trent stuck his head in the door. "What's up, Eddie?" He shook Eddie's hand. "Still doing good work with our kids, I hear."

"Hanging in for the cause," Eddie said.

"That's what we need. Now who is Jade? Lovely name by the way." Trent folded his long, lanky frame into a chair beside Eddie. He looked from his older brother to Eddie.

Damon shrugged. "A lady I'm dating."

"O-ooh. So that's who made your nostrils flare when we talked about three weeks ago." Trent grinned at him.

Eddie stifled a laugh. He got up when Damon gave him a cutting look. "Ahem, time for me to get going. See ya, Trent. I'll be in touch, Damon."

"Bye, man." Trent winked at him then turned back to Damon. "So things have progressed nicely, it seems. What's her full name?"

"Jade Pellerin." Damon shifted in his chair. That pesky heat wave moved through him just saying her name. What kind of spell had she cast? Not even Rachelle had brought out this reaction.

"Hmm, don't know her. But I'm glad you're back in the saddle, cowboy." Trent gazed at him with approval.

"Don't be crude. Jade is a fine person. She's intelligent, caring and—"

"If you could see your face right now." Trent threw back his head and laughed.

"You haven't grown up even at twenty-eight," Damon grumbled at him with a surly look.

"You got it bad and that's good." Trent did not let up despite the dangerous look he got from his older brother.

"Cut it out." Damon's frown melded into an abashed smile. "Eddie was just ragging me about it, too."

"Seriously, go with it. I'm happy for you, bro."

"Mama and Dad weren't so enthused about it." Damon scratched his chin. "You know how they can be."

"Yeah, snobs." Trent did not hesitate to express his thoughts. He was the brash younger son in sharp contrast to Damon.

"They value tradition," Damon said.

"Hey, don't try to dress it up. They're snobs. What is it? Her family not rich enough?"

"Her father is a successful businessman."

Trent nodded. "I get it. The wealth doesn't go back far enough up the old family tree. Yeah, they love old-money families." He gave a grunt of disgust.

"Our parents aren't that bad, Trent. It's how they were raised. Everyone we socialized with while growing up was the same way." Damon remembered the birthday parties with a group of children from only certain families—the care his mother took to steer them into the "right" crowd. His grandparents had been the same way with their children. "They really think it's best for us."

"Get real, Damon. They think we're better than other folks because of our family and money. Like I said, snobs." Trent was not going to budge on this issue. It was one they'd debated before.

"Well, that's one area where you're on safe ground. Carliss is more than acceptable to Mama." Damon thought of the quiet young woman who seemed to balance his brother's brazen flair. She was a center of calm for Trent.

"I don't date Carliss because it suits Mama or Dad," Trent snarled. "She's not poured from the same mold as the rest of those privileged, spoiled-rotten African princesses we hung around with from Hampton Heights."

"True. It's just your good luck she's from one of the oldest families in St. Landry Parish," Damon replied. Carliss Mouton's family could be traced to France and west Africa. "Mama won't question your being with her."

"Don't tell me you're going to let them dictate who you date?" Trent folded his arms.

Damon's eyes flashed with anger at the suggestion. "Definitely not. I let them know it, too."

"Good. Hang tough, big brother."

"But it's not an issue. Really," Damon put in when Trent gave him a look of skepticism. "We had a little talk, and Mother seemed to understand."

"Seems strange she gave up so soon." Trent shook his head to indicate he did not believe it.

"I'm not ten years old anymore. Mother knows better than to meddle in my private life. No, interference from them is not what worries me."

"Then what is it?"

"For a long time, I was so in love with Rachelle—or thought I was—that I just didn't see her for who she really was. She played so many games on me, man." Damon remembered the honeyed lies he believed for years. Rachelle had wanted him for money and prestige. She manipulated to get her own way and made life miserable when he resisted. "I don't want to be caught up like that again."

"I hear ya. I got dumped on before I had sense enough to get with Carliss. Maybe not as bad as you, but it hurt." Trent sighed. "But you can't live in the past. Get on with life. Besides, Jade sounds like a very different kind of woman."

Damon thought of the lilt of laughter that came from smooth brown lips. Jade's warm brown eyes the color of pecan pie lit up when she talked about helping poor people realize their dreams. Not once had she ever talked about shopping or going on expensive trips, subjects that usually came up with other women he'd known. Damon was well used to having such hints dropped, sometimes on the first date.

"She's one extraordinary lady. In fact, I was beginning to think women like her didn't exist. Except for Carliss, of course."

"You got that right. Bet they'd hit it off. Why don't we get together soon?" Trent said.

"Maybe when we get back." Damon wore a shy grin at the reaction to his words.

Trent's eyebrows arched. "Things are really moving ahead. Get back from where?"

"There's a conference in Washington, D.C., on serving at-risk populations. Since Eddie can't go, I'll be there to get information for the center." Damon's grin became a wide smile. "It just so happens Jade will be going. She works for the Department of Health and Hospitals."

"What did you use to bribe Eddie into not going, man?" Trent let out a guffaw.

"It was his decision. But I have to say it gave me the perfect excuse. Especially since I was trying to think up a halfway plausible explanation for going anyway." Damon joined him in laughter.

"That's great, man. And I can't wait to meet the lady who got to you." Trent's eyes twinkled.

Only a month ago, Damon would have been adamant that no woman would get to him. He was convinced that the intense romantic in him had been killed off, a suicide of sorts. Damon worked hard at ridding himself of all such notions. Jade Pellerin had revived that part of him that wanted long walks, evenings of soft music and words of love. The cynical survivor of a painful relationship went down in the first round. Not to mention the way he wanted her. His need to feel that satin milk chocolate skin pressed against his bare chest, to caress the full breasts that seemed to call out for his touch left him dazed at times. The wonderful sensation of how they filled his mouth like ripe fruit was a sweet memory. Though his want of her was much more than on a physical level, his desire for her was a quiet storm that never subsided.

"I have a feeling this trip is going to be the best one of my life."

"From the look on your face, I'd say you already have some sweet memories." Trent clapped his hands with delight when his older brother wore the guilty smile of a kid caught in mischief. "Bull's-eye. Now how about it? When can I meet her?" He got up to leave.

Damon walked with him to the lobby. "I'll ask her tonight. Maybe this weekend?"

"Sounds good. Bye, big bro." Trent winked at him and ambled off chuckling.

"What's so funny?" Damon called after him with mock irritation.

"You, Mr. Cool. All it takes is a mighty good woman." Trent turned around to face him, wearing a big grin.

"Out." Damon started toward him with a frown then laughed when Trent hastened his steps as if frightened.

Damon sang a soft tune the rest of the day. He was amused at the way his employees kept watching him with puzzled looks. At one point he even nodded his head in time to a jazzy beat on the FM station that played music in the lobby.

"You okay, Mr. Knight?" Helen, his office manager, stared at him hard as though trying to recognize this new person. Ten years his senior, she had been with the company twenty years. She was a valued confidant.

"Simply wonderful," Damon said, waving his hands with a flourish. "The end of a great day, the beginning of a great evening."

He went back into his office and left behind several astonished folks. Like a successful practical joker, he laughed at the effect of his intentional dramatic exit. Damon was not surprised at their reaction. The boss they knew was all business and stern. Since meeting Jade, the world did not seem the same hard place at all. After being hurt by Rachelle, he believed romance was the road to being used, and love was for fools. He'd known her for years, and look how much good that had done. So he vowed *never* again—never again would he be stupid enough to think all those pretty words of affection meant everlasting love. Now he realized he was wrong. Well, Jade made him realize it. Jade. The way their bodies connected with the same precision as their personalities was nothing short of beautiful.

"Bye, Mr. Knight. I was determined not to leave until I entered that last set of figures into the database." Helen came in and placed a stack of papers on his desk. "You workin' late like me?"

"No, I'm leaving right on time." Damon took a deep breath. He thought of his evening ahead.

Helen glanced at the pendant watch that hung from a chain around her neck. "No, you're not, it's already quarter to six. This office closes at five last time I checked." Her plump face dimpled with mirth at the way her boss jumped up. "You late for an appointment?"

Damon scrambled to straighten his desk and check to make sure no task had been left undone. "Uh, yes—no, I mean not yet if I move fast."

Damon was the picture of a frustrated man trying to hurry. He was dismayed to realize there were important documents on his desk that had to be locked up. Helen clucked in soothing tones. She helped him put the most sensitive files away.

"No, that goes in this file cabinet. Here, let me," Helen said.

"Okay, but just let me—" Damon opened an envelope. A cascade of paper slid from his fingers onto the floor, then scattered as he tried to catch them. "Man!"

"Stay cool now. We gonna take care of it." Helen gave him a big-sister pat on the shoulder.

Damon paused. "You're right. This is nothing to get upset about. I'll just make a quick phone call so Jade will know I'm running late."

Helen did a double take. "You sure got mellow lately. Time was, you'd be stomping 'round here mad at the least little thing. Here we had a delivery van in an accident, prices go up on some products we ordered without the vendor telling us, and you're still smiling."

"Yep." Damon shrugged as if to say it was no big deal.

"Well, I haven't met this lady. But, sugar, I like her already." Helen laughed. Damon threw back his head and joined her.

"Knock, knock. Hello there." A high singsong female voice stopped them both short.

Rachelle Balleaux Knight swept into the room without waiting for an acknowledgment. She stood still in a pose. Wearing a taupe jacket with a silk scarf draped over one shoulder, few would deny she was beautiful. The hem of her navy skirt was well above her knees to show off her shapely legs. Gold button earrings shone bright against her caramel skin. Rachelle flashed her signature alluring smile.

"Cat woman rides again," Helen muttered with a deep grimace.

Rachelle's bright smile dimmed a bit when she noticed Damon was not alone in his office. "Hi, Helen. Working late as usual—such dedication. Hello, Damon." She recovered and moved in to stand close to him.

"We were just leaving. Finished up for the day." Helen gave her a pointed look. Rachelle ignored it.

"Damon, you work much too hard. You should learn to take it easy sometimes." Rachelle put a hand on his arm.

Helen pursed her lips and glared at Rachelle. "You ready, Mr. Knight? Remember that *appointment.*"

"Thanks, Helen. I'll see you tomorrow," Damon said. He tried not to smile at the way she was giving him eye signals.

"You sure? I can finish up those last invoices." Helen looked like a mama tigress prepared to protect her young.

"I'm sure. I'll be leaving in a few minutes." Damon raised at eyebrow at Rachelle when Helen left. He waited to speak when he heard Helen's retreating footsteps down the hall. "So you're obviously doing well."

Rachelle stepped back and did a half turn. "Glad you noticed. After the divorce I went back into marketing. I've gotten a top position with my cousin's firm."

"I know." Damon gazed at her with an impassive expression. "I saw Edward at the last Chamber of Commerce meeting. He told me what a fantastic job you're doing."

Edward Balleaux had actually spent most of the time complaining about having been strong-armed by his father and aunt, Rachelle's mother, into hiring her. While Rachelle was intelligent and talented in her profession, she also had a knack for antagonizing people with whom she worked. In the last year, two of his best staff had quit.

"I've gotten him three big accounts in the last nine months alone." Rachelle lifted a shoulder. "All in a day's work as they say. You're doing very well yourself." She waved a hand at plaques decorating his wall given in recognition for his success in business.

"We've had a good couple of years." Damon stared at her with mild interest, like a scientist examining a minor curiosity.

The long brown hair was just as perfectly styled. It was pinned up in a french roll. Her perfect size seven figure was just the same. And she still moved with the grace of a woman secure in her attractiveness and abilities, a woman accustomed to privilege. This was the same woman who had kept his emotions on a roller coaster since the day they'd met as juniors in college. Yet here she was, as stunning as ever, and he felt nothing. Not quite true, he confessed to himself, he was impatient for her to leave.

Rachelle watched his expression. "Well, it's been a long time. Maybe we could go out to dinner. No reason we can't be on good terms."

"I have plans," Damon said. He looked at his watch. "And I'm late now. Was there something specific you wanted to see me about?"

"My goodness. I was on my way back from a meeting and decided to drop in to say hello. I didn't think I'd be pushed out on the sidewalk so fast." Rachelle affected the pout that in the past had crumpled his resolve to be firm.

"Sorry, I don't mean to seem rude. But I really do have to go. It was nice of you to stop by." Damon picked up his briefcase and jacket.

Rachelle walked up close to him. "Maybe we can get together when you're not in such a hurry. I really need to talk to you, Damon," she said in a voice filled with meaning.

"Rachelle, we've been all through this."

"All through what? I need to tell you how I feel. After the

years we spent together, you could at least agree to have dinner with me.''

Damon looked into her eyes. ''Rachelle, we don't need to keep going over the same old battles. I don't want to talk about what happened between us anymore. Okay?'' he said in a clipped tone.

''Okay. Then I'll say it right now. I'm sorry for the selfish way I behaved. I should have been honest with you. By the time I had sense enough to realize what I'd lost when we broke up, it was too late. I only hope you can forgive me one day.'' Rachelle spoke in a quiet, earnest voice. ''I'll go now.'' She turned to leave.

Damon had never seen Rachelle act so subdued. In fact, she had never apologized for anything in the time he'd known her. Maybe she had finally grown up.

''Wait. Look, I'm sorry for being so cold-blooded. I'm sorry for all the angry words we both said in the past.'' Damon felt a burden lift. Now he could go forward to a new life with Jade without bitterness from the past weighing him down. He could close this chapter and go on.

Rachelle turned back and hugged him. ''Thank you, darling,'' she murmured. ''I'm so happy to hear you say that.'' She stepped back. ''Now how about lunch Wednesday?''

''Well . . .'' Damon frowned, still unsure of her motives.

''We can do good things for Knight and Sons. I've got a dynamite plan to show you—and you know I'm familiar with your business.'' Rachelle spoke up quickly.

Damon laughed at the smooth shift to business. Rachelle gloried in her ability to influence people. ''All right then. And according to my calendar, I'm free.''

''Excellent. See you then.'' Rachelle's expression softened. ''And Damon, thanks again.'' She put a hand on his arm for a few seconds then left.

* * *

Jade bustled around nervous to make her first dinner cooked for Damon go well. She fussed at herself for letting the chicken get too brown.

"I hope it doesn't taste burnt," Jade mumbled. She gazed at the roasted meat in dismay.

"Jade, honey, relax. It looks just great to me." Damon joined her at the toaster over. "Smells great."

"Oh, I forgot to put in the rolls!" Jade fumbled with the package.

"Here, let me." Damon sliced the rolls down the middle and spread a dab of butter inside. "Now, we pop them in the toaster oven for seven minutes like so, put the oven on warm for the meat and . . ." He took her by the hand and led her to the bar stools set at her breakfast counter near the kitchen. "We take it easy with a glass of wine."

"When did you do this?" Jade said. Two wineglasses were set up and between them lay a beautiful red rose with a gold ribbon tied around the stem. Beside the rose was a gift-wrapped box.

"You were so busy fretting about the food, you didn't notice. Besides, I kept talking while I worked. Now hush and open your present." Damon gazed at her with fondness.

"A gift? But it's not my birthday." Jade enjoyed the anticipation of holding the box. She shook it.

"I know that." Damon shrugged.

"And Christmas is long gone." She shook the box again and then sniffed it.

"Open it, and you won't have to keep guessing," Damon said.

Jade unwrapped the box. "Have mercy." She held up a twenty-four-inch gold chain. It held a gold pendant in the shape of a key. "It's beautiful. Oh, Damon."

"When I saw this necklace, it seemed perfect for you." Damon stroked her long black hair. "You are the key to my happiness." He gazed at her with eyes filled with desire.

"I love it." Jade gave him a kiss. "Thank you, babe."

"You're welcome. Now one more thing," Damon murmured with his lips pressed to her neck.

"Yes?" Jade closed her eyes at the blissful sensation of his caresses.

"The rolls are ready," he whispered close to her ear.

"So am I," she replied. Jade guided his hands to her breasts and ran her tongue around his mouth, causing him to groan. "If you didn't want them to burn, you shouldn't have turned up the heat in here."

"I'm not all that hungry anyway." Damon pulled her closer to him.

Jade slipped out of his grasp. "Oh, no, you don't. I've been slaving away in the kitchen, and you're going to eat this food." She wagged a forefinger in front of his nose.

Damon grabbed for her. "Come back here, woman."

"No way." Jade eluded him and went to the oven. "Dinner is served." She laughed at the theatrical moan of frustration he let out.

All through the meal, they played a sensual game of double entendres. Damon commented on the firm breasts and how tasty they were, while Jade commented how much she preferred hard rolls. By the time they finished, both were weak from giggling at the outrageous puns they'd made up.

"We won't get the dishes done, if you keep being such a tease," Jade said. She stood at the kitchen sink. Damon followed her and put his arms around her waist.

"Me? You bring me to a boil then calmly insist we have dinner. And you've got the nerve to call *me* a tease?" He made a pretense of being indignant.

"Help me load the dishwasher, then I'll give you a special treat." Jade batted her eyelashes at him.

Damon cleared the counter in record time. Jade had tears in her eyes at the comical sight of his rushing about. Soon the kitchen was tidy.

"Now I want dessert." Damon flung the dishcloth he held aside. He stared at her with fire in his eyes.

Without speaking, Jade began to undress to the beat of a

blues tune playing on the stereo system. She started by slowly unbuttoning the blue cashmere sweater she wore. The matching skirt was pulled off and thrown aside.

"It landed on top of the refrigerator," Damon said in a strangled voice. He stood riveted by her performance.

"I'll get it later." Jade stood before him in nothing but a bra and sheer pantyhose. "Now it's your turn."

Damon gasped when she opened his shirt and began to nibble at the smooth brown flesh. He began to help her by unbuckling his belt. Soon clothes were scattered from the kitchen down the hall. By the time they were in the bedroom, nothing was between them as they embraced. A slow dance of passion began. First Damon held still while Jade caressed him until he was dazed. Then Jade closed her eyes as he used his hands and mouth to bring her to the edge of ecstasy only to pull back. Damon stood up to kiss her face. Jade moved toward the bed, but he stopped her. He kneeled, lifted her and held her against the wall.

"I want you like this," Damon whispered.

Jade let out a shuddering moan as he entered her. With each powerful stroke, a bolt of sexual excitement coursed through him. When she wrapped her legs around him, Damon let himself go beyond consciousness to where there were no boundaries between them. There was nothing else in the world, no one else in the world, but the two of them. They joined in a magical world of pleasure and love. Damon felt a frantic need to be inside her more deeply than he had ever dreamed possible. He was suspended for a luscious eternity in the sensation of velvet heat. As their matched rhythmic motion reached a crescendo, they seemed to lose all reason. They gripped each other, crying out for more. Jade climaxed first, and the force of it left her panting. She clutched him. Damon moaned her name over and over with each thrust. Somehow they stumbled to the bed and collapsed, still holding each other. Jade rested her head on his shoulder with a contented sigh.

"Only a few months ago, I'd have sworn this kind of happiness was found only in fairy tales,'' Jade said in a voice soft with emotion. She looked up at Damon. ''Is this a dream?''

Damon threaded his long fingers through a lock of her hair. ''If you mean am I for real, the answer is yes.''

He thought of the lies, machinations and half-truths that had marked his marriage. Now he had a sense of freedom from the past. Seeing Rachelle had only convinced him more that letting his experience keep him from grabbing true joy made no sense. Damon cradled her to his body.

''But you know what my new philosophy is?'' He spoke in a serious voice.

''What?'' Jade grew very still. A flutter started in her stomach.

''Love makes the world go 'round,'' Damon said. A deep rumble of a laugh shook his chest.

Jade gave him a small poke in his side. ''Very deep, Socrates. But really, you're not afraid we're getting involved too fast?''

Damon stopped laughing and stared into her eyes. ''I couldn't stop this feeling even if I wanted to . . . and I don't. Are you unsure?''

''No,'' Jade said without hesitation. No fears or doubts could withstand the force of her craving to be with him.

''Good. Now that's settled, let's move on to a more difficult decision.'' Damon grew serious again.

This time Jade was not fooled. She nestled down next to him and closed her eyes. ''Which is?''

''Are we going out for breakfast, or will we eat in?''

''Who was that on the phone?'' Oliver Knight frowned slightly at the noise distracting him from the newspaper article on the state of black businesses in Louisiana.

''Rachelle. She's having lunch with Damon in a couple of days.'' Marlene tapped a manicured fingernail on the hardcover novel she held.

''Hope you know what you're doing.'' Oliver stared at her

for a few seconds. "Interfering this way could do more harm than good."

"Nonsense. I intend to stop that Pellerin girl from worming her way into this family. Clarice no doubt passed on her social ambitions to her daughters." Marlene wore a sour look.

Oliver lowered the newspaper and stared ahead. "Not all poor girls are mercenary," he said in a quiet voice.

There was a long silence as Oliver seemed to slip into a reverie of his own. Marlene put the novel down on the end table at her elbow. The loud thump made Oliver blink as though awakened from a dream.

"I know the type, Oliver. Remember?" Marlene's voice was laced with acid.

He avoided her gaze. "Damon thinks she's nice."

"Nice? Oh, please spare me from nice poor girls of humble origin," Marlene snapped.

"Marlene, please don't start on—"

"Don't worry. I'm talking about the Pellerin girl." Marlene wore a look of contempt.

Oliver sighed. "Fine. Then let Damon make his own choices."

"Family interests come first." She gave him a heated look. When Oliver did not respond, she gave a short laugh. "Damon is sensible. He'll see Ms. Pellerin for what she really is."

Chapter 8

Jade tried hard not to fidget under the hostile scrutiny of Kathy Lang. "Bill is still tied up with those legislators. He could be in there until lunchtime."

Kathy bared even white teeth. "I'll wait a little longer. It will give us a chance to chat. It's fascinating to see a young African-American woman so close to power. You must be exceptional in many ways."

"Thank you," Jade said in a controlled voice. She swore once again not to assume everything Kathy said had a double meaning that hinted at an insult. "I've worked hard to understand how the department operates."

"Don't you find this work dry and boring?" Kathy cast a glance at the bookshelf filled with huge policy manuals. "My goodness, pages and pages of tiny print. Some bureaucrat had a field day coming up with it all."

Jade relaxed a bit. Kathy's comment seemed to confirm that she wanted only to pass the time. She was simply restless and maybe more than a little lonesome. "But that's the challenge, making the system work to help people even with all the red tape."

Kathy seemed to become interested. "Like what?"

"Hmm, let's see. There are a ton of rules about getting disabled people into a program to keep them at home and out of institutions. With input from families and the people who get the services, we've begun a process to change the rules."

"But that takes a long time. Even I know that from listening to Bill complain."

"Usually it does, but we can publish an emergency declaration that there are people at risk. That way we can start a much shorter process than the usual way."

"So being in the system can be helpful sometimes. I never thought of bureaucrats in such a light." Kathy raised a shapely eyebrow in amusement.

"We have our moments." Jade gave a short laugh.

"Jade, you seem nicer than my husband's other assistants. You actually can hold a conversation with complex sentences," Kathy said. Her pretty face twisted with a trace of bitterness.

"Oh, come on." Jade couldn't help but chuckle. "I've had male bosses before. And people always gossip if he's nice to you or tries to help you advance. Maybe you're being too hard on them."

Kathy shook her head. "No, and I'm not mistaken, either." She studied Jade for several seconds. "So you pretty much know your way around all these regulations and such?" She nodded at the mounds of paper around them.

"Sure. After over ten years, I should." Jade glanced around then back at Kathy.

"Then you know the requirements to do things according to laws and stuff like that?" Kathy tapped a perfect lacquered nail on the arm of the chair she sat in.

"Well . . . yes."

"Did you know Bill before he came to this job?"

"No, not really. Of course I'd heard of him." Jade was curious about the direction of this conversation.

Kathy seemed to come to some decision. "Listen, I feel like we could get along. Be very careful. Bill doesn't always follow rules."

"Most people who make things happen don't. Radical for us bureaucrats." Jade smiled. "But he knows that change sometimes has to come from within a system."

"No, I mean—"

"Kathy, what are you doing here?" Lang stood in the door, wearing a frown of displeasure. "I've got a very full day and so has my assistant."

"I was just nearby and . . ." Kathy's voice trailed off at the look of disbelief on his face. "I thought we could have lunch."

"Impossible. Mike expects me to have lunch with him in the capitol dining room. We have to discuss several issues before our next meeting." Lang looked at Jade. "Did you get the file from Chester Howard's office?"

"Nothing was in the morning mail."

"See if Chester Howard's assistant has it. They promised we'd have it by eleven, and it's almost eleven forty-five." He seemed to have dismissed his wife.

"I'll do it right now." Jade flipped through her Rolodex for the number.

"Thanks, Jade. You're priceless," Lang said. He stood next to Jade with a hand on the back of her chair. He reached across to retrieve a sheet of paper. "Oh, here's that memo from Secretary Chauvin. I was looking for it."

Jade looked up to find the cold glare of dislike back in Kathy's light brown eyes. "Uh, I have to go up to the eighth floor for something else anyway, so I'll stop by and get it." She rose from her chair and moved away from Lang.

"I seem to be in the way here." Kathy got up and blocked Jade's exit. "It has been very enlightening observing you in action. Sorry to interrupt your important work," she said in a soft voice.

"No problem. Really. Drop by anytime." Jade did not want this woman to be her foe.

"Yes, I plan to." Kathy stared at her for a few seconds then faced her husband. "Remember we're meeting the Ricards for dinner at six thirty."

Lang seemed relieved that she was leaving. "Of course. I'll

be home by six, and we will drive over to the restaurant. Now bye, dear.'' He cupped her elbow and guided her down the hall.

Jade took a deep breath. Before she could leave, Lang came back to her office.

''I hope my wife wasn't rude to you, Jade.'' He came in and closed the door.

''Oh, no, Bill. Just small talk.'' Jade tried to make her response casual.

Lang gave a slight shake of his head. ''You're very gracious, but I know my wife better than that. Look, you and I are going to be working very long hours in very close quarters. We might as well get this out on the table. Kathy is very jealous—and for no reason, I can assure you.'' He ran a hand over his neatly cut hair. ''I'm sorry for anything she might have done.''

''She wasn't out of line, honest.''

''But she was questioning you, admit it.'' Lang eyed her.

''She asked about routine department business.'' Jade lifted a shoulder. ''Very harmless stuff.''

''But she wanted to know if you were qualified or were just window dressing. She's caused me no end of grief with her obsessive suspicions. But if she ever upsets you, let me know.'' Lang wore a look of concern.

''She wasn't that bad.'' Jade felt a twinge of guilt talking about Kathy this way. Not to mention her desire not to get involved in her boss's marital strife.

''But she did take a few digs at you?''

''Listen, I—''

''I knew it.'' Lang took a deep breath. ''I really care for Kathy, but her behavior has begun to worry me. I want to help her. But I spend most of my time defending myself or apologizing for her.''

Jade shifted from one foot to the other. She wasn't sure what to say, but she tried to think of some way of getting out of this discussion. ''Well, things can get rough in a marriage. I hope you can work it out.''

''Sometimes I just don't know,'' Lang said in a quiet voice.

"Thanks for being so understanding." He squared his shoulders. "I'm sorry for dumping my chaotic personal life in your lap. You certainly didn't sign on to be my therapist."

"Don't worry about it." Jade thought of how she'd felt when her marriage began to shatter. Lang looked so worn down, very much unlike the usual dynamo filled with purpose and confidence. "Hang in there. Like the song says, trouble don't last always." She gave him a pat on the arm.

"Thanks." Lang gave her a weary smile. "Guess I better get over to the capitol to meet Mike. I'll see you this afternoon."

"Okay, Bill." Jade watched him leave.

Poor Bill had his hands full with such a paranoid wife dogging his footsteps. Jade knew the heartbreak of an unhappy marriage all too well. Unhappy? Miserable was more accurate. Angry, ugly fights that led to nowhere only made going home a dread. Instead of love and refuge, there was resentment. Yet thinking about it now did not cause the sharp ache it once did. Now she could look forward to the sweet embrace of a wonderful man. Damon brought her a kind of peace and calm that no man had ever inspired. His slightest touch was like a full body massage. Tension melted away at the soothing sound of his rich, deep voice—and soon they would go on their first trip together. She intended to make it very special, too. Jade's mood became bright as she thought of her plans to be with him. Bill's marital woes slipped from her mind.

Lanessa came into her living room with a glass in her hand. She moved with a deliberateness as though afraid she would trip. When the doorbell rang, she jumped. "Damn, it's six already. Gotta get rid of this."

She darted into the kitchen and started to pour the liquor out. After pausing for only a second or so, she downed the rest of her drink and put the glass in the dishwasher. The doorbell sounded again.

"Just a minute," she called out. She went to the hall bathroom on her way to the front door and sloshed mouthwash around in her mouth before spitting it out. "I'm coming."

Alex stood at the door with an impassive look on his nutmeg brown face. "Hello, Lanessa." He made no move to enter the hallway.

"Hi there. Well, don't just stand there—come on in." Lanessa swung the door wide.

He walked past her into the spacious living room done in warm beige, green and red. The room was made even more inviting by the fire that filled the fireplace. Lanessa moved with practiced grace, a sensuous sway in her hips. The satin lounge belted jumpsuit she wore was ocean blue with the Victoria's Secret emblem stitched on the chest pocket. Though it fit loosely, the lush curves of her body were clear beneath the fabric. Alex sat down on the large sofa.

"Can I get you something?" Lanessa stood poised to serve him.

"No, thanks." He gazed up at her then looked away. After several seconds, he cleared his throat. "So how've you been?"

"Okay, I guess. You know the drill, work all day and crash at night." Lanessa sat down next to him. Alex seemed about to move away then stopped.

"Yeah, same old treadmill of the working masses." He gave a hoarse chuckle that sounded more like a cough.

"What about you?" Lanessa relaxed against the sofa pillows. She stretched an arm across the top of them.

"No different. We've taken on a new contract with the state to develop a financial application to handle purchasing, payroll, contracts—the works. We'll be working twenty-four-seven for at least the next nine months." He pulled at his tie. "I'll be really busy."

"I see. No social life for you, eh?" Lanessa clucked her sympathy. She rubbed his shoulder. "Poor thing."

"Yeah, well I'm pretty used to it." Alex went rigid when she touched him. "But it's great for business."

"Wonderful." Lanessa moved closer to him.

This time Alex did inch away from her. "But I've got an

early day tomorrow. Uh, what was it you wanted to talk over with me?''

Lanessa smiled. She seemed not to notice his reluctance to be near her. "Last time we were together, we parted on a sour note. I don't feel like we really talked."

"I think we did." Alex did not look at her. "We'd been talking for months, Lanessa."

"That's not true. You lectured me for months," Lanessa snapped. Seeing the reaction to her tone, she softened her expression. "I mean, maybe we can take a different approach this time."

"Like what?" He looked at her.

"Listen, we all have our little faults. I nagged you about wanting to go on nice trips to Houston or New Orleans. I can't help it if I love the theater, concerts and exciting nightlife. You would, too, if you'd give it half a chance."

"I'm just not a nightlife kind of guy, Lanessa. You've known that about me since we were both in college." Alex shrugged. "But that's not—"

"Maybe I can compromise. I suppose I can be a little selfish sometimes. We don't have to go every weekend." Lanessa shrugged. "In fact, maybe nice quiet evenings alone are just what we need." She slid up to him and rubbed her body against his. "Used to be you couldn't wait to get me alone."

"Lanessa, it's goes deeper than whether or not we go out or stay in. You want the fast lane in everything. Expensive nights out, shopping at Lord and Taylor's, Neiman Marcus, the best restaurants. I'm into the simple things." Alex gripped his knees with his large hands. He seemed not to be affected by her provocative behavior.

"Baby, we can work it out," Lanessa whispered in his ear. Her hand moved up his thigh.

"We've been through this a hundred times," Alex said. "I'm willing to talk about us. But you know what I want to hear first." He stood up and looked down at her.

"What is it with you?" Lanessa jumped up to face him.

"It's up to you, Lanessa."

"Just who do you think you are anyway? Just because you're one of the famous St. Romaine clan, that makes you better than everyone else? I don't think so," Lanessa said in a scornful snarl. She paced in front of him.

"This isn't about my family, and you know it." Alex's eyes narrowed slightly at the veiled insult.

"Like hell it isn't. As far back as I can remember, your family has been looking down their noses at everybody, including me. Your sisters especially." Lanessa hurled words at him like arrows.

"Lanessa, my three sisters have been more than nice to you—something you know very well also. I won't even argue about that with you again." Alex got up to leave.

"I practically beg you to come over here, and now you want me to crawl." Lanessa stopped pacing and faced him again. "That's what you want, isn't it? Me on my knees? It's payback time."

"You've lost me." Alex stared at her with a look of genuine puzzlement.

"I broke up with you over a year ago and dated Maurice Whittington. Now you're getting back at me, right? The male ego can't take rejection."

"Don't push your luck, lady." Alex's voice was even, but his jaw muscles twitched. "I've taken crap off you for eight long months, overlooked a lot. But it's never enough for you."

"Oh, please," Lanessa snorted.

Alex reached out to touch her then jerked back his hand. "Lanessa, I've cared for you since we were kids. But you've always taken for granted that I'll come running back whenever you crook your finger and whistle."

"Yeah, make it all my fault." Lanessa turned her back to him.

"No, maybe a lot of it is my fault. You've been under my skin for so long that taking you back was easy."

"How noble of you to shoulder some of the blame!"

"This isn't some competition to prove who's righteous," Alex shouted. "Everything gets twisted when it comes out of your mouth. You don't know the first thing about sharing affection with a man."

"What does that mean?" Lanessa shouted back at him. Her eyes blazed with fury.

"Swinging your butt and wearing tight pants isn't all there is to being sexy. That's what I mean."

"You didn't complain all those nights you climbed into my bed."

"A real woman knows how to give, not just take and take all the time. You're always grasping for more of everything."

"Are you calling me a prostitute?" Lanessa screamed at him. She balled her fist up so tight the knuckles were pale.

"And as for my family, you love showing up at all the best parties, hanging on to a St. Romaine. All I've been to you over the years is a wallet and a trophy date. I want more, Lanessa."

"This is unreal! I've been better to you than any woman." Lanessa took a step back from him. "You should be grateful—"

"You really don't get it, do you?" Alex said. He swung his arm out for emphasis and knocked over a row of small African wood sculptures on the table behind the sofa. Both were so angry, they did not notice the racket it made.

"How can you act like this?" Lanessa shouted in a tearful voice. "I can't believe it!"

Jade started up the stone walkway to Lanessa's front door. She was still humming a love song that had played on the compact disc in her Camry. Loud voices made her stop for a few moments. Was that coming from next door or from Lanessa's house? Then she recognized her sister's voice raised in anger. A shadow, it was a female form, moved behind the light beige panel that hung between the drawn-back draperies of heavier dark green material. A larger figure swung out in aggression. Jade did not wait for more. She ran and pounded on the front door.

"Lanessa, are you alright? Open this door," Jade shouted.

She pulled on the doorknob then struck the wood with the flat of her hand.

"What's wrong?" The man next door stopped in the act of putting out the garbage. He dropped the bag then crossed the lawn in long strides.

"I think Lanessa's in trouble"—Jade's voice trembled—"maybe we'd better call the police. Something is very wrong." She banged on the door again. "Lanessa, can you hear me?"

The door jerked open. Lanessa swayed just a bit to the left then right. "What in the world is going on out here? Somebody get murdered or something?"

"Are you hurt?" Jade rushed forward and examined her from head to toe.

"Course not. Hey, Terry." Lanessa waved at her neighbor with a crooked smile.

"Hi, Lanessa. Party must have gotten out of hand—again." He shook his head then went back to his house. He mumbled something to his waiting wife, and they both went inside.

"I heard angry voices. It sounded like a fight." Jade looked around at the room. Her eyes narrowed when she saw Alex picking up the table. "Just what happened in here?"

"A little spat that got out of hand," Lanessa muttered into a glass. She drank down the last drop and went to the bar for more.

"How dare you!" Jade faced him. "Lanessa, you should press charges against this—"

"Jade, you've got it wrong." Alex's eyes went wide with shock as he realized what she was thinking.

"I don't think so, Alex." Jade pointed to the windows. "The draperies were open. You hit my sister." She stabbed a finger at him.

"Forget it, Jade." Lanessa rubbed her eyes. She dropped her hand. Her eyes were red and glassy.

"Despite everything, I care deeply for Lanessa. I would never do anything to harm her." Alex stared at Lanessa even though he spoke to Jade. "I never raised a hand to Lanessa. Never."

"Unbelievable. You could go onstage with that act," Jade snarled at him. "My sister will have you charged with assault for this. Lanessa, tomorrow we're going down to the district attorney's office."

"No," Lanessa said in a weary tone. "I said forget it. Alex is right. Nothing happened. It's over, right?" She stared back at him with tears rolling down her face.

"Yes, it is. I didn't want it to end like this, Nessa. If you'd only—" Alex a step toward her.

Jade blocked his path. "Get out. She's lucky to be rid of you."

Alex sucked in air. He threw up both hands. "All right. Goodbye, Lanessa. You can always call me. Think about what I said . . . please."

Lanessa turned her back to him. "Yeah, sure."

"She won't need to call you. Now if you don't leave, I'll call the police myself." Jade stomped over to the front door and yanked it open.

Alex paused before walking out. "You need to open your eyes, Jade. Lanessa needs help. Serious help."

"Yeah, and dumping you is a big step in the right direction." Jade glared at him. She slammed the door when he was barely outside. "He's got some nerve acting righteous. You really need to haul his behind into court."

"Hey, that's more trouble than he's worth. I don't need him always criticizing me. To hell with him." Lanessa put her head down on the bar and sobbed.

Jade crossed to Lanessa in two quick strides and embraced her. "I know what it's like having a man who constantly browbeats you. He's got to make himself feel big by making you feel small." She rubbed Lanessa's back.

"He's right, you know. I'm no good," Lanessa wailed. She slumped against Jade for support. "No good."

"Now you listen to me, Lanessa Elise Pellerin Hampton Thomas you've got more going for you in the tip of one little finger than ten of him." Jade put a finger under Lanessa's chin and forced her to look up. "You got that?"

Lanessa only nodded. She put her head back on Jade's shoulder. "I haven't made good choices though. Even you've told me that before."

"Hey, I married Nick Guillory. I could be crying my eyes out right along with you if I think about it too long," Jade quipped. "The point is, we all make mistakes. It doesn't mean we're bad people, Nessa."

"You know, Mama is right. You're the smart one." Lanessa gave her a weak smile.

Jade went to the guest bathroom and came back with a box of tissues. "Here, wipe your eyes. Let's go down to Catfish Town to the Creole Café."

This was a new favorite late-night hangout in the downtown area. The café stayed open all night serving café au lait, beignets and other goodies. Lanessa loved going there. Jade hoped this would help lighten her sister's mood. But Lanessa shook her head slowly.

"I don't feel like being around people right now. You go on home. I'll be okay."

"Nessa, you shouldn't be alone tonight. I'll stay with you." Jade did not like the pale, shaky way she looked. "I'll fix us some nice herbal tea."

"No, Jade. You've done enough for me. Go on and get some rest. You have to get ready for your trip."

"Hey, you know how obsessive-compulsive I am. I've got everything ready—so I'm staying." Jade started for the kitchen.

"Jade, just leave me alone! I don't need a baby-sitter," Lanessa said, her voice high pitched and tense. She took a deep breath at the surprised, hurt expression Jade wore. "I'm sorry, my nerves are stretched to the limit. Please, I need time to get myself together. I'll call you tomorrow, I promise."

"Sure. I understand." Jade kissed her on the cheek.

Lanessa hugged her tight. "Thank you, little sister, for being here for me. I do love you." Her eyes filled with unshed tears.

Jade touched her face. They had never talked about their feelings like this before. Not even through both of their bad marriages. "I love you, too, big sister," she whispered. "One thing about it, Nessa. You've always been straight up with me. I'd wrestle alligators for you, girl.''

"Oh, now don't get carried away." Lanessa brushed back her thick hair. She wiped her eyes with a wad of tissue. "Go get your rest. You'll need it to whip more good lovin' on that man."

"What makes you think . . ." Jade felt like a teenager caught with birth-control pills by her parents. "I mean—We, uh . . .''

"Jade, come on. You glow whenever he's mentioned. That look means one thing: good sex." Lanessa stepped back and put both hands on her hips. She examined a flustered Jade for several seconds. "Whoa! Make that great sex!"

"Everything about us seems to fit. Know what I mean?" Jade gave up on trying to conceal how serious things between she and Damon had become.

"Yeah, in tune, on the same wavelength kinda thang," Lanessa said with a sad smile. "I've felt that way only once in my life.''

"But it worries me, Nessa. Look at Alex, a perfect example of how wrong I can be about men. Not to mention Nick. Maybe Damon is too good to be true."

Jade went over their times together in light of the scene she'd witnessed between Alex and Lanessa. Alex was—or appeared to be—a kind, considerate man. Nick had acted as though he cared about her, desired her above all women. Could she be deceiving herself again?

"I see those wheels turning." Lanessa put an arm around Jade's shoulders. "Now listen up, what did Mama teach us as kids?''

"To eat our vegetables and never wear chipped fingernail polish because it makes you look cheap," Jade quipped.

Lanessa gave her a playful swat on the arm. "Funny. No, what she drilled into us was that we should never condemn a group of people for what a few have done. Even though she was talking about race relations, it applies to men."

"Lanessa, get serious. I've heard you dogging men out a hundred times at least."

"True, but that was just girl talk. Besides, I've grown up since then." Lanessa lifted her nose.

"Yeah, right," Jade retorted. "Ouch!" She jumped when Lanessa pinched her arm.

"I'm older and wiser, so pay attention." Lanessa sat down with her on the sofa. She wore a solemn expression. "Don't be too quick to judge Alex harshly. I've given him good reasons to want out. So give this man a chance, and don't compare him to Nick for goodness' sakes."

"Maybe you've got a point. But—"

"Hey, don't argue with me, missy. Now go home and dream of all the ways you can make that fine man wanna holler." Lanessa gave her a sassy wink.

"Since you insist on kicking me out, I'll go." Jade gave her a hug. "And thanks, Nessa."

Jade thought about Damon driving home, through her shower and as she sat before the television. She did not see any of the programs that flashed by as she punched the channel button on the remote. Lanessa was right. Damon should be considered based on his own actions, not some other man's. And so far his actions had been right on time. Every touch and every word told her he was the one. Now all she had to do was fight down that nasty voice of suspicion that kept saying not to believe it. A musical refrain from the television caught her attention. Roberta Flack sat at a piano, singing in that rich voice of hers. Roberta crooned as though her song was aimed at Jade.

For a magical moment, this was Jade's song. She sat caught in a haze of memory at the wonder of discovering how beautiful making love could be—a discovery Damon had led her to with sweet tenderness. At the last note of the song, Jade sighed. She no longer had a choice in the matter. Her body and heart were on automatic pilot. Destination Damon Knight.

"Hey now," Jade called out in a cheery voice to her friend. She sat in a booth at Uncle Joe's, drinking a diet cola. "Haven't seen you in a while. New love keeping you busy, eh?"

"You should talk. At least we haven't let our Friday nights fall by the wayside. But other than that, you've been scarce." Shaena ordered then handed the menu back to the waitress. "What's up?"

"Just rushing around trying to get ready to leave on Sunday. Every time I think all the loose ends are tied up, one of 'em gets untied. It's so aggravating." Jade gave a resigned shrug and sat back with a contented look.

"Well, you look awfully mellow. I know how much you crave order. Or maybe this is the new you." Shaena lifted an eyebrow.

"Lanessa is right. I should learn not to get so intense about things. Take it as it comes." Jade took a sip of cola.

" 'Scuse me? You're taking advice on life from Lanessa? Now I know your brain is fried from passion."

"Lanessa has had her ups and downs, but she's got some good ideas." Jade shook a finger at Shaena. "And let's not forget your track record."

"Let's do," Shaena said with a grimace. "You're right, at least Lanessa got great divorce settlements from her mistakes. And then there's Brad." She shook her head in dismay.

"Oh, no, Shaena. Trouble already?" Jade tried not to think "I told you so" at the mention of the handsome white attorney with an attitude.

"His family and mine are not taking this well. His parents were cool but polite. But it's his brother and two sisters who are being real nasty about it. And Thanksgiving at my parents' house was a study in how not to entertain guests."

"Not Mama Lula and Papa Jake. They're so sweet." Jade was truly surprised.

"Papa took one look at him and whispered, 'Tell me this is a joke, baby.' Mama kept apologizing for my sister's kids being rowdy. She was so nervous around him, she just clammed up. It's been truly awful."

"Well, both your families just want the best for you. They'll come around." Jade tried to console her.

"That's not all of it. I don't know if what we feel is strong enough to withstand all this pressure. Then there are the stares and remarks from strangers.''

''Amazing that we're almost in the twenty-first century, and folks still think like it's 1897 instead of 1997.'' Jade gave a grunt of disgust.

''The sad bottom line is, we may be history real soon. But this time I'm philosophical about it. I'm to the point of accepting true love and happy ever after is not in the cards for me.'' For a few seconds the tough persona slipped, and Shaena seemed vulnerable.

''I'm sorry, babe. Now it's my turn to lecture you. It's time you examine if you want him enough to take the rough spots. Some serious soul searching is in order.''

''I want him bad, girl. I'm just so afraid he doesn't want me bad enough to be shunned. This race thing is hard to take. He's had people who were friends for years act distant toward him. And it's because of me.''

Jade took a deep breath. ''Brad is going to learn just how much secure status he may give up. Most whites don't have a clue until they cross the color line. But on the other hand, Brad Pittman is not known for letting others dictate how he lives his life.''

''He is a rebel. That's one of the things I love about him.'' Shaena's lips curved into a smile of affection.

''Then talk about what you two will face, I mean long term. From the way you sound, this isn't just a dating thing. Sounds like the *C* word has come up.'' Jade pursed her lips.

''Yeah, and *he* brought up making a commitment.'' Shaena looked thoughtful.

''There you go. It may not be smooth sailing, but then what relationship is?'' Jade stopped long enough to let the waitress put their food in front of them. ''I've decided that love is a crapshoot, and there's no way around it. So go for it.''

Shaena blinked at her, dumbfounded. ''Jade, is that you?''

''I know, I know. It's not easy, but I'm going to give this thing with Damon my best shot.''

"Great. Then if you can, so can I." Shaena lifted her glass. "A toast," she said.

Jade held up her glass. "To giving love another chance."

"And to wonderful, thoughtful, sensitive men," Shaena replied. Their glasses clinked together.

"Hear, hear." Jade took a drink.

"And sex hot enough to make you sing opera like Leontyne Price." Shaena wiggled her eyebrows Groucho Marx style.

Jade choked on the mouthful of diet cola. "Girl, you almost made me spit this stuff three feet." Both of them giggled until tears flowed. Several minutes passed before they could look at each other without starting to guffaw all over again.

Shaena patted a napkin to her forehead. "My oh my, that felt good. I think we'll need a sense of humor around the office in the next few months."

"What's up?" Jade took a bite of her broiled catfish fillet.

"Brad says there are a few tremors about several department programs, especially in Medicaid-funded services." Shaena's face grew serious as she leaned across the table. "Your boss's name keeps coming up. You got a whiff of anything stinky?" she said in a low voice.

Jade held her fork still in the act of taking another bite. "Nothing. Bill has been going strictly by the book. What exactly have you heard?" A lump of unease settled in her midsection.

"Nothing too bad about him. Just that maybe he's being too nice to some of the staff left over from the previous administration. Brad says right now the talk is that he needs to reorganize more."

"For crying out loud." Jade frowned with indignation. "The man can't perform miracles in a few months. Some of those folks have been in state government for years."

"Shh," Shaena whispered. She glanced over her shoulder then turned back to Jade. "Some folks from the fifth floor one table over. You know how they are, ears like high-tech radar."

"But you know what I'm saying is true," Jade went on with no less heat but in a much quieter voice. "Those same people are masters at making things appear to change while it's business as usual. Bill really is working hard to follow all the rules. Even the ones that don't make sense.''

"Hey, I'm just the messenger. I didn't say I thought the guy was up to something.''

"And those that don't make sense, he's trying to change. We've been working our buns off. And this is the thanks we get!'' Jade sat with a scowl, her meal forgotten.

"Will you take it easy? Brad says it's no big deal right now.'' Shaena continued to pop fried shrimp into her mouth even as Jade fumed. "It'll all blow over probably. Being invited to Washington, D.C. Lang gets mucho respect for that.''

"And that's another thing,'' Jade jumped in again. "We beat out twenty other states to get one of only seven grants nationwide.''

"It's one of the reasons they didn't take it any farther, the talk I mean.''

"Just who is *they?*'' Jade said it as though "they'' were beneath contempt.

"Brad would say only that they're some of the big dogs, guys we underlings don't see very often.'' Shaena took a swig of her cola.

"Yeah, well, I'll just bet they couldn't say much more. Results speak louder than any rumors.''

"Which is why I said to take it easy. But still keep your head up.'' Shaena pointed a french fry at her. "My experience has been where there's smoke, there's a smoldering inferno waiting to bust out.''

"No way. I'd have noticed something funny by now,'' Jade said with force, but a tickle of doubt went through her all the same.

"Like I said, be careful.'' Shaena cocked an eyebrow at her. "Bill Lang does have that reputation.''

"I have been keeping my ears open. I just hope Bill doesn't put too much trust in that sleazy Mike Testor,'' Jade said in a very soft voice. This time it was she who glanced around.

"He's another reason I don't like this questioning of your

section. Testor is a guerilla fighter when it comes to department politics. Lang would do well to dump the dude.'' Shaena wrinkled her nose in distaste.

''Yeah, he gives me the creeps. He always wears a greasy smile, like he's just looked up my skirt.'' Jade gave a shiver.

''Ugh, what a worm. Then there's Tavis Collins—handsome and with a mind like a razor.'' Shaena spoke with admiration.

''I can't quite read him.''

''He's considered up and coming by those in the know. Hey, let's not start worrying for nothing. Like I said, Brad doesn't think there is anything heavy to it.''

''Right. Bill is pretty sharp himself. I'm sure he won't let those people pull any shady stuff.''

Jade tried to feel as confident as her words. But like Shaena, she had been in state government enough to be troubled by this development.

''Rachelle, I'm involved with someone.'' Damon gazed at her with dismay. He thought of ways to quickly cut his losses.

From the moment they sat down in Copeland's, he sensed this so-called lunch invitation was more than a friendly pitch for business. Rachelle turned heads in the deep red wool suit she wore with a paisley silk scarf of red, white and gray. For fifteen minutes, while they waited for their meal, she'd hinted at how lonely life was without him. Finally he blurted out his declaration of being serious about another woman in hopes she would back off. He was wrong again.

''Of course you are, darling. I wouldn't expect you to be celibate for goodness' sakes. I know how large an appetite you have,'' Rachelle murmured with a glint in her eyes.

''It isn't like that with Jade. We're very close, Rachelle. She's special to me, very special.'' Damon stared down into the cup of now cold black coffee that sat in front of him. He looked forward to their trip to Washington more than ever.

Rachelle studied him for a good thirty seconds before she spoke. ''By that dreamy look on your face, I'd say she's definitely made an impression on you. You didn't even look this strung-out when we were new loves." A tight line along her jaw made it obvious she was not happy.

"Look, I'm sorry if you got the wrong impression. Can't we at least be on good terms?" Damon dreaded a scene. Rachelle was well known for her dramatic scenes when her ego was bruised, particularly by a man.

"Certainly, sugar." She flashed a warm smile at him and patted his hand with a look of indulgence. "We've both successfully moved on with our lives. No need to nurse old bitterness. Here's to you and . . ." Rachelle let her voice trail off.

"Jade," Damon added. His smile grew wider. "Jade Pellerin."

"Yes, how nice." Rachelle's top lip curled up for a split second. She lifted her cup of coffee.

They finished their meal, and Damon hurried back to his office. He tried not to act impatient to be gone, but he thought of all the last-minute details at the office he wanted to double-check before the trip. He left her still nursing her second cup of coffee. Rachelle wore a dour expression at his retreating back.

"Goodbye," she muttered. "And thanks for nothing."

"Rachelle? I thought that was you," Nick called from a nearby table. "Haven't seen you since the last Delta Sigma Theta ball. Looking good as usual."

"Oh, hello, Nick," Rachelle mumbled. She stared at the door through which Damon had hurried off away from her. "How've you been?" Her upper-class manners kicked in even when she was aggravated.

"Fine, fine. I hear tell you're big in public relations these days." Nick sat relaxed in his expensive suit on an extended lunch break from his grandfather's thriving insurance office.

"Marketing," Rachelle corrected.

"Umm, yes of course. Listen, since your date is gone, why don't I join you?" Nick put his head to one side.

"That was no date, that was my ex-husband."

"I thought I recognized the famous Damon Knight." Nick watched her face. "He's dating my ex."

Rachelle looked at him for the first time. Her face eased into a beguiling expression, like a cat coaxing a bird from a tree. "Nicky, dear, you most certainly can join me."

Chapter 9

"I'm so glad we were *finally* able to have you over," Clarice gushed to Damon.

"Give me strength," Jade muttered. Her father wore a look of sympathy for her.

Jade and Damon were in her parents' spacious den after dinner. Jade stood next to her father, helping him to gather the trays bearing the coffee, cups, sugar and cream. All through the meal, Clarice had been the gracious host. With the skill of a brain surgeon, she had extracted family history from Damon without seeming to pry. Jade's jaw ached from gritting her teeth.

"So am I," Damon said. He pressed his lips together in an effort not to laugh at the flash of irritation on Jade's face. "Things have been so hectic in the last couple of weeks."

"Mama, I told you I've been working lots of overtime, what with the legislative session coming up—"

"That's not for another month or more, dear," her mother cut her off smoothly. "Cream and sugar, Damon?" Clarice beamed at him.

Jade swallowed a tart reply and counted to five. "We start

preparing much more than a month in advance, Mama.'' She bit off the last few words in a restrained tone of reproof.

''Oh, I see. Well, you're here now. So, Damon, tell me more about your fascinating family.'' Clarice turned to him in rapt attention.

For the next hour, Jade and Damon sat side by side on the sofa, she chafing at the need to find an opening to leave. Damon seemed completely at ease. He even seemed to enjoy talking to Clarice.

''Have you met Lanessa? We should get together again and invite her over,'' Clarice said.

''What for?'' Oliver shot his wife a sharp glance.

Jade gazed from her father to her mother. Her senses went on alert when the undercurrent became clear. ''I guess Lanessa will meet Damon sometime, Mama.'' She wondered what was going on here.

''Since you'll be coming over here for dinner again soon, might as well be then. Say a few days after you get back. When will that be?'' Clarice popped up to get a calendar.

''Mama, for goodness' sakes, we don't have to plan it now.'' Jade felt the tug of an unpleasant yet familiar old feeling.

For as long as she could remember, her mother had a habit of arranging for Lanessa to end up with the best of everything. At first Jade had not understood that it was more than coincidence that Lanessa got the fancier dress or brightest hair ribbons. Her mother had always said, ''This style is better suited to Lanessa, dear'' or ''This isn't your color, Jade.'' But by the time she was ten, it was clear that Clarice had different plans for Lanessa. Plans that included a glamorous life. For Jade, a life of quiet study and achievement was stressed. Jade felt a spike of anger go through her as she remembered all the dashing young men Clarice steered to Lanessa.

''*Mama*, I'll decide when to introduce Lanessa to Damon.''

Jade gazed at her mother steadily. Everyone else grew quiet. Damon wore a puzzled look at the sudden tension. Clarice blinked at her in surprise. They stood watching each other for several seconds. Clarice wrung her hands twice in a jerky motion.

"Yes, of course. Plenty of time." Clarice smoothed her blouse and patted her hair. "Oh, here I'm rambling on and forgot to bring in dessert. I made a special apple spice loaf, Damon." She left for the kitchen.

After another thirty minutes of strained small talk, Jade and Damon left. Back at Jade's home, they sat holding each other and listening to music. Jade pushed away resentful thoughts of her mother's behavior toward her. She reminded herself that she was grown and did not have to feel intimidated by her mother anymore. Damon seemed to be reading her mind.

"Honey, don't let your mother spoil our mood tonight," Damon said in a low voice as he kissed her ear then cheek. "I've learned to ignore my mother's attempts to control me. It's gotten easier in the last, oh, six months." He chuckled softly.

Jade wanted to laugh it off, but she could find no humor in this. "Mama can be very thoughtless sometimes. Especially when it comes to me." Her voice wavered a bit.

"Lanessa is the princess, like my brother Trent was always 'Mama's little man.'" Damon nodded with understanding when Jade looked up at him. "Oh, yeah, been there."

"But it's so awful. Sometimes I still resent Lanessa. We've only just begun to get close. I don't think they realize how they've pushed us apart." Jade was torn between worship and dislike for Lanessa even now.

"You said it right: thoughtlessness. Your mother and mine have a lot in common. They just seem to forge ahead, thinking only of what they want, convinced they're right. But we won't let them make life difficult for us."

Jade felt a new source of anxiety take hold. "Your mother has said something to you about seeing me?"

"My mother never wanted me to divorce my first wife. She has this very eighteenth-century idea of marriage. While we were little, she actually picked the three families she expected us to choose our wives from."

"You're kidding." Jade shook her head, amazed. "And I thought my mother was bad."

"Baby, nobody tops Marlene Cormier Knight when it comes to wanting her way. Except maybe Rachelle." Damon gave a grunt of scorn after saying her name.

"So Rachelle was one from one of the 'right' families?"

"First on the list." Damon got up to get them both a glass of red wine.

"I guess so. The Balleaux family is so old money, I'll bet some of the coins have whiskers." Jade thought of the proud handsome men and elegant women who bore that name. They were prominent in south Louisiana.

"Don't be too impressed, sweetheart." Damon sat next to her and handed her the wineglass. "They're just as flawed as the rest of us. Believe me, I know."

"But you're part of that world, too. The Knight family goes back for generations. And your mother's family . . ." Jade's voice trailed off. She reviewed the idle gossip she'd heard over the years. The Cormiers descended from a Thérèse, an African slave woman left a large tract of land by her owner, for whom she'd had seven children. The legend was still fresh after two hundred years.

Damon put down his glass then took hers. "Listen to me, I'm thirty-four years old. My parents don't dictate to me. I did marry Rachelle out of a stupid sense of duty, sure. But I honestly thought I loved her."

"And you didn't?" Jade had almost blurted out the question in present tense. She had seen Rachelle Balleaux Knight several times at social functions. Rachelle had a kind of picture-perfect beauty most women wanted badly.

"I loved the woman I thought she was, Jade. Beauty on the outside doesn't mean a thing if it's just an empty shell." Damon gazed off.

"That's kind of cold. She can't be that bad."

"You're right." Damon thought for a few seconds. "Rachelle just has no concept that what she wants isn't best for everyone else. She can be engaging and even generous."

"So she isn't a complete witch," Jade said with a shade of disappointment in her voice.

"Is Nick a total wash as a human being?"

Amusement tugged up the corners of her mouth. "No." Jade had to admit that Nick was great with children. In his fraternity he always played the clown when they treated inner-city kids to special parties for major holidays.

"See what I mean? Of course I'd like you to remember what a no-good bum he was as a husband," Damon said with a teasing note in his voice. He lifted her face to his.

"And you just remember your ex-wife's most annoying habits, mister." Jade brushed a forefinger across his full lips.

"I can't think of much when I'm holding you like this," he whispered. His mouth covered hers. He touched his tongue to her lips, stroking them lovingly as though savoring fine wine. "Wanting you is the only thing on my mind."

The soft jazz music was an enchanting accompaniment to their lovemaking. He guided her down onto the sofa. Damon caressed every part of her body as he undressed her slowly. Jade panted in delicious impatience yet was hypnotized by his actions. She watched him touch her breasts with the tip of his tongue and move his hands down her stomach. Jade arched to him when his fingers touched her. Like a brush of fire, his fingers caressed her into mindless pleasure. His lips traced a line between her breasts down until they tickled the soft flesh of her mound. Jade cried out and gripped his shoulders. For what seemed hours, he brought her to the brink of ecstasy only to ease her back from the edge. Finally Damon groaned with his own need. He mounted her with a quick motion that brought a gasp from them both. Jade wrapped her arms around him and matched his gentle rocking motion, her mind filled with him. This love was like a deep ocean welling up inside her, leaving her breathless. She swam with the current and reveled in the sensation of having him inside her, surrounding her. Damon was everywhere at once. For one bright, shattering moment as the orgasm rippled through her, she lost a sense of being separate from him. Jade screamed his name, and he answered with his own release. They drifted off into a semiconscious state of sexual contentment for an hour, happy to feel completely cut off from the world.

"You see, baby," Damon said, his fingers laced through the tangle of her hair. They lay quietly holding each other. "It's you, just you."

"But what about in the cold light of day, Damon? What happens when your parents, and mine, start to press in, dragging all that old baggage back with them?" Jade wanted to believe, but they could not live isolated from their families. She knew how important family was to Damon. It was one thing she knew he would always have in common with the Knight-Cormier dynasty. Could he resist the pull of tradition?

"We'll stand together and face them all, Jade. It won't be pleasant at times, but I'll never let them drive a wedge between us." He gazed into her eyes. "Never."

Marlene stretched and enjoyed the feel of satin on her skin. The antique gold sheets had been a gift. She got up from the bed. The master bedroom had a beautiful view of the Mississippi River in downtown New Orleans. Tourists with cameras slung around their necks, some with children in tow, strolled toward the Riverwalk to gaze at the new trendy shops. With a contented sigh, she pulled on the black silk robe that matched the teddy and black lace panties she wore. A glance in the wide mirror set on the teakwood dresser pleased her. For a woman of fifty-four, she could easily pass for forty-four, or younger. Her body was fuller, true, but the generous hips curved out from a still relatively small waist and she was firm. Brisk walks and swimming at the club assured that.

"Where are you going, sweet thing? Get back in this bed," a voice rumbled from beneath the fabric.

"I didn't tell him I'd be here all night." Marlene belted the robe and gazed back at the bed. "I really should be going. It's almost five now."

"Okay." A muscular brown arm pulled back the fabric to

reveal a body to match of flawless bronze. His lips curled up at the way she stopped in the act of picking up her dress to stare at him. "Guess you should leave. Since it's still early, I'll hang out and see what's up at the House of Blues tonight."

"Do you have friends here?" Marlene said with a slight crease in her forehead. She tried to sound casual. The difference in their ages mattered to her, especially when she saw good-looking younger women watch him with hungry eyes.

"Sure, you know I do. I went to Dillard here, remember?"

"Of course. I just meant—never mind. I've got things to do anyway," Marlene said in a voice that sounded like a child pouting. "I don't exactly sit around waiting to breathe, until I can see you, Tavis."

"I didn't say you did." Tavis rose from the bed without one bit of self-consciousness that he was naked. "Now let's not argue. No strings, no questions. That's what we agreed." He ran his long fingers down her arms.

"Yes." Marlene sagged against him with her eyes closed. "I'm sorry, darling. Our time together is too precious. You make me feel so alive, so . . ." She shivered when his hand rubbed her buttocks.

"Oliver must be more attentive now that his retirement has forced you two to be together." Tavis wore a sly look that Marlene did not see, even when her eyes were open.

Marlene pressed against him. "What do I care?" Her voice was too sharp.

"Sure, baby." Tavis suppressed a laugh at her expense.

He knew quite well that Oliver Knight, even stricken with a mild stroke and eighteen years older than he, occupied her every waking thought. Each lover she'd taken in the last twenty years had been with an eye to getting revenge against him. Tavis had a grudging respect for the distinguished old man who still looked good despite his ill health. Oliver Knight could hold a woman in a viselike grip. All without the use of physical force, but with the mind. He was better at it than most men. Except Tavis of course.

"Besides, I want to talk to Damon sometime this weekend

before he runs off to be with that girl.'' Marlene allowed herself
another few minutes of luxury against his hard torso before
she began to dress.

Tavis drew on his bikini briefs then the jeans that hugged
his narrow hips so well. ''Damon and Bill seem to hit it off
very well. Damon has gained a lot of respect for his work at
the center, too.'' He spoke with studied nonchalance.

Marlene let out a puff of air between her plum-colored lips.
''Wasting his time away from the business with that silliness.''

''Has he mentioned anything to you about the grant?'' Tavis
ignored her reference to head off a tirade.

''He mentioned something about how much more could be
done in that neighborhood.'' Marlene tossed off the comment
in a distracted manner.

''Did he say anything about Bill? I mean, they didn't exactly
admire each other in school from what I understand.''

''He said something about maybe Lang had changed. Frankly
I didn't pay much attention. I couldn't think of much else once
it was clear how that little hussy has him fooled.''

Tavis chuckled. ''Some fine young thing has my boy's nose
open, eh? Well, let him have his fun.''

''If he was only having fun, I wouldn't care one bit about
her. But he's stupid enough to think he's in love. With Jade
Pellerin of all people.''

''What did you just say?'' Tavis looked up with a jerk of
his head.

''Jade Pellerin has her hooks in my son—but not for long.''

''Damn! Jade and Damon doing the do,'' he murmured low.
Tavis rubbed his jaw. A wide smile stretched his face as the
implication of this bit of news hit him.

''Something's got to be done about her.'' Marlene pursed
her lips. ''Damon can't see past his hormones, like most men.''

''Man oh man. Life is about to get real interesting.'' Tavis
nodded.

''What does that mean?'' Marlene noticed his expression for
the first time.

''Nothing. I was just thinking about department business.''

Marlene studied him for several minutes out of the corner of her eye. "You're buddies with Bill Lang, right?"

"We've known each other for a while, sure. He's helped me a great deal since we hung out together in grad school. I was the older student who'd worked before I could go back." Tavis grunted.

She winced at the reference to the years between them. Tavis was forty-one, only a few years older than Damon. And he was ambitious. Marlene knew her connections had been as attractive as her experience and skill in bed. A suspicion formed in her mind.

"Damon is working with Lang on this grant thing. And this isn't the first time you've asked me questions." Marlene walked over to stand in front of him. "Don't get any ideas about using my son, Tavis. You're not that good, and I'm not that stupid."

"Hey, baby, I'm not even in that section of the department. I'm just curious is all." Tavis put his arms around her waist. "Lang and I don't have anything going."

"Oh, really?"

"I'm in the policy and planning office, babe. I write those dull manuals stuffed with rules for the civil service worker bees to follow." He slid a hand up her thigh. "I rarely even see Bill these days."

Marlene gasped at the touch of his fingers on her. She shook her head to clear it. "I knew that," she said in a husky voice. "Just don't get any ideas."

"Oh, I've got ideas all right." He pulled her down onto his lap.

Kathy crossed her arms. A fierce look made her girlish features look menacing. Bill was seemingly intent on packing. Expensive folded shirts fresh from the laundry were lined up in the deep suitcase as were several silk ties. A garment bag held three suits.

"You could help. But I guess that would be asking too much." Bill did not look at her.

"So you can conserve your energy for that assistant of yours?" Kathy spat out the words.

"This trip is all business." Bill pressed his lips together. His expression was one of amused contempt.

"I'm glad you're enjoying yourself." Kathy threw the clothes brush she was about to hand him down to the floor. She stomped out of the combination dressing room and walk-in closet into the huge master bedroom.

Several minutes passed while Bill completed his preparations with unhurried motions. He followed her but only to retrieve more items to pack. "Kathy, don't be such a pain. Give it a rest."

"You'd like me to be a smiling doormat," Kathy spat out. "I'd have to be blind not to see what's going on."

"This is getting so tedious." Bill brushed past her but stopped when she grabbed his arm.

"Tell me it's all lies then. The whispers and rumors about you two." Kathy's voice was like a rubber band pulled too tight.

"There's talk about Jade and I?" Bill seemed more intrigued than upset. "Wonder who . . . ?"

"Nina says—"

"Good old Nina. Your best friend with too much time on her hands. I should have known. Instead of occupying herself in some useful way, she floats from one luncheon to the next, scooping up more garbage than the city trash collectors," Bill said with disdain.

"And she's rarely wrong." Kathy stared at him. "Take that last little escapade of yours."

"How Nina keeps a top job at the legislature is a mystery to me. When does she work?" Bill ignored Kathy's attempt to delve into past affairs.

"Her job is to archive and do research. Gathering information is her business, Bill. You'd do well to remember that." Kathy spoke in a level tone, her eyes narrowed.

Bill froze in the act of splashing on Calvin Klein cologne.

"What was that?" He held the opened bottle in one hand, the top of it in the other.

"Nina knows quite a lot about the goings on in state government. And the Department of Health and Hospitals is a major topic of discussion down at the capitol these days."

"Let me tell you something, Kathy." Bill crossed the room in one long stride and jerked her to him. His face was only inches from hers. "Don't ever threaten me again. I'll—"

"You'll what, Bill?" Kathy stiffened in the face of his wrath. She swallowed hard. "Hit me if that will make you feel like a man." Seconds passed as no words were spoken.

"When I get back, I'll be talking to my lawyer." Bill let go of her. "I'm sick of putting up with your tantrums." He turned his back on her and picked up a tortoiseshell hair brush.

"You wouldn't dare!" Kathy blinked as though he had hit her with a stinging blow.

"Don't be so sure." He brushed his glossy dark brown hair with long strokes. "You've spoiled my last Saturday afternoon."

"What about our assets? The family real estate? I'll take you for all you're worth."

Bill sneered at her in the mirror. "Take it. It'll be worth every penny."

"You can't mean it." Kathy's defiant stance crumpled. "We're talking about more than three million dollars in—"

"You're forgetting something, babe. Part of my inheritance is in a family trust—most of it in fact. You can't touch it." Bill chuckled. "My grandfather had a shrewd lawyer, don't forget."

Kathy glared at him. "But *my* money has made you even richer. Not to mention how your family benefited from my brother's investment advice. All that will dry up the instant you walk out on me."

"You overestimate your value, as usual. I don't need your brother, or you."

"You slimy b—" Kathy raised a hand to slap him. He caught it in midair.

"Tsk, tsk. You better learn to control that temper." Bill squeezed her small hand tight.

"Let go," Kathy gasped. A frown of pain twisted her face.

"Now that we understand each other . . ." He straightened the collar of his shirt.

Kathy spoke in a quiet voice, her expression unreadable. "I will not give you up, Bill. Understand? I'll do whatever it takes to keep you."

"Drama was always your best subject in college, Kathy. You really should have gone on the stage." Bill laughed at her.

"Don't you dare leave. I'm not through talking!"

"I'll be at the club, playing golf. I might even stay there for dinner. Have a nice day." He sauntered out without looking back.

Kathy went into the den and sat fuming for several minutes. She picked up the telephone. "Yes, this is Kathy. About that information your friend is interested in . . ."

Jade felt cramped and tense after the flight. The ride to the hotel was even more unpleasant because she was wedged between Damon and Bill. Bill's good humor vanished when Damon arrived with her at the airport in Baton Rouge. The displeasure stamped on his face was clearly directed at Damon. But why? Jade had never mentioned Damon would attend the conference, but then there was no reason for it to come up. She was certain the look Bill had given her was one of censure. It was as though she'd offended him in some way. Damon noticed something was wrong. By the time they arrived at Hotel One Washington Circle, Bill was barely speaking to them. Damon adopted a what's-his-problem? attitude that did not help matters. Thankfully there were no problems with their hotel reservations.

"I'm going to take a rest before the keynote speech." Jade was eager to escape them both for now.

"Sure, honey." Damon placed an arm around her shoulders.

"We'll take a stroll around later. I want to show you Washington in all its springtime glory." He pecked her on the cheek.

"Don't forget to fit this conference into your schedule," Bill said with a tight expression that tried to be a smile.

"Oh, we've got it all planned—right, babe?" Damon pulled Jade closer to him. "We'll soak up lots of knowledge from the workshops, then have a good time. I know all the things Jade would enjoy."

Bill stared at him for several seconds. His face relaxed. "I've got a killer headache. The meeting with Chester Howard Friday afternoon was not good. I'll tell you about it later, Jade."

"Sure, Bill." So that was it. Jade felt a flood of relief. He was uptight because he'd not been able to talk to her in private. "Why don't we plan to at, say, four. I'll get us a small meeting room."

"That won't be necessary. I have a suite." Bill turned to sign the credit card receipt handed to him by the desk staff.

Jade glanced at Damon. He was busy registering. The last thing she needed was for him to hear Bill inviting her to his room, no matter the reason.

Bill followed her gaze. He seemed about to speak when Jade cut him off.

"See you later, Bill. Damon, I'm going to take a short rest first." Jade grabbed Damon's arm and walked with him to the elevator behind the bellboy pushing a cart with their luggage.

Damon had a slight crease in his forehead. "I thought we'd have lunch together at this little restaurant nearby. They've got great soups and sandwiches."

"Not just yet. I need to unwind." Jade gave his arm a squeeze before leaving for her room.

"See you later then," Damon called after her as he walked several doors down the hall to his suite.

By the time she came down for the first speech, Jade was feeling much better. She scanned the crowd streaming in to hear Marian Wright Edelman start them off with words of inspiration. Everyone seemed excited at the prospect of hearing from one of the leading children's right advocates in the world.

International leaders from at least six other countries would speak on child labor, sexual exploitation of children and poverty. Damon joined her, and both looked over the list of workshops that would be presented over the next three days.

"I wish I could go to everything," Jade said in exasperation. "Look, a presentation on self-help groups for teen mothers. And here's a program in New York that arranges after-school programs. Darn, they're at the same time."

"Yeah, and I wanted to hear the panel discussion on Rawandan war orphans. I thought the kids at Gracie Center might organize an aid drive. We could incorporate it into our African studies program." Damon flipped through pages of the program.

"That's a wonderful idea, Damon." Jade sighed. "How am I going to choose?"

"Tell you what, let's divide up all the good stuff. Then we can share information." Damon led her to two empty seats around a table with four people already engaged in animated conversation.

"Perfect."

For the next hour, they were riveted by the dynamic woman who had come to symbolize all their aspirations to improve the plight of children in America and the world. Jade sat in awe of the speaker. Yet her thoughts strayed to the man beside her. Damon was so intent on the words of Marian Wright Edelman that he leaned forward as though he did not want to miss even one. The profile of his strong jaw sent a tingle through Jade. Damon had everything going for him. He was a member of a prominent wealthy family—handsome, intelligent and a successful businessman. Damon could easily have confined himself to once-a-year charity, like most other men in his position. But he made time to really get involved in the lives of people in a neighborhood far removed from the way he'd grown up. Jade wondered why.

Later they sat in the hotel restaurant having coffee before her meeting with Bill. Jade and Damon mapped out their strategy for the conference.

"Now except for a couple of presentations, we've got all the workshops covered between the two of us. That's teamwork." Jade sat back satisfied and took a sip from her cup.

Damon placed a hand on her thigh underneath the table of their booth. "Yeah, we're a perfect fit in more ways than one."

"I'm impressed with you."

"Oh?" Damon's eyes glittered.

"You're really dedicated to making a difference. You want to be hands-on with the center." Jade relished the intimacy of being with him even in a strange restaurant surrounded by people. She wanted to share even more with him. "Why?"

"Wardell Coates is why."

"Who's he?" Jade was intrigued with his answer.

"A guy I made friends with while I was doing volunteer work. Wardell Coates was something. He had fifteen brothers and sisters, most of them in foster care. His mother was on welfare, and his father was in prison. Three of his older brothers were big-time drug dealers, a couple of others small-time thugs. But he was trying to escape."

"Sounds like he was a special young man," Jade said.

"He was real special. Wardell had been through some bad stuff, but he survived with good humor. His foster mother was part of the reason. He had a good heart, you know." Damon smiled at the memory of his friend.

"Amazing how some children can survive hell and come out beautiful, caring human beings. I've seen it before, working with abused kids." Jade remembered her days working with child welfare agencies through the Louisiana Children's Cabinet.

"That was Wardell. He was working after school and helping old folks get home-delivered meals on the days he didn't work. He got a scholarship through the United Negro College Fund with help from a black fraternity. He was going to be an engineer." Damon spoke with pride as though Wardell was his brother.

"And he inspired you. So Wardell is somewhere helping to run a place like Gracie Street Center in his spare time?"

Damon's face became stiff and grim. "He probably would be if . . . Wardell never gave up on his brothers. One night he was standing in their old neighborhood, talking to one of his younger brothers, Quince. Seems Quince had a feud going with another dealer. A car drove up and there was gunfire. Wardell died on the corner of Gracie and Eighteenth Streets."

"Oh, no, Damon. I'm so sorry." Jade put her hand over his on her thigh. She hated to see the pain in his eyes. "Quince was hurt, too, I suppose."

"No, not a scratch." Damon took a deep breath. "He's on death row at Angola State Penitentiary. He killed one of the boys who took part in the drive-by shooting."

"Violence is a vicious cycle, isn't it?" Jade felt a kind of despair at the waste of life.

"Kids, Jade. Quince was sixteen, the boys who killed Wardell were between fourteen and seventeen." Damon looked at her. "Doing nothing would have been like saying Wardell meant nothing to me. Doing nothing was not an option."

"I understand," Jade said in a soft voice.

"The first time a kid I helped graduated from high school and go to college, I was hooked. It was such a good feeling."

Jade was hooked, too. No words could express the love she felt for him at this moment. But no words were needed. Damon pulled her to him, and the rest of the world just went away for a few magical moments.

"You've made a difference. And with the grant, you'll be able to do even more." Jade wanted to smooth away the sadness from his dark brow.

"We're sure going to try." Damon gazed at her, his brown eyes lit with affection. "Thanks."

"For what?"

"For listening, for being here, for being you." Damon brushed his lips across her forehead.

Jade closed her eyes. "Anytime, babe, anytime."

Damon drew back. "Speaking of time, don't you have a meeting to attend?"

"Darn it." Jade groaned. The last thing she wanted was to

discuss work. "I wish we could start our tour right now." What she really wanted was to make love to him hard and fast.

"We'll be together in just over an hour from now." Damon touched her lips with his fingers. "And tonight is going to be all ours. Now go on and help steer the ship of state." He gave her a gentle nudge.

"From the look on Bill's face, I'd say we might need to start bailing water hard and fast," Jade quipped. "Wish me luck." She waved goodbye as he gave her a thumbs-up sign.

"Come in, Jade," Bill said. He glanced at the gold Rolex watch on his wrist.

"Sorry I'm late." Jade felt a flicker of guilt, showing up fifteen minutes after their appointed time. She was surprised to find Mike Testor with Bill. "Hi, Mike."

"Hello there," Mike said. He managed to make a simple greeting sound like a dirty suggestion.

"As I was saying . . ." Bill shot a Mike a testy look of warning. Mike cleared his throat and wiped the slight leer from his face. "The latest round of cuts will have a big impact on the mental health clinics. Advocacy groups have been swarming over the capitol, collaring every legislator they can get their hands on."

"So?" Mike seemed unconcerned.

"Our increase in hospital beds is being questioned. The Mental Health Alliance says we should be concentrating on community-based services." Bill looked at Jade.

"That is the trend nationally, Bill. Best practices in most helping fields is to avoid institutional placement." Jade made a mental review of the literature she had read in the last year. "Some of what we're doing is inconsistent with that."

"Well, that's just one issue we have right now." Bill waved away the issue. "Howard wants us to submit a truckload of documents to the inspector general." His brows came together, and he rubbed his temples.

"When?" Mike sat up straight. He lost his disinterested glazed expression.

Charles Dumaine had been appointed as inspector general in response to the public's outcry that little changed in the huge state bureaucracy even with reform governors. Dumaine was well known as a stickler for following the law. A former economics professor at Louisiana State University, he'd been advisor to two presidents and three governors. Lobbyists and other influence peddlers gave up on trying to gain his favor within the first year of his appointment.

"That will overwhelm poor Aline without me there to help." Jade had no doubts about the propriety of their actions to date. "Just let me know what he wants."

"Documents related to the psychiatric hospitals, home health care rules we've proposed and a few other things." Bill clenched and unclenched his hands. "Like the grant monies we've gotten."

"You mean like memos and executive bulletins related to policy decisions?" Jade was writing notes as she spoke.

"Yes."

"Okay." Jade looked up at the two men. A prickle of apprehension raised chill bumps on her arms. Bill and Mike seemed worried, very worried. "Is there something else we need to do?"

"You don't think he—" Mike stared at Bill.

"It's no big deal really," Bill cut him off. He forced a smile. "Mike and I can tell Aline what to do. Dumaine wants them in the next two weeks. You don't have to worry about it, Jade."

"Are you sure? I've handled quite a few of those projects with you. I really should help gather those documents." Jade was baffled by his attitude.

"No, we've got day-to-day details that I need you to handle." Bill gave her a nod of confidence. "That's where you could be the most help."

"But, Bill . . ."

"Jade, Dumaine is on a search-and-destroy mission. I'm where the buck stops on these issues." Bill squared his shoulders and looked grave. "He'll be expecting me to answer the hard questions, and I'm fully prepared to take the heat."

Jade felt a little relieved. Maybe she was imagining things. Working in state government had made her too suspicious. The fact that Bill was going to handle the inspector general's request made her feel better.

"Listen, let me handle the details. I'm wrapping up work on the new program for public health. That way you'll be free to meet with the assistant secretaries." Jade saw no reason why she should not at least prepare his report.

"We do have that big health care forum coming up, Bill. Remember, we're gearing up for that pilot project to test managed care for welfare recipients," Mike put in.

"We can probably anticipate any questions based on what's gone on before," Jade said. "As long as Dumaine gets his questions answered, he's satisfied. Bill, I really can make this easier on us all."

"She's got a point." Mike nodded.

"Besides, the grant project is well under way. Eddie's proposal sailed through the review committee. It complies with all of the requirements," Jade added.

"You've spent a lot of time on that one." Bill stared at her.

Jade shrugged with more than a touch of embarrassment. "There were a lot of details to work out."

"Hmm." Bill sat unmoving for a while. "Sure more overtime at the office won't put a cramp in your social life?"

"Oh Damon understands—" Jade broke off. Bill's eyes narrowed for an instant. "I mean, it's okay."

Bill's lips stretched tight. "Fine. Mike and I will just tie up a few other things now."

"Of course. I'll see you at the first session tomorrow morning." Jade gathered her notes and left.

"I don't like it," Mike blurted almost the instant the door closed behind her. "Dumaine doesn't sniff around unless he's on to something."

Bill sat brooding, his eyes on the door. "Forget Dumaine. I've all but neutralized him. The great Chester Howard happens to hate his guts, a clash of the mighty self-righteous egos. We're going to pull the rug right out from under that windbag.''

"Then that's good," Mike said with a lopsided grin.

"Yeah, sure."

Mike paused in the act of pouring himself a shot of vodka. "Now what's wrong? And why the act in front of sweet stuff?" He jerked a finger in the direction Jade had disappeared.

"Damon Knight is a problem."

"So he's a do-gooder. So what? He'll get his pay off and not think twice about anyone else, just like all the other hypocrites." Mike took a gulp from the shot glass.

"Not Knight." Bill spoke in a low voice with a frown on his face.

Mike snorted. "Believe me, when the going gets tough, they all try to protect their little pet programs. Just tighten the purse strings like we've done before."

"You don't know him like I do. He's a man of principle," Bill snarled. He got up and poured himself a scotch and soda.

"Then we'll just have to deal with him, too," Mike said in a flat, grim voice.

"What do you have in mind?" Bill turned to him with a look of anticipation.

"Everybody has skeletons, right? It just takes knowing where to dig." Mike raised his glass in a silent toast.

"Damon Knight with something to hide? I don't think so." Bill lost his animated expression and scowled again.

"I've heard a few rumblings about his old man and deals he cut to get state bids. You might even want to ask Tavis about it." Mike wore a leer.

"Tavis? What would he know?"

"Tavis uses all his assets to improve his standard of living." Mike threw back his head with a loud guffaw that eventually trailed off into a hoarse chuckle. "I've booked a flight out tomorrow afternoon, earliest I could get on short notice. But I'll get stated by making some phone calls in the morning. By the time I get back to Baton Rouge, I'll have a solid lead."

Bill raised an eyebrow at him. "I don't want all the details, just fill me in if there are any concerns that others might be interested in.''

Mike wore a look of shrewd satisfaction. ''Sure. I'll take care of things my way. Count on it.''

Thinking of Damon, Bill paid little attention to the tone of Mike's last statement. ''I want Knight out of my way, out of my business.''

''Sure, but this sounds very personal.'' Mike let the unasked question hang in the air between them.

''Knight and I go back aways. He has an annoying habit of popping up to give me trouble.'' Bill's face was stiff with anger. He stared ahead as though seeing his adversary. ''Thinks he's better than me. The mighty Knight family.''

''Hmm. Jade seems to be fond of the guy. She won't be happy.''

''Jade won't give him the time of day once he's exposed for the fraud he is. He's just a carpet salesman with an inflated opinion of himself. Besides, her interests lie with me.'' Bill gazed at Mike. ''Her name is on some of those bulletins and policies.''

''I'm sure she'll soon realize how much you two have in common.'' Mike chuckled again.

Bill raised his glass to take a sip of his drink. ''Yes. When we get back to Baton Rouge, I'll make sure of it.''

Chapter 10

The cool night was beautiful. Jade savored the view of Washington Harbor from Tony and Joe's Restaurant. To her delight the music of the Neville Brothers began to play from the sound system. "This is fantastic, Damon."

"Glad you like it. Tomorrow I have a special treat. We can leave the conference at two and visit Affrica." Damon watched with pleasure as her eyes lit up.

"The gallery that has traditional African art? Cool! And somehow we've got to get over to the Smithsonian, the Bethune Museum and Archives, the—"

Laughing, Damon held up a palm. "Hold on, we won't be spending the rest of the year in this town."

Jade sighed. "I know. Four days isn't nearly enough time."

"Maybe we can stretch it out." Damon placed an arm around her.

"The galleries stay open only until five or six. I don't see how we can do everything we want in just a few days."

"We can if we stay longer," Damon said in a quiet voice. He wrapped a tendril of her hair around one finger. "The conference ends Thursday at noon. We could stay over until the following Wednesday.''

"Oh, that's not possible. Not after that meeting with Bill.''

"Not another project,'' Damon said. "We promised not to be so driven, remember?''

"Hey, don't blame me. I've got a new task now thanks to Charles Dumaine. Bill said I didn't need to handle gathering all the materials. But no-oo, I had to insist.''

Damon tensed at the mention of the inspector general. "Dumaine is asking questions about Lang?''

"The department's handling of certain programs, not just Bill. It's no big deal, just a lot more work.'' Jade wore a look of regret. "And it means staying here a few extra days is out of the question.''

"What exactly is Dumaine asking about?'' Damon's brows came together.

"Some of the Medicaid services and stuff like that. Look, it's all dry and boring. We'll give him piles of paper to sift through. That'll make him happy.''

"So you think it'll probably be over once he's got the documents you send?'' Damon rubbed his chin. He did not like the sound of this at all. He was a fool to have believed Bill Lang had changed. Charles Dumaine did not chase after smoke unless he had good reason to know he'd find fire.

"Sure. No matter what folks say, Bill has followed all the rules.'' Jade noticed the frown he wore. "Damon, you don't trust him, do you?''

"We've got some history. The Bill Lang I knew wasn't above breaking the rules to get something he wanted. And what he wants most is money, power and control over people. He particularly likes having control over women. Be careful,'' he said in a deep, somber voice. Damon remembered the young women in college who'd suffered at his hands. They were bright, attractive and educated. But Bill Lang had a way of putting a psychological noose that held them captive, frantic to keep him.

Seeing the grim set to his jaw and the note of something

shadowy in his voice, Jade shivered. "You make him sound like an evil mastermind grabbing for everything he can get his hands on."

Damon snapped back from his dark thoughts. He did not want to frighten her or spoil the evening. "Hey, listen to me taking the fun out of my own party. I'm sure you're right about this being no big deal. Right?" He tried to push down that nagging doubt still stuck in his chest.

"Nah, it'll be over in no time. I'm just sorry I won't get to spend more time at the Smithsonian." Jade propped her chin on one hand and looked forlorn.

"Hey, wait a minute. You mean the chief attraction to staying was the exhibit on prehistoric art?" Damon affected a look of wounded male ego. He sat back. "Thanks a lot."

Jade draped an arm around his waist. "Hey, I would have had some extra special attention for my own precious find," she murmured close to his ear.

"Don't try to make it up to me now. I'm playing second fiddle to million-year-old finger paintings."

"Think of us strolling hand in hand in front of breathtaking art, enjoying the feel of being close and thinking of the evening to come." Jade wiggled against him with a seductive sigh.

Damon breathed a little faster with each movement of her body. "Sure, I'm just an escort to the interesting stuff." He blinked at the feel of her hand on his thigh.

"No, indeed, you're the main event. The art museums are only the warm-up acts." Jade kneaded his firm muscles. "Feel better?"

"Yeah," Damon mumbled. He gazed into her eyes. "Now let's make this a private party."

During the cab ride back to the hotel, Jade savored the anticipation of finally being alone with Damon. They sat together, enjoying the heat of being close in the dark.

"Hmm, I feel like a kid again." Damon planted a kiss on her neck.

"Really?" Jade closed her eyes. Her body ached to be touched by his strong hands.

"Yeah, I finally got you in the backseat of a car," Damon whispered.

Jade laughed out loud, causing the cabdriver to glance into the rearview mirror. Frank curiosity danced in the eyes of the man.

"Stop it. The driver is watching." Jade felt a thrill of fire when Damon's hand cupped her left breast. The feel of it through her sweater made her squirm. "Wish he'd drive faster." She ignored the man as she pulled Damon to her for a deep kiss.

Once in the hotel elevator alone, Damon pressed her to the wall as soon as the doors closed. He murmured endearments as he rubbed her thighs, lifting up the blue wool skirt she wore. Damon lowered it again with reluctance when the elevator bumped to a stop. An elderly couple stared with disapproval at their rumpled clothing. It was clear they guessed the cause. Jade giggled as they went down the hall to her room, feeling not the least bit contrite. She marveled at her lack of decorum, but it was no mystery. Damon Knight turned around all her old habits and ways of thinking when it came to men. Where she had been restrained even with Nick, just that certain look in Damon's beautiful eyes caused her to grope him shamelessly in public!

"You're going to have my reputation in shreds by the time we leave this conference," Jade said with a sigh once they were in her room.

Damon shrugged off his overcoat and jacket with quick motions. He took her coat off as well, too impatient to wait for her to undo the buttons alone. "So should I leave?" He massaged her thighs and buttocks with one hand while pulling her blouse out of her skirt with another.

Jade's hands tightened their hold on his biceps at just the thought of having him pull away now. "No—oh, no," she whispered between his steamy kisses that made it hard for her to think straight.

The urgency of desire sent them into a mindless rush of undressing each other. Naked and breathless, they clutched at each other hungrily. Their bodies rubbed together, causing a friction that made them moan in a kind of passionate harmony. Jade took great pleasure in feeling his erection against her skin. Damon walked her backward to the bed and they sank onto it. His mouth and tongue caressed every inch of her. When he began to suck her nipples, Jade dissolved in a haze. Love washed over her like a tidal wave. There were no other sensations except the touch of his mouth and hands. Her whole being vibrated with longing for him.

"I've never wanted anyone as much as I want you," Damon murmured.

Jade could only reply with a strangled cry of joy as he entered her. They hung suspended in ecstasy without sensation of time or space. Their bodies moved with the smooth rhythm born of a need for physical and emotional union. At first they made love in slow motion, relishing the union of flesh. But soon their hunger for each other raged, pushing them into frantic, faster movements. They seemed to crash together with the force of a powerful storm as though they were caught in a whirlwind. When Damon stiffened inside her, he called her name over and over. Jade wrapped her legs around him and held on with all her might. Her orgasm began as an insistent pounding deep inside with each thrust, then tore through her. Jade arched her back with such force, she lifted them both clear of the bed for a few seconds. Every muscle in her body went rigid. Damon moaned as he climaxed. His release sent Jade back over the edge into an impossibly intense second orgasm. After an eternity of gasping for air, they lay together trembling.

"Damn." Damon still clutched her tight to his chest.

"My, my," Jade panted.

"You keep this up, lady, and I won't make it to thirty-five." Damon lifted himself from atop her with care and settled next to her.

"Oh, you'll make it all right. I'll see to it."

"That a fact?" Damon rested his head against hers.

"Yes, indeed. I'm going to put you on an exercise schedule and a heart-healthy diet." Jade nodded.

"Wait just a minute—"

"I expect you to stay in shape so you can keep on giving good love." Jade laughed.

"I ought to spank you for that." Damon gave her arm a sharp squeeze.

Jade gave him a daring giggle. "Promise?"

Damon grew serious when he look into her eyes. "I promise to always cherish you, baby. For once my head and my heart agree."

Jade thought of her doubts. They seemed silly when they were holding each other like this. Yet even the glow of their potent lovemaking could not blot out the real world that lay just outside her hotel door. "Are you sure your head isn't in the right place after all?"

"I have no doubts. If you do, then I plan to love you long and hard until they're all gone," Damon said in a voice strained with emotion.

It took all Jade's strength to resist the urge to let go and once again be swept into their own private world of love. "Damon, we don't live in a vacuum. Your parents don't even want to meet me. I think they'd rather see you get back together with Rachelle."

"That's not true." Damon did not return her gaze. "We just haven't been able to coordinate. Both of them keep pretty busy, and Dad is even threatening to start work again now that his recovery is almost complete."

"Nice try, honey. But I can tell from the way you talk that your mother isn't happy with us being together." Jade put a forefinger on his full lips to cut off his protest. "Don't bother to deny it, Damon."

Damon let out a long breath. "Mother is stubborn. She thinks I didn't put forth enough effort to save my marriage. But she didn't have to live with Rachelle's tantrums and self-centered behavior."

"I just thought of something. Our mothers are alike. My mother can be overbearing, even bossy. And your mother is. . . ." Jade hestitated to go further.

"I'll say it, she's a dictator in a designer silk dress." Damon laughed. "Oh she rarely raises her voice, but Marlene Cormier Knight has a will of steel. Another reason we understand each other."

"Now that's something we definitely have in common." Jade nodded and sighed. "It's funny how our parents see things." She thought of her mother. Clarice was so sure she knew what her daughters needed.

Damon shook his head. "Amazing that they want to control us even at this age."

Yet Jade wondered at his reaction to Rachelle. Could he still have feelings for her?

"Sometimes the past is hard to leave behind." Jade gazed at him steadily. "What's that song say? It's never as good as the first time."

"Not one of my favorites. Besides, you just blew that myth out of the water." Damon returned her gaze for several seconds. "And you?"

Jade thought for a fleeting moment that this was an evasion. But the soft look of longing in his eyes touched her. "It was over long before the divorce. I need to be with someone whose commitment to me will stand the test of time."

Damon responded to the question in her eyes. "Then I'm your man."

Jade rested her chin on his chest and closed her eyes. "Lucky me," she whispered.

"This isn't fair, Jeanne!" Lanessa shot up from the chair across from her supervisor's desk. "I've been working here for seven years, busting my butt!"

"I'm concerned about you, Lanessa." Jeanne Proctor remained calm. Her voice was even and low. "Sit back down . . . please."

After a few seconds, Lanessa dropped into the chair but crossed her arms in a defensive pose. "Yeah, sure. I just bet you care about me."

"Listen, you've been a rock around here. More than anyone else, I could count on you when push came to shove. But—" Jeanne took a deep breath.

"Yeah, here it comes."

"Your work performance has been slipping for months. And you come in late as many as three days a week."

Lanessa scowled at her. "Why are you picking on me? What about the rest of the staff? I could tell you a few things about some of those folks."

"We're here to talk about you, Lanessa. Now I've got your attendance record right here. You've been late nineteen times in the last thirty days alone."

"I told you, I've had some personal problems. My ex-husband has tried to cut my alimony." Lanessa wrung her hands.

"I went back over six months. You call in sick frequently, Mondays and Fridays most often. This is the fourth time we've talked about this in the last year, Lanessa." Jeanne pushed the open folder toward Lanessa with her sign-in sheets and record of leave taken from the office. "See for yourself."

Lanessa did not glance at the papers. "Look, I know I've been late a few times—okay, a lot. But cut me some slack, Jeanne. I'll do better, honest."

"That's what you told me the last two times." Jeanne closed the folder.

"Oh, so you're getting all your ducks in a row to fire me, right? It figures." Lanessa slumped in the chair.

"No, I could have done that months ago. I want to help you save your job. But with the mistakes you've made and your attendance record I've got to see a change." Jeanne leaned forward.

"What do you want me to do?"

"Call the State Employees Assistance Program. Get counseling." Jeanne handed her a pamphlet.

"I don't need counseling. Soon as I show my ex he can't push me around—"

"Lanessa, this is not a request. Your job is on the line." Jeanne stared at her with a firm set to her jaw.

"I'm a civil service employee. You can't push me around like this."

"I've got documentation of the times we've talked about your tardiness and calling in sick. You just completed a supervisory plan. The results of my review are not good. I could legally take formal personnel action right now."

"Listen, Jeanne, I'm doing my best." Lanessa pressed her fingertips to her temples. "I just need time."

"Call the number, Lanessa." Jeanne did not soften as she had so many times before. "It's for your own good. I really believe that."

Lanessa stared at the pamphlet for several long moments before taking it. Without speaking, she left Jeanne's office.

"We're talking about millions of dollars at stake here, Mike. I don't want any mistakes." State Representative Sherman Ortego spoke in a mild voice, but the hard glint in his eye told a different story. "I don't want that rule change to go through."

"Senator Ortego, relax. We've got to cut the daily payment rates for a short while until the heat is off. In a few months, we can quietly push them back up," Mike Testor said. He tried to maintain his cool demeanor, but being under the scrutiny one of the state's most powerful men was unsettling.

They sat having drinks at the City Club in Baton Rouge. The exclusive club had an air of old money, old family and old connections. Memberships could not simply be bought by anyone who could afford the considerable fee. For seventy years politicians and businessmen met here for the comfort of being able to speak freely. After all, once they passed through its polished oak doors, no one knew who they shared a table with inside. There were no prying eyes. Businessmen could sit with a friendly state legislator or U.S. congressman and not worry that a reporter would make wild accusations.

"The cuts don't bother me as much as the moratorium on nursing home expansions." Ortego lowered his voice. Even here he was reluctant to let it be known that he had business interests in the string of lucrative nursing homes in south Louisiana. "The cut won't seriously affect profit."

"And that won't be for long—a few months, like I said," Mike put in quickly. He was anxious to reassure the formidable man.

"Just make sure Lang understands the importance of issuing those certificates. We all stand to lose if these reformers get their way." Ortego glared at Mike as though it were his fault that advocates for the elderly and disabled wanted more public funds diverted from institutions.

"Listen, those folks don't have clout—we do, no matter how many grandmothers they roll down to the state capitol building."

"With recent scandals about conditions in nursing homes and state institutions for the retarded, who knows? That report on *60 Minutes* didn't help one damn bit. Now the feds are coming. We've got to get those beds before the Justice Department orders the state to make drastic changes." Ortego fingered his glass of scotch but did not pick it up.

"The feds will take a long time to get their report back. Then the state will have a month or so to reply. Hell, we can do all kinds of things by that time." Mike smiled with satisfaction.

"Don't kid yourself, young man," Ortego snapped. His words wiped the smug expression from Mike's face. "The governor does not play ball, Mike. And he's surrounded himself with men who do not share our views."

What Ortego meant was the governor's top officials had no financial interest that made them partial to business as usual in the state. The power brokers, used to the previous administrations, were dismayed to discover that public talk did not change behind closed doors. The new cabinet members said the same things in private: cut costs and no favoritism.

"But there is just so much he can do," Mike protested. He looked uneasy. Sherman Ortego was the quintessential insider. If he said there was reason to worry, then things were bad. "I mean, they can't be everywhere at once. If we can get them onto some other problems—say, the Department of Insurance, or what about the Department of Transportation and Development?'' He wore a look of hope.

Ortego glowered at him. ''You haven't been paying close enough attention. The governor and his people are not stupid! They already have a handle on those things, too.''

''Oh.'' Mike looked deflated.

''Chester Howard, the commissioner of administration—all of them know the moves we can make.''

Mike pulled a meaty hand over his face. ''Then what are we going to do?''

''Get Lang to act and act quickly. Supply Dumaine with what he wants, drown him in paper. And shut Franklin up, or I'll have someone I know take care of him.'' Ortego spoke in a low, menacing voice.

Mike turned pale. ''You mean . . .'' he croaked. He'd heard of Senator Ortego's dangerous temper. His ancestors had been known to hire assassins.

''Don't be a fool, man! I'm talking about putting the state auditors on his trail. The idiot plays fast and loose with his books. Tell him about my concern. He'll get the point. He's not that much of an idiot.'' Ortego sneered. He seemed pleased at the prospect of making Franklin squirm.

''Yes, sir.'' Mike Testor suddenly lost his taste for the fine wine he'd been enjoying.

Rachelle crossed her legs and lifted her shoulders back. The knee-length skirt showed her shapely legs to advantage. Her curves were made more pronounced by the contrast with the black pin-striped fitted suit jacket she wore to match it. A crisp white shirt and tie completed the outfit.

''So, Nicky. Are we all set?'' She gazed at him.

''*We* are nothing, Rachelle. And quit calling me Nicky.'' Nick ignored her attempts to entice him. He turned his back to prepare a drink at the bar in his spacious town house. ''Jade will be at the restaurant.''

"How can you be so sure of yourself?" Rachelle retorted. She wore a look of irritation at his dismissal of her. "Why should she even listen to you? With your record of stretching the truth, I sure wouldn't." She got up and snatched the drink from his hand.

"Because she's basically a suspicious person." Nick looked down to watch the ice cubes bounce as he swirled his drink.

"Humph, who wouldn't be with you for a husband," Rachelle retorted. "But even she's not that gullible."

"We have some joint property still. I'll tell her we need to discuss business."

"That's it? That's your grand plan to get her there?"

"Yes."

"Please! She blew you off the last time you tried to sweet talk her. I've been wasting my time." Rachelle put all the contempt she could muster in her voice.

"She'll be there. And when I tell her you've been seen with Damon more than once, Jade and Damon will be history." Nick wore a nasty smile.

"A pretty thin strategy, if you ask me. They'll fall back into each other's arms in no time." Rachelle gave a disgusted grunt at the thought.

"Have you been reading the newspapers lately?" Nick said.

"No, and what does that have to do with anything?"

"A scandal is close to coming to a boil at the Department of Health and Hospitals. Within the next few weeks, things are going to get hot for Jade's boss and his buddies. He—"

"Spare me the boring details. So Jade will have a tough time for a while, which will be fun to watch. But so what? Damon will run to her side and play the devoted lover. I want her out of his life." Rachelle's pretty mouth turned down in a rancorous expression that transformed her features.

"I'm going to see to it that they turn *on* each other, not *to* each other." Nick gave her wink.

Rachelle looked up at him sharply. "How?"

"Leave that to me. My uncle is a very well-connected man. He has lots of inside information."

"What in the world are you talking about? What—"

"All you need to know is that I can make it happen, sweetheart. Believe me, when I'm through Jade won't give Damon Knight the time of day." Nick's face took on a hard, scheming look. "And he'll be just as suspicious of her."

"Nick, you're more devious than I thought." Rachelle spoke with new admiration. "But Jade might decide to remain loyal to him."

Nick shook his head slowly. "She'll spit in his face. I know Jade."

"Maybe you don't know her as well as you think. Damon certainly changed." She gave a slight frown of true puzzlement. "He's different somehow."

"You mean waving your butt in his face didn't make him sit up and beg." Nick gave a snort of scornful amusement. "You've always overestimated your ability to conquer the male libido, Rachelle. Besides, your little escapades did quite a bit to tarnish your shiny veneer."

"You didn't complain back in college. As I recall, you did beg for it more than once." Rachelle raised an eyebrow at him. "I still remember what you like."

Nick still wore a look of detachment. "Hmm, and you screamed like a banshee when I used to give you those long strokes."

"That's enough," Rachelle said in a raspy voice. She swallowed hard and wiped her face with a napkin. "Don't be crude."

"But, sweetheart, that's how you like it." Nick walked to her slowly and put his drink down on the coffee table. He stood looking down on her.

"You make me sick. I ought to—"

"Don't mess with me, Rachelle. Damon knows only about one affair. I could fill him in on much more. You even had him fooled before you got married."

"And I could tell Miss Too-Good-to-Be-True Pellerin about the other girlfriend of yours who has a baby by you. A father twice, all within two years of your wedding." Rachelle raised an eyebrow at him.

Nick tensed, alarm flickered across his face. "How did you find out about—"

"Never mind. Look, let's call truce. We won't get far by clawing at each other. Damon's mother is going to talk to him again about being on good terms with me."

"His mother doesn't despise the way you misused her darling son?" Nick looked skeptical.

"Trust me, Marlene wants us together for purely selfish reasons. Money and family name. Besides I don't think she knows all the details of my . . . our marital problems." Rachelle stood and smoothed down the fabric of her suit.

"You're good, I've got to give you that much." Nick laughed. He raised his glass to her in a mock toast. "Nobody does it better."

"Just make sure Jade shows," she spat at him. "I can't wait to see the look on her face. What he sees in her is a mystery to me."

Nick swallowed some of the Courvoisier. "Jade is one helluva sexy woman. She's got a sweet, warm kind of quality that makes it nice coming home to her. It's hard to explain, especially to some people." Nick gave her a look from head to toe.

"Save the sappy act for someone who doesn't know what a dog you are, okay? Just do your part. If we're lucky, we both get what we want." Rachelle picked up her leather Coach purse.

"Yes, dear," Nick said in a false voice like a man subdued. He chuckled at the angry oath she uttered before slamming the door behind her.

Lanessa sat nursing a drink at Club Monaco. The elegant old bar catered to the well-to-do and pretenders to wealth in the black community. The bar was of a rich, dark varnished oak as were the tables and chairs. A first-class restaurant was on the other side of carved swinging doors.

The clink of dinnerware could be heard. But Lanessa was intent upon her own troubles.

"Hey, Lanessa. How's it going?"

"Wonderful. Everything is just peachy," Lanessa muttered. She did not bother to look at her new companion.

"The wheels of state government still rolling along smooth eh? Heard your sister is movin' on up. You still working with what's-her-name in documents, I guess." The man leaned closer to her.

Lanessa turned to him. "Well, well. If it isn't Glenn Curtis, ace reporter. So my star falls while Jade's rises. Trust you to dig up all the dirt you can find," she snorted. "Still freelancing and sending tidbits to the national trashloids, right?"

"Here, let me buy you another one of those." Glenn signaled the bartender. "I'm into legitimate news stories, babe. *Times-Picayune,* Baton Rouge *Morning Advocate* to name a few."

"Yeah, right, and I'm engaged to Prince Charles. Queen Elizabeth is fit to be tied about it." Lanessa gave a short, rough laugh.

Glenn ignored her joke at his expense. "So like I said, Jade is runnin' with the big dogs. Bill Lang is a real powerhouse. She ought to do well."

Lanessa gripped the glass in her hand. "Yeah, she's making important decisions. His top assistant. What have I done with my so-called career? Nothing."

"Hey, get Jade to help you out. She's positioned just right to get you in near the top." Glenn watched her take a long pull of her drink. "Jade in on the big stuff. Figures. She always had brains."

"Sure. That's my little sister. Mother always said Jade had all the brains. Me? I'm skating on my looks." She gazed at herself in the mirror. "What's left of 'em. Jade got looks *and* smarts."

"Yeah, she's something else. Listen, is she in on the hospital expansions and Medicaid decisions? They say Lang even lets her attend top-level meetings."

"Jade is in the driver's seat. Signing off on all kinds of rules, reviewing policies to make sure they're what Lang wants—

while I'm just a gofer for every jerk on the sixth floor of the state capitol building." Lanessa was deep in self-pity.

Glenn hitched closer to her. "So she's got delegated authority. Little sister is in on the real deal."

"Yeah, she's in D.C. First class all the way. Jade is—" Lanessa seemed to snap out of a fog at the eagerness in his voice. "Wait a minute, what's your interest? I'm not saying anything you can use to smear my sister."

"Hey, we're just talkin' casual-like. Chill." Glenn wore a placating smile.

"Like hell we are. You little chump-change scribbler! Selling out our community. I saw the article you wrote on black welfare mothers." Lanessa scoured him with a look of distaste. "You played to every stereotype with that one."

"That was a solid piece of journalism—and it was about welfare, not black welfare mothers." Glenn drew himself in anger at her words.

"Just a coincidence everyone you interviewed was black with lots of kids, I guess."

"Hey, I go where my information leads."

Lanessa gave a grunt of derision. "No wonder we called you the worm-mouth back in grade school. You'd slink around keyholes, then blackmail people."

Glenn sneered at her. "Your baby sister is up to her neck in some shady dealings. Should make quite a splash when my story hits."

Lanessa clutched the fabric of the wool checked jacket he wore until it was balled into her fist. "You listen to me, you little—"

"And I'm not the only one on it, either. Major investigative reporters from the *Shreveport Times*, *Times-Picayune* and the *Morning Advocate* right here are working up stories. I'll get my own byline outta this one." Glenn cackled.

"Not with anything from me you won't." Lanessa was breathing hard. She looked desperate as she tried to remember just what she'd said to him.

"You confirmed what I suspected all along. All I needed

was a little bit to tell me where to look next. Thanks for the help.'' He pulled free of her grasp.

''I couldn't have—'' Lanessa pressed her fingertips to her temples.

''Here, have another drink on me. Best price I ever paid for information.'' Glenn walked with a swagger as he went through the exit door leading to the parking lot.

''Oh, God.'' Lanessa clamped a hand over her mouth. She stared glassy-eyed with agony at the rows of liquor bottles on a shelf behind the bar.

''Glad to see you made it back to see us Mr. Knight. You folks okay?'' The waiter hovered over her shoulder ready to please.

''Everything is marvelous, perfect.'' Jade smiled at him. ''Thank you.''

''Thanks, Charlie. We're fine.'' Damon nodded at him. ''So how do you like my suggestion?'' He swept a hand around the dining room.

Jade gazed out the window at the breathtaking view of Georgetown. They were in The Roof Terrace restaurant at the top of the Kennedy Center. Elegant was the best way to describe every detail down to the fresh flowers on their table, a simple arrangement of white carnations with pansies of deep purple. A jazz ensemble was playing a sampling of favorites from the great Miles Davis.

''Damon, I've never had this much fun on vacation. I'm going to think of ways to have you come on my next business trip.'' Jade giggled.

''All I need is a day's notice, sweetheart.'' Damon laughed.

''The conference was outstanding. I've learned so much from the speakers. And the exhibits were the best I've seen. My bags are stuffed with great pamphlets. I grabbed up everything I could carry.''

''I had a chance to spend time with a director and board member from an agency in Chicago called Bright Futures, Inc.

Man, the things those men are doing for black kids! I can't wait to tell Eddie about it.''

"We've had the best of both worlds for the last few days. Thank you for showing me so much of this city. Especially the African-American art galleries and historic sites.'' Jade knew she would never forget the joy of strolling hand in hand with him, gazing at art that dazzled them both.

"I aim to please, ma'am,'' Damon said in a smooth voice.

"Sir, your champagne.'' The waiter placed the ice bucket with the bottle on their table. He poured the bubbly liquid into long-stemmed goblets.

"Damon, I'm speechless.'' Jade's eyes were sparkling with delight.

"This is a celebration.'' Damon took both her hands in his when the waiter was gone. "You're the best thing that's happened to me in a long time.''

"I tried hard not to like you that first day we met. I thought to myself, 'This is the last thing I need.' '' Jade shook her head. "But you didn't cooperate. You were so sincere about the center and so intriguing—not at all the self-centered black upper-class snob I wanted you to be.''

"Sorry to disappoint you.'' Damon grinned.

Jade lifted a hand to his face. Her fingers brushed his cheek, then traced the outline of his lips. "Oh—no, indeed. One thing you haven't done is disappoint me, Damon Knight.''

Back in Damon's suite, they undressed each other with tenderness. Their lovemaking was slow. Their bodies moved in concert, matching the throbbing tempo of craving deep within. Damon kissed her, his tongue moving around the soft, sweet inside of her mouth. Then he drew back and looked into her eyes.

"I love to watch your face when I'm loving you,'' he whispered.

"Damon, kiss me again,'' Jade said in between gasps for air.

She moaned and dug her fingers into the flesh of his back. The hunger for more of him seized her, sending shudders through her hips and thighs. Faster and faster the whole world seemed to go, spinning them both into ecstasy. Later they lay wrapped in a soft cushion of contentment, tired but wide awake.

"I hate to go back home to the real world." Jade nestled in the bend of his strong arm, her head on his chest. "Let's run away to a Caribbean island."

"I'll book a flight." Damon reached for the phone.

"Stop that! We can't just take off." Jade pulled his arm back.

"What's to stop us? Listen, we can spend the weekend and head on back to Baton Rouge." Damon pushed her hand away. "I've got a pal who's a travel agent right here in town. He can make it happen on the internet and have the tickets here by morning."

"Don't be ridiculous, I can't do that. Bill is expecting me to start getting all those policies and stuff together." Jade felt alarm tinged with excitement. This man was incredible.

"Look, Bill told you yesterday he didn't expect you to work this weekend." Damon's hand rested on the phone.

"True, but there is some preliminary work I could do."

"Obviously starting this weekend isn't necessary then, right?"

"Ye-es, but . . ."

"Then there is no reason we can't have a long weekend in Barbados." Damon picked up his wallet. "Here's the old trusty Gold Card."

"But I don't have clothes for a warm climate. And my swimsuit is at home." Jade began making a mental list of things she'd need.

"Then we'll go shopping once we get there. My friend Harmon and his wife can tell us the best places to go for shopping, dining—the works. They spend two weeks there every year, they love it so much."

"I'll need to call my parents to let them know, and where did I put my Visa Gold Card?" Jade sprang from the bed then stood stock still. "This is insane! A crazy impulse." She gazed at Damon.

Chapter 11

"She went where?" Bill Lang spoke in a tight, angry voice. He was the picture of barely contained fury.

Tavis did not lose his mild expression. "Barbados. His mother would like to strangle Jade for seducing her son into acting so wild."

Bill was so incensed, he did not even question why Marlene Knight confided in Tavis. "No wonder I couldn't get hold of her Friday night. And she left a message that she would take a personal day, which is why she isn't here."

"Right. They left Friday morning and will get back this afternoon." Tavis examined his neat fingernails. "Bet that was some long weekend."

"Damnit, I must have been brain dead to tell her she didn't have to rush back to work on that stuff Dumaine wants." Lang slapped the desktop in frustration. He stood up and turned to stare out the window at the scene spread before him.

"Man, what is it with you? You're losing focus. The business at hand is getting those policies implemented, remember? We didn't throw in with our associates to not make money. Forget Jade." Tavis gazed at Bill.

Bill remained silent for several minutes. When he faced Tavis again, his expression was cold and hard. "I don't need you or anyone else to tell me how to handle my business, personal or otherwise. Mike has been working on gathering everything we need. Dumaine won't be a problem."

"Mike can't be trusted, Bill. He's been meeting with Ortego. Has he told you about that?"

"When? Where?" Bill did not move.

"I saw him coming out of the City Club Friday right behind the good senator. Now if he doesn't tell you about it today, then something is up."

"So Mike and the good old boys think I'm a fool, think they can set me up." Bill rubbed his jaw. He seemed excited by the challenge rather than worried.

"Or let you take the fall while they benefit. It's been done before. Your name is on those rules and memos." Tavis sat forward.

"But I won't go down alone. And I intend to make sure they know that." Lang paced the length of his office. "No, I've got ways to tie them up so tightly to my fate, they won't dare let me go down."

"But how—"

Lang held up a palm. "Just let me handle it, okay?"

Tavis stood up and smoothed down his jacket. "Okay. But remember, I'm in this with you. I don't want my position in jeopardy. My boss would hang me out to dry if he found out I've got an interest in SAMCO."

"He won't," Lang said with a wave of his hand. "SAMCO has other business holdings that indirectly lead to the nursing homes and hospitals. No way will anyone care enough to track back through the maze of corporate tangle even if they could."

"I hope you're right." Tavis did not sound completely convinced.

"Not even Mike knows as much as he thinks he knows," Lang said. The corner of his mouth lifted, giving him a look of sly satisfaction.

"Really? Good. Very good." Tavis nodded with approval. "I was beginning to think . . ."

"Tavis, you've known me long enough to know I'm no fool. Mike and I have worked together on a lot of things, but I haven't forgotten who he is and who I am." Lang sat down in the leather chair behind his desk. "No, indeed."

"Carry on, brother. Carry on." Tavis gave him a firm handshake then left.

"I will," Lang said once the door closed behind him. "And my plans include Jade. Damon Knight be damned."

Kathy wore dark sunglasses. She kept looking over her shoulder. "I don't like this at all. We're too out in the open."

She sat across from Glenn Curtis and John Savoie. The roadside Waffle House restaurant was across the river in the small town of Port Allen. The two reporters exchanged a harried glance.

"Mrs. Lang, it's okay," Savoie said. "Listen, you picked out this place because you were sure no one would know you here. Relax."

"Why do both of you have to be here? I thought I was just meeting you, Mr. Curtis." Kathy leaned across the yellow table. "Then you show up with him."

"John is an investigative reporter for the *Morning Advocate,* Kathy. He needed to hear your story for himself." Glenn's expression said he was not happy to be sharing the source. But he had no choice.

"I know who he is!" Kathy hissed at him. "That's the only reason I'm still here. In fact, Mr. Savoie, since you're the reporter with clout at the *Morning Advocate,* we don't need him," she said, jerking a thumb at Glenn.

"Call me John, ma'am," the blond-haired man said with an engaging smile. "Since Mrs. Lang is so uncomfortable, maybe we should talk alone."

"Hey, hold up," Glenn protested. "This is my story—"

"Glenn, I've been developing this for nine months now.

You'll get a shot at the local angle, like I said. But I got most of what I need without you. Mrs. Lang was on my list of key people to contact anyway.''

"Yeah, but I got you the interview." Glenn thumped his chest. "Without me, you wouldn't have gotten this close to Lang." He glared at Savoie.

"Listen, you two work out your squabble another day," Kathy snapped. "Do we talk or do I walk?" She looked from one to the other.

"Glenn, come here a sec," Savoie said, tapping Glenn's arm.

When they were a few feet away, he turned his back to the booth where Kathy sat. "Listen, she's jittery enough as it is. You'll still get a piece of this. Just take off."

Glenn huffed for several seconds. "Sure. You got all the cards, like you said. What choice have I got?" He stomped out of the restaurant.

Savoie went back to the booth and sat down again. "Now let's start with what I already know . . ."

"You just got back from where?" Shaena stared at Jade with an amazed expression. She had stopped by Jade's condo right after leaving the office. "Here I'm having the usual manic Monday and you're grinning like a Cheshire cat."

"You heard right, sugar. Barbados. Three magical days with Damon." Jade dropped down on her sofa with a sigh. "A dream come true."

"You dropped everything at the last moment and flew off to Barbados? Just like that?" Shaena sat down. "I can't believe it."

"Quit looking at me all googoo-eyed like I just announced I flew to Jupiter. I can be spontaneous, too." Jade lifted her nose in the air. She popped up and went into her kitchen. "I've got some iced raspberry herbal tea."

Shaena followed her. "Fine." She took the glass and sipped from it. Still dumbfounded, she wandered back into the living room behind Jade. "Have mercy. Tell me everything. I mean *everything*."

"The hotel was beautiful and—"

"Beach view from the bedroom? King-sized bed, too, I'll bet." Shaena gulped in air at Jade's gleeful nod. "Whoa! Then what?"

"We ate at an enchanting restaurant called The Boatyard. It's on the outskirts of Bridgetown." Jade's eyes glowed at the memory of holding Damon's hand across the table, listening to the melodic steel drum band.

"Oh, skip the G-rated stuff, let's get down to the nitty-gritty. What does he like when you—"

"Shaena! That's too much in my business, girlfriend. I do not kiss and tell." Jade smirked at her over the rim of her tea glass.

"Oh, come on!"

"Forget it."

"Fine. I wasn't really interested in details anyway." Shaena affected a tone of disinterest. She relaxed against the back of the love seat.

"The reverse psychology routine is tired, baby. You're dying to hear all about it." Jade eyed her.

"Ooh, I could strangle you, Jade Pellerin." Shaena shot her a dirty look. "Just tell me this, did you do it on a secluded, lovely beach?"

"No way! You've been reading too many romance novels," Jade said with a laugh. "Those folks would have arrested us for sure."

"Another fantasy shot down. Seriously though, I think it's great that you're so happy." Shaena beamed at her. "Didn't I tell you? Giving in to the feeling doesn't always mean losing out."

"Shaena, happy doesn't begin to describe how I feel. In fact, words fail." Jade shook her head.

"And now you're back to the old grind. I assume you're going to work tomorrow." Shaena raised both eyebrows. "I mean, you haven't quit your job to run off to this island paradise forever—"

"Do I look like I've gone completely nuts? Don't answer that." Jade cut her off.

"I hate to spoil your good mood, but things are getting strange down at the department." Shaena sat up with a serious expression. She put her empty glass on the end table at her elbow.

"How do you mean?"

"Dumaine is asking all kinds of questions. Computers are being moved around, and all of a sudden none of the attorneys in legal want anything to do with writing rules for Bill Lang." Shaena ran fingers through her braids. "I don't like it one bit, Jade."

"Bill told me about Dumaine while we were in D.C. It's all routine at this point. And as for that other stuff, you're seeing conspiracies again." Jade shrugged. She went into the kitchen to get a bowl of nuts and chips.

"Brad says things are happening at higher levels, too. A lot of meetings with the purpose kept vague. He'd heard talk that there are serious questions about policies out of your office."

"Déjà vu, girl. Like I said before, there is no smoking gun. I've tracked everything, and it's all been done in compliance with rule-making procedures. I wouldn't be sitting here so cool otherwise."

Shaena took a deep breath. "Okay, this is the real reason why I wanted to talk to you away from the office. Brad swore me to secrecy, so don't repeat this or I'll deny it."

"Check, I'll swallow poison from my secret ring if they try to get it out of me," Jade said in a stage whisper.

"Will you cut that out? Word is Bill has somehow gotten lots of money from decisions made." Shaena nodded slowly as the playful expression melted from Jade's face.

"I don't believe it." Jade tried not to feel uneasy.

"Only a few real insiders are even willing to whisper this."

Several minutes of silence stretched between them as Jade chewed over this new information and Shaena chewed on several snack foods from the bowl. Bill did not seem like the underhanded type. Sure he overdid the charm sometimes, but that was just Jade's personal preference. Since Nick, men with too much polish did not appeal to her. And after all these were just rumors. Her previous boss had been tainted by false accusations that were never proven. Jade remembered the long hours working with Bill. He was truly dedicated. He could have profited in dozens of ways but did not attempt to do so. Despite the whispers, Jade was not convinced.

"Bill Lang may not be a saint, but if he was that crooked, I'd have smelled a rat by now. Since that last near fiasco, I've kept my eyes wide open, sugar." Jade went to the hall closet for her coat.

"I hope you're right, for all our sakes. Every time there's a shake up, everybody gets hit by the flying shrapnel. The good suffer with the bad."

"You're telling me? It takes forever to get even a minor contract through review since that last little scandal. You'd think these guys would learn. Reporters love to read public records." Jade gave a grunt of distaste.

"Yeah, they used to slip it by them all the time. Keep it under fifty thousand and word it just right. Throw your old frat brothers a plum contract. That way no review by the legislative auditor, contract review or the inspector general." Shaena gave a short laugh. "Gotta hand it to 'em, they're slick."

"But I'm telling you, Shaena, Bill hasn't pulled any tricks. And you know I've seen it all." Jade stood before her. The more she thought about the last few months, the better she felt.

"Like I said, I hope you're right."

"Look, I'm not going to lose my jazzed-up feeling from this weekend." Jade pushed department worries from her mind. "There is life outside that eight-story box downtown."

"There is? Why didn't somebody tell me?" Shaena cackled.

"Girl, you and Brad are both workaholics. I'll bet you'd sleep down there if they let you." Jade shook a finger at her.

"Well, we didn't exactly *sleep* on Brad's desk late one Thursday night," Shaena said with a sassy wink.

Jade's mouth flew open. "You didn't! His desk?"

"Overtime has its benefits."

"Have mercy."

"Whew! Just thinking about it makes me hungry. How about the all-you-can-eat buffet at the Red Dragon?" Shaena stood up.

"I'm with you. Boy, you are something else." Jade stopped and stared at her friend, then shook her head.

"Hey, we got caught up in the moment. Just like you and your honey. He's something else, I'll bet."

Jade's smile returned. "Yeah, Damon is the original Dr. Feelgood."

"Brad ain't no slob, either." Shaena moved her hips seductively. She hummed and snapped her fingers.

Jade belted out the words, doing her imitation of Aretha Franklin. They danced out the front door, giggling and singing off key. Still they did not fully recapture the buoyant mood left over from her Barbados weekend. Jade made a decision that she would speak to Bill about the rumors at the first opportunity. She was sure he'd heard at least some rumblings by now. Even if he had made a few poor judgments, Jade could not stand by and watch another talented black official suffer an unfair career setback. Yes, she would definitely talk to him.

Two days later Damon sat stone-faced in Eddie's office at the center. He did not like what he was hearing.

"I should have known," Damon said. He slammed a fist down on the desk. "That sleazy bum."

"Keep your voice down, man." Eddie got up and closed the door. "Anyway, it's all unsubstantiated rumors right now."

"William Jefferson Lang, III, is a rotten, lying—" Damon broke off at the look of reproof from his quiet-spoken friend. "Sorry. It's just that we need people in those high positions so much for the sake of communities like this. But what we keep getting is Bill Lang and his sort."

"I know how you feel. But like I said, this is just talk going around certain circles. My buddy that works downtown in the Medicaid office swore me to secrecy.'' Eddie watched his friend. ''What is this with you and Lang anyway?''

''Let's just say I've seen his handwork, man. Lang is a master at orchestrating shady schemes. But he always manages to escape without a scratch.''

''He'll need every ounce of skill to get out of this if it hits the fan. *If* they can trace it back to him.''

''At least the center isn't involved.'' Damon started to relax until he noticed the look on Eddie's face. ''What?''

''Uh, more bad news. Questions are being raised about the way decisions were made on several grant programs.'' Eddie held on to the arms of his chair, braced for a new outburst.

''Then we'll just show them that Gracie Center is squeaky clean.'' Damon did not raise his voice, but it was obvious he was struggling to control his temper. ''We've got to protect the at-risk teen programs we just started.''

''You might as well know it all,'' Eddie muttered. He ran a hand over his short haircut. ''The contract we have to operate our AIDS prevention program and drug programs are being criticized. It's not just the new grant.''

''That's almost one quarter of our budget. This is bad, Eddie. Really bad.'' Damon, in true fashion, began to worry about the people being served. He forgot about his anger toward Lang.

''Reverend Little is going to say 'I told you so' real quick if we lose that money.''

Damon let out a groan at the mention of the stern, young Baptist preacher. ''Over a year ago, Ted brought up that we shouldn't be so dependent on state money. And we got into a hot argument that stretched over three meetings.''

''This is my fault. I should have pursued grants from Greek organizations, the Links—and others. I've let myself get too wrapped up in the day-to-day running of this place, going from one crisis to another.'' Eddie let out a long breath.

''Don't talk nonsense. You've done an outstanding job,'' Damon said with intensity. ''You can't be everywhere at once.''

''I don't know, man. Maybe my focus should shift to being

a better administrator.'' Eddie shook his head. ''Just the thought of losing those programs because I didn't take the time to go after more money makes me sick.''

''Eddie, if you put in more time at the center, Beverly would never see you. You work late on a regular basis and come to weekend center activities. Beverly comes with the kids as much to see you as to help out,'' Damon said with a grin.

Eddie smiled at the mention of his family. ''Yeah, she's one of a kind. Bev is what makes our house a home.'' He grew grave again. ''Lots of kids don't have that, Damon. I feel like this center is a lifeline. We've got to protect it.''

''And we will, man. We will.'' Damon clenched his fist again. ''Gracie Street Center and the Heritage Foundation have over ten years of credibility in this city. Not to mention a powerhouse board backing it.''

''Like Reverend Little,'' Eddie said. ''He's not just fiery in the pulpit. He may fuss behind closed doors, but when the chips are down, he'll be behind us all the way. Still I'm going to make a few phone calls to the River City Links president, AKA, the Deltas and a few others today.''

''They can't give us the kind of money we get from those grants. We'd have to scale back, even eliminate programs.'' Damon got angry again. ''No, we have done nothing wrong, so our community center should not suffer.''

''Good. That's exactly what we'll need to say when we get dragged before a legislative committee,'' Eddie said. He seemed resigned to rough times ahead.

''Let's hope it doesn't get to that point. But if it does, we'll be ready.''

''Bev could definitely give us pointers on that score. Her courtroom skills have saved me many a day. The woman has nerves of steel—which comes in handy with our little rascals.'' Eddie laughed.

Seeing the soft light of affection on Eddie's face as he spoke of his wife made Damon think of Jade. What was her role in all of this? How much did she know? Damon silently chided himself for the small prick of suspicion. Of course she had nothing to do with Lang's crooked dealings. There was no reason to think Jade and Bill Lang were involved in wrongdoing together. None at all. Still he could not resist asking.

"Anyone else in the department mentioned in the talk you heard?" Damon tried to keep his voice neutral. "Mike Testor or . . ."

"Or Jade," Eddie finished for him. "No, at least not by name."

"What do you mean?"

"Listen, don't get yourself worked up over this. It's all DHH scuttlebutt. It could mean nothing." Eddie tried to sound convincing and failed.

"Eddie, you wouldn't waste time on gossip. Now tell me." Damon wondered if he really wanted to know even as he spoke the words.

"My friend just said that there are questions about how Lang's office has been handling things. His key people will be asked to provide explanations on some recent rules."

"And Jade is one of his key people," Damon said in a low voice. His jaw muscles worked.

Damon tried not to think of Jade and Bill Lang linked in any way. Yet they did work together. Jade would somehow be painted with same broad brush if a scandal broke.

Eddie squirmed under Damon's gaze. "Look, I wouldn't even mention this, but . . . well, it's talk and you might hear it anyway. But take it for what it's worth. I mean, people are always running their mouths."

"Tell me." Damon sat very still.

"They say Lang and Jade are extremely close. She's got a lot of power because of Lang. They work a lot of late nights and—look, man, this is all probably a bunch of garbage." Eddie tugged at his tie.

"What else have you heard?" Damon wanted to hit something. He wanted to pound the table in rage. But he pushed down the visceral reaction to Eddie's words. "Are they having an affair?"

"Supposedly that's how she got the job without much experi-

ence at such a high level. They say she's very ambitious."
Eddie tried to lessen the impact of the ugly gossip. "Look,
people are always saying things."

Damon thought of all the evenings Jade worked late, how
distracted she'd been. Was it just pressure at work, or was she
bored with him? Maybe he'd been only a welcome diversion.
And Jade herself had talked about wanting to move up to make
a difference. Could he have misjudged her? The memory of
touching her, making love to her rushed back. It was true that
nothing mattered when he was in her arms. Which meant he
could have seen what he wanted to see, not the real woman.
And she was working late tonight. No, it had to be just vicious
gossip.

"It's all lies. I know that," Damon said with force.

"Sure. Chill out. Besides, Lang may have done nothing
wrong."

"Bill Lang has always loved beating the system. I wouldn't
put anything past him." Damon felt his dislike of the man
crystallize into loathing. "If he's made even one suggestive
remark to Jade or involved her in his scams—"

"Hold on, my brother." Eddie looked worried at the menace
in his quiet assertion. "Don't go off on him before you know
he's guilty."

"Bill Lang hasn't changed one bit. Making the center lose
out is one thing—but if Jade gets dragged through the mud
because of him, he'll be very sorry. I'll make sure of that."
Damon gazed ahead with a look of cold, hard determination.

"Goodness, your new lady friend seems to be having a bit
of a problem." Marlene turned down the sound on the television
news cast. She brushed back her hair. It was cut in a new style
that made her look younger.

"Mother, the report was about the department she works
for, not Jade." Damon felt as though a tender spot had been
touched.

"She's the top assistant to Bill Lang. Seems they are very

close.'' Marlene spoke in a quiet voice. She glanced at her son then away. "Well, I'm sure it's nothing.''

"Nothing at all,'' Damon said in a strained voice. That was all he could manage.

He hated the pictures that came to mind, that had been rolling around like the reel of an old movie for the last few days. Bill and Jade. Damon saw her at odd times, but she still worked late much too often.

"You've been seeing quite a bit of her lately. Isn't that nice.'' Marlene seemed to be clairvoyant. She studied his face for a long time.

Not nearly enough was the first thought that sprang to his mind, but he was not about to voice it. "Yes, we have. Listen, is Dad around?'' Damon said to change the subject.

"Yes, I am. Hello, son.'' Oliver came in and gave Damon a pat on the back.

"How are you feeling?'' Damon was worried at the grayish tinge to his dark skin.

"Tired. I went to the store in Lafayette this morning. Gave the manager hell for letting those salespeople lounge around like they're on vacation.'' Oliver eased down into his favorite chair.

"Don't push it, Dad. Just because the doctor said—''

"The doctor advised me to keep active. Okay, that's exactly what I'm doing. Look at this.'' Oliver flexed his right hand to show the side most affected by his stroke was stronger. "I'm doing fine. You better keep an eye on Tessier.'' He pointed a finger at Damon.

"Yes, sir.'' Damon respected his father's judgment. He'd take a closer look at the store manager. "Dad, what did you think of the marketing ideas?''

"Good solid information. Son, I built my business on being able to change with the times. Go for it.'' Oliver nodded.

"Rachelle did the work for you? How wonderful. And she is looking just lovely these days,'' Marlene put in.

"Yes, those figures mean the home renovation should be on

solid ground as soon as a year from now." Damon sidestepped mentioning Rachelle directly.

"You know, she still cares a great deal for you." Marlene spoke before her husband could reply.

"Rachelle cares a great deal about Rachelle, Mother. Look, I have to go."

Damon made a quick exit before his parents could start on their old familiar theme. The last subject he wanted to explore was his ex-wife and failed marriage. For the rest of the evening, he fought hard against troubling questions about Bill Lang. And Jade.

"Told you it would be a breeze." Lang smiled at Jade.

"You were right. After three days Dumaine was satisfied with our documentation." Jade was relieved and happy. "I just wonder why he decided to investigate our section."

"Who knows? Dumaine seems to randomly select agencies to scrutinize. But since we have nothing to hide, we don't care how many documents he asks for. Right, number-one assistant?" Lang gave her a pat on the shoulder.

"You got it, chief."

"And I've got a treat as a reward for all your hard work. A trip to Hawaii."

Jade gave a short laugh. "Yeah, sure. When will the limo pick me up?" She did not bother to look up.

"I'm not kidding, Jade." Lang came to stand beside her. He held a brochure in front of her face. "See for yourself. Four days with plenty of time to see the sights."

"Oh, gee, I don't think . . ." Jade was uncomfortable with the implications of this. She took the brochure and glanced through it. "A conference on community-based care for troubled children. Who else would go?"

"Just you and I." Lang went on despite her small frown at this. "It's going to be great. Hawaii has implemented a coordinated care system across disciplines. There is single point of entry, which means the family of a child who has multiple problems only has to call one number to have all his needs addressed.''

"Sounds very interesting, but I just came from a big conference. I'm still shoveling through the paper that collected on my desk.'' Jade moved away from him.

Bill followed to stay close to her. "The conference isn't for another three weeks. June is a great month to be in Hawaii, Jade. The colors are so vibrant, and the waterfalls are magnificent.''

"Maybe some of the others should go this time. I don't want to hog all the plum trips,'' Jade said with an uneasy smile.

"The state doesn't reward the way corporate America does, Jade. It's one of the few perks you get being at this level. Take advantage of the chance.'' Bill went back to sit behind his desk. "Besides, the secretary is very interested in moving DHH toward just such a system.''

"Yes, I know.'' Jade could not deny that Dr. Chauvin had made breaking up centralized service delivery one of his priorities. "He feels strongly about placing decision making at the local level.''

"And we're expected to take a very active role in making such changes. This isn't just an excuse to hit the beach.'' Lang wore a charming smile. "Hawaii just happens to be lagniappe. Now are you feeling better about it?''

Jade felt reassured the more she thought about it. "Sure thing, boss.''

"Good.'' Bill kept his voice light. "All you have to do is pull out those island outfits you wore on Barbados.''

"Listen, Bill, about that—''

He held up a palm. "We've been over this more than once. We didn't have one problem while you were gone.''

"So you don't need me around here?'' Jade chuckled.

"Of course we do. But you've got my office so well organized, we both can be away for a few days, and the well-oiled machine keeps going.'' Bill tapped a manicured fingernail on the blotter of his desk. "Knight's business must be run just as well for him to be gone.''

"He's got great managers." Jade felt a rush of pleasure at the thought of Damon.

"Yeah, he's got one impressive set of stores. I hear he's branching out into home remodeling soon. He's a smart businessman." Bill watched her closely. "And lucky to have you."

"Thanks." Jade felt shy at the vague reference to their relationship.

"Anyway, let's get that meeting set up for Tuesday if we can. Oh, and here are some more policy changes." Bill shifted into business mode again.

Jade worked with him for another hour on a host of pressing issues that had to do with funding cuts. When Mike Testor knocked, they were finishing a memo to the managers of each of the major programs.

"Hi there, Jade." Mike ignored the sour glance his chummy greeting brought from Bill.

"Hi, Mike. How are you?" Jade gathered up her notes. She wore a friendly expression. Jade had decided he was okay, at a distance. He could not help it if he was less than charismatic.

"Fine now that I've had a breath of fresh air from a pretty lady." Mike did a bow.

"Aren't you the charmer this morning, or should I say afternoon." Jade turned to Bill. "I'm going to lunch with a friend. We'll be at Uncle Joe's if you need me."

"Don't worry, I won't interrupt a much deserved break." Bill waved her out.

"Lucky friend," Mike called after her as she went out.

"Give it a rest, Mike." Bill glared at him when the door shut. "Or *I'll* encourage her to file sexual harassment charges."

"Just being sociable, nothing more. What about your motives for being so nice to Ms. Pellerin?" Mike's dark eyebrows went up to form arches above his eyes.

"You don't know me that well." Bill pointed an index finger at him.

"Hey, don't get so wound up about it. Take it easy, Bill." Mike lifted both shoulders. "I'm sorry."

Bill sat back in his chair, but still wore a tight expression. "Well, what about the hearing?"

"Scheduled for the week of June tenth like I thought."

"Good." Bill nodded.

"Representative Roubique will ask for information on the community centers. When that hits the papers, you know what will happen."

"Certainly, advocacy groups will make plans to pack the committee room. Are you sure those centers we talked about are included?" Bill stared out the window.

"Yeah. Listen, Damon Knight will hit the roof. He'll be there for sure to tell the legislators what he thinks." Mike poured coffee into a styrofoam cup.

"Yes, indeed," Bill said. He turned his leather captain's chair around to get a full view of the state capitol building in the distance. "I'm sure he will."

Chapter 12

"Jade, Lanessa was just telling me she's got a chance at a much better job." Clarice gave Lanessa a proud look. "That's my girl."

Lanessa gave a shrug. "I need more of a challenge. I've mastered everything there is to know down in the documents section. I'm bored."

Jade sat down on the large sofa in her parents' den. She threw her purse onto the matching ottoman. "What job, Nessa?"

"In the Secretary of the State Office Archives section. They take care of important materials, some dating back to the Spanish colonial governors." Lanessa gave a sharp flick of her wrist. "Pay is right, and I will pretty much work on my own. Perfect." She leaned back and stretched.

"Sounds like it. Congratulations. When do you start?" Jade could only marvel at the way Lanessa seemed to find cushy jobs.

"Not soon enough. I told that witch all about it." Lanessa chuckled. "The look on her face was priceless." She made a face with eyes wide and her mouth hanging open.

"I thought you got along great with Jeanne—" Jade said.

"She didn't appreciate Lanessa. I always said so," Clarice broke in. "Probably scared Lanessa would get promoted ahead of her," she sniffed.

"Mama, Jeanne is not like that. Besides, she encouraged Lanessa to apply for top positions. Right, Nessa?"

Lanessa gave a snort. "At first she was okay. But she changed. For the last year, she seemed to have it in for me."

Jade wore a frown of surprise. "Really? That sure doesn't sound like the Jeanne I know."

"I think she envious of my clothes, my car. Guess when her husband dumped her she got bitter."

"I saw her a couple of months ago, and she seemed fine. We had lunch and—"

"What did she talk about?" Lanessa cut her off. She sat up straight.

"Oh, I don't know, the usual casual lunchtime chitchat. And she talked about her ex-husband as though they were on good terms. We even shared dating horror stories." Jade laughed.

Lanessa squinted at her. "So you didn't talk about me?"

"No, Lanessa. Believe it or not, we actually had other things to discuss." Jade rolled her eyes. "Talk about vain."

"Yeah, she better not have been talking about me. I would sue her for breach of employee confidentiality." Lanessa relaxed against the sofa cushions again.

"Jeanne is a professional. She wouldn't do that, Nessa." Jade stared at her older sister with an expression of puzzlement. "You're awful touchy today."

"Jade, I'd think you would take your sister's side in this. It's obvious the woman is jealous and tried to use her position to punish Lanessa."

"Mama, I'm not taking sides, for goodness' sakes. I was only . . ." Jade let her voice trail off when she saw Clarice was not listening. "Forget it," she murmured.

"Anyway, Lanessa tells me she broke up with Alex. She's on the dating scene again." Clarice sipped her hot tea. "What you need, Lanessa, is a man who can give you security."

"I'm going to really take my time this go-round, believe

me.'' Lanessa took out her compact to examine the state of her makeup.

"Too bad things didn't work out with Alex. Such a distinguished family," Clarice said.

"Well, onward and upward is what I always say." Lanessa snapped the compact shut, satisfied with the condition of her lipstick.

Clarice gave a wistful sigh. "Such a fine old family." She brightened. "Speaking of fine old families, how is Damon?"

"Great." Jade did not want to discuss her love life with Clarice at all. "We're having dinner Thursday as a matter of fact."

"Such a dashing young man. Why, he's dated all the most beautiful girls in town." Clarice raised an eyebrow. "Quite a reputation after his divorce."

"So I've heard." Jade clamped her mouth shut. Trust Clarice to remind her that Damon had his pick of glamorous women from old-money families. *But he's with me now.* Jade tried to ignore the insistent self-doubt trying to take hold as usual when in her mother's company.

"So tell me, Jade—has Damon a brother for me?" Lanessa said.

"He has a younger brother. But—"

Lanessa raised an arched eyebrow. "Hmm, how much younger?"

"Twenty-eight. And he—" Jade began.

"Hmm, six years. Not too bad. I'd love to meet him if he's even half as fine as Damon." Lanessa took on the look of a cat stalking prey.

"Don't get excited. He's deeply in love, won't even glance at another woman." Jade held up a palm.

"Humph, get real. Sugar, some of my best boyfriends were deeply in love with someone else when I met them." Lanessa winked at her.

"Damon hasn't met Lanessa, has he?" Clarice put in.

"No." Jade looked at her mother.

"Then maybe we could have a get-together so we can all

meet.'' Clarice tapped a finger against her cheek. "Yes, that would be nice. Oh, of course his brother could come.''

Jade felt a tightness in her chest. "Mother, what did you have in mind?''

"Something simple, intimate. Lanessa, you could bring that wonderful crab dip you make." Clarice grew animated.

"Mother, I buy it from the deli department of a grocery store near my house." Lanessa brushed her hair.

"He doesn't have to know that," Clarice replied. "What about a week from Saturday?" She looked at Lanessa.

"I planned to see a concert in New Orleans."

"Are you sure?" Clarice looked disappointed. "I don't want to wait too long."

Jade felt as though they had stepped into a time machine. She was fifteen years old again and Lanessa was the most popular girl in her high school class. That year, Jade had a huge crush on Ronnie Johnson. Ronnie was a track star with a dazzling smile that left girls weak. Jade almost fainted when he asked her out. They met several times at the movie theater. Then Ronnie insisted that he pick her up for their next date. The moment Ronnie stepped through the door and saw Lanessa, Jade knew their budding relationship was doomed. Clarice seemed to be an accomplice. Two weeks later a tearful Jade went to her mother for consolation. Clarice said maybe it was for the best. He was too mature for Jade, according to her. Jade flashed back to the feeling of betrayal and anger as though the incident had happened yesterday.

"Just what the hell is going on here?" Jade raised her voice over the back and forth planning of the two women.

Clarice blinked at her in shock. "Jade! What in the world . . . ?"

Lanessa's mouth formed a wide circle. "Whoa, Jade-girl, chill. You are tripping."

"Mama, why are you so hot to have Damon meet Lanessa?" Jade brushed aside their reproaches to get to the point.

"I wanted him to meet us all and—"

"He's met you and Daddy already." Jade's eyes were hard.

"But Lanessa wants to meet him . . . and his brother."

"But you really want her to meet Damon," Jade persisted.

"He's a nice, mature young man. Why shouldn't we all get together?" Clarice lifted a shoulder.

"I see. He and Lanessa ought to hit it off," Jade retorted. "She can ladle on that thick charm you're so proud of. Is that why?"

"Uh, Jade, is there a problem here?" Lanessa said.

Jade did not hear Lanessa, only Clarice pushing her aside once again. "No, I'll tell you why. You think he's a better match for Lanessa than he is for me. He's too good to be wasted on me. Right?"

"Don't be silly!" Clarice gaped at her in astonishment. "I said no such thing!"

Jade jabbed a forefinger at her. "So you want them in the same room so Lanessa can pull one of her old tricks. Like she's done to me before."

"Now hold on, I never ..." Lanessa's voice died at the withering look from Jade. "It was only a couple of times. We were kids back then!"

"You're right, Lanessa. But we're not kids now. And Damon isn't some horny teenage boy. Grow up! Both of you." Jade snatched her purse from the ottoman. "Damon won't run sniffing after you just because you wag your tail."

"Jade, really! You've gone too far, young woman." Clarice stood up.

Jade stood to face her. "Mama, I could put up with your favoritism toward Lanessa. I've always been proud of her, I even wanted to be like her. But just once you could consider me."

"I do not play favorites," Clarice protested. "That's not true," she stammered.

"Not being the center of attraction doesn't bother me. But couldn't you just once think about *my* feelings? Damon is the best thing that's ever happened to me. Instead of being happy for me, you're thinking up ways get him interested in Lanessa." Jade's voice quivered. She was fighting the urge to cry but fast losing the battle.

Lanessa reached for Jade's hand. "Listen, honey, you know I'd never try to hurt you."

Jade gazed at her. "You never mean to, Nessa. Somehow you just always think of yourself first." Lanessa pulled back from her with a stricken expression.

"Now this is too much. Jade Pellerin, don't you ever speak to me like that again!" Clarice glowered at her.

"Mama, I'm grown now."

"Well, being an adult doesn't give you the right to insult your mother," Clarice shot back. "You've got some nerve behaving like this in my house."

"Then I won't visit your house until I get the same respect and consideration you expect me to give." Jade turned to leave.

"What nerve!" Clarice followed her. She grabbed Jade's arm to stop her. "You apologize to us right now."

Several seconds of tense silence stretched between them. "Goodbye, Mama," Jade said in a quiet voice.

For the rest of the evening Jade tried to tell herself she'd done the right thing. Yet within a few minutes of closing her mother's front door behind her, all the familiar self-doubts came rushing back. Jade felt like the plain little girl again—except for the first time in her life, she had stood up to her sister and mother. Hundreds of times she had wanted to say those things to them but never found the courage. Unlike those girlhood fantasies of standing tall, she did not feel the least bit of satisfaction. She felt alone and unsure of herself. Was Clarice right? Maybe she was foolish to think Damon was serious about her. Wherever they went, attractive women did a double take as he passed by. Until now Jade had quieted her feelings of inadequacy. Could she be deceiving herself? Was she hiding from the truth like she'd done before? *Stop it. It was you Damon made love to all night. You he took to Barbados. Don't let Mama get to you the way she has all your life.* Jade spent the rest of the evening bolstering her battered self-esteem.

*   *   *

"Where the hell is he getting all this garbage?" Bill shook the newspaper in his hand. He glared at Mike, Tavis and Steve Franklin.

"Reporters are scum. They nose around like pigs in the mud then piece together half-truths to make a flashy headline. This'll blow over." Steve Franklin's flushed face was shiny with sweat. He glanced at the other two men in a plea for confirmation. He was disappointed.

"Hate to say this, Steve, but you shot off your mouth once too often." Mike smiled at him without a trace of real humor. "They mentioned your name at least twenty times."

"Why me? My company has operated in accordance with all regulations." Steve mopped his brow with a linen handkerchief. "I'm going to sue that damn paper."

"Don't waste your money, Steve." Tavis looked at him in mild disdain. "We all know everything he's said is from public record." He dismissed Steve and addressed Bill. "What bothers me is this smells of an in-depth series. It reads like a novel with an open ending."

"And the question is what comes next?" Bill stared at the newspaper as though trying to get the answer from it.

Mike shrugged. "More exposé on greedy health care providers. Then it'll die down like it's done before."

"But only after the private company suffers." Steve gulped in dismay. "They suggest we give back 2.3 million dollars at least. That would ruin us."

"Will you be quiet?" Mike said with scorn. "The department has always been willing to work with conscientious providers to arrange a reasonable payment schedule. Right, Bill—"

"Step carefully, Bill," Tavis broke in. "There's talk that Dumaine has serious questions about the last agreement we negotiated. Community Care, Inc., has paid pennies compared to the one million dollars owed. If that gets out . . ."

"He doesn't refer to any other companies by name." Bill rubbed his jaw.

Steve pointed to the newspaper. "Yeah, just me. I won't

stand idly by and be slandered. Like you said, other companies have problems and—"

"Will you shut up?" Mike spoke through clenched teeth. "Babbling on like an idiot is what got you in this fix. Let's keep Community Care out of this."

"You'll give this reporter more reason to dig deeper. And you do not want him to get on that particular trail." Tavis eyed him steadily. "You'll have a lot more to worry about than unpleasant press."

Bill dropped the newspaper onto his desk. "Let's not get carried away. This is only one article. No need to imagine all kinds of disasters at this point. We've taken measures to be within all regulations."

"Smooth." Mike wore a wily grin. "No need to mention how the regulations have been . . . molded." He gazed at Bill with admiration. "You'll do nicely when that reporter finally calls for a statement."

"He already has. We meet Friday. He's coming here." Bill did not show one bit of concern. "The more I think about it, this may be an opportunity to wring some advantage out of this."

Steve Franklin hopped from his chair with a look of horror. "What are you planning? You can't just throw me to the wolves like this. I know what you're going to do: lay all the blame on me."

"Get a grip, Steve," Bill snapped at him. He turned his back to the still shaky man. "Mike, have Errol in communications come down here. We're going to have a nice string of press releases over the next two to three weeks."

"Press releases on what?" Mike wore a puzzled expression, his brows drawn together.

"Our efforts at AIDS prevention, changes to improve health care for infants in low-income families, how much money we saved with rule changes—to name a few subjects." Bill smiled at him.

"Very good." Tavis gave an appreciative nod.

"John Savoie is one reporter who won't be sidetracked by that," Mike said.

"Dumaine is satisfied. I'll be sure to bring that up to him. We need lots of good press as a cushion just in case." Bill appeared relaxed now. He brushed a hand across the newspaper still on his desk. "If he is working up to criticizing the department, we'll need it. Especially with the legislative session coming up."

"Excellent," Tavis said. "You can't stop him, but you can dilute the negative impact. By the way, I've got that information you wanted on—"

"Good, stay here." Bill stood up and took Franklin's elbow. He guided him to the door. "Steve, relax. Everything will be fine."

"This is serious, Bill. Two other reporters have called my office for quotes," Franklin blurted out.

"You did well saying you would work to correct any problems. Mike, set up a meeting with Errol for this afternoon." Bill opened the door as an obvious invitation for the two men to leave.

"Sure." Mike walked slowly past Tavis. He raised an eyebrow at him then glanced at Bill. "You need me to come back?"

"No, I'll see you later." Bill shut the door on them. "Well?"

"Oliver Knight had some very good friends in high places. Still does to some extent." Tavis examined his designer tie. "The bid process was suspended quite a few times. He's installed carpet in over fifteen state offices in the last twenty years at considerable profit."

"Tsk, tsk. Damon won't be so quick to join the chorus of criticism when we let him know his father could get burned. But . . ." Bill formed a steeple with his long fingers.

Tavis studied him for several seconds. "What are you up to now?"

Bill leaned forward. "Jade might find it interesting. Let her see that Damon Knight isn't Mr. Clean."

"Remember, he has influence independent of his father. Damon Knight is no pushover, Bill. Neither is his family."

"You should know about the Knight family." Bill's lips curved up.

Tavis assumed a blank look. "Should I?"

"Don't bother with the innocent act, Tavis. You've been doing Marlene Knight for the last nine months at least."

"Eleven, but who's counting."

"Talk about living dangerously. Oliver Knight may be sick, but he's no fool. And he most certainly does have powerful buddies." Bill rocked back in his chair to gaze at Tavis. "Hope you know what you're doing."

"I never start anything without knowing exactly what I'm doing, brother." Tavis stood up. "Someone I know will make sure the press gets that information."

Bill looked satisfied. "Just make sure it's published in the next few days."

"Rachelle, I've got to admit I'm impressed." Damon looked at the colorful sketches in the presentation folder. "And with our expansion, we really do need to update our marketing strategy." He had barely touched the plate of broiled fish in front of him.

"Of course, sugar. Knight and Sons has to establish its own niche in the marketplace. These figures show just where your customers are and how we can best appeal to them." Rachelle moved closer to him. "Look on page eleven."

"Yes, that sounds like a great idea." Damon's thoughts raced ahead to the wider implications. "Bereniece Howard could do interior decorating consultations. I've done a little work with her before."

"The number of upper-class folks, especially African-American, is on the increase in Baton Rouge. They've got the disposable income to spend on their homes. Especially all those aspiring society women who host club meetings in their homes." Rachelle winked at him.

Damon put down the proposal and started on his lunch. "Rachelle, I have a confession. I didn't take you seriously about doing market research and a plan for Knight and Sons."

"I'm always serious about making money, sugar. Always." Rachelle took a sip of diet cola.

"Don't I know it. I went through a divorce settlement with you, remember?" Damon said, one dark eyebrow raised.

"Now, now. Let's not go there." Rachelle chuckled. "Truth is, my uncle saw the possibilities, but he was afraid to approach you."

"I don't have any reason to be angry at him."

"Exactly what I told him. Anyway, I'm going to start on this for you right away." Rachelle lifted her hands in the air.

"Perfect. This lunch didn't turn out at all the way I expected." Damon looked at her with an amused gleam in his eye. "This has been a surprising afternoon."

Rachelle dabbed the corners of mouth with a cloth napkin. Her lips were painted with a creamy red lipstick that perfectly matched her outfit. "You have no idea how surprising, sugar. No idea."

"Jade, sweetheart." Nick tried to kiss her cheek. He beamed a forgiving smile when Jade put a restraining hand on his chest.

"Make this fast, Nick." Jade sat down at the table. The lunchtime crowd in LeBlanc's downtown was thick as usual. She'd agreed to see Nick only because the restaurant was near her office—and he'd said something about needing her signature on some papers. "What about the duplex apartments?"

"Well, you know my lawyer says after sorting through the tangle ... By the way your lady lawyer is one clever legal detective." Nick did not seem at all angry.

"I'll tell her of your deep admiration," Jade retorted. She wondered where he was going with this. "Why couldn't I just sign the papers at Bevry's office? We didn't need to meet." She gave him a sour look.

"I asked Kevin not to mail them." Nick stopped while they ordered lunch from the young waitress. "I wanted to see you."

"I can't imagine why, Nick." Jade was on guard. "If you think I'm going to take less money for the sale—"

"No, no. I have no intention of fighting you on this." Nick smiled at her again.

"Then why are we here?"

Nick grew serious. "Seeing you the other night made me realize how much I've missed you. We—"

Jade's sharp laugh cut him off. She crossed her arms. "You've got to be kidding. After all this time, you can't really believe your boyish charm will work on me. You haven't exactly been lonesome from what I could see."

"Sure, I've been dating—but nothing serious. Not since you." Nick assumed a sincere look.

Jade picked up her purse from the empty chair next to her. "Nick, I'm going to do you one last favor. I'm not going to let you waste your valuable time on a *lost cause.*"

He rested a hand on her arm. "Wait, don't go. I want us to be friends at least. We've known each other since we were little kids. We were best pals long before we got married. We could be again."

"How long have you been having these hallucinations, dear?" Jade used two fingers to lift his hand from her arm.

"Look, I made a terrible mistake. But couldn't we put that behind us now after all this time? Do you hate me that much?" Nick started to touch her again then thought better of it after the look she gave him.

"Nick, I don't hate you. Matter of fact I'm not even angry anymore. I was as much at fault. I jumped into marrying you as a way to feel good about myself. You only let me believe the fantasy I wanted to believe."

Jade knew it was true. Nick was there to give her all the attention she'd missed at home. He said what she needed to hear. Because of her hunger for affection, she had closed her eyes to his true nature.

"I guess we've both grown over the years. To tell you the

truth, I'm burned out on all those empty relationships. A warm body next to me just isn't enough anymore."

"Oh, really? What bolt of lightning completely changed your personality?" Jade shot him a cynical look.

"Since my mother died, I realized there was not one other woman I cared enough about to share how I really feel about things." Nick stared off with a thoughtful expression.

"Yeah, I was really sorry about Miss Telma." Jade now felt like a heel for being so flip with him. Though she thought Nick walked on water, his mother had always been kind to Jade. Jade had gone to the wake services but stayed in the background. "She was a sweet lady."

"She really liked you, too." Nick gazed at her with fondness. "So can't we let all that old history go and learn how to be buddies again?" Nick put a hand on the back of her chair. "Come on."

Jade did find that Nick seemed different somehow. Losing his mother could well have forced him to look at his life. But still his treatment of her could not be so easily forgotten.

"Nick, I have no animosity left toward you, but we can't go back to where we were before."

"That's a given, Jade. Time has changed us both. But we can be friends on a whole new basis of mutual respect for who we are now."

"I guess so." Jade could see no reason not to be cordial to him.

"Well, just think about it." Nick seemed relaxed already in his new role as friend. "Besides, we'll see each other again."

"Now wait a minute. I never said that." Jade scowled at him.

"We'll be business partners so to speak. We could make a good deal of money on the sale of this property to an industrial complex." Nick took an envelope out of his inside jacket pocket.

"I'll get my check and that will be the end of it, Nick. No more business." Jade was curious despite her distrust of Nick's motives.

"My uncle and I want to lease part of the property at a greater profit. And we can have an interest in the other businesses who want to locate on it."

Nick launched into a description of the possibilities. Jade listened carefully, interrupting often to ask questions. She was definitely impressed with the proposition.

"Okay, get the legal documents to Bevry, and I'll get back to you after talking to her." Jade took a final bite of her shrimp remoulade.

"Good." Nick watched her for a few seconds, a smile on his face. "This was really nice. Unfortunately I've got to leave—a charity committee meeting . . . Say, isn't that your friend Damon Knight? And that's Rachelle Knight with him." Nick glanced at her sharply. "She's still a knockout."

Jade followed his gaze to see Damon throw back his head to laugh at something Rachelle said. "Yes, she is."

Rachelle was dressed in a brick red power suit trimmed in navy and a crisp white shirt underneath. Her brown hair was twisted up in a french roll. Jade compared herself to the elegant woman standing next to Damon. If Rachelle was back in Damon's life, Jade would be no match for her. That little green-eyed monster called jealousy pounced at the sight of his arm on Rachelle's.

"They were a hot couple at one time. Man, he was crazy about her." Nick cleared his throat. "You still seeing him?" He put just a touch of doubt in his tone as he darted a glance at Jade then back at the laughing pair. They'd paused to talk to a group of businessmen eating lunch.

"Yes, I am." Jade tried to sound casual. "He's probably just being nice. I mean, you and I are having lunch."

"I'm sure you're right. Gossip doesn't mean a thing. What's that old saying? 'Believe half of what you see and none of what you hear'." Nick went back to eating his pasta with crabmeat.

"What gossip?" Jade said sharply.

"Well, they've been seen together a couple of times. People are saying maybe they plan to reconcile. Now I know better since you two are still together, right?'' Nick shrugged. ''Obviously my sister and her friends are dead wrong.''

''Obviously.''

Jade's lunch seemed to be congealing in the pit of her stomach. She struggled to conceal her shock at seeing Damon with Rachelle. But she knew Nick well enough to know he was not fooled. His comment about the gossip was too perfectly timed. Yet even as she felt sure Nick was manipulating the situation to his advantage, Jade could not help but wonder how much was true.

''I don't mean to sound sexist, but women talk too much. Felicia said—''

Jade stood up. She did not care to hear what his sister had to say. ''Nick, I've got to get back to the office.''

''Sure, babe. I'll get the check. You go on.'' Nick took his napkin from his lap then stood also. ''Let's get together again. I enjoyed myself very much.''

''Thank you, Nick. Goodbye.'' Jade left without meeting his gaze.

''Goodbye, Jade. I'll be seeing you.'' Nick sat back down with a smug expression. ''Real soon.''

Chapter 13

"Hey, what's the emergency?" Shaena hurried inside Jade's apartment and looked around. "You sick?"

"No emergency. I've got some herbal tea brewing." Jade went into the kitchen.

"Say what? You called me in the middle of one of my favorite *Get Christy Love* reruns, tell me you really need to talk to me and then offer me a cup of herbal tea." Shaena put both hands on her hips. "Girl, please. I'm going to have to hurt you."

"And I baked some angel food cake muffins. A perfect low-fat, low-calorie treat." Jade did not seem to hear her. She was too busy darting around gathering cups, saucers and napkins. "Go sit down."

"Oh-oh, you've been baking. This *is* an emergency. Who died?" Shaena said in a hushed voice.

"Nobody has died. I just wanted to talk."

"Jade, quit stalling." Shaena snatched a stack of napkins Jade was about to stuff into a holder on her counter. "Give it up." She sat down on one of the breakfast stools and pulled Jade down on the one next to her.

"Our tea is getting cold." Jade reached for the steaming cups.

"No, it's not." Shaena slapped her hand. "Start talking."

"Damon's leaving me," Jade blurted out. "It's over."

"Oh, honey, I'm so sorry. When did he tell you?" Shaena shoved a muffin in front of Jade then patted her back.

"Well, he hasn't. Not directly." Jade drew in a ragged breath.

"Damon is leaving you," Shaena said.

"Yes." Jade bit her lip.

"But he hasn't told you yet."

"Right."

"I'm missing something here." Shaena blinked rapidly. "Let's start again."

"I saw Damon with his ex-wife. They were having lunch. More than that, they were having a good time." Jade could see Damon's hand on Rachelle's back. "A real good time."

"Well, that might not mean a thing. Maybe they had some kind of business," Shaena offered.

"The thing is, now I'm beginning to think I've seen only what I wanted to see in him. No man has made me feel as special as Damon." Jade knew this was an understatement. Damon touched her like no one else.

"Damon made you glow all over, honey. See? Just saying his name has you lit up."

"Maybe he's just a better class of player than the rest."

Shaena propped an elbow on the countertop. "I can think of a dozen completely innocent reasons for them to have been together. Did you speak to them?"

"No. Nick was with me, and I didn't want to give him any more satisfaction. He was gloating enough as it was." Jade groaned. "He pointed them out to me."

"So you were with your ex-husband, but of course you're above suspicion." Shaena crossed her arms.

"You didn't see the look of pain in Damon's eyes when he talked about Rachelle. Or the way he smiled at her when I saw them today." Jade felt a hollow sadness. "Everybody talks about how in love they were. Even Damon said so."

"And you and I know even 'solid as a rock' love affairs end. Look, you don't need to talk to me. You should be talking to Damon." Shaena pointed to the cordless telephone. "Call him."

"And say what?"

"Hello is a nice start." Shaena got up.

"That's your wise advice? Shaena, you've got to help me think of what to say. Why do you think I got you over here?" Jade pleaded.

"Oh, no." Shaena shook her head. "You don't want my help. Somehow I always end up with a blunt object in my hand."

"Don't you dare walk out on me, Shaena Greene." Jade advanced to block her exit.

"Look, when it comes to men suspected of lying, I go a little nuts. I have these awful flashbacks, sorta like druggies get from old LSD trips that turned bad." Shaena backed away from her. "Just let me know how it turns out."

"Thanks a lot." Jade looked forlorn.

Shaena put both hands on her shoulders. "Jade, if you want this to work, then you've got to be up front with him. Don't stew about it. If he's lying, you'll find out. We've both been there before."

"That's what I'm afraid of, Shaena—that I'll hear the famil-iar false note in his denial. The 'Oh, come on, baby, you know I wouldn't do that' line."

"Damon doesn't impress me as the type to put on such a sleazy act," Shaena said.

"We've both been wrong before. Spectacularly wrong," Jade said with a grimace.

"You're judging him based on your experience with Nick. Don't make up your mind before you talk to him. Otherwise, it won't be a conversation but an inquisition." Shaena spoke in a logical tone.

Jade raked her hair with her fingers. "This is the reason I didn't want to fall in love. You're always one step away from misery."

"And a heartbeat from heaven. Love brings a lot of happiness, too," Shaena said in a soft, sympathetic voice.

"I know," Jade murmured.

"I meant what I said. You call me anytime." Shaena gave her a hug.

"Thanks, Shaena." Jade held her tight for a second before letting her go. "Even if you are deserting me in my time of need."

"Don't give me that bull, call him." Shaena pointed to the telephone. "Goodbye."

"Yeah, yeah. Call him." Jade stared at the phone as though it were a coiled snake she was afraid to touch.

Damon sat drumming his fingers on the dark green tablecloth. As usual, Ethel's was packed. The unassuming little soul food restaurant was an institution in the city. Strong, delectable smells of jambalaya, corn bread and fried chicken filled the air. A strong contingent of Southern University students and professors, here for the good prices as well as the good food, made up a large portion of the chattering crowd. But Damon did not notice the enticing scents. He waved at friends with a distracted smile.

"Well, this place brings back memories." Bill shook his hand and sat down. "How are you? Whew, food still looks good." He waved to the tall, stately owner, Ethel's granddaughter, behind the counter. "Hey, Rose, you looking good, cher."

Rose beamed at them as she approached. "Well, how you doin', Mr. Big? Damon, I love how my new tile looks. Your workers did a fine job. You boys keeping outta trouble, I hope." She winked at them.

"Yes, indeed." Bill winked back. "Haven't we always?"

Rose threw back her head to laugh out loud. "You devil, ain't changed one bit." She called out to a young waitress to take their orders before she went back to work.

Bill took a long drink of iced tea. "So I hope things at the center are going well. That grant should help a lot."

"Yes, it does. In fact that's the reason I wanted to talk to you." Damon sat forward.

"Away from the office and prying eyes? What is this about, Damon?" Bill did not seem upset, merely curious. He also had the demeanor of a man humoring an old acquaintance.

"I know you're very busy," was Damon's only reply by way of an apology. "About the hearing coming up, what's the real story?"

"Nothing to worry about. With the new administration, every project or program is under scrutiny. We'll give them the information they want, and that will be the end of it."

"But Dumaine is asking all kinds of questions."

"Which were answered to his satisfaction. Listen, if that's your only concern, then we can have a pleasant lunch."

"Bill, there are persistent rumors about impropriety in the way certain programs and funds are being administered. Now if Dumaine is satisfied, why am I going to a Senate hearing before the Health and Welfare Committee?"

"Oh, that. These things are routine in preparation for the legislative session. You should know that." Bill maintained his relaxed posture. He toyed with his dinner fork.

"Except that these whispers won't go away, Bill." Damon struggled to hold on to his temper. This condescending attitude was wearing his patience thin. "I've seen more than one huge scandal start with one whisper about something being out of place. Now level with me." His brown eyes bored into Bill.

Bill heaved a sigh as though indulging him. "All right. There have been a few questions on how we've administered some funds, questions that they haven't been put to good use." He returned Damon's gaze with a slight smile. "But Jade and I worked hard to prepare evidence to show otherwise."

"Then you have a paper trail." Damon stiffened at the mention of Jade but chose to ignore Bill's reference to their late nights. "And you use the word evidence like you expect to go on trial."

"Bad choice of words. Let's call it documentation." Bill's good humor slipped a notch under the persistent questioning.

"Jade has done an excellent job of putting together information for me. She's meticulous, best assistant I've ever had. With her by my side, I can't go wrong. With her ability and ambition, she'll go far."

Damon wanted to smash his fist into Bill's face. He was shocked at his strong reaction. The man had a right to praise his employee. But was there an undertone of something more in his words?

"Yes, Jade is good at what she does," Damon said.

"The best." Bill smiled at him.

Damon bit off a sharp reply when the waitress brought them steaming plates of food. Bill tasted a forkful of his red beans and praised them to the waitress. She blushed then bustled off a happy woman. But Damon did not notice the spicy aroma of fried catfish that usually tempted him. A female voice made them both look up.

"My goodness, what a small world." Kathy stood in front of Bill. She gave him a sour glance before turning her attention to Damon.

"Kathy, this is Damon Knight. He—"

"So nice to meet you." She flashed a smile that faded quickly when she looked at her husband again. "So can I expect you home this evening, or does your lovely assistant require attention again tonight?"

"My wife," Bill said to Damon with a look of resignation. "Kathy, let's not go there again. Yes, I may have to work late."

"Oh, the job benefits that come with being high in state government." Kathy's face clouded over. "This is getting old, Bill. I won't stand for it."

Damon sat stunned by her veiled accusation. He was sickened by them both. "Maybe I should just leave."

"No, Mr. Knight. I don't want to interrupt *real* business." Kathy stared at Bill hard. "I'll expect to see you this evening at a reasonable hour—to talk about a certain newspaper article."

"The one that came out? I've seen it, Kathy. It's nothing serious." Bill relaxed again.

"No, the one that *will be coming out soon.*" Kathy grinned at the startled look that flickered across his face. She gave a slight nod. "No later than six, my darling. Enjoy your lunch."

Both men sat for several minutes of tense silence after her departure. Damon stared at Bill, who sat blinking rapidly, his gaze darting around the restaurant.

"I, uh, listen . . . is that all you wanted to talk to me about?" Bill rubbed his jaw with a nervous jerky motion. He glanced at his watch. "I've really got to get back to the office." His food was untouched.

"Sure." Damon wanted the man gone from his sight before he did something foolish.

After Bill left, Damon sat trying to convince himself not to come to the obvious conclusions. Jade was very ambitious, this he knew. Had he fallen for the wrong woman again? He thought of the way her eyes sparkled when she laughed. Was that special look only for him? Or was she a clever actress like his ex-wife, like his mother? Damon gave up trying to eat after a few minutes. Bill Lang was an accomplished liar. Why should he believe anything the man said or even implied? But then there was his jealous wife. Damon felt as though needles were sticking him with each question that popped into his head. There was only one way to get rid of them, he knew. Somehow he must approach the subject, or it would eat away at the trust between them like acid.

"Hello, Jade." Alex sat down across from her.

"Gee, Alex, did I say you could join me?" Jade shot him a venomous look. He'd interrupted her thoughts of Damon—Damon and his leering smile at Rachelle, at least that's how Jade now thought of it. The last thing she wanted was to look at another man with a penchant for hurting women.

"I knew you'd say no. I really need to talk to you." Alex did not give any indication that he would leave.

"Alex, we don't have anything to discuss." Jade was reassured only somewhat by the fact that they were in a public place.

Since the night that she'd walked in on his terrible fight with Lanessa, Jade had nothing good to say about him. Alex St. Romaine was tall, attractive though not handsome in the usual sense. He dressed in conservative dark colors. Sitting across from Jade in a booth at Uncle Joe's, he seemed the exact opposite of the violent man she'd seen at Lanessa's house. True, she and Lanessa were not on the best terms these days, but that did not cool her anger toward Alex. Lanessa was still her sister.

"Thanks for coming. Listen, Jade, about that night at Lanessa's—" Alex did not meet her gaze.

"Don't tell me—it wasn't what I thought it was," Jade cut in.

Alex leaned forward. "No, it wasn't. I have never raised my hand to hit any woman. I certainly would never hurt Lanessa."

"Her furniture knocked over was a figment of my imagination, I guess. Or did a strong wind sweep down the chimney?" Jade folded her arms across her chest and sat back to be as far away from him as possible.

"That was clumsiness—not because I attacked Lanessa. Listen to me, did she have any bruises or say I'd hit her?"

"I didn't see any bruises. But then I didn't strip her down. And of course she'd deny it if she was scared enough." Jade bristled. "Surely you don't expect me to buy that?"

"Jade, listen to me. Lanessa is . . . She needs help." Alex stopped when the waitress came up to take their orders for soft drinks.

"Lanessa needs help? This is too much! I walk in on you knocking my sister around and *she* needs help?" Jade fought to keep her voice down.

"Jade, I—" Alex blinked as though her words were blows to his face.

"The only help she needed was out of an abusive relationship. Now that she's dumped you, that problem is solved." Jade stabbed a finger at him.

Alex shook his head slowly. "I broke off with Lanessa when she wouldn't listen to reason and get help."

"Bull. Lanessa got fed up with being used as a punching bag. You couldn't stand not being in control."

"Shut up and listen to me. I've never hit Lanessa, damn it! We were arguing because your sister is an alcoholic. I've been trying for the last year to get her into treatment. She won't admit to having a problem." Alex spoke in an burst of angry frustration, his voice rising with each word. Then he realized diners around them were staring. "I'm sorry. It's just I've been going crazy for a long time, trying to find a way to help her."

"That's a lie," Jade said in a quiet voice. Her throat went dry.

"You've suspected something was wrong. I can tell by the expression on your face." Alex regarded her with a steady gaze. "Admit it."

"I've never seen Lanessa drunk. She has a drink in the evening, but . . ." Jade remembered how Lanessa seemed never to be far away from a bottle of alcohol. But she shook off the label Alex was trying to put on her older sister. "No, Lanessa has her problems but being a drunk isn't one."

"Jade, Lanessa hides how much she drinks. She keeps a bottle in her bedroom. Sure she doesn't stagger around, but not every alcoholic reacts the same way. That's a widely held misconception."

"But Lanessa goes to work every day." Jade shook her head. "She's careful about her appearance. If what you say is true, she wouldn't do those things."

"Lanessa is a well-functioning alcoholic. She's so far been able to maintain some semblance of a normal life on the surface. But she's sliding down. That's why we were arguing." Alex stopped talking and seemed reluctant now to go on.

"What are you talking about?"

"She's always in debt. Have you ever wondered why she has to work when her last divorce settlement was so generous? Lanessa is doing a juggling act with all her bills. I've loaned her money several times in the last year alone." Alex took a sip of cola.

"This doesn't make sense. Lanessa is always dressed nice and shops at the best stores." Jade did not like the cold lump forming in her stomach.

"She's shopping on credit, usually mine. I want her to have nice things, but not so more of her money can be spent on drugs." Alex rubbed his eyes.

"Drugs? Now wait a minute, you said—" Jade sat bolt straight with alarm.

"Alcohol is a drug, Jade. But about three months ago, I found out she's been taking prescription drugs. She goes from one doctor to the next, trying to get them to give her refills." Alex's light brown eyes were filled with apprehension. "But doctors these days are alert to what they call drug-seeking behavior. I'm afraid she's going to connect with street dealers next."

Jade felt as though the room was twirling around her. How could this be? Lanessa was always so cool, so in control. She had beauty, brains and charm. Using drugs was an escape. But why would Lanessa Pellerin Hampton Thomas, a woman envied by other females most of her life, need the kind of escape drugs provided?

"You're just trying to make Nessa look bad in case we file charges against you," Jade said, grasping at straws.

"Then why would I risk more trouble by seeing you? Look, do what you have to. But don't keep hiding from the truth." Alex gripped his glass, tense with the effort of trying to convince her.

"I'm going to talk to Lanessa about this," Jade said.

"Fine. Let me tell you exactly what's going to happen. I should know, I've been through this with her at least a hundred times or more."

Jade did not want to hear the awful things Alex was saying about her sister. Yet his words were like missing pieces of an elusive jigsaw puzzle. A picture was forming that scared her. The last times she'd been with Lanessa, she noticed a kind of stretched tight quality to her behavior. Her laughter had a note of threatening hysteria. Lanessa did not so much seem happy as she seemed busy being happy. Her anger of two weeks before evaporated in the face of such a terrible threat to her sister. With her stomaching churning, Jade left the restaurant and headed straight for Lanessa's house. A strange car was parked in the double driveway. Jade went to the front door and rang the bell. A young man wearing a gold necklace answered.

"Hey, baby. What's up?" He looked at Jade in a suggestive way. "O-wee, come on in even if you at the wrong house."

"I'm looking for my sister." Jade wanted to knock that silly leering grin from his face. "Where is she?"

"Come on in, baby girl." He stepped back just enough to let her pass, but so that she had to brush against him as she did so. "Ump, ump. Sweet stuff."

"Jade, what are you doing here?" Lanessa was still dressed in a suit from the office. "Uh, this is Malik."

"Jade, huh? Fine name for a fine honey." Malik bobbed his head up and down.

Lanessa smoothed down her wrinkled blouse. "Malik, thanks for coming by. I'll talk to you later." She could not keep her hands still.

Malik seemed about to protest, then shrugged. "Okay. I got places to be anyway. See ya, Lanessa." He gave her a half smile that was not pleasant to see. "You know how to get in touch with me if you need to."

Jade watched him saunter out with the bravado of a young turk who owns the world. After locking the door behind him, she turned to Lanessa with both eyebrows raised. "Who was that?"

Lanessa's glance slid sideways. She picked up a bottle of vodka and poured it into a glass with grapefruit juice. "A friend of mine. We met at a party."

"You met *him* at a party given by one of your friends? Which one?"

"Uh, Verise I think. Or maybe Rodney. Oh, I don't remember." Lanessa took a long drink.

"He sure doesn't look like anyone your upscale pals would invite to their homes. Looks like a character from one of those gangsta rap videos." Jade put down her purse and walked over to sit beside Lanessa at the bar. "He seems kind of young."

"What is this anyway? One minute you're not speaking to me, next thing it's the third degree. You act like I've got to explain my social life to you. Well, I don't." Lanessa banged the glass down. She got up from the sofa to pace in front of the fireplace.

"I'm just curious because he's very different from the other people you hang with, that's all. Lanessa, come back and sit down." Jade did not want to start an argument. "Please."

"Mother sent you over here to spy on me, that it?" Lanessa shook a cigarette from a crumpled pack.

Jade took it from her. "Lanessa, you promised to quit after that last bout of bronchitis."

Lanessa threw the empty package to the floor. "Look, you want to mother somebody, adopt. I'm grown, and I don't need another mother—especially not with the one I've already got."

"I can't believe you're talking like this." Jade was surprised at the bitterness in her voice. "Did you and Mama have a fight?"

"I'm tired of her pushing me. What clothes to wear, what makeup to use, how to style my hair, what men to flirt with . . . all so she can brag and play the socialite bourgeois mother. I'm sick of it." Lanessa jumped up again. She swung her arms wildly as she spoke. "And I don't need you to ride me, either."

Jade could not believe her ears. "Lanessa, Mama just wants the best for you." She could not think of more to say, so shocked to hear Lanessa express such resentment against their mother. "I mean, you were always so close. You both love the same kind of fashions, the same kind of parties. I was always the one reading books and trying not to be noticed."

"Lucky you. At least she left you alone." Lanessa barked a bitter laugh. "How I envied you. No pressure to perform."

"Nessa, I had no idea you felt this way. All these years . . ."

Jade wrestled with this astonishing new view of their early family life.

"Oh, don't give me that. You loved being the one with brains, always showing off your latest triumph in academia. You know what one guy told me? 'That's what I like about you, Lanessa, you're uncomplicated.' Dumb is what he meant." Lanessa opened a drawer in the coffee table to pull out a fancy box filled with cigarettes. She threw Jade a defiant glare. "Well, I don't give a damn. I've done fine for myself. I'm not so dumb I couldn't get great divorce settlements."

"I have never, ever thought of you as being dumb."

"Yeah, yeah. You with the big job. I'll be lucky if I can keep being a glorified file clerk with that witch on my case." Lanessa was not listening to Jade. She was too intent on her own inner voices. "To hell with her anyway. I'm going to get that property Mr. Gerald Maxwell Thomas, IV tried so hard to snatch back." She cackled with glee.

"Nessa, tell me what's going on with your boss." Jade tried to get control of the conversation. "Wait a minute, I thought you got a new better job?"

"Jeanne told them a bunch of lies. By the time I got to the second interview—"

"You told Mama and I you had the job, almost wrapped up," Jade broke in.

"I did, almost. I mean all they had to do was check my references. I really busted butt to follow her stupid rules, and still Jeanne slammed me." Lanessa switched back to a bitter tone.

"Oh, Lanessa."

"I'll tell her to stuff that lousy job. Then I'll be living it up." Lanessa ground out her cigarette but reached for another immediately. "Maybe I'll go to Vegas for a little vacation." Lanessa spoke rapid fire, punctuating her words with hand gestures.

"Nessa—"

"My lawyer says that property has doubled in value in the last ten years. Gerald is already backing down because he knows I'll win." Lanessa looked pleased with herself. "Yeah, I'm going to get a nice income. Plus I own land out in West Feliciana with sand and gravel a company wants to dredge. So I don't have to put up with her crap."

Jade wanted a way to avoid confronting her older sister. Maybe this was not the right time. She watched Lanessa continue her harangue of injustices done to her. Even as part of her wanted to avoid a painful subject, just watching Lanessa confirmed her worst fears that Alex was right.

Jade grabbed Lanessa's arm to get her attention. "Lanessa, hush for just one minute. I need to talk to you about something."

Lanessa sat in a limp posture, leaning back now. She seemed to have wound down after ventilating. "Sure, sure. Hey, you oughta go with me to Houston for a shopping trip."

"Lanessa, listen to me. Alex talked to me today about your drinking and the pills you've been taking." Jade steadied herself for an explosion.

"Alex talked to you." Lanessa sat very still. Her eyes glittered with anger. "You and Alex got together. So how long have you two been sneaking around?"

"You can't be serious!" Jade's mouth dropped open in shock. This was the last thing she'd expected.

"Sure. He's one fine man, gotta give him that. And you've been hot for him since you were fifteen years old."

Jade took a deep breath. "Lanessa—"

"Go on, admit it. It's payback time, huh? For all those boyfriends of yours I stole." Lanessa sat straight now. Her voice was dry and rough.

"This is crazy, Lanessa. Alex loves you. He's worried sick." Jade regretted the harsh things she'd said to him. It was now clear just how much Alex loved her sister. He alone had tried to pull her back from self-destruction. "And so am I. Lanessa, you're addicted and you've got to get help."

"Get out." Lanessa stood over her with balled fists.

"Lanessa, please. Let's talk about this calmly. I'll go with you to the first appointment. You need to see a substance abuse counselor. I'm sure the department has a list of the best African-

American therapists in Baton Rouge.'' Jade stood to face her. She placed a hand on her shoulder. ''Honey, we'll be here for you. Alex, Mama, Daddy and me.''

''How sweet of you to have my welfare at heart.'' Lanessa jerked away from her. ''All ready to have me checked into some hellhole to dry out. My how comforting to know you'll be there on visiting days.''

Jade ignored her sarcasm. ''Nessa, we don't know what the first recommendations will be. It could be outpatient treatment. I've toured several hospital programs. Even our state facilities are top rated.''

''You've gone so far as to look at hospitals!'' Lanessa screamed.

''As part of my job, Nessa. It had nothing to do with you.''

Lanessa gave a loud grunt. ''You're lying, Jade. You've been plotting all along—listening to Alex's outrageous stories. He only wants to make himself look good to you.''

''Okay, Lanessa, you want the truth?'' Jade shouted at her, her frayed nerves giving way. ''I didn't even suspect, didn't have one clue that you were addicted. I was wrapped up in seeing what you wanted me and the rest of the world to see.''

''I am not addicted to anything. I drink because I want to. When I decide to stop, I will.''

A crystal clear realization flashed into Jade's mind. ''Then why didn't you quit for Alex? Why? Don't tell me you don't care about him. After all this time, I think you finally realize he's the one man who's loved you for who you are, not what you look like or what you own.'' She lowered her voice. ''He didn't want to leave, Nessa.''

''You have no right to say these things to me. No right.'' Lanessa's voice broke.

''Lanessa, let's face this together.'' Jade took a step toward her.

''You don't get it. There is nothing to face.''

''Then going in for an assessment won't hurt, will it? Let's make an appointment now.'' Jade went to get the phone book.

''No! I've put up with your self-righteous attitude long

enough. Who the hell do you think you are anyway? I don't
have a problem with alcohol, my prescriptions are for migraine
headaches.'' Lanessa snatched the phone book from Jade's
hands. ''Now leave.''

''Nessa, stop hiding from the truth.'' Jade could see that she
had failed to reach her sister. The elegant cocksure Lanessa,
her facade of control in place again, was back.

''Jade, it's past your bedtime.'' Lanessa lit a cigarette and
took a long pull from it. ''Go home,'' she said in a taut voice.

''Okay. But I'll be back. There is nothing you can say or
do to make me stop loving you. And if that means making you
mad at me, so be it.'' Jade kissed Lanessa on the cheek despite
her rigid stance. She looked back one last time before walking
out the front door.

Lanessa's mouth trembled as tears came down within minutes
of hearing Jade's car start. ''Don't be so sure you can forgive
anything, Jade girl. Don't be so sure.''

Chapter 14

"Thanks." Jade took the cup of coffee from Damon and smiled up at him. She concentrated on the dark liquid.

Jade suppressed a sigh. Dinner had been strained with conversation coming in spurts punctuated by awkward silences. Thoughts of how to bring up the subject of Rachelle without sounding like a jealous woman kept her distracted most of the evening. She decided not to bring it up in the restaurant, but now that they were alone in his apartment her tongue was frozen.

"So how is work?" Damon still held his mug without drinking.

"Hectic." Jade felt a little relieved to have an excuse to discuss something else. "But we can finally start working on the budget now that Dumaine is off our backs." She eased back against the cushions. "Bill handled it well, I thought."

"Dumaine hasn't asked for more documentation?"

"Not yet. Guess he's preparing for the session, too. Thank goodness. We don't need him snooping around." Jade thought of the mountain of forms coming in from all the offices with requests for new budgets. "We've got our hands full."

"What about the hearings? I understand there are going to be hard questions asked. I'm planning to testify about the funds the center gets." Damon chose his words with care. "Bill's name keeps coming up."

"Bill hasn't taken one step over the line." Jade waved a hand in a dismissive gesture. "Just sour grapes because he's smart and accomplished."

"So there is nothing to the rumors?" Damon studied her expression.

"What have you heard? Wait, don't tell me. That Bill is somehow setting himself up to benefit, and funds are being funneled to his pals." Jade recited the rumors in a singsong voice.

"Something like that."

"Baloney. Bill and I have spent hours together. He's never suggested we do anything but follow the rules." Jade brushed back her hair. "No, Bill's doing the right things."

The simple gesture of smoothing back her hair while referring to Bill Lang set Damon's teeth on edge. Damon had an image of Rachelle tossing her long hair unconsciously while she lied without batting an eye.

"Yes, but maybe he's not telling you everything." Damon clutched his mug tightly. "I don't think all these rumors are about nothing, Jade. Are you sure there isn't at least some truth to them?"

Jade shrugged. "Bill is a charmer who enjoys skirting convention. But so far it's only been to help the poor people who depend on us for services. We've come up with some innovative approaches."

"Yeah, he's a real charmer." Damon sat still next to her. "Must have made all that overtime easier to take."

Jade came back from her musings with a jolt. "Say what?"

"I mean, there are questions being raised about some of the decisions coming out of that office. And you keep defending him," Damon said in a taut voice.

"I'm defending him because he hasn't done anything

improper from what I can see. And just what are you implying?'' Jade kept her voice even.

''Working long hours with the man, sometimes at night, isn't a good idea, Jade. In fact, it's a real bad idea. Those rumors you're so ready to dismiss aren't going away easily. I just think—''

''You just think what, Damon?'' Jade's voice was stretched taut. This was the man who'd laughed with and touched his ex-wife with such intimacy. And he had the nerve to question her behavior!

''I don't like all the late nights you've been hanging around with him,'' Damon blurted out.

Jade moved an inch away from him on the sofa. ''I haven't been hanging around with him, I've been working. Or don't you believe that?'' Her brown eyes glittered with fury even though her voice remained even.

''I do, it's just . . . Look, the man isn't known for honesty or fidelity to his wife. I just don't want you to get caught up in nasty talk. Bill Lang is well known for chasing women.'' Damon gazed at her. ''And your decisions coming out of the department have been mentioned in some rumors, too.''

''So I'm a slut?'' Jade gave him a look that could melt steel.

Damon put his mug down with a bang. ''Honey, of course not! I'd never say such a thing about you—''

''Oh, so you don't think I'm a slut, just stupid,'' Jade said in flat voice. ''And possibly dishonest.'' She wanted to toss the hot contents of her cup into his lap. The nerve of him!

''You know I don't think you're stupid or dishonest.'' Damon floundered for a way to untangle himself from his own words. ''But maybe you put too much trust in the man. You said yourself he's charming.''

''So I'm gullible enough to be taken in by his charm, which is only one step away from being stupid as far as I can see.'' Jade turned away from him.

''Jade, listen, let's back up. I'm putting this badly.'' Damon rubbed his forehead in frustration. He was digging the hole deeper by the minute.

"Now that's the first thing you've gotten right so far," Jade retorted.

"Jade, not only do I care for you but I have the utmost respect for you as a professional," Damon pressed in order to make her see he was sincere.

"I see." Jade was unmoved.

"It's just that sometimes appearances give a bad impression."

"I know exactly what you mean," Jade snapped. "Who you spend time with can cause people to speculate about your actions."

"It's not always fair, but you're right. So you understand where I'm coming from?" Damon's handsome face brightened, but only for a second when he saw the storm gathering in her brown eyes.

"Oh, yes, I understand perfectly." Jade faced him with a sharp turn that made him jump. "For example, I could have concluded that you were still having the occasional fling with your ex-wife when I saw you having lunch with her."

"Now wait—"

"Oh, you were in a public place all right. She must have been especially amusing the way you were laughing it up. And some would say your hands were all over her like a cop doing a body search. But of course the fact that you didn't think I'd see you had nothing to do with your behavior, did it? I mean, it wouldn't be fair to assume just because I know you'll be seeing her again that something is going on." Jade spoke in a rapid-fire delivery.

Damon's jaw muscles worked for several moments before he spoke. "That's not at all the same thing. Rachelle's marketing firm is doing work to help expand our customer base. That was business."

"So is my work with Bill Lang," Jade replied. She returned his gaze.

"After the times we've spent together, how could you think I'd lie to you?" Damon said in a quiet voice.

"How could you believe gossip? You must have assumed

some of it was true, or you wouldn't have asked me about it,"
Jade replied.

"Look, I'm sorry. I was out of line to bring up those rumors."

"Yes, you were." Jade still wore an unyielding expression.

"I never meant to suggest you've done anything questionable." Damon took a deep breath. "Let's just end this right
now. I don't want an ugly argument."

"Neither do I," Jade said with conviction.

She'd had too many dramatic scenes with Nick. Once they
were divorced, she vowed not to get involved in any relationship
that included shouting matches and accusations. The arguments
never solved anything anyway. Damon seemed to read her
thoughts.

"I've had my fill of finger-pointing in relationships," he
said in a tired voice.

Jade could think only of how he cut off discussion once the
subject of his being with Rachelle was brought up. It was fine
to dissect her relationship with Bill, but it seemed he was
anxious to avoid a closer look at his feelings for his ex-wife.
She felt a taste of bitter loss at the notion that the beautiful
promise of love was an illusion. Wrapped in sadness, she turned
away from him. Once the seeds of suspicion were planted,
things went sour. Eventually she would find out the truth. There
was no smoke without fire. Arguing was useless. But how she
had wanted this time to be different!

Jade was determined not to cry. "I have an early day tomorrow. A lot to do." Her voice was dead, dry of expression. A
long moment of silence stretched between them.

"Yeah, I've had a long day, too" Damon gazed at her with
a look of expectation. When she did not return his gaze or
speak, he cleared his throat. "Guess I'll let you get some rest."
He rose from the sofa.

Jade nodded. She could not trust her voice. A voice in her
head screamed *don't let him walk out!*. But the image of all
the times she gave up her pride to hold on to Nick cut through
as a strong force holding her back. No, she'd had her fill of

compromising her pride for a few moments of affection. The short-term payoff never equaled the long-term misery.

Damon did not move. He seemed poised, waiting for something. "Good night, Jade."

Jade stood and walked to the door. She steeled herself not to react as he passed her. Yet the smell of his skin, a mixture of soap and aftershave cologne, delivered a solid blow to her resolve. His physical effect on her had not diminished. How could she live without feeling his solid body molded to hers? The image of them entwined in a love knot, hips moving in concert, caused a sharp hunger to slice through her. She sensed this was an ending. *If he walks out this door, girl, you'll lose that.* Jade gripped the doorknob. A combination of lust and romantic illusion would not be enough. *I will not be a fool twice.*

"Good night, Damon." Jade managed to glance into his eyes for a moment before looking away. And he was gone. The soft sound of her front door lock clicking into place seemed to echo through her head.

Damon sat in his car in the parking lot outside her condo. He was in a mild state of shock. The words *it's over* played in his head like a broken record. How had this happened? Sure, he'd avoided an ugly shouting match. But this ending had been more painful in a way. As crazy as it seemed, he now began to think Jade's quiet reaction meant she did not care enough to waste energy being outraged. *Man, you're outta your mind. Go home.* He drove away, all the while wrestling with the urge to stay. Maybe it was better this way. No, maybe he should go back. Maybe . . . A blast of a horn brought him up sharply. Damon slammed on the brake in time to avoid ramming into a car. He'd gone through a stop sign. *Damn, get it together!* Damon steadied his nerves and drove on. To hell with this. Jade had defended Bill Lang. And she had always said, even bragged, that she was ambitious. It could well be that she had made her decision to stick by Lang. Every conversation they'd ever had about her work and Lang took on a new meaning. Damon slapped the steering wheel with the flat of his hand. He'd been blind once again, it seemed. Now all he had to do was forget about her. Just the thought made his body react. Longing took hold in his groin. Her sweetness flooded back to him. Jade had been more than a luscious body. She was thoughtful, caring, the kind of woman he wanted to talk to at the end of his day. Or at least he'd thought she was that woman. Now . . . *it's over*.

"You can forget that little tryst in Hawaii." Kathy cackled. She waved her glass of wine in the air. "The Senate committee isn't cooperating these days, Billy boy?"

Kathy leaned against the open door to his office at home. She was dressed in a pale pink satin lounge pant set, the tunic shirt open at the throat. Bill shuffled through papers on his desk.

"What the hell are you obsessing on now?" Bill threw an irritated glance at her before resuming his search for something among a stack of files.

"I wasn't dumb enough to think you wanted to attend another conference on the less fortunate. You don't give a damn about anybody else but yourself." Kathy came into the room and wandered around, gazing at the books in the wall-to-wall bookshelf. "Amazing how you've risen to power in a state agency that has nothing but social welfare type programs," she said as though thinking aloud.

"I worked hard to help start the most innovative services in this state. I've done volunteer work since college to help nonprofit agencies aid disadvantaged groups." Bill held up a file then pushed the others aside and sat down. "Based on my brains and hard work, I've advanced."

Kathy put down her empty wineglass and clapped her hands. "Bravo. Your delivery is perfect, Bill. As usual." She slid down into a chair of rich dark brown fabric.

"And your harping is getting on my nerves as usual," Bill retorted in a gruff voice. "Please leave. I've got work to do."

Kathy ignored his remark. She wiggled into a more comfortable position in the stuffed chair. "That article in the paper wouldn't be the reason your wonderful trip is canceled, is it?"

"What do you mean?" Bill tapped a finger on the manilla folder in front of him. His jaw clenched.

"Well, that reporter did seem to have uncovered a lot of not so flattering facts about you." Kathy lifted a shapely shoulder. "Some of it could make people think you've been up to no good." Her lips twitched in an obvious expression of suppressed delight.

"Is that how you see it?" Bill said.

"Um-hmm. And apparently I'm not the only one. Senator Langlois seems to be a bit peeved about that hospital certificate thingy." Kathy picked up her wineglass from the table next to the chair. She frowned at the small drop of liquid left. "Darn."

"You're enjoying this. In fact, you seem to know quite a lot about the details of this story." Bill stared down at the scatter of sheets before him.

"All I know is what I read in the papers," Kathy said with a grin. She stood on unsteady legs. "I'd love to continue this fascinating conversation, but I'll need to get a drink first."

Bill crossed the room in three long strides to grab her. "What have you been doing? Huh?" He shook her like a rag doll. "It hadn't occurred to me until now that you could have been his source."

Kathy tried to break free of his hold. "Let go of me! I don't know what you're talking about."

"Like hell you don't! In the third paragraph, he talks about my ties to Franklin and mentions a deal that I never discussed at the office. We met here two years ago, Kathy. Right in this office. How long have you been spying on me?" Bill squeezed her arms. "How long?"

"Leave me alone." Kathy pushed him away. She tugged at her clothes and brushed her hair back into place.

"I want an answer." Bill glowered at her.

"Oh, now you want to talk to me," Kathy said with a snort. "Now I've got your undivided attention. Lucky me."

His face twisted with rage, Bill raised a fist to strike her. "I'm going to—"

"My father will see to it that you can't get a job selling shoes in this state. My brothers would beat you to a pulp." Kathy watched him with cold, fearless eyes.

The full import of her words brought him up short. "You're not worth dirtying my hands." He stepped back from her. "And your little scheme to ruin me won't work."

"Don't be so sure," she snapped. "That article is just one in a long series. Unless of course you're agreeable to renegotiating how this marriage works."

Bill gaped at her. "You did all this because I haven't paid enough attention to you? I always knew you were nuts. This proves it. With the stuff they're raking up, I could go to jail for malfeasance in office."

"On a good day, you ignore me. Most of the time you treat me like nothing, less than nothing. You stopped pretending to care about me right after the honeymoon. You married me for my family's money and influence." Kathy's angry voice sliced through the air like a knife. "The worst part is, I didn't care. I wanted you so much, I didn't care."

"Now you hate me and want revenge."

Kathy wiped tears from her face. "Yes, I want revenge, but I don't hate you. But just once I want to be in control. You're mine, bought and paid for."

"Why you cold-blooded ..." Bill murmured. A lustful gleam came to his eyes. "I've never seen you like this."

"First, you're going to get rid of Jade Pellerin. You know the drill. Your assistant acted without your knowledge. Agency bigwigs have used that line to wiggle out of trouble for years." Kathy gave a short, hard laugh. "She'll probably end up as a file clerk."

Bill ran his fingers over his dark hair. "No one is going to believe she didn't get clearance from me." It was clear he was already considering his escape routes.

"Yes, they will. Just say she was too emotionally attached to you and got carried away. Make them believe it." She fixed him with a look of cold steel. "You've pulled off far more difficult performances before. Our wedding day, for example."

"Kathy, you know that's not true." Bill softened his scowl into contrition. "I know I've made mistakes. And yes, I've been unfaithful. But it was my weakness for a momentary fling, nothing more. You're the only woman I really care about." He reached for her hand and pulled her to him.

"Do you?" Kathy watched his hands move down the front of her shirt to caress her breasts. She opened her mouth to accept his kiss.

"You know it, baby. It's always been you." He moved them over to the sofa. "Come on, baby, let me show you."

Kathy grabbed his hands. "You'll see to it that Jade Pellerin is destroyed starting tomorrow?"

"Yeah, sure," Bill rasped. He was eager to push her down onto the dark wine leather.

Instead, Kathy shoved him down on his back. "Good. And don't forget, I'm in control," she said as she climbed atop him.

"Marlene, it's his life. Stay out of it." Oliver stared at her with a determined expression. "Damon should choose the woman he wants to be with."

"He's a fool like most men when it comes to women." She glared at him.

Oliver got up and got another glass of apple juice. "Damn stuff. I need a good cup of strong coffee." He sipped the juice with a frown. "Listen to me, Damon is happy for the first time in years. To tell you the truth, I was glad when he escaped the claws of that scheming little harpy."

"I don't remember your being so choosy when her father suggested you two go in on those business deals together." Marlene wore an expression of disdain. "So much for supporting the cause of true love. Your practical side won, just like before."

Oliver stiffened at her last statement. "I couldn't very well refuse Eugene's offer without insulting the man. Besides, that has nothing to do with it. Damon thought he was in love with Rachelle. He *wanted* to marry her."

"After I made sure they stayed close from the time they were in junior high school," Marlene said. She laughed. "You both think it was a coincidence that they went to the same functions, that I served on all those committees with her mother? Just proves that men are dense."

"Good Lord, woman. That you've manipulated your sons' lives isn't something to be proud of." Oliver shook his head. A look of weariness and disillusionment crossed his drawn face.

"Don't give me that morally superior attitude. You married me for less than pure reasons."

"Please, Marlene, don't start that again. It's been almost twenty years." Oliver turned from her.

"Lisette Honore. Your one true love." Marlene spat out the words like acid. "Lots of long, black hair and big brown eyes. Unfortunately her family not only had no money, her father was a drunken dirt farmer."

"You're still jealous of a dead woman." Oliver slumped down into his recliner. "Lisette died years ago. You talk as though we've been lovers all these years."

"You have, Oliver. You don't think I know how you've nursed those memories? I can see it in your eyes." Marlene's voice choked. "It's why you've never been able to look at me when we make love."

"That's not true," Oliver shot back.

"It is! I know it."

"I've tried to give you a good life. I treated you with respect and tried to be considerate in every way."

Marlene closed her eyes. "That's all you had to give me. But she had your love, your passion. I settled for being treated with consideration."

"I'm sorry," Oliver mumbled. He sank back in his chair. "Is that what you want to hear for the thousandth time, Marlene?"

"I don't want your pity." Marlene banged down her cup of tea so hard the brown liquid splashed across the carpet.

"I see," Oliver said in a quiet voice. "Is that what those affairs were about? And this latest one with Tavis Collins? Does that even the score?"

"Only a little," she snarled. "At least I know they want me."

Oliver rose with effort and crossed to sit beside her. "Marlene, I never pretended to feel passion when we made love. I care about you." His voice was deep with emotion. "Please believe me."

"Nice speech, Oliver. Your acting skills have improved with the years." Marlene was unmoved. She got up and got a damp cloth. Without looking at him, she blotted the stain from the green carpet.

"I wasn't acting, Marlene." Oliver stared at her with resignation. "But it seems you'll never believe me."

"Keep trying, darling. I might swallow it one day . . . right after I start believing in the tooth fairy again." Marlene laughed. She looked up to find Damon standing in the doorway. "Oh, hello, Damon."

"Tavis Collins is one of Bill Lang's pals."

Marlene's eyes went wide with alarm. "Who?"

"I heard it all, Mother."

"How dare you sneak into my home to eavesdrop!" Marlene stood before him in outrage. "You don't have any right to pass judgment when you've skulked around and think you know—" She turned away from his hard stare. "Don't ever walk into my house uninvited again."

"I knocked on the back door before I used my key, Mother— something Trent and I have done since Dad got sick." Damon looked at his father's stricken expression. "But you're right. I'll wait to be let in from now on."

"See that you do." Marlene hurried from the room. After a moment they could hear the door to her bedroom slam shut.

"Son, sit down."

"I'm sorry for you, Dad. I've known Mother was insensitive—a snob, even, but now ...'' Damon felt sick to his stomach.

Was every woman in his life manipulative and deceptive? A long time after their marriage, he'd been forced to admit that Rachelle was very much like his mother. He had always been thrilled to see the light of approval in Marlene's eyes. To him she was one of the most elegant, beautiful women in the world. But there was the unpleasant fact that she had to have her way. Was that why he had been so drawn to Rachelle? And Jade? Was she in the same mold?

"Damon, don't judge your mother based on things you don't understand.'' Oliver looked as though he was aging before Damon's eyes.

"She lies and is having an affair. I think I understand that real well!'' Damon threw his keys down on the end table. He jammed his fists into his pockets. "How long have you known?''

"Awhile. Listen to me, son, your mother is younger than her age. Physically I haven't been able to ... I mean, my medications—'' Oliver broke off with a look of dejection.

"Dad,'' Damon said with a catch in his throat. He put a hand on his father's shoulder and squeezed hard. For several minutes he could not speak. "That's no excuse. If anything, she should have been more devoted. But Marlene Cormier Knight isn't like that. She thinks only of herself.''

"This is as much my fault.'' Oliver held up a hand to stop Damon from interrupting him. "Sit down, son. I can't let you go away thinking your mother is the only villain in this sordid situation.''

"You're one helluva man to have put up with her all this time.'' Damon threw a hostile glance in the direction his mother had gone.

"Now stop it!'' Oliver barked in a loud angry tone to get his attention. "I will not have you showing disrespect for your mother.''

"Dad I—'' Damon jerked around to stare at him in surprise.

Oliver took a deep breath. "Damon, I hurt Marlene terribly. I've been callous and selfish for the last thirty-six years."

"You've treated her like a queen." After a few moments of thought, Damon sat back on the sofa. "Wait a minute. Did you have an affair, too?"

Oliver looked away from him for the first time. "I married your mother out of family loyalty, Damon. It wasn't just my parents but my grandparents—Very strong-willed people. I should have shown more backbone but . . ."

"What are you saying?" Damon was confused by this thread.

"Lisette Honore was from a poor family that lived outside of town. Back in those days, there were only a few high schools for blacks. So kids from all over traveled to the nearest one. Lisette rode one of three buses that brought kids to the old McKinley High School. She was so beautiful. When she didn't have her long hair in a braid, it would fluff out like dark shiny wool around her head, soft with big thick curls." Oliver seemed lost in the memory for several moments. Then he blinked back to the present. "My grandmother saw us together one day. There was no question that we could get married. After pleading from my mother didn't work, my father laid it on the line. I was seventeen and the only job I would get without family connections was as a janitor back in those days. At least that's what I thought."

Damon could not believe what he was hearing. "You cared more about your social position?"

Oliver hung his head. "That's not the worst of it. Nasty rumors about Lisette started circulating. Rumors that her drunk of a father had molested her and her sisters. I turned my back on her like all the rest. Years later I found out my family helped expose his behavior not to help Lisette, but to destroy any chance I might marry her despite their objections."

"What happened to her?"

"She moved away for a while to live with relatives in New Orleans. Her father was stabbed to death in a Catfish Town juke joint a month later. She came back about six years later to teach." Oliver wore a sad smile. "Lisette even forgave me

for being so cowardly. I don't think your mother even guessed
we had a brief affair. But Lisette wanted a home and children.
She broke it off and married a nice man. She died about ten
years ago, cancer.''

"Why did you bother to stay together?'' Damon stared at
him.

"For you boys, for appearances, our families . . . for a lot
of reasons. But mostly because I really tried to make up for it
to Marlene.'' Oliver stared ahead. ''And for some crazy reason,
your mother has always loved me.''

"How can she love you yet have an affair?''

"It's all so complicated, so messed up.'' Oliver shook his
head. ''I don't have any answers for you, son. We just keep
doing the best we can.'' He gazed at him. ''Don't give up
someone you love. Look what it's done to our lives.''

"It's a dead issue at this point,'' Damon said. ''Mother will
get her wish.'' The dull ache returned. ''We won't be seeing
each other again. I'm sure of that.''

Oliver studied his son for several seconds. ''Damon, take it
from me. When you love a woman with all your heart, there
isn't a damn thing in this world worth keeping you apart.'' He
rose with stiff movements. ''Now I'm going to go to my room.
I'm so tired.''

Damon watched him walk away with slow, shuffling steps.
Oliver J. Knight had never looked small or defeated, until now.
Damon wanted to make it right for his father. But events that
had taken place before he was born made that impossible.
Damon sat deep in thought for a long time with nothing but
the ticktock of the antique grandfather clock down the hall to
keep him company. After a while, he rose to leave. There was
much for him to think about.

"Lady, you've had more than enough,'' the burly bartender
said in a gravelly voice. ''Last thing I need is the cops comin'
down on me.'' He turned away without filling her glass with
more whiskey and soda.

"Look, I've got money. Now give me another drink." Lanessa tossed back her hair. She straightened the expensive jade green jacket she wore over matching slacks.

A tall, muscular man in a blue shirt at the other end of the bar was listening to their exchange with interest. "Come on, Joe. Give the lady another one. The cops don't care what goes on in this dump." He barked a husky laugh.

Joe walked to him and bent down to whisper in the man's ear. "Looka how she's dressed, man. I don't need no grief behind some bourgeois broad getting wasted in my place, Ray." He eyed her again. "Probably got some high-powered daddy who'll use his influence to shut me down."

"She ain't the regular skanky female you got comin' in here, that's for sure." Ray licked his lips.

"Look, I done warned Malik and them to keep it on the down low. Now this I don't need." Joe jerked a thumb in Lanessa's direction.

Ray studied the leather purse and shoes. He gave an appreciative wink at the curves beneath the fine fabric. "Listen, I'll take care of this, honey. You just keep 'em comin."

Joe followed his gaze. He handed Ray a bottle. "Just keep it quiet. You can use one of the rooms upstairs to help her sleep it off if you want." He gave Ray a crude wink.

Ray strolled over and sat on the bar stool next to Lanessa. "Here you go, ma'am. Joe just kinda concerned for your safety. But I assured him you was okay." He gave her a wide grin.

Lanessa reached for the bottle. "My hero."

Ray did not let go of it. "What's your name, pretty woman?"

"My throat's kinda dry. I'll talk better after a drink." Lanessa pried his fingers loose and poured some of the whiskey into her glass.

"Hey, what about the soda?" Ray laughed as he signaled to Joe.

"Oh, yeah." Lanessa giggled. "Soda." She found this funny and continued to laugh.

"Yeah, let's cut this some or you'll end up out cold." Ray raised an eyebrow at the bartender.

"From the looks of it, she can hold lots of straight booze."
Joe gave a knowing grunt. "Yep, she ain't just started puttin'
away a lotta liquor." He walked away.

"I don't like his attitude," Lanessa said with a scowl. "I
don't have to spend my money here, you know," she called
out at Joe's retreating back. He only waved a hand in dismissal
as a reply.

"Ah, that's just how Joe is. Hey, you some kinda fine woman.
How you got loose tonight without your man?" Ray leaned
toward her.

"Real easy." Lanessa's eyes filled with unshed tears. She
swiped at her face with the back of her hand. "I don't have to
ask permission from anybody for what I do," she said with
force. "To hell with him."

"I know what you mean, baby." Ray poured more whiskey
in both their glasses. "Woman like you needs the right kinda
man. Somebody gonna treat you good."

"Uh-huh." Lanessa took a deep drink. "It's too hot in here.
Hey you, turn on the air conditioner," she yelled at Joe. "And
turn down that music while you're at it."

"Say, listen, it's hot 'cause it's too crowded up in here. Let's
go where we can really talk." Ray took her arm with one hand
and picked up the bottle with the other. He pulled her through
a door leading down a dim hallway.

"Where we goin'?" Lanessa hesitated.

"Our own private bar, babe. With soft music. Come on,"
Ray urged in a soothing voice. "I'm going to take care of
you."

Lanessa gazed up at his smiling face. "I just want time to
get myself together, you know? Everything is rushing at me at
once." She let her body slump against his imposing bulk. "You
understand, don't you?"

"Sure, babe. I understand just what you need."

Ray walked her into a dingy room and shut the door. Illumi-
nated by a single table lamp with a dirty shade, the room was
furnished with a couch that sagged in the middle and several
ragged chairs. A fold-out single bed, covered with a faded blue

bedspread worn almost to holes in spots, was in one corner. Lanessa plopped down onto the sofa before Ray could get her over to the bed.

"Where's the bottle?" Lanessa pushed back her hair.

"Give me a kiss, and I'll give you a drink." Ray stood in front of her.

Lanessa smiled and wagged her finger at him. "Now don't play games with me, Ray." She got to her feet, wavering a little. "Where's that drinky?"

Ray laughed and danced backward with the bottle held behind him. "Guess. Come on, babe." He moved away from her in time to the music that could be heard from the barroom. "You give me what I want, you get what you want."

"Okay, you asked for it." Lanessa lunged at him. She put both arms around him and touched the bottle. "Now give it up." She took it from him.

"You first," Ray said in a husky voice. He grabbed her to him as he fell onto the bed. "Some fine." His hands worked with amazing speed to undo the buttons on her jacket.

"Now don't be in such a hurry," Lanessa said. She tried to wriggle out of his reach. "We've got plenty of time." His groping became more insistent, his fingers digging into her flesh. "You're hurting me. Stop it!"

"Feel this." He guided her hand to his crotch. "I'm ready now. Don't try to tell me you don't like it rough. I know your kind."

"Let go." Lanessa's voice rose in panic.

"Come down here for a little ghetto excitement. I got it for you, sugar." Ray groaned at the sight of her beige lace demi-cup bra. "Oo-wee," he muttered.

"I said, let me go." Lanessa slapped the side of his face hard. Her long nails scraped skin from his cheek.

Ray snarled as he jumped up from the bed. "You really wanna play, huh? Then you got your wish." He hit her with a backhanded blow.

Lanessa staggered back in stunned horror. Suddenly she remembered the bottle in her hands. "Stay away from me."

Her voice trembled. She held the bottle upside down sloshing the remaining whiskey down her pants.

"I'm going to show you something, pretty woman." Ray wore a nasty smile. "Right after I take that from you." He advanced to her.

In a blind panic, Lanessa swung the bottle. The crunch of the heavy glass on his scalp shook her arm. Ray stumbled a bit before he reached at her with like an enraged bear, his fingers curled into a claw. Lanessa hit him again harder. The bottle broke and blood flowed down his face. Ray screamed at the realization that the blood was his. He fell hard against the sofa then fell to the floor. Lanessa backed away and looked down at him. He did not move.

"My God!" Lanessa was shaking. She grabbed her purse. "Gotta get out of here."

Once out in the hallway, she ran blindly to a door. With a cry of relief, she found herself outside. Somehow she found her car. It seemed to take forever to get the car open. Her hands shook so hard, she dropped the keys three times in her attempt. Finally she got them and drove off the parking lot at top speed. The dark highway curved ahead, causing her to jerk the wheel more than once. Oncoming headlights left her blinking away the spots that danced in front of her. Which way was home? She had to get to her refuge. But she had no real refuge. Everywhere was pain. Tears streamed down her face further reducing her vision. There was nothing at home but emptiness, nothing at home to comfort her. The car lurched to the left. With a spray of gravel, the tires hit a soft shoulder. Lanessa screamed as the world spun around like a carousel.

Chapter 15

"Calm down. They didn't say she was . . ." Shaena's voice trailed off. She drove at the speed limit but leaned forward as though urging the car faster.

"Please let her be okay, please let her be okay," Jade mumbled the prayer over and over. Jade was glad she'd been with her friend when she called home to get her messages. Her mother's frantic voice on her answering machine saying Lanessa was hurt had left her shaken. Shaena had declared she was in no shape to drive. Now they were still ten minutes from the small hospital in Plaquemine where Lanessa had been taken. What was she doing at a bar across the river? Jade thought once more of how little of Lanessa's life she knew these days. She had spent the last few minutes assessing just how much of this was her fault.

"I should never have left her that night, Shaena," Jade said in a tearful voice. "Alex said it was bad, but I didn't believe it could be . . . I never thought about . . . I was too wrapped up in my own problems."

"You couldn't follow Lanessa around twenty-four hours a day. And you couldn't force her into treatment she didn't want."

Shaena took one hand from the steering wheel to place it on her arm. "Stop blaming yourself."

"I should have made her go into a clinic or had her committed. Anything."

"Jade, you know what Fred told you. That's a last resort," Shaena said.

She was right of course. Jade had spoken in confidence to her friend who headed up the Office of Alcohol and Substance Abuse. He had encouraged her to get Lanessa in for an evaluation. Only if she was considered an immediate danger to herself and others could she be committed by the coroner's office.

"I know. She wasn't threatening to kill herself or anybody else—so we just had to let her self-destruct." Jade began to cry softly.

They drove in silence for another ten minutes. The parking lot at Riverwest Hospital flashed with the red lights of an ambulance. Both of them jumped from the car the moment Shaena cut the engine. Jade raced ahead of her to search for her parents. Her father met her just beyond the automatic doors and gathered her into his arms.

"What did they say?" Jade's heart pounded like a drum. All surrounding sounds became muffled as she waited for her father's answer.

"She'll live, but she's going to have a long recovery. The air bag saved her since she wasn't wearing a seat belt. She was tossed into the backseat sometime while the car was still rolling." Alton took in a long breath. "But she's going to make it. Thank God." He held Jade to him in a tight embrace.

Jade welcomed the reassuring warmth of being in her father's arms for several minutes. Then they went through the emergency room to where Lanessa was being treated. Two nurses, a blonde and redhead, emerged from the small room. The door closed behind them with a soft *whoosh* sound.

"Only immediate family, two at a time." The short, plump blonde spoke in a calm voice.

"This is my other daughter," Alton explained. "I'll wait out here, baby." He kissed the top of Jade's head.

"I'm Lisa. You holler if you need me. I'm gonna be right down there." There was compassion in her blue eyes. "But she's going to be okay." She gave Jade's shoulder a pat before she bustled off.

Jade was afraid of what she'd see. She took a few seconds to steel herself before going in. Her mother sat next to the bed, holding one of Lanessa's hands. Jade forced herself to look at her sister. Bruises covered her face. A tube was in her nose and an IV tube snaked down to the needle stuck in the back of her left hand. A cast was on her right leg from the thigh down.

"My baby's going to be fine," Clarice said. "Come here, Jade. Lanessa has been asking for you." Clarice got up and put an arm around Jade's shoulders. The effort was too much. She sagged against Jade and began to sob.

"Mama," Jade sobbed with her. Then she pushed Clarice back. "Look at us. We're just crying when we know she's going to be okay. She's going to wake up and panic if we don't get it together."

After a few more moments of sharing tears, they broke apart. "You're right." Clarice dabbed at her eyes. "Lanessa will be back to her old self, just like before, in no time."

Jade gazed at her sister. She thought of what Fred had told her about a crisis being the best opportunity for change. Pretending the only problem was recovering from her injuries seemed wrong. "Mama, we don't want Lanessa back to being just like she was before."

"What do you mean?" Clarice looked up at her sharply. "Of course we do." She bit off another remark when the redheaded nurse came back into the room.

"Let's step outside for a minute. All three of us need to talk." Jade led her outside.

The nurses showed them to the waiting area for families. A separate section with a television was empty. Jade turned down the sound on it.

"Jade, what is this about?" Clarice asked soon after they were seated.

"Mama, Daddy . . . Lanessa is chemically dependent—on alcohol for sure and maybe even drugs. Alex—"

"It's a lie. Alex is angry that Lanessa broke up with him!" Clarice cut her off.

"No, Mama. Lanessa has been having problems at work, and she's deep in debt. Alex says—" Jade tried again.

"Alex? Why in the world would you listen to him?" Clarice shook he head with vigor. "Lanessa is not a drug addict or an alcoholic. Not Lanessa."

Alton placed a large hand over his wife's. "Clarice, we've got to face the truth. The police have ordered a blood test to see if alcohol was a factor. But she smelled of whiskey when they brought her in. And that's not the worst of it."

"Oh, no. Someone else was hurt in the crash?" Jade felt a dread that Lanessa had not only hurt herself, but someone else. And Jade felt the burden of that responsibility, too.

"Not in the crash." Alton gripped Clarice's hand tighter. "Lanessa was in a bar and she attacked a man. He's in here, too, getting his scalp stitched up. Apparently . . ." He glanced at his wife's stricken expression.

"Daddy, go on. We've got to face the whole truth now," Jade prompted him.

"She was drinking heavily with this man, and they ended up in an upstairs room of the bar. They got into a struggle." Alton looked down. "I think maybe he was too rough, and Lanessa fought back.

"You can't mean she was going to—No, no." Clarice's expression hardened. "Not Lanessa. End up with some bum in an upstairs room of a bar like a prostitute? It's all lies—" Her voice broke. "Lies." She looked at her husband, her eyes desperate for some sign he agreed.

"No, baby. It's true. Lanessa's got a big problem, and now she's hit bottom. She could be charged with aggravated assault and driving while intoxicated." Alton swallowed hard. "Clarice, no more hiding from the truth. No more." He wrapped his sobbing wife in his arms and rocked her gently.

Jade looked up through the glass enclosure to see Lisa approaching. She opened the door.

"You Jade?" She smiled.

"Yes." Jade stood.

"You sister's askin' for you, sugar. Come on." Lisa gestured to her.

Jade entered to room to find Lanessa awake. "Hi, Nessa," she said in a soft voice.

"Hey. I'm glad to see you. Hell, I'm glad to see," Lanessa said with a pained smile that lasted only a moment. Her voice was raspy and low. "I sure messed up this time, didn't I?"

"Nessa . . ." Jade's voice failed her. She caressed Lanessa's face with care not to hurt her. "I'm sorry for not being there for you."

"Like you put the drink in my hand? Forget it." Lanessa gazed at her. "This isn't your fault, Jade."

"But I've been so busy being a jealous sibling that—"

"Shut up," Lanessa broke in. "We competed for the prize of most stupid sister, and I win hands down. So don't dare try to horn in on my moment of glory. You know how I hate that." She reached with effort to take Jade's hand.

Jade gave her a gentle kiss. "I love you, sister."

"Me, too, Jade-girl. Now how bad is it?" Lanessa's expression said she wanted the hard truth.

"You could be charged with drunk driving."

Lanessa's bottom lip trembled. "Did I . . . was anybody else hurt when I wrecked my car?"

"No, no other cars were involved." Jade shook her head.

"Thank you, Lord. I owe you one." Lanessa let out a sigh of relief. A tear slid down one cheek.

"But they say you attacked some guy." Jade still found this to be the biggest shock of the night. "Lanessa, you've never even swatted a fly in your life."

"Wha . . . ?" Lanessa wore a perplexed frown. "Wait a minute. Things are kinda fuzzy." She tried to sit up. "Oh, now I remember."

"Take it easy." Jade put a hand on her shoulder. "No sudden moves."

"That bastard got rough with me, and I gave him a crack on the head. I'd do it again, too." Lanessa showed a spark of defiance.

"That kind of talk won't help in court. I think you could be charged for it." Jade wondered at how they would get through the next few weeks. Shaena could help them find an attorney.

"Then I'll face it. Being a drunk is no license for rape." Lanessa went limp against the pillow. "Well, I finally said it out loud, Jade-girl."

"We're going to be with you all the way." Jade felt hopeful about Lanessa's future for the first time that night.

"Oh, no—Mama and Daddy." Lanessa closed her eyes. Tears flowed down her cheeks. "They must be so ashamed."

Jade wiped away her tears tenderly. "No, Nessa. They feel only love and joy that you're going to be all right. And you will be. More than all right. Better."

"I don't care how much it hurts, give me a hug," Lanessa whispered.

Jade still had both arms around her in a loose embrace when their parents came in. The blonde nurse stuck her head inside, and after seeing the family together, gave the thumbs-up that it was okay.

Later Jade went home tired and scared. Her whole life was a disaster, like an earthquake. The ground seemed to shake and crack beneath her feet. There was nothing solid she could hold on to these days. Tears flowed down her face as she cried silently. How she needed arms around her now. Damon's arms. But that would not happen. The career she had cherished seemed in jeopardy, her sister was almost killed because she lacked the courage to act . . . and then there was Damon. She'd pushed him right back into his ex-wife's arms. For the rest of the night, she stared at the television screen without seeing the succession of salespeople on a twenty-four-hour shopping channel.

* * *

"Jade, you handled this process. I think you'll need to be at the hearing with me." Bill handed her a stack of vinyl folders with labels on them.

"Sure." Jade gazed at him in speculation. "I'll take it with me when I leave early today."

"Oh, that's right. Sorry to hear about your sister." Bill spoke in a monotone, automatic courtesy manner. "And the section on Magnolia Hospital, too."

"I'll pull my file on it." Jade left him still staring at the mounds of paperwork on his desk.

For the last two days, she'd noticed a difference in him: a coolness, a distance that had not been there before. And she kept getting instructions to pull all correspondence dealing with the hospital certificates. Bill no longer had a casual, confident attitude about the legislator's questions. Now that three articles had been published in the *Morning Advocate*, his good humor regarding the accusations was gone. But what was up between them?

"Hey, Jade. How's it going?" Shaena came into her office with a breezy smile.

"Fine, I guess." Jade glanced back at Bill's office.

"Lanessa's doing better every day. That's great." Shaena spoke loudly. She looked around her.

"Yeah, she's doing great." Jade wondered what she was doing.

Aline, Bill's secretary, stuck her head in the door. "I've got all the files from out here, but where's the one on Health Tech?"

"Oh, I think those are in those big file cabinets against the wall, Aline." Jade pointed to section used for storing documents.

"Thanks. I'll see you later." Aline's voice faded as she walked off.

Shaena closed the door after checking the hallway once more. "Have you seen this?" She pulled a cut out section of newspaper from her pocket. "I just so happened to pick up today's *Times-Picayune* down at the City Newsstand."

Jade scanned the article: TOP DHH OFFICIAL USES CONNECTIONS. A chill crept up her spine as she read on. "Bill Lang has gone on cruises aboard the luxury yacht of hospital magnate Theodore Kingsly. Shaena, this says they've been meeting for the last six years!"

"Uh-huh. If you ask me, Bill's been working on this for a long time." Shaena plopped down in the chair across from Jade.

"This is unbelievable. It—"

"Stinks to high heaven. Bill was contacted and quoted as saying those trips were as a friend to Kingsly's family." Shaena pointed to a section in the long article that Jade had not read yet. "And he 'delegated certain decision-making authority to his subordinates who he is confident acted within established policy. But of course, some errors could have occurred,' end of quote."

Jade did not have to be told what that meant. "He's setting me up to take the fall." Her hands shook. So now she understood the cool behavior.

Bill Lang was signaling to outward observers that perhaps he had lost confidence in her since probing had uncovered indications of wrongdoing. The rumor mill in state government operated with the efficiency of a well-honed high-tech communications system. A subtle change in their working relationship was bound to be duly noted and reported up the line, even to certain legislators. Like many who had risen through the ranks, Bill understood the game and played it with great skill. Jade knew the game, but could she compete with Bill Lang and hope to win?

"What are we going to do?" Shaena sat forward and spoke in a quiet voice.

"We? Listen, you stay away from me through all this."

Shaena tossed her long braids. "No way. Some friend I'd be to slink off and let you face this on your own. Hey, mess with my friend, you mess with *me*."

"Don't be crazy, girl. It doesn't make sense for both of us to suffer professionally. Things can get real dirty." Jade remembered how her former boss had suffered. Even longtime friends who'd come to her defense had been vilified in the press. Their personal and private lives splashed across headlines read all over the state.

"There's talk about charging someone, girlfriend. We're wasting time, Jade. I'm in." Shaena's pretty brown face was set in a stubborn expression. "Now let's think what our next move is going to be."

For well over an hour they talked. Finally Shaena suggested they start by going over every major decision that had come out of their section since Bill came on board.

"Yeah, we can probably see which way this is headed. I mean, we know the general direction this reporter is taking. Psychiatric and nursing home beds. That's what we'll really look at." Shaena paced the floor like a lawyer preparing for a big case. She seemed excited.

Jade rubbed her forehead with a sigh. "Like my great-aunt Gloria used to say: 'If it ain't one thing, it's two.' " A name on the small print of the article caught her eye. A sharp pain pierced her chest. "Damon Knight, well-known businessman, denies that his family ties to members of the legislative black caucus influenced funding of programs at the Gracie Center," she read aloud.

There it was again, an empty feeling whenever she thought of Damon. Through all the nights of sitting with Lanessa, Jade could not help thinking of him—a fact that made her feel even more a fool. With all the turbulence in her life, the last thing she needed was to waste emotion on a man who could leave her without a backward glance. Damon Knight. He was a creature of the old-money, old-family, black upper-class after all—a world Rachelle belonged to without question. The only kind of woman men from his world would consider marrying. Yet heated dreams of being in his arms, of his voice whispering words of love, would not go away. More nights than she cared to remember in the last three weeks had been filled with restless sleep.

Jade raked fingers through her thick shoulder-length hair. She had to get him out of her mind. *And out of your heart, too.* A voice, her voice, sounded clear as a bell inside her head.

"Jade, you should call him." Shaena, her female soul mate, could read her like a book. "About seeing him with Rachelle . . . I think maybe you jumped to conclusions."

"No, I've thought about it a lot. They behaved like a couple, Shaena. Nick says they've been together quite a bit." Jade felt the sting of tears. Stupid to cry for a man who was so shallow. She blinked them away.

"Nick? What does he know about it?" Shaena raised an eyebrow.

Jade closed her eyes and saw a vision of Damon holding Rachelle in his arms, passionately kissing her. She had to stop doing this to herself. "You know he travels in the same circles. He knew her in college, I think he said."

Shaena rubbed her chin. "That a fact? And you were having lunch with Nick the day you saw them together."

"Yes." Jade opened her eyes back on the real world. She did not need any more reminders of that day. She picked up a stack of binders. "Nick is such a pain—like all men. He's so transparent now."

"Umm, Nick likes pulling tricks." Shaena opened her mouth to say something more.

"I'm embarrassed I couldn't see through him years ago. Oh, well, the folly of youth."

Jade pushed away those thoughts. She needed all her energy for standing by her sister and now defending her reputation, maybe even her career. Men! She became very angry all of a sudden. Did she have a bull's-eye painted on her back? The men in her life seemed to think she was an easy target these days. Well, Bill Lang was in for an unpleasant surprise.

"Listen, Jade, I've got an idea that Ni—" Shaena started to speak, but Mike Testor opened the door without knocking.

"Jade, Bill needs to see all memoranda related to the increase in nursing home payment rates. We'll be in his office." Mike

stared at Shaena with a question in his eyes. "Ten minutes."
He left the door open a few inches when he withdrew.

"Well, I'll see you later," Shaena said in loud, staged voice.
"Maybe we can have lunch tomorrow." Then she stepped close
to Jade. "Don't let them team up on you," she mumbled low.

"Don't worry. I've got a plan," Jade whispered. "Yeah,
call me later. I mean it."

Seeing only a green silk tie through the peephole, Jade opened
the door with a wild hope—a hope that faded when she saw
her ex-husband. Nick stood looking very sure of himself. She
tried to deny she'd wanted to see Damon standing outside her
door once again. But her reaction to the doorbell was no different than the way her heart pounded whenever the phone rang.
Hadn't she learned her lesson yet? Here was a very good reason
to dislike men.

"Nick, what is this?" Jade stared at the flowers in his hand.

"A bouquet, lovely and fragrant. Like you, sweet thing."
Nick's famous perfect smile flashed like the bulb of an expensive camera.

For a second Jade mused at just how little effect it had on
her now. Once she would have melted at the mere lift of his
mouth. "Whatever," she deadpanned. With a bland expression,
she took the vase from his hands. "Come in."

"My, my. Things have changed. You're going to let me into
your apartment." He gazed around in appreciation that was
genuine.

"Don't get excited. I'm being polite. What do you want?"
Jade was more bored than annoyed.

"Great colors. Love these Tanner prints." Nick walked
around the living room as though he belonged there.

"Nick, get to the point."

"The property is going to bring in top dollar as expected.
You should get a healthy check every quarter as your share.
I'm working with a contractor to build three big warehouses
that will be leased."

"Perfect." Jade could at least count on more than her paycheck. This was the first bright spot in her personal life in weeks. "Thanks for coming by to tell me that." She went back to the front door and opened it. "Next time a phone call will do."

"Baby, that's no way to act. I could have stiffed you on this deal. My lawyer said—"

"Your lawyer advised you that I'd clean your clock in court if you tried." Jade batted her eyelashes at him and smiled sweetly. "Or words to that effect, *baby.*"

"I don't remember your being so cynical, so bitter."

"Nick, it's been a rough two weeks. So let's not pretend." Jade's hard outer shell began to weigh heavy. When she went over all she'd been through, the fight began to seep from her. She needed a breather.

"Okay, enough with the flip attitude. I'm sorry." Nick raised both his hands palms out. "Listen, let me know if I can help in any way. I know you've been spending a lot to time with Lanessa and all." He seemed sincere.

"Thanks, but right now I'm holding together." Jade tried to smile and failed.

"Just barely by the looks of it. Tell you what, no games for the next hour at least. I'll fix us some coffee." He went into the kitchen.

"Nick, get out of there." Jade marched in behind him.

"Great, you've got that gourmet blend. You know I have a special touch with coffee. Now just let me whip up some for us." Nick searched through her cabinets. "Ah, yes. You haven't changed much." He drew out package of beignet mix.

"You have a lot of nerve, Nicholas Lane Guillory." Jade planted fists on her hips.

"By the way, you could at least have waited a few years before dropping my last name. That was the cruelest cut of all." He grinned at her.

Jade leaned against the counter and watched him go through familiar motions. Nick had always been a great cook because, surprisingly, he enjoyed it. Jade wondered why she did not throw him out on his butt. The truth was, his antics were mildly amusing. And for almost a month now, very little had appealed to her sense of humor. Damon. The name popped back into her head. How long would it take to get over him? Somehow she knew the answer and felt the return of sorrow.

"Listen, it's better to find out these things early on." Nick stirred the batter in a large blue mixing bowl.

"What?" Jade swam up from her deep thoughts to focus on his words.

"I mean that Damon Knight dude. Him and Rachelle go back a long ways. She's his type, if you like shallow self-centered women who happened to be gorgeous." Nick shrugged as though they both knew what he meant.

Jade gave a grunt. "I've seen some of your ladyfriends, pal. They're about as deep as a baby's wading pool."

"Unfair. That description doesn't apply to you at all." Nick beamed at her. He turned back to concentrate on the task of pouring oil in a deep pan. "Look, Rachelle is just using business as a means to get next to the man. And he's falling for it pretty good."

"Guess she's got the right plan for him in more ways than one." Jade swiped at a spill of milk harder than necessary.

"Hey, she dangled two things in front of him he couldn't resist: making his company more money and sex."

Jade paused in the act of pushing back her ceramic canister set after handing him the one with sugar. "Is that a fact? You know all about it, do you?"

"Rachelle has a natural talent for making sure things go her way. Why once she sets her mind . . ." Nick's voice died. He gave a nervous chuckle. "At least when I knew her a *long, long* time ago."

Jade grabbed his arm, making batter fly across the kitchen. "Just coincidence we happened to be at the same restaurant, was it?" She backed him against the counter. "Just happen to know all about her plans to use business as an excuse to get to Damon?" She picked up the large wooden mixing spoon and held it under his nose.

"Ba-baby, please," Nick stuttered. "This violent side of you is so unbecoming." His expression changed to a slight leer. "And kind of a turn-on."

"Really?" Jade brought her knee up to his crotch with a quick motion.

"No, now you don't want to do that," Nick yelled out. Beads of sweat budded on his top lip.

"You and Rachelle orchestrated that little scene," Jade said through clenched teeth.

"Well, I . . . I knew he was no good for you the moment I saw the guy." Nick spoke in a rush of words. When Jade stepped back from him, he blew out a gust of air.

"You slimy, lowdown lying—"

Nick tried to recover some masculine dignity. He straightened his shirt with care. "Nobody forced him to grin all up in her face or put his hands all over her like that."

"You know what? I think I'm going to let the child support folks know just how much money you're making on this deal." Jade nodded at him slowly. "*Both* mothers of your children would be quite interested."

"You know about—" Nick clamped his mouth shut.

"Have for a long time, Daddy dearest."

"Now, baby, let's not be vindictive." Nick rubbed his mouth. "That would cut into both our profits."

"My attorney says it will come out of your half of the community property." Jade smiled at him. "Your check, not mine. Now get out of my apartment."

"Fine. Be alone if you want. Because no matter how they got back together, Rachelle has her hooks in your precious Damon again. And you can't pry him loose," Nick said in a voice heavy with rancor.

"Out!" Jade pointed to the door.

She watched him stroll out then sagged against the counter. What he said rang true. And she might have pushed Damon even farther into Rachelle's arms by overreacting. Look how easy she'd made it for Rachelle by stepping aside. Three weeks since that night. Not a phone call from him. Nick was right.

Her pride had prevented her from making the first move. Any chance they had was gone now. Or was it? The cordless phone seemed to pull her like a magnet.

"Rachelle, you didn't have to come over here this late," Damon said. "Thanks, Helen." He suppressed a smile at the look of disapproval his secretary gave Rachelle.

"That urgent call you were expecting might be coming in any minute." Helen raised her eyebrows and gestured at him in sign language. "You know the one I mean."

"Thank you, Helen," he replied in a stern tone. "But I doubt it will. Now if we want to be out of here by midnight, type up that final inventory report for tax purposes." He jerked a thumb at her to leave.

"Call loud if you need help." Helen threw one last hostile glance at Rachelle before leaving.

"Why you don't get a real secretary is beyond me." Rachelle sniffed at the closed door. "Helen has always been more trouble than she's worth."

"Helen has the kind of business sense that you can't learn in any MBA program. She's more than a secretary." Damon brushed aside Rachelle's snippy comment. Helen had disliked Rachelle at first sight. And the feeling was mutual. "Now let's see what your graphic design artist came up with for a new logo."

"Alonzo outdid himself this time, Damon." Rachelle pulled out the large drawing with a flourish. She stood close to him.

"It has a certain . . . something to it." Damon continued to study the picture without sitting down. A large dark blue *K* with shadow below it was drawn on a soft gray background.

"Like a commercial giant looming on the horizon. See the shadow effect as though the letter is standing in sunlight." Rachelle draped herself against him, her arm resting on his. "Ready to thrust forth." She pressed her hips to him.

Damon glanced over his shoulder at her then moved away.

''Uh, yeah. I like this. It really makes an impression. Let's see the rest.''

For the next fifteen minutes, Damon reviewed sketches for a complete campaign that included billboards and print advertising.

''I'm so glad you're pleased.'' Rachelle leaned forward, causing her knee to touch his.

Damon rose from the table set in the corner away from his desk near the window. ''I'm more than pleased. Alonzo did a fantastic job capturing the essence of where I wanted to go with this.''

''Listen, I haven't had dinner. Why don't we get something to eat.''

''No. I mean, thanks but I've got more work to do.'' Damon moved to his desk. He hoped it would signal Rachelle that their meeting was over.

''We don't have to go out, in case you don't want your little friend to see us again.'' Rachelle wore a catlike smile. ''We could order in. There's a new gourmet pizza place that delivers.''

''Rachelle, I—''

''Jade Pellerin got you on a short leash these days?'' She spoke in a tone designed to needle him.

''Not exactly.'' He looked away.

Damon came back to the grim reality of how much he missed Jade with a solid thud. Sure he could keep the demon at bay for sometimes as long as an hour these days. That was some progress, if not much. *By the year 2000, I should be able to sleep through the night without . . .* The ache in him was like an ice pick. He could not bear to finish the thought. Yet the memory of how she tasted on his lips—sweet and salty at the same time—was like a flame licking at his groin. Damon had never experienced this kind of wanting before in his life—a craving that left him weak and bathed in sweat in the middle of the night.

"Damon? Hel-lo." Rachelle waved a hand in front of his face. She wore an expression of annoyance. "Goodness. Little Miss Priss certainly has your nose open."

"That subject isn't up for discussion between us, Rachelle." Damon's jaw muscles worked.

"We don't have to talk. I've got something that can still make you forget everything else." Rachelle opened her jacket to reveal a low-cut lace bra.

Damon stared at the flawless mounds of flesh the color of fine teakwood and felt . . . nothing. Not one twitch, not one thrill. All he could think of was how to get her to button up and leave. His thoughts must have been mirrored in his eyes. Rachelle's lascivious smile drooped as she continued to gaze at him.

"Uh, Rachelle, I've got these reports and—"

"You must have some kind of problem these days." Rachelle jerked her jacket together and jammed the buttons through the holes. "You can't perform or something?" She stomped over to snatch up her leather purse and matching portfolio.

The implication that he was impotent was an obvious bid to restore her feminine pride. Damon felt a kind of guilt to be the source of her embarrassment. After all, Rachelle was not accustomed to men *not* being turned on by her body. He rubbed his jaw.

"Look, Rachelle, it's just with all this work and stress I'm preoccupied. Besides, it's been over between us for a long time." Damon tried to be honest yet a gentleman at the same time. It failed.

Rachelle spun to face him. "You're welcome to your little wannabe upper-class cow with the soulful eyes. Tell her to lose the innocent act. Nobody is fooled." She had missed a button on the jacket, making it hang crookedly.

"You didn't have to go there," Damon said. He smothered a laugh at the spectacle of Rachelle's obvious envy. He pointed to her clothes. "You need to fix th—"

Enraged at the being the butt of humor, Rachelle squinted

at him. "I'd like to have you fixed. Go on, run back to what's-her-name. She's more your speed."

Damon stopped smiling as a notion popped into his head. "Rachelle, you said something about me not wanting Jade to see us again. How did you know she'd seen us together?"

"You must have mentioned it when I saw you last time." Rachelle tossed her hair back in defiance. "What does it matter?"

"I didn't mention anything about Jade to you. Wait a minute." He snapped his fingers. "Nick Guillory and you know each other."

"I know a lot of people," she snapped. "Look, go sniff after Jade Pellerin if that's what you want. That is if Nick hasn't got her legs in the air by now." Rachelle's mouth twisted in a spiteful curve.

"Dumb. So dumb of me not to have figured it out by now." Damon glowered at her. "You arranged it so carefully, didn't you? Covered your tracks well, as usual."

"What are you talking about?" Rachelle lifted her nose in the air.

"Just like you managed to hide your affair with Gregory Carrington." Damon nodded slowly at her. "Yes, I eventually did figure that one out."

What he did not say was that by the time he knew of the affair, it no longer mattered to him. He had already decided to leave her. She had killed whatever feelings he'd had with her selfish behavior.

Rachelle's mouth hung open for a few seconds before she recovered. Damon could almost hear the wheels turning as Rachelle calculated what response would best serve her. It seemed denial and outrage won.

"You're imagining things. Don't come scratching at my door when you realize she's back with Nick. He's got a certain way with women, and she was stone cold crazy for him."

Damon felt a wave of revulsion for this woman. How could he have ever thought he'd loved her? "Goodbye, Rachelle. I'll deal directly with your uncle from now on."

Rachelle snatched up her leather briefcase. "Drop dead." She strode from his office.

Helen wore a delighted grin when she came into his office. "Wo-wee! Miss Thang flew outta here like a cat with a fire cracker on its tail. Please tell me you got her told."

"We had words, yes." Damon could think only of how to undo the damage she'd done. He had a lot to apologize for as well. But what if Rachelle was right about Jade and Nick? He'd been stupid to leave the way clear for Nick to step back into her life. Now it was probably too late to do anything about it.

"Won't know until you call her, boss." Helen broke through his musing.

Damon started at her words. "Are you psychic?"

"Don't need a crystal ball to know something went wrong with you and the new lady. Not the way you've been brooding lately." Helen pulled a long face in obvious imitation of him. "Now call so I don't have to keep looking at this all day." She gave a nod of approval when he picked up the phone then left.

With another second of hesitation, Damon punched in the numbers. He anticipated the musical sound of her voice with a mixture of excitement and anxiety. The phone rang six times then picked up. He heard her voice.

"Damn!" Damon groaned in frustration as her recorded voice told him to leave a message at the tone. A cold knot formed in his stomach at the thought that Jade was with Nick. He put down the receiver.

Jade sat in the car, feeling numb. She'd hung up without leaving a message on Damon's answering machine at his apartment and made a bold decision. She knew he was more than likely at his office, working late what with the new business. His car in the building's parking lot was a welcome sight. After parallel parking on the street directly across from the entrance, she started to get out when Rachelle emerged. With a toss of her hair, she disabled the car alarm on her Mercedes. Jade watched her slam the car door hard and drive away. Now she sat wondering would it make a difference to see him. Her own angry words from that last night came back to her. In a haze of gloom, she started the car with mechanical movements. *No reason to stay here, girlfriend.*

Chapter 16

"Can you believe this zoo?" Shaena gazed around at the packed hearing room.

Jade and Shaena were seated in the row right behind the table where those giving comments sat. The chairs were empty for now. A microphone was poised for those who would speak. Some yards away, directly facing these tables and the audience, was a raised dais. A long table in the shape of a half-moon, with microphones dotting its surface, was for the state senators. Soon all seven members of the Health and Welfare Committee had bustled in. Dressed alike in varying shades of gray, brown and blue suits, they all strove to look like serious statesmen on a mission.

"And just think. We still have the Finance Committee to face." Jade felt her nerves stretch tight at the very thought of having Senator Baham, the glowering chairman, fix her with his steel gray eyes.

"Let's fasten our seatbelts, babe. It's going to be a bumpy ride," Shaena muttered low so as not to be overheard by those surrounding them.

"Thanks for coming with me. I know you've got other things

to do.'' Jade gave her a look of profound gratitude. She had not protested when Shaena announced she would accompany her.

''Hey, most of the grunt work is being done by the baby sharks now.'' Shaena referred to the pool of young attorneys fresh out of law school who were subordinates. ''I wouldn't miss this for the world.''

''Hi there.'' A tall woman with red hair and pale white skin stood over them, wearing a smug expression.

''Hello, Zelda,'' Jade said with a slight frown. The woman had been antagonistic toward her ever since she'd been promoted ahead of her four years earlier. This day was going south fast.

''Smart move, bringing your lawyer. From what I read in the papers, you might need one soon.'' Zelda moved away before Jade could respond.

''Sheesh, you'd think with that hairdo she'd at least try for Miss Congeniality,'' Shaena called out in raised voice. Several snickers came from onlookers. Zelda shot back a poisonous look then dropped down in a seat near the back.

''That was so immature,'' Jade said. She giggled with delight.

''Yeah, but it felt good.'' Shaena grinned back at her. ''They're about to start. Bill and Mike just slithered in,'' she whispered close to Jade's ear.

Jade looked around to find Bill Lang watching her steadily as he made his way down the center aisle. He nodded to her with a curt dip of his head but passed by before she could acknowledge the greeting. They took their places at the table, apparently knowing they would be first.

The chairman, Senator Thibodeaux, announced the agenda in a voice with a Cajun lilt. ''Now before we get started, Senator Raymond has some opening remarks.''

''Thank you, Mr. Chairman.'' Senator Raymond cleared his throat—a signal that the conservative from north Louisiana was about to pin someone to the wall.

After the first few sentences deploring the waste of the taxpayers' money, Jade tuned him out. This was a familiar thread with the humorless crusader. Jade felt an urge to glance around. Damon stepped through the double doors, closing them behind him just as she turned. He did not see her and moved to stand against the wall since all seats were taken. This was the first time she'd seen him in almost a month now. She wanted to look back again but resisted. Shaena leaned an inch closer.

"Raymond is out for blood," Shaena mumbled. "And he looks like he expects a nice meal."

Jade's mind was full of memories that had nothing to do with work. She glanced back to find Damon gazing at her. He smiled and her heart turned over. "What? Did you say something?"

Shaena followed her gaze. "It's about time. He's probably been just as miserable as you. I hope you two—" She broke off when Bill spoke into the microphone.

"Thank you, Mr. Chairman. First just let me say that we have provided each of you with the final report of Inspector General Dumaine. Many of your questions, Senator Raymond, have been answered." Bill spoke in an even tone. He was the picture of calm. He delivered a bold offensive strike by anticipating the most difficult issues and addressing them first.

Jade could not help but admire his audacity. It was a risk, but one that seemed to be paying off. Many of the committee members' frowns were replaced with expressions of attentive thoughtfulness. But she also recognized in his words the escape clauses should wrongdoing be proven. Bill was careful to remind them that he relied on top staff for day-to-day operations. He expressed full confidence in their actions.

"I will do everything I can to solve the Medicaid crisis." Bill wore the serene look of a man with nothing to hide.

"Mr. Lang, I have some specific questions," Senator Raymond rumbled in his best statesman voice. It was obvious he was not impressed with Bill's performance.

Much as she tried, Jade could not keep her attention on the proceedings. Just knowing Damon was in the room acted as a magnetic force, drawing her away from everything else. Why was he here? *To see me?* Her heart rate increased. Something

Bill said caught her attention. He was referring to the grant funds. *The grant to Gracie Street Center is why he's here. Besides, he would have called if he wanted to see me.* Jade pressed her lips together. She would not make a fool of herself running after the man. He and Rachelle Balleaux Knight deserved each other!

Damon could sense the pull between them even across the room packed with people. More than once the voices of Bill Lang and the committee members faded to a distant hum as he stared at Jade. Even the smallest things, like the way her hair moved when she turned her head, ignited a glowing ember in his lower body. He wanted to make this crowd vanish so he could be with her. They had much to talk about. Yet he could sense a resistance from her, too. Was it because she was angry about Rachelle? Then he would talk to her and make her see Rachelle meant nothing to him now. Or was Nick firmly back in her life and heart? Maybe Rachelle was right. He tried to remember every expression, every nuance of Jade's voice when she had talked about him. Could Jade still be in love with Nick? *Stop driving yourself crazy with these questions! Damn, let's get this thing over.* Damon knew he should be concentrating on the hearing since the future of Gracie Street Center could hang in the balance. But all he could think of was getting to Jade.

"Damon, I'm so glad to see you."

Damon blinked back to his surroundings to find himself being addressed. He glanced around. "Mrs. Wilson, so nice to see you."

"Now look here. You're just the one we need on our task force to fight these budget cuts." Mrs. Wilson launched into a whispered description of her latest crusade. The sixty-something social activist was in her element, taking aim at the powers that be.

"If there is nothing further, we'll adjourn until Friday afternoon at two thirty." The chairman dismissed the hearing.

"Let me call you after I check my calendar," Damon said. "I'll be in touch." He glanced to see Jade still seated behind Bill Lang. If only Mrs. Wilson would stop talking, he could go to her.

"Wait a minute, let me tell you this." Mrs. Wilson put a hand on his arm.

Damon suppressed a groan of despair. The woman rattled while he tried not to make his impatience too obvious. Even more exasperating, the crowd lingered to discuss the interesting exchange between Bill and Senator Raymond. Damon was tempted to shout her name when Jade began moving in the opposite direction to the doors set at the other end of the hearing room. Surely she must see him.

"You ought to go over there, girlfriend," Shaena mumbled to Jade so Bill Lang and Mike Testor could not hear. "Just go on over there and sort this thing out."

"Did you forget what I told you? She was coming out of his office swinging her hips and acting like she owned the place." Jade doused the fire in her body Damon had started with the cold memory of Rachelle.

"Will you get off that? Even I know that her uncle's marketing firm is tops with black businesses in a four-state area." Shaena tucked her brown leather portfolio under her arm. "Even *I* believe it was just business. And, honey, you know how suspicious I am."

"He hasn't hurt himself trying to get to me. And the phone lines haven't been down for the last two weeks." Jade made it a point to keep her back to where Damon stood. She headed for the doors at the other end of the hearing room.

Shaena grabbed her arm. "Come back here, you. I'm tired of this mess. You're going to talk to that man today, or I'm going to whip both your butts for acting crazy."

"Jade, we need to get back to the office. Might as well plan on a late night. Thanks to Senator Raymond, we've got more documents to gather for the next hearing with this committee."

Bill Lang's hold on his unruffled exterior was beginning to slip. Worry lines were etched across his forehead.

"Sure, Bill." Jade shot an irritated look at Shaena. "Cut it out," she said low enough so only she could hear. She yanked free of Shaena's hidden grasp on her arm to follow him.

For the rest of the day, Jade's emotions swung crazily. She went from supreme satisfaction that she had not given in to the desire to approach Damon to crushing uncertainty. Had she made the right choice? He looked so fine in that navy blue suit. If she closed her eyes, she could smell his brand of cologne. The rows of cream-colored file folders faded before her. Jade stood just outside Bill's office where anyone looking would think she was intent on searching for something she needed. In fact she was several miles and days away back in Damon's apartment.

"Jade, get me the file on Care Systems, Inc." Bill's voice cut through her musings.

"Okay." Jade was so startled, she jumped. She shut the file drawer and started down the hall.

"Jade, you seem out of it. Want to talk about what's troubling you?" Bill eyed her with speculation.

"Just tired from reading page after page of tiny black print. I'm fine." She spoke over her shoulder before continuing on.

For once Bill's clipped instructions that kept her occupied all day were a welcome distraction. Never mind that he was probably using mountains of paper to bury her while clearing an escape route for himself—which brought her back with a jerk to her predicament once more. In the last few days, she had not seen any direct evidence that Bill had singled her out to take the blame, yet her gut instinct told her to beware. Despite the odd moments when he seemed poised to confide in her, Jade sensed something wrong. She continued to gather her own set of files as protection she hoped she would not need.

Jade had been a sincere admirer of Bill Lang—another disappointment that stung. Add to that the difficult family therapy she and her parents had begun as part of Lanessa's treatment, Jade felt a desperate need to have someone she could turn to right now. The file room became blurred before her. Jade swiped at the tears before they trailed down her face.

"Jade, Bill wants me to run up to legal for something. I'll be back in a minute. One of the student workers will get the phones." Aline stood in the open door.

"All right." Jade sniffed. She kept her face away from her.

"Is there anything I can do to help?" Aline stepped in the room. "I mean . . ." She glanced over her shoulder. "I know where some other papers are that might help you."

"I've got all I need. Thanks."

"Yeah, but these are folders on Health Tech you really need to see." Aline spoke each word with emphasis.

Jade turned around to look at her. "Really?" Something in Aline's eyes made her know that she was giving her some kind of message.

"Things that might come in handy later." Aline closed the door behind her. She pulled out a sheaf of photocopies folded and held against her side. "I've been trying for days to slip you these. I'll deny it if you tell where you got them."

"I won't. Never." Jade gave her hand a squeeze. "Thanks, Aline."

"Listen, of all the folks I've watched pass through here, you were one of the few that didn't treat us secretaries like servants. Watch your back." Aline opened the door again. "Okay, I'll be right back," she said in a normal voice intended for anyone passing by.

Jade nodded to her then turned her back to scan the pages. "Thank you very much," she murmured.

"Hello, Mother," Damon said in a stiff voice.

He had never felt this uncomfortable in his parents' home. The revelations from his father had placed his parents in a whole new light. Oliver had always been the driven entrepreneur, his mother the graceful, socially well-connected wife of a successful man. He had never thought of them as having frustrated passions or dark secrets. Like most children, he'd seen them only in terms of himself. Their outward appearance seemed all there was to see. An appearance that before now, he would have sworn was real. Of course now he knew different. Oliver Knight, gruff workaholic, had once been a young man caught in a tragic love that was worthy of a Shakespearean play. Marlene Cormier Knight was so desperate to have him, she had married Oliver despite knowing he loved another woman. Damon clenched his jaw. But that was no excuse for adultery.

Marlene patted her hair with a nervous motion. "Hello, Damon. Have you eaten yet? I could fix you something." She started to leave the den.

"No, thank you. I had something right after I left the office."

"Oh." Marlene, eager to please, was disappointed.

Damon let the awkward silence lengthen. He searched for something to say. "Where's Dad?"

"He's out with his friends. I . . . I wanted to talk to you alone." Marlene got up from the chair. She twisted her hands. "Damon, whatever has happened between your father and I has nothing to do with you or Trent."

"Okay."

"We have things to work out." She rubbed her forehead.

"I'm sure," was Damon's terse reply. He wore a frown of censure as though he were the parent of a wayward daughter.

Marlene did not miss the message. She spun to face him. "How dare you pass judgment on me, young man. I'm still your mother."

"Yes, ma'am." Damon put all the sarcasm he could muster in his reply. He sat stone-faced, not looking at her.

"Don't do this to me. I've had it from your father for the past thirty-five years. I can't take it from you, too." Marlene's shoulders shook. "Oliver shut me out of his heart and a big part of his life. I married him thinking somehow I could push her out of his mind. Even when he found out about her father and how he treated her, Oliver still deep down wanted her. Once when I tried to confront him, he just sat looking at me, cold as ice. And now you." She shivered.

Damon felt a rush of regret for being so unyielding. His

mother looked so lost and unhappy. He was in no position to judge her. How could he know what her life had been like? She'd spent years trying to win his father's love and attention away from a memory. Damon was reeling with the new knowledge that her cool, elegant exterior had hidden a deep agony.

"Mother, come here." He got up and led her back to sit next to him on the sofa. Marlene rested her head on his shoulder.

"I've done terrible things. But can you imagine what it's like to realize that no matter what you do, the one man you love will never love you back?" Marlene sobbed quietly, her hand pressed to her mouth.

"Mother . . ." Damon did not know what to say. The only person who could answer her was his father. "I'm so sorry for you both."

Marlene wiped her eyes one final time. She sat up with her head held high. "I'm sorry for going to pieces like that. This isn't something you or your brother should be burdened with." She held up a hand to cut off his protest. "I meant what I said before. This is between your father and I."

Damon took her hand. "I understand. Of course you're right." He kissed it.

"Thank you." Marlene's eyes pooled again with tears. She smiled at him with gratitude. "But I want to tell you how it's been for us."

"You don't have to. Dad told me a little." Damon patted her back.

"He told you about Lisette?" Marlene's eyes went wide with surprise.

"Yes, he blames himself for making you so unhappy."

Marlene hugged herself as though for warmth. She stared off. "She was beautiful, but I suppose he told you that. And I hated her on sight. From the first time I saw them together, I knew Oliver was infatuated. I thought it was only because she was loose. There were girls who did and girls who didn't. Boys were expected to chase after girls who did. But they married nice girls from the right families."

"Sort of like what you want for Trent and I," Damon said in a low voice.

Marlene wore a sad smile. "Yes, it's how we were raised. But Oliver really loved Lisette. In a way he never loved me. I was glad when her name got dragged through the mud. But even dead, she has more of Oliver than I've ever had." Several minutes of silence followed as they both thought about the long-ago events that seemed to still shape their lives in a dramatic way.

"Mother, Dad really wants to talk to you about all this—in a way he's never done before. I know it." Damon put his arms around her waist.

"There is so much I want to say to him. After all these years, we've got to find a way to each other. Before it's too late." Marlene took a deep breath. "But I owe you an apology."

"For what?" Damon rubbed her arms in a comforting way.

"Damon, the one lesson I should have learned is how dreadful life is without the one person you truly love. Instead I let my snobbish attitude, inherited from a long line of fancy-pants Creoles, rule once again. But at least you stood up to me. Good for you. I can tell you love Jade Pellerin with all your heart." Marlene put a hand on his face in a gesture of maternal love. "I'm happy for you, baby."

Damon felt the familiar despair creep back. His mother was right to say he was like his father. Like Oliver, he'd left important things unsaid. Instead of facing the problems between he and Jade head-on, he'd avoided them. Now it was probably too late.

"Jade and I aren't seeing each other anymore. At least not for the past month. We had an argument. Well, more of disagreement really. We—"

"About what?" Marlene raised her shapely eyebrows at him. The elegant sophisticate returned.

"Well, she thought Rachelle and I were seeing each other again. And we had words."

"And are you seeing Rachelle?" Marlene gazed at him.

"Only for business. I don't have one bit of warm feeling

left for her, Mother,'' Damon said with a shake of his head. He remembered the look of chagrin on Rachelle's face as she stood with her jacket open. ''No, that's over.''

''I see.'' Marlene bit her bottom lip. ''I have another admission.''

''What?''

''Rachelle called you with my encouragement. Another misguided attempt to control your life.'' Marlene gazed at him with an anxious expression.

''It's okay, Mother.''

Damon knew Rachelle had needed little prodding to try and worm her way back into his life. But Jade filled up his mind, heart and senses so completely there was no room for another woman. Jade. How he missed her. He wanted to savor the rich sweet taste of her on his tongue.

''No, it's not okay. I cost you the woman you love.'' Marlene put her head to one side. ''But that can be remedied.''

''I'm sorry, Mother. What did you say?'' Damon was awash in memories of being wrapped up in Jade's silken arms and legs. He blinked in embarrassment, sure that his mother could tell what he was daydreaming by his face.

''I said, get up off your butt and go find Jade. Tell her you were wrong. Tell her she's the air you breathe, she's what makes getting up each morning a joy, tell her—''

''I get the message, Mother. But what if she won't see me?'' Damon wavered in the face of rejection. Jade could well be angry or worse, indifferent.

''Oh, she'll see you. Of that I'm sure.'' Marlene smiled with the supreme confidence of a woman used to getting her way. ''Now get out of my house.''

''What?'' Damon stared at her bewildered. ''I thought we could spend a little time together.''

''Don't think you're going to hide out over here to avoid facing her. Get out and don't come back without Jade on your arm.'' Marlene tugged him to his feet. ''I mean it, Damon.''

''Okay, okay.'' Damon laughed. He walked ahead of her to the front door with Marlene's hand planted firmly in his back, urging him forward. "Mother, you really have a most unique approach to matchmaking."

"And don't screw it up." Marlene shook a finger under his nose. Her expression softened. "I love you, my baby."

Damon hugged her to him. "I love you, too."

"As your best friend I have to tell you this. You're nuts." Shaena stood in Jade's living room with her fists on her hips.

"Thanks for the pep talk," Jade retorted. "Now sit down and eat." She pointed to the cartons of take-out Chinese food.

Shaena did not move. "So she was at his office yesterday. So what?"

"So they're seeing each other." Jade gazed up at her. "Now will you sit down? I'm getting a pain in the neck looking up at you."

"Good, 'cause you're giving me a pain in the butt being so hardheaded." Shaena plopped down on the chair that matched Jade's sofa. "She was at his office conducting business, which is what he told you. Hel-lo?"

"Maybe but . . ." Jade wanted to believe that more than anything. But uncertainty kept rearing its ugly head.

"No maybe, no but. Grrr . . ." Shaena dug into her lemon chicken. "You can be so stubborn sometimes." A glob of sauce plopped on her blouse. "Oh, no, not my new outfit!" She dabbed at it.

Jade got up. "You need a bib, girlfriend. I'll get more napkins."

"Don't change the subject," Shaena yelled. She started at the sound of the doorbell.

"Get the door," Jade called from the kitchen. "They would be pushed behind something," she complained. She stretched to reach the top of her pantry shelf for the package of napkins. A solid feeling of warmth was suddenly at her back.

"Let me help," Damon said. He moved his body close to hers and reached up to easily retrieve the napkins. "Here you go." He handed them to her.

"How . . . ?" Jade turned to find herself within inches of his broad chest. She stood immobilized by the sensation of being near him. His ebony eyes were the most beautiful and welcome sight she'd seen in weeks.

"Shaena said to tell you she'll see you at work tomorrow." Damon gazed at her.

"She's gone?" Jade murmured.

"Yes. We're alone. Jade, I'm sorry." Damon put his arms around her.

"Sorry?"

Jade tried to focus. Feeling the hard muscles of his biceps pressed to her was wonderful. She had sorely missed his touch. Yet the thought that he had something to be sorry about brought a stab of anxiety. That he had a reason to apologize could mean only one thing.

"You and Rachelle." She looked away from his gaze.

Damon put a finger under her chin to lift her head back up. "No way," he said in a firm voice. "I'm sorry for not fighting harder to make you believe the truth. The only reason I met with my ex-wife was because of business. My father has done business with her family for years."

"I see." Jade did see. She saw the truth in his eyes and heard it in his voice.

"You're the only woman I want, Jade. The only one," Damon whispered as he lowered his mouth to hers. He ran his tongue along her lips as though she were candy he savored. "Say you believe. Please." His hands pulled her to him in a tight embrace.

"I do, Damon. I do." Jade gave herself up to the yearning to feel his kiss. She melted inside when he pressed against her, his erection fanning a flame that spread through her. "Let's get out of this closet before we have all my dry goods on the floor," she said with a soft giggle.

"Good idea." Damon grinned at her. Still he pulled back from her with great reluctance. "As long as you promise to save my place."

"It's a deal." Jade led him by the hand to her living room.

Once they were seated on the sofa, she snuggled against him. "I'm sorry, too, Damon. I shouldn't have been so quick to assume the worst about you."

"Well, aren't we something? So worried about getting hurt again, we backed away from each other." Damon rested his chin on the top of her head.

"Is that what we did?"

"At the first sign of trouble, we let the past influence how we reacted." Damon caressed her arms with tenderness. "At least that's what I did. Men always complain that women treat them like all the men who mistreated before. Well I did the same thing. I judged you based on Rachelle."

"Sometimes it's hard to forget the past. But things aren't always what they seem." Jade was thinking not only of her failed marriage, but her family. "I'm learning that more and more."

Damon held her for a few moments in deep thought. "I know what you mean." He kissed her head.

"Damon, so much has happened in the last three weeks or so. It's made me realize how important it is to hold on to those we love."

Jade told him about Lanessa. Fears and guilt she had held in, even from herself, flowed out. Yet with his strong arms around her, she knew it would be all right. She could face all the problems with hope.

"I'm so sorry, Jade. I should have been here for you." Damon cradled her gently in his embrace.

"You couldn't have known. Thank goodness it wasn't in the papers. We've been trying to pick up the pieces. Now I know how Humpty-Dumpty felt." Jade rested her cheek against his chest. The hard muscles were reassuring.

"You can do it, baby. And I'll be right there by your side." Damon trailed kisses down the side of her face until their lips met.

Without another word, only sighs and moans, they undressed each other slowly. They paused only to explore each area of newly exposed flesh with their hands and tongues. And for hours their bodies moved in perfect harmony. Long languorous moments of teasing each other to new heights of pleasure were interspersed with bone-shaking ecstasy that left them both breathless. They moved from the living room sofa to Jade's bed somewhere in-between.

"Umm, that feels wonderful," Jade said in a husky voice.

Damon was on top once again, his turn in a delicious game of tit for tat. She arched beneath him. The feeling of him inside her was too delicious.

"More, faster." Jade clung to him.

His hardness thrust deep inside, causing ripples of delight that spread with mind-bending intensity through the rest of her. She let out a long shuddering sigh. Damon cried out her name in response as his own orgasm took control of him. He kept calling her between ragged breaths. After an eternity, they sagged together still clutching each other tightly. Damon shifted his weight, then rolled off her.

"Woman, you're going to kill me. But if I'm going to die young, this is how I want to go." Damon lay flat on his back and pulled her to him.

"Like I told you before, I'm going to see to it that you stay nice and healthy," Jade murmured. "Now get some rest. You've got a big morning ahead of you."

"Yeah, I have a meeting. But how did you know that?" Damon was enjoying the way her hair felt between his fingers. He closed his eyes and drifted into sleep.

"I'm talking about before you leave here." Jade chuckled softly. She placed her thigh across his legs.

"Have mercy," he murmured.

Chapter 17

"Sit down, Jade." Bill gestured to one of the two leather chairs facing his desk. "Let's talk."

Jade had come just inside the door and stood with pad in hand. Most of the staff had gone for the day and she was about to leave when Bill called her. It was a struggle not to betray her feelings of suspicion and distrust when they worked so closely. Jade had been sure she was successful. Until now. This request to see her without a reason made her uneasy.

"Did you go over my summary of all the reports sent in by the regional managers?" Jade sat down and crossed her legs. "I tried to include all the key points you might want to know."

"Yes, yes. I've glanced through it. Very complete." Bill sat against the cushioned back of his chair, one elbow propped on its arm. His gaze drifted down to her legs.

"And the reports on new beds and rate changes?" Jade uncrossed her legs but resisted the temptation to tug her skirt hem down.

"Fine. Listen, I thought we should talk about the current situation." Bill shifted in his seat. "With all these allegations being made, I want to make sure you're okay. I mean, a lot of unfavorable things are being said about us."

"True." Jade did not trust herself to say more.

Unfavorable was an understatement that would have been funny if the accusations were not so serious. In recent weeks the newspaper accounts had carefully outlined a trail through a maze of incorporation papers and ownership disclosures. A trail that led to several former top state government officials. And though Bill Lang's name was never found on any of the documents, his connections to those involved were exposed. The report was clever in comparing agency decisions to the impact they had on certain agencies owned by these same politically connected former officials. These agencies had bene-fited to the tune of millions of dollars in the last five years. The top executives of these agencies made exorbitant salaries.

Worse still, Jade's name had appeared in the latest article. Two memos under her signature authorized the increase of rates for two nursing homes. Of course it was mentioned that this was in accordance with rate changes. But the implication was clear. Her actions were shown as one example of questionable activities going on in the department. Bill's quoted response, that he would look into it, angered her. Since he had initiated both memos, why should he have to look into it? Now references to malfeasance charges kept popping up with her name not far away.

"I don't want us to get a siege mentality around here. We've got to support each other." He affected a solemn expression. "Because *we* know they're false, don't we?"

For a few seconds of heavy silence, they gazed at each other. Jade wore a slight smile. She could play this game, too. "Of course, Bill. No rules were broken . . . to the best of my recollec-tion." A trace of surprise then amusement flashed across his face.

"Smart and gorgeous. A lethal combination." Bill stood up. "I think we'll do okay together. We make a good team."

Jade stood to face him. "Thanks. Is there anything else?"

"What's the rush? Jade," Bill said. He took her hand. "I

want you to know how much your support means to me. For the past few months, you've made having this position bearable."

"I've just tried to do my job, Bill. But I appreciate the compliment." Jade tried to move away but he still held her hand.

"Wait. No matter how bad things seem to be, I won't let your career suffer. Do you understand what I'm saying?"

He stood so close, she could feel his breath on her face. Jade stared into his light brown eyes. She read the unspoken message. He would pretend to abandon her but make sure she continued to have a top job in state government—a quite common practice. Once all the controversy died down, none but a few would know that all the players still held positions of authority, high-paying positions at that. Jade resisted the urge to jerk back her hand.

"Yes, I understand exactly what you're saying," Jade said in a neutral tone. She wanted to slap the sly smile that tugged his lips up.

"We're a magnificent team. I'm about to separate from my wife, you know." He stroked the palm of her hand.

Jade was fascinated with the way the man operated. Gone was the sincere, conscientious public servant. "That's too bad."

"I've tried to ignore her jealous outbursts, even to the point of violence. But now I need a different kind of relationship, a different kind of woman," he murmured.

The door to his office swung open. "Late meeting on vital issues, I presume?" Kathy sneered as Bill jumped back from Jade.

"Eavesdropping Kathy?" Bill was quick to regain composure.

"Excuse me." Jade started past her. She wanted no part of a nasty scene.

"Don't leave, Ms. Pellerin. I have something to tell my husband that I want you to hear, too." Kathy came into the office and slammed the door shut.

"Mrs. Lang, I really don't think—"

"No, sweetie, screwing around with my husband means you

definitely have not been thinking,'' Kathy snapped. ''That line about leaving me is one he's used a dozen times at least. It won't happen, not in this life. Got it?''

''Kathy, I'm sick of you. I've already moved out most of my things.'' Bill laughed at the look of shock in Kathy's eyes. ''That's right. I don't need your money.''

''I'll make sure those investments dry up. That reporter will be very interested to hear how you've met with Steve Franklin and those other crooks to feather your nest,'' Kathy shot back.

''You can't do a thing, and we both know it.''

Kathy spun to face Jade. ''He'll let you take all the blame if things get too hot, you know.''

''Is that so?'' Jade said as she looked at Bill.

''Baby, she's lying. She'll say anything to come between us.'' Bill lifted both hands.

''Bill, please don't do this.'' Kathy's tough facade crumpled. ''I need you, honey. I'll do anything you want.'' She wrapped her arms around him in a tight grasp. ''Listen, I didn't tell those reporters about Senator Ortego. What they have so far won't seriously hurt you unless they find out about that.''

Jade was appalled. The poor woman would go to any lengths to hold on to a cold, self-centered man who cared only for himself. Kathy only wanted him to love her, but she was willing to settle for binding him to her out of necessity if that was all she could get. Jade turned away on the pitiful sight of her begging him not to leave her.

''Kathy, take your hands off me.'' Bill held himself rigid, not returning her embrace.

''You slut. This is all your fault,'' Kathy screamed at Jade.

''That's it. I've had enough.'' Jade threw the pad and pen down on the floor. ''Bill and I have never even come close to having an affair. It's true!'' she said at the contemptuous look of disbelief on Kathy's face. ''But I really don't care what you think.''

Bill gave a repellent laugh. ''Tell her, Jade.''

''You're welcome to him.'' Jade jerked a thumb at Bill.

''Take it easy, baby.'' Bill lost his amused expression.

"And you," Jade said as she jabbed a forefinger at him. "I'm not stupid or blind. I'll take care of myself."

Kathy stared at Jade for a few seconds with a thoughtful expression. "Good for you."

"Jade, what are you talking about?" Bill did not like this turn of events. He glanced from his wife to Jade.

"Just what I said."

"I expect an answer right now." Bill glared at her. "I'm still your boss."

"I'm going to do my job as usual, Bill. Don't ever touch me again, or I'll add a sexual harassment charge to all the other problems you've got." Jade marched out of the office.

Once alone, she took a deep breath. She had come close to tipping her hand, something that would have been a serious mistake. If Bill thought she knew of his plans, he might take steps to do her career serious harm before she could defend herself. Better to let him think she was enraged about the clumsy advances he'd made. Jade headed out of the building, hoping Bill would not think too hard on their exchange. With her mind in a whirl, she went to the inpatient clinic where Lanessa was being treated. At least tonight there would be no emotion-packed therapy session to face. Lanessa was in her room, sitting on the bed, when Jade arrived.

"Hello, Nessa." Jade kissed her forehead.

Lanessa twisted the hem of her shirt. "Hi." She was thinner, and there were circles under her eyes. "What are you doing here? We don't have a session tonight."

"I came by to visit. I can see you outside of therapy, you know." Jade sat next to her on the bed.

"Oh, goody, a private sermon. Number one hundred and two at last count," Lanessa said with resentment.

"No sermon, Nessa. I just wanted to see how you're doing," Jade said in her most patient voice. After the scene with Bill and Kathy, this was the last thing she needed.

"Don't talk to me like that!" Lanessa shot back. "Everybody uses that singsong voice like I'm some nut case. I can hear you talking about me: 'Just try not to upset her, or we'll have to slap the restraints back on.' ''

"Nessa, stop it."

Jade watched her go back and forth. She still was not used to her outbursts. There was no way to predict what mood Lanessa would be in these days. The social worker had said that sometimes issues brought out in her individual therapy session might leave Lanessa agitated for a time.

"You don't know what it's like caged up in here. I hate it." Lanessa pulled at her hair with trembling hands. "You waltz in and out of here like Rebecca of Sunnybrook Farm without a care in the world."

Jade felt a rise of irritation at her older sister. Her raw nerves jangled at being attacked. "Well, at least you're not out getting yourself wrapped around trees in your car."

"Great, bring that up. Is this your idea of a cheery visit?" Lanessa hissed at her.

"No, it's not. But getting beat up every time I visit you isn't my idea of a pleasant way to pass the time, either—especially after the day I've had. I've got folks hinting that I'm a crook, my boss probably planning a way for me to take the fall and an interview with Dumaine. Trust me, I've got problems."

"Oh, Lord. I'm sorry for what I've done to you." Lanessa sobbed into her hands. "I'm so sorry."

"Come on now, it's all right." Jade left the bed and put her arms around Lanessa. "I'm sorry, too. I know how rough it is. And here I'm laying all my troubles on you."

"It's my fault," Lanessa said in a muffled voice. Her face was pressed against Jade's shoulder.

"Don't be silly. I was in a lousy mood when I got here."

"No, Jade. It *is* my fault those stories are in the newspaper." Lanessa pulled away from her. She turned her back on Jade to stare out of the window that faced the clinic parking lot.

"What are you saying?"

"You remember Glenn Curtis? The little jerk was in grade school with me." Lanessa seemed to sag inside her skin. She walked back to sit down on the edge of the bed.

"Short stumpy guy that was always hanging around the popular crowd telling dirty jokes." Jade frowned. She had a vague memory of a young man with a shifty expression permanently stamped on his boxy face.

"That's him. He's a reporter. The worst kind." Lanessa twisted the hem of her blouse again with jerky motions. "One night I was drunk"—she snorted—"like that was unusual. Anyway, I was rambling on, telling him how you had moved up and had so much authority. I resented your success, Jade, but I swear, I didn't mean to give him damaging stuff to use against you. By the time I realized he was pumping me for a story, it was too late. One more thing that qualifies me for a spot in the Hall of Shame."

"Oh, Lanessa." Jade shook her head slowly.

Lanessa sobbed harder, unable to face her. "It's not enough I've ruined my life, I had to ruin yours, too."

"Listen to me," Jade said.

"I don't blame you for hating me." Lanessa rocked back and forth.

"I said stop and listen to me." Jade sat next to her and put an arm around her shoulders. "What little I ever told you about my job is public record. Savoie would have found out that and more if you'd never spoken to Glenn. They were already digging for damaging information."

"But I gave him a lead on where to look. Glenn said so." Lanessa wiped her nose with a wad of tissues.

"Believe me, Nessa, Savoie didn't need Glenn to point the way. He's one of the sharpest investigative reporters in the South. He knew exactly what to look for. This isn't his first time tracking down scandals in state government."

"You're not just saying that?" Lanessa gripped Jade's arm with a look of hope. "I didn't hurt you after all?"

"No, Nessa. You didn't." Jade brushed a wisp of her hair away from her eyes.

"Thank God. At least that's one thing I didn't do. But not through any virtue of mine." Lanessa looked grim and hollow-eyed. Her shoulders drooped with self-recrimination.

"Lanessa, you've made mistakes. But you're still the bestest big sister in the world." Jade hugged her.

"Oh, please. I'm just grateful you never used me as role model. Instead of setting an example for you, I've done everything wrong." Lanessa waved a hand in the air. "Mama didn't call you the smart one for nothing."

"The only reason I know anything about style is because of you. Remember those times you spotted me going out the door dressed in some strange getup?" Jade wanted to coax her back from despair.

"Yeah, I seriously wondered if you were one of the fashion-challenged. Those checked pants you bought one weekend . . ." Lanessa gave a comical shudder.

"You'd drag me back inside and say 'Girl, you are not representing me out in public dressed like that!' I still think my pants were cute." Jade giggled when Lanessa gave a shriek of dismay.

Lanessa grabbed her by the shoulders. "Tell me you're not wearing those things, please!"

"Come on now. I learned something from you." Jade gazed at her sister with affection. "Nessa, there were times when I felt down on myself that I'd think, 'Now Lanessa wouldn't let them mess with her' or 'Lanessa would handle it this way.' You were a great role model when it came to being assertive and commanding respect."

"Jade-girl, you're beautiful inside and out." Lanessa kissed Jade's cheek.

"So are you," Jade said.

"No, I'm—" Lanessa shook her head.

"*Yes,* you are," Jade cut her off firmly. She held Lanessa for the rest of their visit, willing her to believe it.

"Hello, Mama." Jade watched Clarice with a wary eye.

They stood in the large laundry room of her parents' home. Since the night of the accident, her mother had been on the defensive. In the therapy sessions, both her daughters' anxieties had centered on living up to her expectations. The result was that Clarice had missed the last two sessions. Now Jade wanted to find a way through to her. No matter how resentful she felt toward Clarice, Jade had never ceased to want a closer relationship.

"Sure you want to speak to me? With me being such a witch of a mother and all." Clarice worked at folding up a pile a laundry, a task she insisted on returning to after having let Jade in.

"Oh, Mama, that's not how we feel, and you know it." Jade set down her purse with a sigh. This was going to be as tough as she'd expected.

"Sure can't tell from the way you talked in front of the social worker. I'm surprised you and your sister haven't disowned me by now." Clarice popped the bath towel in the air with a sharp flick of her wrists then folded it.

"Mama, let me—"

"It's all my fault. You don't like yourself because I made you feel ugly. And Lanessa is in trouble because I pushed her to it."

"Mama, Lanessa is an alcoholic. She has an addictive personality. Even she admits she was sliding into illegal drug use." Jade took a cue from the therapist and pressed the truth on her. Clarice still resisted the fact of Lanessa's substance abuse.

"Everything is laid at my door. Well, what about your father? I was left to raise you girls alone when he was out working twelve hours a day, sometimes nights and weekends." Clarice yanked another towel from the stack. "Did anyone mention that? How I stayed up nights nursing you two through fevers, chicken pox and all kinds of illnesses? No!"

"Mama, we don't blame everything on you." Jade tried to think of something to say that would diffuse her anger.

"Well, thank you so much, Jade!" Clarice whirled to face her. "How very nice of you not to place *everything* on my shoulders." Her voice broke. "You accuse me of pushing Lanessa until she almost killed herself. Now I'm supposed to feel better because you don't blame me for everything."

"Mama, Lanessa has to take responsibility for her life. You didn't put the drink in her hand. When all is said and done, she can't use any of us as an excuse to get high." Jade approached her mother. "She's an alcoholic and at the edge of being a drug addict."

Clarice sat stiff with grief. She trembled as tears flowed down her face. "Oh, Lord, what have I done to my children?"

Jade led her into the kitchen to the breakfast table. "Mama, you raised us with love and did everything you could to help us. We all need to stop beating ourselves up. The one thing we have is that we love each other dearly." She made soothing noises while her mother cried for a few minutes. Finally Clarice gained some control.

"When I was coming up, my parents didn't have much. Oh, Daddy worked hard, but things were tight. Those girls like Marlene Knight used to laugh at us right to our faces. Our clothes were old, we didn't have money for fancy makeup or trips. I hated it. Mama made us wear hand-me-downs even when we had money to buy new clothes." Clarice looked back to her past as though she could see herself as a young girl again.

"Yeah, Grandmama was a little tight-fisted. Daddy used to say she pinched her pennies so hard, Lincoln had a frown on his face." Jade smiled at the memory of her brusque but lovable grandmother.

"Mama never understood how it felt to walk down the hall at school while kids were snickering at you. She didn't want to hear it. She'd say, 'When they start buying your clothes, then start listenin' to them.'" Clarice wore a frown traced with bitterness after forty years.

"So you blamed your mother, too?" Jade said in a soft voice. She saw her mother in a whole new light. Clarice even looked younger. Jade could almost see traces of the teenage girl humiliated at how she looked.

Clarice seemed not to notice Jade anymore, so deep was she in her past. "I wasn't good enough to be asked to the dance in seventh grade. All through high school, the teachers favored the girls from so-called good families. I swore they would never look down on me again. And I would make sure my daughters had everything I'd never had.''

"We did, Mama. You did a wonderful job." Jade patted her hand.

"I don't think so, baby. I never thought you were ugly." Clarice place a palm on Jade's face, cupping it lovingly. "You're the most beautiful child in the world. It's just you had the looks and a kind of inner strength. Since you were a baby, you struck out to find things on your own. Your sister was a fearful little thing. So I tried to give her confidence, you know. Lanessa is more . . . vulnerable.''

They sat pondering her words for a long time, listening to the kitchen clock tick. Jade knew that there was no magic wand that would make things all right for her family, but at last they were on the right path. She could feel it. For the first time in her life, she felt a true kinship with her mother. Clarice had never spoken to her so openly about her past hurts. Her mother's conflict with her own mother was a revelation.

"Seems like mothers are always trying to do what's best for their children." Jade thought of generations of mothers and daughters stretching back through time. She felt a connection to all those beautiful strong black women. "But one legacy we have is the love and dignity they gave to us.''

"Yes, Mama was a strong woman. She could walk into a room of teachers and professors without feeling the least bit intimidated." Clarice's face shown with pride. "You know what, let's call your grandmother. She's got pictures of her grandparents and great-grandparents. I'll bet Lanessa would love to see those, too.''

"Yeah, that would be wonderful! Then we can get Mama Rose to talking about *her* mother." Jade chuckled.

"Lord, don't get her started about Granny Adele. You know Mama and her sister Loretha didn't speak to each other for two years after Granny Adele let Auntie Loretha wear the best dress to a school function.''

"Get outta here! Two years?" Jade cackled.

For the rest of the day, they sat talking about family history and sharing confidences as never before. Jade poured out all her feelings for Damon. Clarice listened to her with the kind of rapt attention Jade had always wanted from her mother. Jade no longer felt like an outsider. And she knew they would get through this horrible time together.

"Don't get me wrong, sweet thing. I'm happy to see you. But aren't you taking a bit of a chance?" Tavis was all feline grace as he poured them both a drink.

Marlene stared at him. "Yes, I know exactly what I saw in you." She watched his every move. She did not return his smile when he walked to her, holding out the glass.

"Really? Tell me about it." Tavis took a sip of brandy. He sat down and patted the cushion next to him on the leather sofa. "I like this game we play."

Marlene put the glass down on the glass coffee table. "I have a bit of news for you. We're through." She stared down at him.

"I see." He swirled the dark liquid around the heavy glass in his hand.

"What we had was entertaining, but . . ." Marlene shrugged.

"But you're trying to tell me the thrill is gone? Get real." Tavis stood up to face her. The muscles of his chest and arms rippled beneath the white knit cotton shirt he wore. Powerful thighs were outlined by the olive khaki pants. "You were begging for more the last time. You know I'm right."

"As I said, entertaining." Marlene was all cool sophistication. Her full lips curved up.

Tavis kept smiling, but his jaw was clenched. "So you've decided to get someone else. Younger than me, no doubt."

"No, not another lover." Marlene arranged the folds of her silk shirt.

"Don't tell me you're going to play the part of dutiful wife." He snorted. "It doesn't suit you. And it won't last." Tavis pointed a forefinger at her.

"What I'm going to do is irrelevant. But there is something you are going to do." Marlene nodded to him to be seated. She sat across from him on a matching chair. "Bill Lang has set up Jade Pellerin to take the fall. But you're going to make sure it doesn't succeed."

Tavis could not hide his surprise at her words. "How did you ... I mean, I don't have one clue what you're talking about." He got up to pour more brandy into his glass, though it was still half full.

"Nice try, lover, but you didn't quite pull it off." Marlene stared at his broad shoulders.

Tavis turned around. "Listen, Oliver might be very upset to know where you've been spending your evenings and Saturdays. I think you have more to worry about than Jade Pellerin."

"Is that a threat?" Marlene did not seem worried at all.

"Baby, come on now. We've had a wonderful arrangement. Good sex and—"

Marlene held up a palm. "And my insider tips whispered as pillow talk helped you jockey into a more visible position. Your career has been enhanced in the few short months we've been seeing each other."

"Hmm, a delicate way to describe what we've been doing." Tavis wore a suggestive smile. "I've got big plans and, well, frankly I need you."

"So until you're through using me, our affair continues?" Marlene spoke in a quiet voice.

"I knew you'd understand. Listen, we both get a lot out of this deal, you know?"

"No. Suddenly it's clear to me that I don't need you anymore." Marlene stared past him, not seeing him for a few seconds. "Empty physical gratification isn't enough."

"Humph! After a couple of weeks with old Oliver, you'll be hot to get back to me. So don't give me some line about being in love with your husband." Tavis waved a hand at her.

"I do love my husband, very much," Marlene murmured softly more to herself than to him. "But as I was saying, we're through."

"Number one, we're not through just yet. I'll see you as usual. Number two, don't ever tell me what to do again. Got it?" Tavis sat down next to her on the arm of the chair. "Now drop the act, and let's go into the bedroom so you can get what you really came here for." He stroked her arm.

Marlene gazed at his hand for a few seconds before she stood up. Tavis smiled at her in triumph. He pulled her close to him with one hand on her hip.

"I knew you wanted it," Tavis whispered.

"Tavis, let me tell you something. My husband knows about us. He has for some time now." Marlene nodded slowly as the full impact of her words changed the expression on his face.

"How did he . . . ?" Tavis stepped back and rubbed his faced hard.

"Oliver is no fool. And he has powerful friends." Marlene smiled at the flicker of anxiety that chased across his handsome features.

"Damn! He could bring me down a little at a time now. I'm not yet in a position to stop him. Aw, man." Tavis ran fingers over his dark hair.

"Fortunately for you, Oliver isn't vindictive. He doesn't care about your little career. So these dirty deals with Lang were going to put you on top, with help from me. Then you wouldn't care about Oliver knowing or what happened to me." Marlene crossed her arms. "Well, you're going to have to switch to Plan B, my dear."

"What are you talking about?" Tavis eyed her with nervous suspicion.

"You're going to *help Jade Pellerin*. Show her where the bodies are buried." Marlene now wore a hard, relentless expression.

"You've got to be out of your mind. Bill would bury me if he found out!" Tavis blinked at her in shock. "No way."

"Bill Lang will be very busy trying to cover his own hind parts, sonny. He won't have time for you," Marlene quipped.

"But some of that stuff could bounce right back on me." Tavis jabbed a finger in his chest. "No way." He paced again.

"My dear, I have every confidence you'll find a means to save your own skin. We're mainly talking about the nursing home stuff, I think. You didn't have anything to do with that part of it." Marlene watched him with her head to one side. "You were mostly in on the medical center expansions and construction contracts."

"How do you know . . . ? What else have you found out?" Tavis stared at her with his mouth wide open.

"Those wonderful connections you cherish so, remember?" Marlene picked up her purse. "So do it, sugar. By the way, be careful. They're going to catch up with you soon."

"Have you heard something?" Tavis pulled at her arm with a jerk.

"I'd start backing off from Harlan Favre. He's a distant cousin, did you know that? Clever but no scruples. I'll be watching the newspapers, sugar." Marlene's amused look was replaced by one of fury. "And don't ever make the mistake of threatening me again!" She swept out of the town house without looking back.

"I'd like to kick his a—" Damon spluttered. His brows were drawn together in a fierce frown.

"Ah, ah. Cool it, baby." Jade stroked his cheek. "Maybe we better keep you away from Bill for a while."

They sat in Uncle Joe's, having dinner on Saturday. The usual weekend crowd flowed in and out. Tables were filled with people enjoying the seafood and Creole dishes. Blues and zydeco played in the background.

"Yeah, if you want to keep him healthy," Damon retorted.

Jade had tried not to let on just how worried she was about the pending interview with top officials. The governor had ordered Secretary Chauvin to conduct a thorough internal investigation. Shaena, courtesy of inside information from Brad, had told Jade more details than Bill had. Jade wondered if her meager notes of meetings with Bill would be enough to clear her name. In recent days her name was mentioned with more frequency in the newspaper articles. She suspected Bill and Mike Testor were feeding the reporter details through a third party in an attempt to take the heat off them.

"I'll be okay," Jade murmured absently.

Damon glanced at her. "Tell me the truth, Jade. Do you have the ammunition you need to fight back?"

"I think so. Well, actually I'm pretty sure," Jade added quickly at the look of concern her response caused. "Don't worry about me. You've got enough on your mind. I can take care of myself." The last thing she wanted was for Damon to become a target. There were already hints from Bill that he would involve Damon.

"I know you can. But I'm going to help you from now on," Damon said. He folded her hand into his. "It's the least I can do after acting like such a jerk—believing stupid gossip."

"We've been through all that." Jade gave him an affectionate poke in the ribs. "No more beating ourselves up, okay? Besides, I don't care about gossip. The people who really matter to me know the truth."

"It just makes me so mad to know he's manipulated this whole situation. He's always figuring an escape route no matter what situation he lands in." Damon wore a grimace as though just talking about Bill Lang made him sick.

"Yeah, and he's done a good job this time. I could even be indicted for malfeasance in office." Despite her best efforts, Jade's voice trembled. Her whole career could be ruined, and she could face criminal charges.

"I won't let that happen," Damon said, his voice harsh and intense. "No way."

"Well, between Mike Testor and Tavis, they've—"

"Tavis Collins?" Damon cut her off.

"Yeah. You know him?" Jade stared into her diet cola with a morose expression. "He's real smooth. They'll cover for each other for sure."

"Tavis Collins, eh? He's a buddy of Bill's. That's right." He snapped his fingers.

"They've been friends for a long time." Jade looked up at him with a curious expression.

"Of course. Tavis Collins." Damon tapped the tabletop with his fingertips. He stared ahead at the crowded dining room without really seeing anyone.

"Damon, remember me?" Jade waved her fingers in front of his face.

"Hmm? Oh, sorry. Listen, baby, I've got an errand to run." Damon stood up.

"Now? We just got here." Jade put her hands on both hips. "Damon Knight, what are you—"

"I've got an idea that just might blow this whole thing up in their faces." Damon nodded to himself. "Yeah, I'm going to have a little chat with my old buddy."

"Damon, what are you talking about? I'm not letting you out of my sight until you explain. Damon?" Jade's mouth flew open with surprise because Damon was already rushing off while she spoke.

"Gotta go, sweet. I'll call you later. But I'm going to make sure everything works out fine." Damon blew her a kiss.

"That man has not been getting enough rest." She shook her head.

Jade stared after him with a befuddled expression. Then she thought about his last words. That was it! She should have thought of it before. The waitress appeared.

"You ready to order?" The young woman, the name LaQuinta stamped on a plastic name tag on her blouse, held a pencil poised over a pad.

"No, thanks, we changed our minds." She paid her for their soft drinks.

Jade glance at her watch. It was only five fifteen. She could make it back to the office in plenty of time before the building closed at six.

"Might as well now that I'm free for the evening," she said. Excitement over her idea pushed her to dash out just as Damon had. Hours later she was home when the doorbell rang.

"Baby, you're all set." Damon pulled her to him and kissed

her. His eyes were bright with enthusiasm. "Here you go." He handed her a large brown envelope.

"Hey, this doesn't feel like a diamond necklace," she quipped.

"It's even better. Take a look."

Jade sat down to scan the papers she took out. "My oh my," she said. "Where did you get this?"

"Doesn't matter. Just use this to bury Bill Lang in his own you-know-what." Damon wore a wicked smile. "Just wish I could be there."

Chapter 18

"Sit down, Ms. Pellerin." Secretary Chauvin gestured to a chair. The top DHH official had the graceful but proud bearing of an old Creole family. His voice held just a touch of an accent. Iron gray hair was swept back from his forehead.

Sitting in the secretary's office in a half circle around the large room were six other men. Jade recognized two top Medicaid officials: Hazel Preston and her assistant director Wilton Trosclair. Bill Lang and Mike Testor sat stiffly next to each other. They did not greet her when she entered. Bill even avoided eye contact.

Chester Howard entered from a side door next to Secretary Chauvin's desk. The heavy, black eyebrows were in sharp contrast to his pale skin. His long face gave no clue as to his mood. He looked as he always did, like a humorless accountant. Known for his dogged stand on conservative spending that kept him ignored through successive freewheeling liberal/populist governors, Chester Howard sat closest to Secretary Chauvin. After introductions were made, Secretary Chauvin got down to business.

"I called this meeting because we have some serious problems in the department. We have a credibility crisis." Secretary Chauvin glanced around the room, watching the others react to his words.

"Sir, these newspaper reporters are digging for any scraps and . . ." Mike Testor's voice trailed off weakly at the slight shift of Chester Howard's eyebrows.

"Not only are we having serious problems with the legislature. Our congressional delegation is reluctant—and that's putting it mildly—to approach the feds on our behalf with the Medicaid shortage we face." Secretary Chauvin glanced at Bill then Jade. Seconds ticked away as the expression on his face made it clear he expected a response.

Bill cleared his throat. "We have tightened controls on several programs that have already resulted in savings. A few programs have been scaled back, others eliminated—"

"Others have been expanded and rates increased, as this Mr. Savoie has taken great trouble to describe." Secretary Chauvin pulled the article from a file folder filled with other newspaper clippings.

"Well, we know that news reporters will print one side of the story." Bill shrugged. "Notice he hasn't mentioned our cost-cutting measures."

"That's not the focus of his investigation." Howard's bland southern drawl came out just above a whisper.

"Exactly." Bill leaned forward. "He's going to slant the story to give it maximum effect. That's what sells newspapers. What we need to do is emphasize what we've done in response to the serious Medicaid shortfall. We can counter the effects of these stories." His voice had the old confident quality.

"Ms. Pellerin, do you agree with your boss?"

"Well, I think—" Jade tried not to fidget under his gaze. Bill cut her off. "We shouldn't be on the defensive."

"So you suggest we all but ignore these articles?" Secretary Chauvin made a tent with the fingers of both hands.

"No, obviously we must answer direct questions. I've put together a report that outlines all our cost-saving activities—some of which were reviewed by the Health and Welfare Committee members before we took them.'' Bill snapped his fingers at Jade, who handed him a small binder. He took the report without looking at her. Secretary Chauvin did not reach for the report, nor did he look at the white vinyl binder in Bill's hand.

''Wilton''—Chauvin turned to one of the Medicaid administrators—''tell me about Health Tech and the nursing home rates.''

Wilton Trosclair shifted in his seat. He glanced at Mike then caught himself. His boss, Hazel, sat impassively next to him.

''Health Tech owns eight nursing homes in the state, ten in Texas.'' Wilton tugged at the tie clipped to his white shirt. ''We, uh, did a review of rates and found the nursing homes were not being adequately reimbursed to cover the cost of care. This is based on—''

''Figures that were provided by the Association of Nursing Home Administrators,'' Howard, his voice still low, finished for him.

''Er, yes, that's true. But we checked them thoroughly against reasonable expense rates in the rest of this region of the country.'' Wilton bobbed his head, seeking some sign of encouragement from someone. No one moved.

''Yet the profit statements reviewed show that Health Tech, taken as only one example, has shown a stable and substantial surplus. Couple this with some scathing survey reports on patient care, and we have to wonder why an increase was granted.'' Chester Howard's brows went up just a fraction.

Hazel Preston, her heavy jaw quivering, flashed him an irritated look. ''We have to respond to their request by state regulation. If the figures indicate an increase, we have to give it. My section has acted totally in accordance with all state regs.'' She clearly meant to show that she was not intimidated.

''I know that, Hazel. I also know that you can use past performance on patient care surveys as a factor in your decision.'' Howard did not raise his voice to match her tone.

''That is not a usual part of the process,'' she clipped back at him.

"These are not usual times, Ms. Preston." Secretary Chauvin stared at her hard. "What about that, Bill?"

"Well, I . . ." Bill glanced at Mike. "To be candid, Secretary Chauvin, Health Tech has worked hard to improve. We know that. Ms. Pellerin worked closely with them."

"So this was a reward for their efforts?" Howard glanced around the room.

"Well, I wouldn't say it like that," Mike put in with a grin. "Let's just say in consideration for future services. Ms. Pellerin could give more details."

Secretary Chauvin turned in his heavy leather chair to stare at Mike. "Is that so, Mr. Testor?" A long, tense silence stretched after his voice died away.

Jade felt as if a trap had closed over her. Here she was caught between two men who would gladly let her take the fall and two conservatives who would just as soon jettison holdovers from a previous administration. Bill was seen as part of the old liberal system. He'd been appointed with reassurances that he would not continue old practices. Now it was clear that Howard had been watching his every move. She was surprised when he turned to Hazel and Wilton instead of her.

"We need a full report outlining the nursing home rates and any other rate changes made in the past eight to ten months." Howard did not blink at the glares the two gave him. "By noon tomorrow."

"Why, we'll need more time than that," she grumbled.

"It's all in a computerized database. I helped set it up two years ago." Howard's heavy brows twitched when Hazel snapped her mouth shut and stomped from the room.

"Yes, sir," Wilton stammered. He scurried after her.

"I'll just leave our report. Let me know if you have any questions." Bill started to leave. A look of relief started across his face then stopped at Howard's voice.

"Wait, Lang. We need to talk." Howard closed the door behind Trosclair. He sat in the chair beside Jade this time.

"What about these disturbing reports that you and Ms. Pellerin have some ties to several providers? We need to know if there is any aspect of your relationship that can be misconstrued." Howard's voice was mild, but it was clear he was asking for loaded information.

Jade felt as though she were the easiest target. Bill and Mike had political connections. What did she have? She fingered the brown envelope in her lap. As though from a distance, she heard Mike and Bill rattling on. Jade could tell that Secretary Chauvin and Howard were not impressed. Using the information she had was the last thing she wanted. Deep down, Jade wanted to close her eyes and make this all go away. But her career was on the line. Jade would not easily accept that years of hard work with the goal of gaining a top position could be swept away. Especially when she'd done nothing wrong.

"Well, it may be best if I speak with Jade and Mike alone. I'll get back to you with my findings." Bill gave a solemn nod.

Jade snapped to attention. "Excuse me, Secretary Chauvin. I feel compelled to say there is nothing questionable about any decisions made in which I took part."

"Jade, we'll talk later." Bill stood up.

"I have a list of all meetings, and my notes to correspond with our response to the inquiry on nursing home rates." Jade opened the envelope and handed Howard a memo sent to Wilton Trosclair. "I also have—"

"Really, they don't want to see any of this now." Mike Testor took the memo from Howard's hand. "We'll send a full report with all the details." His voice indicated that Jade was out of line and all the "guys" understood that.

"I'd like to see it actually." Howard retrieved the paper from a flustered Mike.

"I have notes of every meeting plus a few documents regarding the hospital certificates granted." From the corner of her eye, Jade could see Bill go rigid at her words.

"What are you doing?" he said in a taut voice. Bill struggled to maintain his composure.

Information from Damon confirmed that Bill's ties were deeper than she or the reporter suspected. Jade was able to follow a trail that someone had tried hard to bury. Only "lowly" clerical staff would know where to look. Jade thought of how excited Damon had been to help her. He'd tracked down his father's friends to get a trace on Tavis and Bill's activities with all the cleverness of a detective. Jade glowed inside at the thought of his gorgeous face soft with love for her. She shot a glance at the men around her. *First things first, babe. You're not out of the woods yet.*

"There is a set of documents in there that sets out an agreement with two providers that indicated expansions needed." Jade handed the papers to Howard.

Howard looked at the dates of one sheet after another. His dark eyes held a predatory gleam when he looked up at Bill and Mike. "Some of these are dated prior to your assuming the position of deputy under secretary. When did your discussions with these providers begin?"

Jade fought to steady her breathing. The papers indicated that Bill was cutting deals even before his appointment was confirmed. She turned to stare at Bill. Greed and arrogance. So eager to get the ball rolling, he had started working with men like Franklin immediately in preparation for his rise to power. No doubt he did not think the obscure paperwork, filed routinely and forgotten in a maze of cabinets on the fourth floor, would ever be found.

Jade had taken a big gamble. Howard and Secretary Chauvin might decide she was expendable. Her stomach tightened as she waited for their reactions. Secretary Chauvin and Howard looked at each other. Howard stood up.

"Let's meet in my office twenty minutes from now, Lang. I need to make a few phone calls. You, too, Mike." Howard turned to Jade. "Excuse us." With that, he dismissed her. He did not look back before heading down the hall.

Testor followed him with a heavy tread, a look of desperation on his blunt features. Bill paused outside Secretary Chauvin's office to confront Jade.

"Why did you do this to me? You know how few of us are in positions of authority," he growled at her in a rough, low voice. He looked over his shoulder.

"You wanted me to bring in a variety of information on decisions made, didn't you?" Jade stood tall, her chin lifted. "I brought all pertinent files. Is that a problem?"

"Damnit, I didn't ask you to go back that far—and you know it. I won't forget this, *Ms. Pellerin.*" Bill spoke through tight lips, his fury barely in check.

"Neither will I, *Mr. Lang.*" Jade met his wrathful gaze without flinching. "Should I help you prepare for this next meeting, too?" she said in an innocent voice.

Bill went pale with the effort not to lash out at her. The veins in his neck stood out. With a muttered curse, he spun away from her and stalked off.

"Well, that was touch and go." Shaena emerged from a small office.

Jade jumped with surprise. "Girl, what are you doing here?"

"On standby. The cavalry so to speak. Brad told me about the meeting."

"And just what did you think you were going to do?" Jade looped arms with Shaena as they walked to the elevator.

"I was going to get his secretary, Vonice, to put in a call to Howard and talk to him." Shaena winked at her. "Back in the days when he was politically incorrect, I helped him out a few times."

"Howard? The conservative? You're kidding." Jade's mouth dropped open.

"Hey, Vonice slipped in to give Secretary Chauvin a message. She said you were too nervous to notice. But she heard enough to know Bill Lang is in deep you-know-what. So I decided just to wait here for you."

"Thanks, my friend." Jade felt a lump in her throat. She pressed her cheek to Shaena's. Jade raised an eyebrow at her. "But you all cozy with conservatives is a bit hard to take."

"Honey, we both know poor folks never did get to see even half the money from a lot of programs. It ended up in the pockets of men like Steve Franklin and"—Shaena dropped her voice to a whisper—"Senator Ortego. With help from some so-called leaders who had their hands in the cookie jar."

Jade took a deep breath. She and Shaena had argued over this many times with Jade defending the social programs. After seeing Bill Lang in action this morning, it was hard to argue with her friend. Still Jade could not agree with the conservative solutions to cut entire programs.

"We have to make those services do what they were intended to, not condemn the recipients for a few greedy jerks," Jade said.

"Some of them are just plain political pork, Jade. You know it." Shaena waded in with her familiar charge. "Spoils for delivering votes to old-boy network black politicians."

"But we can't let that keep people from getting the services they need. No, we have to fight the devastating cuts and men like Bill who use programs for their own benefit."

Shaena steered Jade through the open doors of the elevators. "Yeah, yeah. And I'm sure we'll be discussing this at great length some time—just not now." She wore a mischievous grin as she waved goodbye.

"What?" Jade turned to find herself in Damon's arms.

"Hello, pretty baby." Damon winked at her. "Going my way?" He kissed her long and deeply as the elevator doors whisked shut.

A deep blue sky overhead, emerald green water below and a warm breeze that tickled her cheek made Jade purr with satisfaction. The soft sand of the beach gleamed in the late afternoon sun. From the restaurant patio, all the beauty of the island seemed laid out just for her. She became even warmer at the sight of Damon approaching. The light green cotton shirt clung to his broad chest. His muscled thighs—dark skin set off against the white shorts he wore—rippled as he walked. Female heads turned, their eyes taking in the sight of such marvelous masculinity on parade. *Down, girls, this one is all mine.* Jade giggled to herself.

"Here we are, sweet thing." Damon handed her a tall glass

with slices of pineapple. "One for you and one for me." He settled down in the chair beside her.

"Paradise. Barbados is paradise pure and simple." Jade took a sip of the rum concoction and wiggled her scarlet-painted toenails.

"Especially with you here." Damon's gaze traveled from her feet up her body to her face. "Hmm, hmm good."

"You sassy thing." Jade pinched his arm. "Seriously, thank you for the wonderful idea of getting away. If you hadn't, I'd still be slogging away in the bowels of state government." She stretched with a languid movement.

"You needed a break after the last few months." Damon did not need to add more.

"Yes, Lanessa has a long hard road ahead, Damon." Jade bit her lip.

Lanessa was far from cured. Jade knew that each day was a challenge for her sister, especially now that she was back at home. Lanessa had insisted on living in her own home. She rejected her parents' suggestion that she live with them or Jade's offer to move in with her.

"Lanessa is determined to make it, Jade. And with all the love and support she's getting from her family, I think she can," Damon said.

Jade remembered her last visit with Lanessa before leaving on vacation. Her older sister had seemed more in charge, more at ease than ever before. "I think . . . no, I know she'll do it. After everything that's happened, at last a glimmer of hope."

"Well, you won't have to worry about Bill Lang for a while at least. He's gone down in disgrace, back to his old position." Damon gave a grunt of approval.

"Sad really, because he's such a smart man. I hear he's pretty much considered poison these days." She stared out over the water.

Jade could not help but feel some sympathy for the man. Bill was back in his old civil service position with little authority to do much—a common type of punishment in state government and one that was painful for someone grown accustomed to power. He was given meaningless tasks, no staff and shared a secretary with employees with less rank. Still he would survive. He had the instincts of a street fighter.

"He'll land on his feet like any good alley cat." Damon seemed to read her mind. "Don't waste any tears on William Jefferson Lang." He put down his glass. "Now let's forget everyone and everything else back home for the next few days."

"You're right. What next?" Jade happily joined in his effort to sweep away serious thoughts.

"Come here." Damon stood up and extended his hand.

Jade's heart skipped at the sight of him reaching out to her. This beautiful man was all she wanted for now and forever. Framed against the lush, tropical background, he was a dream come true. She put her hand in his. Damon led her down onto the soft sand. Music from a steel drum band in the lounge began to play as though on cue. He swept her into his arms around in a circle to the sensuous Caribbean rhythm, their hips swaying in time to the beat.

"Jade, will you marry me?" Damon whispered in her ear.

"Oh, my goodness." Jade pressed her forehead against his chest.

"I want to be with you for the rest of my life." Damon brushed his lips against her earlobe. "I want to make love to you in our bed. Will you marry me, baby?"

"My goodness," was all she could manage. She felt a dizzy, marvelous kind of intoxication that did not come from liquor.

"I love you with all my heart." He lifted her chin and kissed her with tenderness. "Now this is the part where you say . . ." he murmured, his lips against hers, coaxing, urging her.

"Yes," Jade whispered. "Oh, yes."

Dear Readers:

I love to hear from you, so please drop me a line. To receive signed bookmarks, send a SASE to:

Lynn Emery
P.O. Box 74095
Baton Rouge, LA 70874

If you are online, write me at MHubb10676@aol.com. Or visit my website at: http://www.geocities.com/Athens/9911

Thanks for the warm welcome and support expressed in letters and via e-mail. I hope you enjoy my stories as much as I enjoy writing them. Wonderful readers like you are why we work so hard at our craft.

Best Wishes,

Lynn Emery

ABOUT THE AUTHOR

Margaret Emery Hubbard, aka Lynn Emery, is a native of Baton Rouge, Louisiana. She lives there with her artist husband. Ms. Hubbard is a social worker by profession.

Her first novel, *NIGHT MAGIC*, was sold to Kensington Publishing Corporation in July 1994. Released in September 1995, it received enthusiastic reviews in Romantic Times Magazine and Rendezvous Magazine. *NIGHT MAGIC* was nominated for Best Multicultural Romance Novel of 1995 by Romantic Times Magazine.

Her second novel, *AFTER ALL*, was released in November 1996. A novella, *Happy New Year, Baby*, was released in December 1996 as part of a holiday collection called *SILVER BELLS*.

Look for these upcoming Arabesque titles:

January 1998
WITH THIS KISS by Candice Poarch
NIGHT SECRETS by Doris Johnson
SIMPLY IRRESISTIBLE by Geri Guillaume
NIGHT TO REMEMBER by Niqui Stanhope

February 1998
HEART OF THE FALCON by Francis Ray
A PRIVATE AFFAIR by Donna Hill
RENDEZVOUS by Bridget Anderson
I DO! A Valentine's Day Collection

March 1998
KEEPING SECRETS by Carmen Green
SILVER LOVE by Layle Giusto
PRIVATE LIES by Robyn Amos
SWEET SURRENDER by Angela Winters

SENSUAL AND HEARTWARMING
ARABESQUE ROMANCES FEATURE
AFRICAN-AMERICAN CHARACTERS!

BEGUILED   (0046, $4.99)
by Eboni Snoe
After Raquel agrees to impersonate a missing heiress for just one night, a daring abduction makes her the captive of seductive Nate Bowman. Across the exotic Caribbean seas to the perilous wilds of Central America . . . and into the savage heart of desire, Nate and Raquel play a dangerous game. But soon the masquerade will be over. And will they then lose the one thing that matters most . . . their love?

WHISPERS OF LOVE   (0055, $4.99)
by Shirley Hailstock
Robyn Richards had to fake her own death, change her identity, and forever forsake her husband, Grant, after testifying against a crime syndicate. But, five years later, the daughter born after her disappearance is in need of help only Grant can give. Can Robyn maintain her disguise from the ever present threat of the syndicate—and can she keep herself from falling in love all over again?

HAPPILY EVER AFTER   (0064, $4.99)
by Rochelle Alers
In a week's time, Lauren Taylor fell madly in love with famed author Cal Samuels and impulsively agreed to be his wife. But when she abruptly left him, it was for reasons she dared not express. Five years later, Cal is back, and the flames of desire are as hot as ever, but, can they start over again and make it work this time?

Available wherever paperbacks are sold, or order direct from the Publisher. Send cover price plus 50¢ per copy for mailing and handling to Penguin USA, P.O. Box 999, c/o Dept. 17109, Bergenfield, NJ 07621. Residents of New York and Tennessee must include sales tax. DO NOT SEND CASH.